Gottfried von Strassburg

TRISTAN

AND

ISOLDE

with Ulrich von Türheim's Continuation

Gottfried von Strassburg

TRISTAN

AND

ISOLDE

with Ulrich von Türheim's Continuation

Edited and Translated, with an Introduction, by
William T. Whobrey

Hackett Publishing Company, Inc.
Indianapolis/Cambridge

23 22 21 20   1 2 3 4 5 6 7

For further information, please address
   Hackett Publishing Company, Inc.
   P.O. Box 44937
   Indianapolis, Indiana 46244-0937

   www.hackettpublishing.com

Cover design by E. L. Wilson
Interior design by E. L. Wilson
Composition by Aptara, Inc.

Library of Congress Control Number: 2020931962

ISBN-13: 978-1-62466-907-1 (cloth)
ISBN-13: 978-1-62466-906-4 (pbk.)

The paper used in this publication meets the minimum requirements of American
National Standard for Information Sciences—Permanence of Paper for Printed
Library Materials, ANSI Z39.48–1984.

∞

To my parents, Bill and Edith,
for a lifetime of unwavering support

CONTENTS

CONTENTS

Introduction

Gottfried in His Time

The story of Tristan and Isolde was well known and, judging from the many versions and manuscripts that have survived, well loved throughout the medieval period. In fact, there was probably no other story in the Middle Ages that gave rise to so much artistic expression, not only in text, but in murals, wood and ivory carvings, manuscript illuminations, and tapestries. Among the many versions of this story is one that exists in a lengthy, although incomplete, text in German written by Gottfried von Strassburg in the first decade of the thirteenth century. The time and place of this composition positions it in the midst of what was for German literature its first era of extraordinary productivity. The time from around 1170 to 1230 was a period of remarkable artistic activity in the German-speaking lands ruled by the Hohenstaufen dynasty, whose patronage of German poetry gave song and verse center stage at its secular courts. Although many poets were of the peripatetic sort, wandering from court to court with their repertoire of songs in Latin, and also in German, Occitan, Anglo-Norman, or other vernacular languages, there was a distinct movement among a small group of writers toward the non-Latin long form in what was rapidly becoming a culture of books and readership. Gottfried considered himself an author of books, which is to say that his writing was intended as much for an audience of readers as listeners, and his rhetorical style and intricate narrative architecture catered to the possibilities offered by books written for a new, noble readership. Gottfried's *Tristan and Isolde* is a masterpiece of the writer's art, at a time when such works were just beginning to claim their place in the literature of the Middle Ages.

The author of this masterpiece does not name himself. He does name a certain "Dieterich" in an acrostic made of the first initials of each of the first ten strophes of the prologue, a name that has been assumed to be a reference to a patron or sponsor or source of the work. All we have is an initial "G," the very first letter of the first line of the first strophe, before the patron's name, to hint at Gottfried possibly being the author's name. This game of hide-and-seek seems at first glance a playful wink to the reader that the author, while refusing to name himself outright, places himself at the head of his work in a way that must first be puzzled out, much as the entire work challenges the reader to discover its multilayered meaning throughout. Perhaps Gottfried would have named himself at the end of his work, much like his predecessor Eilhart von Oberge did in his treatment of the material some thirty years earlier, or like his successor Ulrich von Türheim, the first poet to complete Gottfried's *Tristan*, did some twenty or thirty years later, but we don't have the ending to Gottfried's own work, and so it is impossible to know if he intended eventually to reveal his identity. For us, Gottfried remains hidden behind an authorial persona and a cryptic letter "G."

The reader will also find very little information about the author, or his time or milieu, in the text itself. Unlike other poets of the period, such as Wolfram von Eschenbach, who refers in his *Parzival* to evidence of a recent battle, local delicacies, and an episode in the *Nibelungenlied*,[1] Gottfried is surprisingly reluctant to divulge personal or local details that might help establish his identity. Outside of the text we have a portrait of Gottfried in the Codex Manesse, the large, illustrated collection of medieval German lyric dated to the early fourteenth century,[2] but like other portraits in the Codex it represents at best an educated guess as to the poet's appearance, circumstances, and activity. Gottfried is portrayed as a teacher, a master, seated with a tablet in his hand and surrounded by five young men gesturing, three seated and two standing. They represent an audience of some kind, perhaps students or other poets or young nobles. Unlike most of the other poets in the Codex, Gottfried's portrait does not display a helmet or shield, and so we might safely infer, given his title of "Master" and the positioning of the portrait toward the back of the Codex, that Gottfried was not a member of the nobility.

Much has been assumed about his education, as it is clear that Gottfried knew French and Latin and was widely read, especially in the classics. The title of "Master" could refer to an academic degree, perhaps from Paris, or it could simply point to his "mastery" of the poet's art. His presumed place of residence or activity, Strassburg, was an important town in the orbit of the Hohenstaufens in the early thirteenth century, but nothing is known of Gottfried's view of events of the time, such as the circumstances surrounding the trials and execution of Waldensian and Amalrician heretics in Strassburg in

---

1. Wolfram mentions the vineyards of Erfurt, trampled by a recent battle. This refers to Landgrave Hermann von Thüringen's military campaign and the siege of Philip of Swabia's troops in Erfurt in 1203. The effects of this action must have been visible for at least a few years, allowing for this part of Wolfram's work to be dated to around 1204–1205. See *Parzival*, 379,18–20. The *krapfen*, or "donuts" in Trühendingen are mentioned (184,24). This refers to modern-day Wassertrüdingen or Hohentrüdingen near Ansbach and also near Wolframs-Eschenbach. There is reference made in *Parzival* (420,25–30) to the kitchen master, Rumolt, and his counsel not to accept Kriemhild's invitation.

2. Heidelberg University Library, CPg 848. The manuscript is digitized and available online.

1211–1212.[3] In short, nothing points with any certainty to a reality outside the author's text itself. It is as if Gottfried intentionally withdraws his readers from the present and leads them into an alternative reality that exists, as he says, only for those "noble, longing lover[s]" who might find edification and solace in his tale. This seems to be confirmed by the "autobiographical" comments that Gottfried inserts into the Love Grotto allegory. He states that he, too, hunted in the wilderness, but that his labors were beset by misfortune, and even as he gained entry to the cave he never reached the ultimate goal of lying on the crystal bed. All of this is, of course, also allegorical, and in the end it seems that Gottfried is more at home within than outside the allegory.

The reader does gain some insight into Gottfried and his art through his commentary on the membership of a small, distinguished company of poets and singers. This commentary, the first of its kind, takes the form of a rather lengthy literary review (ll. 4589–821) of his German colleagues. The placement of the review, inserted in the middle of the scene of Tristan's knighting ceremony, is not coincidental. Like everything in Gottfried's *Tristan*, this first major disruption of the narrative is carefully managed to manipulate the readers' experience of the story. The knighting ceremony is one of the most conventional scenes in medieval literature. It represents the early success and crowning social achievement of a young man and his companions, but Gottfried seems intent to deny Tristan even this most familiar observance of chivalric success by claiming that he is inadequate to the task of portraying the ceremony properly. Gottfried juxtaposes his own task of adequately—that is to say, joyfully—describing the elaborate preparations being made for Tristan's knighting ceremony and his own inadequacies as a poet. This modesty trope is introduced with the observation that any description of courtly ritual and extravagance has already been presented so often that he has little to add that might bring joy to the hearts of his audience. The detailed and lengthy descriptions of events such as knighting ceremonies have been overdone to the point of spoiling any possible delights that might still be gleaned from further poetic treatments. The reader is made aware that Tristan, although seemingly on the path to a "normal" career as knight and courtier, must be denied even the trappings of the joyful celebration that would launch just such a career.

It is in the company of his colleagues, past and present, that Gottfried exposes himself as poet and critic by praising, and disparaging, those whom he names and those whom he does not. A closer look at this grand digression into the state of German letters around 1210, often referred to as the "Literary Excursus," reveals something about Gottfried's concept of the poet's

---

3. For more details on this period in Strassburg's history, see Michael Batts, "Gottfried's Strasbourg: The City and its People," in Hasty, 2003, 55–69.

vocation and his own place therein. Gottfried begins with poets who, like himself, are best known for their longer works, which is to say their books. The first poet he mentions, and the one for whom he obviously has the most respect, is Hartmann von Aue. Hartmann is praised for his lack of artifice, unassuming manner, and precise style. He is the greatest poet because he is able to infuse form with meaning while maintaining clarity and directness in his language. Hartmann leads his readers with ostensible simplicity along a path to a meaning both clear and edifying. The next poet is the pretender to the crown. He is unnamed but assumed almost unanimously to be Wolfram von Eschenbach. He is the foil to Hartmann, that is to say, he is the rabbit's friend[4] who meanders and wanders and jumps back and forth, leading the reader on a wild goose chase in search of a meaning that may or may not even exist. As a result, the narrative suffers from a kind of self-importance effected by nothing more than smoke and mirrors. To reemphasize his point about the importance of directness of style, Gottfried next summons the example of Bligger von Steinach. Bligger harmonizes form and content with a brilliant turn of phrase and sense of artful poetics. With what has been thought to be a reference to an unknown work, possibly titled *Umbehanc* (or "Tapestry"), or to his interwoven style, Gottfried sees in Bligger a colleague of immense talent and "soaring" language.

Gottfried calls out Heinrich von Veldeke as the man responsible for bringing the art of vernacular love poetry from the French courts into the orbit of the German language. He is referred to in the past tense, and it must be assumed that he was no longer alive as Gottfried wrote these words. Heinrich epitomizes for Gottfried the confluence of epic poetry and courtly love poetry, or *Minnesang*. Hartmann and Wolfram were known primarily for their longer treatments of Arthurian romance, and Bligger presumably may have worked in this genre, but all three were also active in writing songs. The first named leader of those who were called "nightingales," a reference to poets known for their "birdsong," or shorter love poetry, is Reinmar der Alte, also known by his presumed town of origin, von Hagenau. Gottfried refers to him specifically as deceased. First in line to take up the mantle of leadership is Walther von der Vogelweide, perhaps the most prolific and versatile medieval German lyric poet of all. His love poetry is singled out, but Walther was active in composing many different kinds of shorter works, from gnomic poetry to political, artistic, and religious criticism. Neither he nor Reinmar is known to have written a longer romance or epic.

This excursus is not just a list of those working in German courts as poets and entertainers around 1210. It defines Gottfried's own stylistic ambitions

---

4. The reference to rabbits most likely comes from Wolfram's most famous work, *Parzival.* See the footnote to l. 4638 in the main text.

by describing the aspects of other poets he finds praiseworthy or objectionable. Among the epic poets he admires are those like Hartmann and Bligger, who write a clear and direct narrative without the use of technical jargon or an over-reliance on circumlocution. What he finds most objectionable in Wolfram and others like him is the superficial creation of hidden meaning with nothing more than rhetorical tricks. He admires the singers for their talents and their ability to move their audiences. What Gottfried admires in others is what is put to best effect in his own work: epic meaning and lyrical affect. It has long been acknowledged that Gottfried was a master of the German language, evoking the claim that "Gottfried wrote in a style so elegant that it was not to be matched in Germany until the late eighteenth century."[5] But it is not just a bag of rhetorical tricks that Gottfried has at his disposal. He matches himself with Ovid and Virgil and other great writers, not just those German colleagues he mentions. Gottfried aims to build a text of epic proportions, not just content, and his work is woven through with meaning on the surface, just below the surface, and at the mythic level deep beneath the surface.

There has been considerable speculation as to whether or not Gottfried wrote any other poems, long or short, and if any of these have survived. Other authors of longer works, as named in the literary review, were active in composing shorter lyrical poems, and so it would not seem improbable that Gottfried was similarly engaged. The Codex Manesse collects three poems as the work of *Meister Gotfrid von Strasburg*. This group of texts under Gottfried's name is not insignificant in scope. It totals eighty-two strophes over eight pages of text,[6] but it is generally agreed, mostly for reasons of language and style, that these three poems, which include a shorter love poem,[7] a praise of Mary and Christ (sixty-three strophes), and a didactic poem about poverty, are not authentic. Mention is made of Gottfried in the works of the generation of poets that followed him, among them Rudolf von Ems and Konrad von Würzburg, both of whom show influence by Gottfried in their works, and those who took on the completion of his *Tristan*, Ulrich von Türheim and Heinrich von Freiberg. Only Rudolf von Ems, however, makes mention in his *Alexander* (around 1240) of another work of Gottfried's, quoting one of its lines, *Gelücke daz gît wunderlîchen an und abe* ("Good luck rises and falls in strange ways"), as having been "sung" (*sanc*) by the *wîse meister Gotfrit*. This seems to point to a poem in the Codex Manesse listed not

---

5. C. Stephen Jaeger, "Foreword," in *Gottfried von Strassburg: Tristan and Isolde*, edited by Francis Gentry, 1988, ix.

6. The portrait of Gottfried is at 364r in the Codex, the text runs from 364v–368r, followed by five blank pages (368v–370v), perhaps in anticipation of yet more to be added.

7. The first five strophes of this poem are also collected under Gottfried's name in manuscript A, Heidelberg University Library, CPg 357.

under Gottfried but rather under the name of Ulrich von Lichtenstein.[8] This fact is not necessarily disqualifying, as many poems in this and other lyric collections were misattributed to one author or another. The text consists of two strophes of twelve lines each. Given the identical metrical form and related content, it is most probable that the two strophes form a single poem, now usually titled by the opening words of the first strophe, *Liut unde lant* ("People and Lands"). The "glass luck" that Rudolf referred to is the topic of the second strophe. The poem of the *glesîn gelücke* ("Glass Luck") attributed to Ulrich von Lichtenstein is now generally accepted to have been written by Gottfried.[9]

Rudolf von Ems points us in the right direction, but there are internal correspondences between the poem and Gottfried's major work that are convincing enough to confirm this attribution, and the poem is included here. Another clue for Gottfried's authorship is offered by the fact that the poem incorporates at least two of the maxims published by Publilius Syrus,[10] a source often cited by Gottfried, especially toward the end of his *Tristan*. Even more convincing, however, are stylistic and linguistic parallels, including the recurrence of certain phrases in *Tristan and Isolde* and the short poem.[11] Several word pairs appear in both, for example, *liut unde lant* (people and lands) occurs twelve times in *Tristan*; *meinen und minnen* (to think of and to love, l. 1113; in the negative 19,146) and *mit handen und mit zungen* (with hands and with tongues, l. 17,209) occur as well. There is an association between the words *vertân* (cursed) and *gîteclîch* (greedily) in the character of the giant Urgan (ll. 16,141–43), and certain phrases are shared: *umbe als ein bal* (around like a ball, l. 11,363) and *wunder uf der erde* (a wonder on earth, l. 688; l. 4332). None of this by itself is proof of authorship, but this common vocabulary begins to make the poem "sound" like Gottfried.

More important for our present purpose is the poem's content and how it both shares in and sheds light on the meaning of Gottfried's main work. The poem is not a love poem but falls under the broad category of Spruchdichtung, or didactic or gnomic poetry. As such it is one of the earlier representatives of this genre, even if we date it to Gottfried's later period around 1210. The first strophe introduces the concept of greed or avarice (*gîte*) as the source of disruption, corruption, betrayal, and instability in the world. Gottfried blames the lust for wealth and power for moral corruption and disloyalty, the central transgressions in his *Tristan*. The desire to possess has the power to

---

8. MF XXIII/I.

9. It is included in Ranke's edition (1949, 246; although with the strophes reversed), as well as in Krohn's commentary, Volume 3, 1980, 209–11.

10. Maxim 280: "Fortuna vitrea est: tum, cum splendet, frangitur," and Maxim 282: "Fortunam citius reperias quam retines."

11. Stackmann (1997) details most of these.

corrupt love as the ultimate good. The second strophe links this denunciation of greed to the fickleness of fortune, conjuring up the well-known image of the vicissitudes of the Wheel of Fortune. What Fortune gives is temporary and never suitably timed, and if it gives too much or takes it back again, the result is always pain instead of joy. Whatever looks most desirable is the most fragile, and the desire to possess ever more proves itself to be both cruel and illusory. Gottfried offers no solution or vision of a better world; this is not moral didacticism. Instead he affirms that aside from being disruptive, greed and the impermanence of good fortune conspire to deny a life without burdens (*âne swere*; l. 2,8).

Isolde, too, is a victim of greed and the ever-changing fortunes of the kingdom of Ireland. She complains as she is married off to King Mark and taken away that her life would have been carefree (*âne swere*; 11,580) had it not been for Tristan. This points to the "careworn" heart that pervades the entire work. The individual's utopian, carefree existence is mirrored in the opening line of the first strophe. All of humanity could live in harmony were it not for greed, which in turn is amplified by the inconstancy of fortune. Gottfried's answer is clear. Such an ideal life (*wunschleben*) can only exist outside of reality, and only temporarily, in the mythical world of the Lover's Cave.

These two themes, greed and the fragility of fortune, are central to the story of Tristan and Isolde. Greed is the chief instigator of all the misfortune that befalls Tristan, beginning with his kidnapping by Norwegian merchants. The episodes of King Gurmun's tribute and his enforcer Morold are clearly motivated by the lust for power and wealth. The seneschal's desire for Isolde and his false claims to have killed the dragon are motivated by his desire to possess the princess. Most of all, the envy and greed of the Cornish baronage prompt Tristan's fears of assassination and his subsequent attempt to find a suitable wife for Mark. Tristan strives to right these wrongs, but Fortune's loyalty is fickle, instead turning what should have been a "life without care" into a life of constant sorrow. The critical episode of the love potion is at its core a case of Fortune's bad timing. The potion was meant to ensure that Isolde and her future husband, King Mark, would truly love each other as man and wife and not just rule as king and queen. A simple case of mistaken identity, the potion for wine, destroys this intention and turns everything upside down. The inherently fortunate spell of love is cast at the wrong time, and therefore on the unintended recipients, Tristan and Isolde.

Tristan's attempts to right wrongs through deception and subterfuge; his lies and disguises; his disloyalty to his lord and later to his wife, Isolde of the White Hands, can be seen as either the causes of his failure or the only means left to Tristan to defeat a fate that is neither rational nor just. While Gottfried's poem decries the prevalence of *valsch und anderunge* (betrayal and uncertainty), it could be argued that Fortune, or Misfortune, can only be confronted with its own tactics. The story of Tristan offers no remedies, and the tragic end for both lovers is fated within the structure of a courtly society that insists on loyalty and obedience in a world that respects neither.

Sources

Gottfried's relationship to his source material is difficult to discern given the fragmentary nature of the manuscript transmission of these earlier works. It is clear, however, that a lively Tristan tradition existed in French and German well before Gottfried took up the story around the turn of the thirteenth century. In fact, by the middle of the twelfth century troubadours in southern France like Bernart de Ventadorn and Raimbaut d'Orange were including allusions to the Tristan matter in their songs, especially the love potion episode. Other French poets like Marie de France were working with the material in the second half of the twelfth century. Her *Chevrefoil* ("Honeysuckle") is a very short account of a secret meeting in the forest between Tristan and Isolde following his exile. The entwined honeysuckle and hazel tree serve as a metaphor for the two lovers who, when separated, both die. The *lai* also makes mention of the name of the story in English and French, implying that the tale was widely known in several languages. Around the same time there is reference in the *Roman de Renart* to a Tristan story, and the great French author of Arthurian romances, Chrétien de Troyes (flourished 1160–1185), claimed to have written a story about King Marc and Ysalt the Blonde,[12] which is unfortunately lost. In one of his shorter poems (*D'Amors, qui m'a tolu a moi*), Chrétien went so far as to compare himself favorably to Tristan as a lover. Tristan's love was caused by a "poison" and was therefore accidental, but Chrétien's love was true because it was intentional. It is not possible in most cases to link these treatments of the Tristan story to one version or another, but there is little doubt that singers and writers in the second half of the twelfth century could assume that their audience knew the story well.

The variety and scope of Tristan narratives is considerable, and several different versions of the story were competing for their audience's attention at the same time. One somewhat simplified organizational principle that has gained currency is the division of the versions into two main branches, one called the "common" and the other the "courtly" tradition. These terms are imprecise at best, but they try to capture both major plot and stylistic differences. The common branch has been described as coarser, more violent in its treatment of the basic story as well as in its use of language and rhetorical devices. The courtly branch is considered to be more refined in these ways

---

12. See the opening line of his Prologue to *Cligés* (around 1176).

and perhaps more sophisticated in its portrayal of the complex relationships between the main protagonists and society. Béroul and his adherents, including Eilhart von Oberge and his German *Tristrant* (around 1170), are assigned to the common tradition, Thomas of Britain and his successors, including Robert and his Old Norse *Saga of Tristram and Ísönd* (1226), represent the courtly version. Both branches were known to Gottfried, but he specifically names Thomas as his source (l. 150), because his version was "accurate" (*die rihte und die wârheit*; l. 156), that is, historically grounded in other sources. It is now agreed, however, that Gottfried also made use of elements of the common version, despite his protestations to the contrary.

Very little is known about Thomas. Gottfried is the only writer who identifies him as von Britanje, which in the usage of the time could mean either "greater" Britain or "little" Britain, or present-day Brittany. He was an Anglo-Norman writer and possibly served at the court of Eleanor of Aquitaine (1122–1204). Although the dates for his *Tristran* vary widely, Thomas could have been working on his text as early as 1160. The transmission of Thomas's text is unfortunately very fragmentary, with fewer than 3300 lines extant of what has been assumed to have been a work of more than 18,000 lines. The main parts that have been transmitted to us in what remains of four different manuscripts happily cover the ending of the story, almost precisely where Gottfried's text breaks off, but unhappily allow for no direct comparison. Two other relatively short fragments, one discovered fairly recently,[13] include episodes from a middle (Tristan and Isolde confess their love and then arrive in Cornwall) and a later part of the story (Tristan's final farewell) and therefore allow for a more direct, albeit still very imperfect comparison between Gottfried's text and his main source. These comparisons provide us with an inexact understanding of how Gottfried used his Old French source, but we can generally say that he tended to expand upon Thomas's original.

Thomas had other successors, most notably a Friar Robert, who in 1226 translated the Old French into Old Norse for King Hákon Hákonarson of Norway (1204–1263). Fortunately, this text has been transmitted in its entirety in two, albeit late, manuscripts. Although it seems from what we can tell that Robert was more willing to redact and cut than Gottfried in his treatment of Thomas, the *Saga* provides the only other work that allows us to conceptualize the Thomas text as a whole. Where gaps exist in Thomas's work, we can try to fill these in with Robert's version, although it is important to stress that we must be mindful that the *Saga* does not represent a literal translation of Thomas but rather the interpretation it received at the hands of Robert. It is certainly also possible, although there is no direct evidence to support this, that Robert knew of and was influenced by Gottfried's *Tristan*,

---

13. The so-called Carlisle Fragment was discovered in 1995.

"T" initial. The chiastic, or crossed nature of this T/I interaction is significant, as it exemplifies the relationship between the two main protagonists as an embrace of "I" or Isolde by "T" or Tristan. That the initials themselves stand for these two characters is made clear in the episode of the coded wood chips, in which Tristan is instructed by Brangane to carve these initials on opposite sides of wood chips that can then float downstream to where Isolde will see them.

Gottfried's primary metrical pattern, as expected for a work of this type and this period, is the rhyming couplet with lines of four stressed syllables. Along with the initial eleven strophes and their unique rhyme schemes, we encounter other four-line strophes throughout the text that are often but not always marked by a large initial. They are always distinctive, however, in their rhyme schemes, either AAAA or ABBA or ABAB, and they are further characterized by the additional complexity of identical rhyme. The insertion of these strophic markers in the text alerts us to a change in content, an organizational transition, or they represent some particularly meaningful kind of introduction to what follows, a mini-prologue if you will. This translation has attempted to make this clear in its own use of rhyme in these strophes. One example should help to illustrate this:

[1865] Such worldly affairs
oft turn to cares,
but then from cares
return to fair affairs.

These four-line strophes with their large initials and unique rhyme patterns work in tandem with other initials. Combinations of letters, marked in this translation with large initials, occur as "T/I" "I/T"; "R/S" "S/R"; "I/O" "O/I"; and "S/L" "L/S." The pairs of letters and their reverse-order repetition are not immediately significant by themselves, however. Only in a different kind of visual pattern as a larger chiastic arrangement do they begin to make sense as the letters that actually spell out the names TRIS(TAN) and ISOL(DE) or ISOL(DEN). That only the first four letters of each name are present can be explained by the fact that we are missing a significant portion of the last part of the text. We must assume, therefore, that the other pairs of letters would later have been put in their proper places, although it is unclear how this would have been accomplished, given the unequal number of letters in the two names.

There is one additional cross-textual acrostic that deserves mention, and that is the continuation of the "G" initial in the very first strophe. The assumption is that this letter stands for the author, Gottfried. This is confirmed by further initials "O" "T" "E" at the head of strophes in positions that precede the other pairs in order. It should not surprise us that the final letters are missing here as well, and we would expect later to find the missing letters GOTE-**FRIT**. It should also be noted that these letters are not found in pairs, that is, they are not followed four lines later by an initial reintroducing the rhyming couplet scheme.

Another way to illustrate this schema is as follows:[16]

Prologue 1–235	1751–869	5069–181	12,183–507	unfinished
G	O	T	E	(F-R-I-T)
DIETERICH				
T	R	I	S	(T-A-N)
I	S	O	L	(D-E-N?)[17]
I	S	O	L	(D-E-N?)
T	R	I	S	(T-A-N)

There are other quatrains with similar rhyme schemes and large initials, especially the final two strophes of the Prologue, l. 233 and l. 237, whose initials spell out "D" "I," with a following "U" initial, and then again l. 11,871, "S" followed by a "D" and finally l. 12,183, "E" followed by an "S," that have not been satisfactorily deciphered, assuming they have any meaning at all.

It remains for us to examine where these initials appear and if their placement is more or less random or if they appear at significant junctions of the narrative; that is, do they simply represent a game of spelling out names or do they mark organizational seams that have meaning. As we might expect with Gottfried, here, too, we find a veritable labyrinth of structure and meaning. As with the numerical and symbolic structure that underlies the construction of the great Gothic cathedrals, so, too, is Gottfried's work constructed on a foundation of hidden numerical relationships. A poet can build words into a literary wonder in much the same way that a builder uses an underlying mathematical and geometric framework to erect an edifice of astonishing proportion and beauty.

---

16. Much of what follows is based on the work of Fourquet, 1963, and Gravigny, 1971, restated in the Haug/Scholz edition, 2012, 2.231–39.

17. There is some disagreement as to the spelling of Isolde's name in this scheme. If the pairs of initials were to be even, then Isolde would need seven letters just as Tristan has seven letters. IsoldeN would represent the accusative or dative case of the proper name. Gottfried never writes the name in this way, however, and other options without the N would leave the name with only five or six letters (Isolt or Isolde). Without evidence from the missing ending, we can never know for sure what Gottfried's intention was in this regard.

The prologue encompasses 244 verses. This is clear given the content and the well-defined organization of this section, which is Gottfried's own and not found in any other source. It therefore follows that the main narrative starts at line 245 with the story of Rivalin and Blancheflor, a commonality of the Tristan tradition. The number of lines between this beginning and the first large initial (l. 1751) of our strophic scheme outlined above is 1506 lines. The "distance" to the next set of initials is 3318 lines, then comes another section of 7118 lines, finally followed by what I have called an "interlogue" or middle portion of 244 lines from ll. 12,187–430. The remaining work from l. 12,431 to l. 19,548 numbers 7118 lines. Given our familiarity now with Gottfried's propensity for chiastic structures, we begin to see a pattern, first of increasing numbers of lines between major initials and strophes until the number 244 is repeated, and then a decrease of the same number of lines initiating what could be assumed to be a similar declining pattern. This structure repeats the number of lines in reverse order, mimicking the rhetorical and graphic usage of chiasmus and further accentuating the concept of envelopment as demonstrated with the T I / I T initials and the spelling of their names.

If this theory of intentional design is correct (although no single manuscript presents the text in exactly this way), then it can be represented as follows:

Section	Lines	Number of Lines
Prologue	1–244	244
First half, part one	245–1750	1506
First half, part two	1751–5068	3318
First half, part three	5069–12,186	7118
Interlogue	12,187–430	244
Second half, part one	12,431–19,548	7118
Second half, part two	(19,549–866)	3318
Second half, part three	(22,867–4,372)	1506
Epilogue	(24,373–616)	244

Because the poem ends with l. 19,548, the presumed remaining sections based on these calculations would have taken Gottfried's work out to a total of 24,616 lines. Another way to look at this is that we are missing 5068 lines, or that Gottfried completed about 80 percent of his work. The total number of (presumed) lines is impressive, but not beyond what could be imagined for such a massive undertaking. Wolfram's *Parzival* consists of almost 25,000 lines, for example, and a few other texts even exceed this. It also gives us pause to think that the final line in our incomplete text is in fact a major fault line between sections and is therefore not random, which is to say it is calculated and not simply where the author stopped working or was taken from his work. None of this can be proven conclusively, but the scheme as hypothesized is intriguing and does not stretch the limits of reasonable supposition. Given Gottfried's use of strophes at key junctures that call attention to a transition of some sort, it is reasonable to assume that the position of these strophes within a chiastic structure could form the narrative skeleton onto which Gottfried erected his poem.

This scheme divides the story into parts that are not only determined by a mathematical concept but also signify divisions of content. The prologue and interlogue are clear in terms of their separate functions. The work is divided into two main halves at the interlogue, which coincides with the episode of the love potion. This is the critical point of the entire work: everything changes with the return to Cornwall and Mark's court. Within the first half of the text there are two subdivisions, the first coming at line 1751, immediately following Tristan's birth. The preceding story of his parents has formed a kind of prologue of its own, and their tragic fates foreshadow his, as told in the naming episode at his baptism. The story of Tristan's childhood commences at this juncture and proceeds until line 5069, or the end of Tristan's knighting. This closes the story of Tristan's youth. After his knighting, he is an adult member of the chivalric order, responsible for defending and protecting his lord, the Church, and the people. It is on the cusp of this success that Gottfried tells us that Tristan's renown was constantly overshadowed by grief and hatred. After attempts to overcome these through vengeance and retribution, and in his attempts to overcome the envy of Cornwall's baronage, Tristan finds himself again in Ireland with a winning strategy to gain the hand of Isolde for his king. All of these divisions in the first half of the poem are both logical in terms of the plot and mark critical points of development in Tristan's journey: lineage, youth, knighthood.

Whether or not the final division, at the end of the present fragment at line 19,548, was meant to be the end of one part and the beginning of another is impossible to say, given the absence of what was to follow. The division would make sense based on a section of 7118 lines, but because neither of Gottfried's continuators, Ulrich von Türheim nor Heinrich von Freiberg, were aware of or chose to follow the overarching organizational design of the main work, we can only speculate. Ulrich continues the story line in the middle of Tristan's monologue, in which he vows in short order to marry Isolde of the White Hands and begin a new life. This is a turning point toward the final stage of the narrative, namely the unsuccessful attempt by Tristan to forget his true love by way of marriage to another Isolde. Other versions, including Thomas's, continue in much the same vein with the story of the "other"

Isolde. Eilhart has none of Tristan's monologue but moves directly from the battle against King Havelin's enemies to Kehenis's (Kahedin's) attempts to convince Tristrant to stay. Gottfried ends the battle at line 18,948. In fact, this is where our main remaining fragments of Thomas's text begin, something that is perhaps coincidental, perhaps not. The two texts converge right around line 19,500 in Gottfried and line 75 in Thomas.[18]

Manuscripts, Editions, and Translations

Gottfried's text is known to us in a total of thirty manuscripts, of which eleven are complete and nineteen are fragmentary. Of this total one fragment is now lost, and one complete manuscript from 1489 exists only in a copy from 1722 (see page 307 in the Appendix for a complete listing of manuscripts by date). This is a fairly substantial number of surviving witnesses, a number consistent with some other major works in Middle High German from around the same time (*Parzival*: eighty-eight manuscripts; *Willehalm*: seventy-nine; *Nibelungenlied*: thirty-seven; *Iwein*: thirty-three).[19] Many important works have far fewer manuscript witnesses. Fully half of the manuscripts known to us were written in the Alsatian region around Strassburg, and of the total twenty-nine manuscripts that we have at present, two complete manuscripts and five fragments have been dated to the thirteenth century, providing us with a significant proportion of early witnesses. The oldest complete manuscript is Cgm 51 (M) in the Bavarian State Library in Munich, dated to the second quarter of the thirteenth century, most likely between 1240 and 1250 because it already contains Ulrich von Türheim's continuation from around that time. This is only thirty to forty years after Gottfried was working on the text himself. The short fragment in Tübingen (t) is of a similar age. The fourteenth century has left us with four complete manuscripts and twelve fragments, and the period from 1420 to 1489 provides us with another five complete manuscripts and one fragment. Three of the manuscripts are rich in illustrations, including above all manuscript M (plus BR).[20] The editorial conventions of the nineteenth century assigned these manuscripts upper- or lowercase single letters, with the uppercase designating the complete manuscripts and the lowercase letters the fragments. Finally, it is important to note that seven of the eleven complete manuscripts contain Ulrich von Türheim's continuation, while three of them have Heinrich von Freiberg's later version,

---

18. The Haug/Scholz edition of Thomas begins the first Sneyd fragment at line 53.

19. Taken from totals of manuscripts listed for each work in the online *Handschriftencensus*.

20. For an overview see Julia Walworth, "Tristan in Medieval Art," in Grimbert, 1995, 255–99. The manuscript M illustrations can also be viewed online at https://daten.digitale-sammlungen.de/~db/0008/bsb00088332/images/

meaning that only one complete manuscript (W) does not include one of the two endings from the thirteenth century.

As is sometimes the case, the oldest manuscript to have survived is not always the most reliable witness of the original text. Manuscripts M and H have both vied for the honor of *Leithandschrift* (lead manuscript) for Gottfried's text. The problem with M is that its scribe took the liberty of abridging the text by cutting out or altering almost a fifth of the whole. This represents in practical terms a significant redaction of the entire work. The second-oldest manuscript, H, from the University Library in Heidelberg (Cpg 360), dated to the fourth quarter of the thirteenth century, is now believed to be closer to the archetype than M. One advantage of H is the fairly consistent and systematic use of large initials in much the same way that we believe Gottfried intended. Also worth mentioning is the Vienna National Library Codex 2707,3 (W) from the early fourteenth century which, although later than the other two manuscripts, represents another branch close to the archetype. The most recent editions, especially that of Walter Haug and Günther Scholz (2011/2012), have preferred the readings of H over M in most cases, especially when supported by W.[21] Fortunately for our work on these manuscripts today, several complete manuscripts (HMBO) as well as some fragments (enpqrt) are available in whole or in part in digital images online.

Gottfried's text suffered much the same decline into obscurity as some other well-known medieval German works. Although the story of Tristan and Isolde still found an avid readership in the fifteenth century, it was not Gottfried's version that eventually made it into printed book form. That honor went to the rival narrative by Eilhart von Oberge, a prose adaptation of which was printed in 1484 by Anton Sorg in Augsburg as *Tristrant und Isalde*. This prose version enjoyed considerable popularity, as witnessed by its repeated publication even into the beginning of the twentieth century.[22] Gottfried's text, on the other hand, seems to have been largely forgotten after the last late fifteenth-century manuscripts were produced, until its reappearance in an edition from 1785. From this publication the story gained the early attention of none other than August Wilhelm Schlegel (1767–1845), who in 1798 announced his own efforts to adapt Gottfried's work, an effort that was published in part in 1811.[23] Schlegel's work remained unfinished, but another early editor, Friedrich Heinrich von der Hagen, was impressed enough by Schlegel's poem to undertake an edition in 1823. Unfortunately, subsequent publication and scholarly attention seems to have suffered from

---

21. For a more detailed explanation of their editorial principles, see Haug/Scholz (2012, 2.228).
22. See *Tristrant und Isalde*, 1966, ix–xvii for a complete listing of printed editions.
23. Schlegel, 1811, 98–134.

an early condemnation in 1820 by the eminent philologist Karl Lachmann in his comments on the suitability of Gottfried's text for students: "the main parts of its effeminate, immoral narrative offered nothing more than extravagance and blasphemy."[24] It seems that this damning judgment led to what has since been a somewhat disorderly editorial history, with some still today lamenting the absence of a definitive edition of Gottfried's work. The period between 1821 and 1888 saw no less than five separate editions, none of which can satisfy today's demands of scholarship and editorial principles.[25] Friedrich Ranke worked on an edition for many years, but his publication of the text in 1930, considered by many to be the best of the twentieth century and the basis for most editions today, unfortunately remained absent a second volume with its variant apparatus. This unhappy situation was relieved somewhat by Werner Schröder's edition of 2004, which included an apparatus of textual variants along with Peter Knecht's fine translation into modern German, but had the disadvantage of being based on Marold's edition of 1906. There is general agreement, finally, that a state-of-the-art scholarly edition has yet to be produced, despite the very good update of Ranke's text with extensive notes in the two-volume edition of Haug and Scholz (2011/2012).

Gottfried's text was translated into German several times in the nineteenth century, and a modern German translation has accompanied most editions of the twentieth and twenty-first centuries. Hermann Kurtz (1844), Karl Simrock (1855), Wilhelm Hertz (1877), and Karl Pannier (1903) were the pioneers in this regard. In fact, Richard Wagner became aware of the text for his opera of the same name (1859) through Kurtz's translation. The seeming disinterest in English-language translations is puzzling, however. Sir Walter Scott took an early interest in a Middle English version of the story and in 1804 first undertook publication of the story titled *Sir Tristrem*, a kind of edition of the single manuscript that contained the text. It seems, however, that the first English translation of Gottfried's *Tristan* was not accomplished until Jessie Weston's book in 1899. In fact, this was not a full translation but instead a highly redacted prose retelling. The first full English translation of the German text did not appear until 1960 in the form of A. T. Hatto's masterful rendition, which also includes a translation of Thomas's French text as a kind of conclusion to the story. Republished in 1988 with some emendations and without the Thomas ending, this translation remains the only complete English translation in print to date. A later translation by Lee Stavenhagen exists online only. It is undoubtedly the high quality of Hatto's translation that has discouraged others from following in his footsteps, but

---

24. Karl Lachmann, 1820, vi.
25. See Dickhut, 2012, 248–70, for a detailed discussion of the nineteenth-century reception of Gottfried's *Tristan*.

even with the repackaging of his work in the 1988 edition by Francis Gentry, the nearly sixty years since its first publication has left Gottfried's text in need of a new effort that takes advantage of the intervening half-century of scholarship.

Continuations

Gottfried's work went out into the world after 1210 still a fragment, and the need to complete the story was felt very soon after work on the text had ceased. It seems clear from the manuscript evidence that nearly every copy of Gottfried's work had one or another continuation following it. The decision in this book to include, for the first time in English, a translation of one of Gottfried's Middle High German continuations is founded on the desire to present Gottfried's text in a more medieval context, which is to say that, while most medieval readers would have recognized Gottfried's *Tristan and Isolde* to be a fragment, one of two continuations or endings to the story would have been available in the same manuscript. The first to take up this task sometime around 1230 was Ulrich von Türheim, followed by Heinrich von Freiberg some fifty or sixty years later. In seven out of eleven complete manuscripts the continuation included is the earlier one by Ulrich, whereas Heinrich von Freiberg's version is extant in three of the manuscripts. Ulrich's version remained popular even into the fifteenth century. These facts, along with the earlier date of Ulrich's version, made the more compelling case to translate and include here the first and possibly most popular continuation, even though Heinrich's version is generally acknowledged to be the more artful.

Ulrich was given his task by Konrad von Winterstetten, an influential Swabian member of the imperial court who died in 1243. Ulrich was not an unlikely choice, as we know him to have written another major work after his completion of Gottfried's *Tristan*, namely a text now titled *Rennewart*, a massive continuation (36,500 verses) of Wolfram von Eschenbach's *Willehalm*. Rudolf von Ems makes mention of Ulrich in his own *Willehalm*. What little else we know about Ulrich is that his family name came from what is now Unterthürheim near Dillingen on the Danube, and that he is attested in Augsburg in documents from 1236 and 1244. He died sometime around 1250.

Ulrich took on his assignment at the urging of his patron Konrad following Gottfried's death, or so he tells us. In his own short prologue, Ulrich praises Gottfried's mastery of language and his "inventive, coherent, and truly exemplary" story. Unlike Gottfried, however, Ulrich chose to use Eilhart's *Tristrant* as his primary source. It is possible that he simply didn't have access to Thomas's version. While staying at first quite close to Eilhart's version, Ulrich later takes liberties with Tristan's several journeys to visit Isolde, combining some while in the process disentangling the narrative flow as the final Nampotanis episode unfolds. This independence from his main source shows some creative impulse, although it must be generally admitted that Ulrich's own language, style, and abilities lag far behind his predecessor, Gottfried.

It also seems that Ulrich was not in agreement with the basic premise of the exemplary nature of Tristan and Isolde's love. He praised the two for their loyalty to each other, even in the most extreme circumstances, but in his commentary Ulrich clearly disapproved of their adulterous relationship. He feared that they could only be saved from the fires of hell through prayer and God's intervention. For Ulrich, love is not redemptive but represents that inexorable force that causes only suffering and that ultimately leads the two lovers to the only possible realm of unification: death. The love potion represents this sinister power that binds the two lovers for life (Eilhart's version, on the other hand, has a limited time span of four years) even as it loses its grip on the couple in death. As Ulrich reveals his name at the end, he does so in a plaint against this unjust, but necessary death. He directs this question to God: Why are the good taken indiscriminately while the bad go unpunished?

Heinrich von Freiberg likewise relied heavily on Eilhart for his plot and, in a composition almost twice as long as Ulrich's, completed Gottfried's fragment in what is generally considered to be a more sophisticated rendition. Heinrich was active in the second half of the thirteenth century and most likely completed his *Tristan* continuation around 1290. The sponsor and patron for his work was Raimund von Lichtenburg (d. 1329), a close advisor to King Wenceslaus II and active at the royal court in Bohemia. The text itself is transmitted to us in three manuscripts along with Gottfried's *Tristan*, and two separate fragments attest to Heinrich's work as well. Nothing else is known of Heinrich except that three other works are attributed to him, although the attribution of any one of these is less than certain.

It remains to mention the major post-Gottfried versions of the *Tristan* legend, none of which seems to have been directly influenced either by Gottfried or his continuators. The Old Norse translation of Thomas's French work by Robert in 1226 has already been mentioned. A lengthy prose version in Old French (*Tristan en prose*) was probably written between 1230 and 1240 and proved to be very popular. This text was firmly rooted in the Arthurian literature of the period, especially the Lancelot and Grail cycles, and thus represents a major revision of previous versions of the Tristan material. While fairly faithful to the traditional story line at first, the narrative loses itself in myriad side adventures as Tristan eventually sets out in search of the Holy Grail, a plot line most certainly added later. The text was copied often and became perhaps the most influential version of the story in the later Middle

Ages, serving as a primary source for Sir Thomas Mallory's treatment of the Tristan legend in his *Le Morte d'Arthur* (around 1470; first printed 1485). Finally, a Middle English adaptation of Thomas's version from the late thirteenth century, titled *Sir Tristrem*, exists today in a single codex, the Auchinleck Manuscript (1330–1340). This somewhat simplified telling of the classic story had little effect on the reception of the legend as a whole.

The Translation

This translation has undertaken to present Gottfried's masterful *Tristan and Isolde* in a number of new ways. It is only the second English translation of the entire work to appear in print, and the first since 1960.[26] Included for the first time is the continuation by Ulrich von Türheim, written only some twenty to thirty years after Gottfried's fragment. The short poem now generally agreed to have been written by Gottfried is included as well, not just for the sake of completeness, but also because it provides us with another window into Gottfried's main work. Finally, the organizational presentation of the work is new and incorporates Gottfried's own architecture with regard to major divisions and transitions. In an effort to maintain a readable acrostic in the prologue in English, certain compromises in word order or syntax were necessary so that the strophe could begin with the correct letter. Given the multiplicity of meaning in the prologue, especially the first ten strophes, there was no attempt to further complicate matters by undertaking the compromises necessary to accommodate a rhyme scheme. The appropriate rhyme scheme was used in the internal four-line strophes, however, because this helps to illustrate the unique nature and placement of these verses and does little to endanger an accurate translation of these more straightforward stanzas. This translation follows Friedrich Ranke's text, mostly as presented in the edition and German translation of Walter Haug and Günter Scholz (2011/2012).

The work is divided into two main parts, introduced by a prologue and separated by an interlogue that ends with line 12,430. The second part begins with what is here Chapter 18, just before Isolde and Mark meet. The chapter divisions are based to some extent on previous editions and translations in English and German but in the end are unique to this translation. Because the original work did not have chapter divisions as we know them today, nor do most medieval texts, the need to divide the text into these shorter parts caters wholly to a contemporary readership. The chapter titles are for the most part my own. One consideration in determining these chapter divisions was the desire to mimic to some extent a sense of balanced design, so

---

26. Revisions were made to Hatto's translation in 1988.

the perceptive reader will note that the various parts and subparts that can be identified as Gottfried's contain an equal number of chapters on either side of the midway dividing line. One last nod to the manuscript transmission, especially through the Heidelberg manuscript (H), is the indication in bold of large initials that are not part of the acrostics or separate strophes. These are so marked in Ranke's edition and have been cross-checked with the manuscript itself. Whenever practical, paragraphs follow the manuscript cues given by the larger initials.

Personal and place names have been spelled in fairly conventional ways, using Hatto's translation mostly as a guide. The name "Tristan" is now fairly common in English usage, with variants such as "Tristram" and "Tristran" also not uncommon. The spelling of "Isolde" is a bit more problematic. Isolde is clearly the modern German equivalent as well as Hatto's choice, while Gottfried himself writes "Isôt(e)" or "Isôlt." This and other variants, such as "Isold" and "Isolt" have been used in other translations and editions. The French variants "Iseult," "Yseult," and "Ysolt" have also found their way into the material but are generally not used for Gottfried's poem. There is some difference of opinion on the spelling of King Mark/Marke. While the final "e" reflects Gottfried's practice, there seems to be no compelling argument against using the modern equivalent of the name.[27] Most other slight changes to naming conventions were made for the sake of ease of pronunciation in modern English.

One of the more difficult decisions turned out to be assigning a title to this book. Most medieval manuscripts and writers, with a few exceptions, did not assign titles to their work as a whole. This is a fairly modern convention. Hatto chose to name his translation (only) *Tristan*; other German translators and editors have followed suit (Krohn, Schröder/Knecht, Weber). The choice is not as clear-cut as Hatto would have us believe, however.[28] It is true that Gottfried indicates that his story is about Tristan and that he is the main protagonist, but it is equally true that the entire work is based on the concept that the two, Tristan and Isolde, become one. Gottfried's own chiastic play with both names and initials makes this clear. There is also the weight of convention, and Hatto's own translation was republished under the title *Tristan and Isolde* (1988). While there is an understandable temptation to avoid confusion between Gottfried's work and Wagner's 1859 opera, also

---

27. The Celtic origin of the name seems to point to a form of "marc," meaning horse. This name was possibly Latinized into Marcus by Gallo-Romans, with Old French variants including Mark, Marke, and Marque. See Okken, 1.63–64, note to l. 423.

28. "Gottfried's story is essentially the life of Tristan, courtier, warrior, and lover, into which Isolde enters only at a later stage. Poets who followed Gottfried refer to his work as the *Tristan*, correctly, beyond all question, and I have followed them in turn, resisting the temptation to name it 'Tristan and Isolde', as readers might have expected" (Hatto, 1960, 7).

titled *Tristan und Isolde*, it seems fair to say that most readers would prefer the more familiar title that includes both main characters.

Commentary on the text and its themes has been relegated largely to the footnotes as opposed to this Introduction. In the footnotes the reader will find indications of passages where translations have differed in their interpretation, with quotations from those translations that will help the reader understand why there is disagreement and also how the text might be interpreted differently. Translations of Gottfried's Old French have been relegated to the footnotes, with modern French appearing in the text, thus mimicking the effect such language might have had on a medieval audience. Historical facts and references to other sources should help orient the reader to some context for Gottfried's text, and the occasional interpretive note is meant only as a guide to some points of scholarly discussion on broader themes.

Gottfried was revered by the generation that followed him for his mastery of language, and it is a difficult task to produce a translation of Gottfried's language that does justice to his complex and subtle employment of and experimentation with the vernacular as it shifted from oral to primarily written form. Even a fairly literal translation is challenged by Gottfried's playful and in many ways unique art of bending syntax and semantics to produce not only new meaning but significant ambiguity. Gottfried chose to tell a tale that, on the surface, is unredemptive. The story of Tristan and Isolde is a tale of deceit, disloyalty, and adultery. Even the next generation of readers and poets had to reject this aspect of the story, as witnessed by Ulrich von Türheim's criticism. Any final redemption could only be found with God. But Gottfried infused his narrative with a deeper meaning, a message of redemption intended for those who could appreciate the beauty of a love burdened with pain and conflict. The question any translator faces is whether or not a more literal approach can adequately communicate not only Gottfried's story but also his persistent efforts at subversion. It is the hope of this translation that a less literal, more free translation might be better able to impart a deeper understanding of Gottfried's art, but in the end any translation of such a complex work can only hope to convey to the modern reader some appreciation of the artist's ability to create multiple layers of meaning that exploit both ambiguity and the playfulness of linguistic experimentation.

This leaves me to encourage every reader to engage with the original in one form or another. The addition of line numbering follows the practice of Knecht's translation, with every ten lines indicated in brackets. This translation's line numbering uses Ranke's system, which as noted is not the same as that used by some other editions. The inclusion of numbers should make it easy for a reader to refer back to the original text, something that any translator should encourage. It is hoped that the translation is itself seamless

Gottfried von Strassburg's

TRISTAN

AND

ISOLDE

Prologue

[1] **G**ive a man no credit
for the good he's[1] done for others,
then all the good done in the world
would seem to be worth nothing.

[5][2] **D**oing good for others
with good intent is what a good man does.
Whoever thinks it anything but good
is acting in bad faith.

[9] **I** often hear disparaged
what should instead be wanted.
Then much is made of mediocrity,
then people want what they don't want at all.

[13] **E**veryone should rightly praise
what is to him essential,
and may it bring him pleasure
for as long as it is pleasing.

[17] **T**o me the man is rare and worthy
who can weigh both good and bad,
who can value me and every man
according to his worth.[3]

---

1. There is disagreement in the manuscripts and editions as to whether the pronoun is singular or plural. Ranke's edition has the singular (*dem*), which follows manuscripts HS, whereas most other editors have the plural (*den*), which follows all other manuscripts (except M). Ranke's singular form is consistent with the "good man" (*guoter man*, l. 5) in the second strophe. If the plural is preferred, then the first two lines would read: "Give people no credit / for the good they've done for others."

2. The D initial continues the acrostic through strophe 10 that spells DIETERICH, widely accepted to represent a dedication to an unknown patron or donor of the work. The acrostic is only obvious and consistent with large initials in manuscript H, where the initials actually spell out DIEDERIKH.

3. The first five strophes (ll. 1–20) employ an alternating rhyme scheme, or ABAB, whereas the following five (ll. 21–40) use an enclosed rhyme scheme, or ABBA, all with the added

[21] Esteem and praise inspire art,
where art for praise is fashioned.
Wherever praise adorns it,
there art in every form will flourish.

[25] Rightly just as something fades away
if not praised or honored,
so it will be cherished given honor
and not denied its praise.

[29] It is these days a common practice
to think of good as bad
and to think of bad as good.
This is not a practice, it is malpractice.

[33] Critical minds and art,
how well they illuminate each other.
Should envy come between them, though,
then art and discernment are extinguished.

[37] Hah, Excellence, how narrow are your walks,
how difficult your climbs!
How fortunate the one who
climbs your walks and walks your climbs.

[41]⁴ To waste my time without reward,
seasoned as I am for living,

---

complexity of identical rhyme. This division seems to reinforce a transition in content from the ethical to the aesthetic, with the first five strophes focused on the importance of external praise and fair judgment for the good works (poetry) of the good man (poet), while the next five strophes transition to the appreciation of art and creativity in general and the role this plays both in memorialization and the pursuit of excellence.

4. The T initial most likely stands for Tristan, the main protagonist of the story. This eleventh strophe (ll. 41–44) completes the first ten, differentiated as they are by rhyme scheme, by returning to the initial ABAB pattern. The rest of the poem, starting with l. 45, continues in an AABB scheme of rhyming couplets. Certain additional quatrains will appear throughout the work in strategic locations, as discussed in the Introduction. The interjection of different rhyme schemes is clearly meant to alert both the listener and reader to a significant passage or transition.

would be to live in this world
not as "worlded"⁵ as I am.⁶

[45]⁷ **I** have set myself a single task: to please the world and bring pleasure
to noble hearts, to those hearts that are one with mine, to that world which
my heart perceives. I don't mean all the world, not those who, so I've heard,
can't tolerate hardship and just want to revel in bliss. May God let them live
in joy! That world and that kind of life will not appreciate what I have to
say, its life and mine are unalike. I have another kind of world in mind, one
that can hold together in one heart [60] sweet bitterness and pleasant pain,
heartfelt joy and the agony of unfulfilled desire, a happy life and a miserable
death, a happy death and a miserable life. To this life let me be devoted. May
I be "worlded" in this world, to perish with it or be saved.⁸ I have remained

---

5. I have decided to leave this word (MHG *gewerldet*) essentially untranslated. The word is
Gottfried's own creation and as such contains multiple meanings not otherwise available to
the poet. To be "worlded" means to have a world, to be in the world, to have a relationship to
the world, that is, to others. This has most often been translated as to be a part of the world, a
part of society, or specifically a member of the court. But it can also insinuate another world,
a world apart from society, as Gottfried infers in his only other use of the word in line 65. As
usual with Gottfried, it is important to recognize the ambiguity and subversion of meaning
with which he confronts his readers from the very start.

6. This entire strophe has proven particularly difficult for translators. Hatto includes the lines
as part of the following main section, despite its distinctive ABAB rhyme and T initial: "If I
spend my time in vain, ripe for living as I am, my part in society will continue to fall short of
what my experience requires of me" (1960, 42). Gentry revises Hatto to read, "ripe for living
as I am, I would not be as much a part of the world as I am" (1988, 4). Krohn (1980) separates the four lines from the following strophe (l. 45 on) and translates: "If I were to waste my
time in idleness, even though I am fit for life, then I would not be so much a part of society
in this world as I truly am" (Wenn ich meine Zeit unnütz vertrödelte, obwohl ich doch reif
bin zum Leben, dann wäre ich in dieser Welt nicht so sehr ein Teil der Gesellschaft, wie ich
es tatsächlich bin). Haug/Scholz (2011/2012): "If I waste my time in my advanced age, then
I am living in the courtly world not a part of it as I am now" (Wenn ich meine Zeit vertue in
meinem vorgerückten Alter, so lebe ich in der höfischen Welt nicht so eins mit ihr, wie ich es
bin). Knecht (2004a): "If I, whose time to live is limited, waste my time, then I am not living
in the world according to my worldly calling" (Treibe ich, dessen Lebenszeit gemessen ist,
meine Zeit umsonst dahin, lebe ich in der Welt nicht so, wie es meine weltliche Berufung ist).

7. The I initial, following the logic of the T initial, stands for Isolde. It brings to mind the
episode in which Tristan is instructed by Brangane to carve the initials T and I on small chips
of wood as a coded signal (ll. 14,421–43). The initials are repeated in l. 131 and l. 135 in the
reverse, I and T. Line 130 of the Prologue demonstrates this in another way by repeating the
names: *Tristan Îsolt Îsolt Tristan*. This chiastic arrangement represents both the interconnected-
ness of the two names and persons, as well as the embrace of the two inner "I's," or Isolde, by
the two outer "T's," or Tristan.

8. Gottfried makes it clear with this sequence of oxymorons that paradox and dialectic is the
leitmotif of the entire work, and indeed his whole enterprise.

Part 1.1

Chapter 1: Rivalin and Blancheflor: Courtship

[245] There once lived a lord in Parmenie,[1] still young in years, according to what I read. He was, as the story tells us truthfully, a peer of kings in birth, as wealthy in land as any prince, handsome and a joy to behold, trustworthy, bold, generous, and powerful. As he was obliged to bring joy to others, this lord was in all his days like a ray of joyful sunshine. He was a delight to all the world, a paradigm for all of chivalry, an honor to his own people, and the promise for the future of his lands. [260] In him was lacking none of the virtues a noble should have, with one exception. Too often he wanted to follow his lofty heart's desire and act however it suited him. This was to bring him much sorrow, because unfortunately it is now and has always been true that these two, flowering youth and great wealth, together lead to arrogance. Tolerance, which many [270] exercise despite their power, was seldom something he contemplated. Repaying evil with evil, responding to violence with violence, that was his way.

It is impossible in the long run to want to retaliate for every offence in full measure.[2] God only knows that often we all need to look the other way in such exchanges, [280] or we will surely get the worst of it in the end. Whoever cannot abide injury will certainly reap only more injury. As with the method used to kill bears, he avenges every strike until he himself is overcome by injuries.[3] I think it was the same with him. He so often took revenge that he eventually harmed himself. [290] His ultimate undoing was not the result of his own meanness, which certainly is the cause of harm for some, but rather resulted from the circumstances of his youth. His struggle against his own happiness, in his flowering youth and with the qualities of youthful nobility,

---

1. Gottfried changed the original *Ermonie* in the sources to Parmenie, which could either be a playful jab at his "loyalty" to his sources or possibly an early scribal mistake that became standard. The first option is more likely. This fictional land is somewhere next to Brittany in France.
2. The original, *mit Karles lôte* (l. 277) refers to a common notion that the emperor Charlemagne's (*Karles*) silver coin was the standard for measuring weight (*lôte*) against other coins, given its presumed high silver content and the high esteem in which Charles the Great was held throughout the Middle Ages. The metaphor therefore works by projecting a common phrase for exact monetary equivalence into the sphere of human experience.
3. This is a reference to a cruel hunting technique in which a beehive was used as bait for a trap consisting of a heavy weight or hammer that swings in front of it. The bear would bat the hammer away, but it would swing back to knock him in the head. Eventually the bear tired and could be killed by the hunters below.

resulted from the careless immaturity and stubborn pride that sprouted [300] in his heart. He acted just like other young people who never think ahead. He didn't think he had a care in the world but just lived on as if there were no tomorrow. As his young life was just beginning, rising as the morning star, he looked out into the world with amusement. He thought that his life [310] would just breeze by in honeyed bliss, but that never happens. No, the days of his youth were soon over. Just as the sun of his worldly joy was beginning to rise, the twilight that had been hidden from him quickly extinguished his morning. [320]

The sources tell us his name, his story makes it clear. His Christian name was Rivalin, his sobriquet was Canelengres. Many people believe that he was a lord from Lohnois and king of that land,[4] but Thomas assures us, and he read it in the sources, [330] that he was from Parmenie. He had received a fiefdom from the hand of a Breton, and for that he owed him fealty. That man was Duke Morgan.

Now Lord Rivalin had been a knight for three years,[5] during which he gained success and great honor. He completely mastered the skills of chivalry [340] and mustered the forces needed for war, for which he had land, people, and wealth. I don't know if it was as an act of self-defense or on account of his conceit, but the story tells us that he attacked Morgan, as if he were to blame. He invaded his lands with overwhelming force and destroyed [350] many of his castles. The towns had to surrender and ransom their property and lives, as much as they loathed the thought. He had by then gathered together enough money and property to increase his military force and [360] impose his will on fortifications or towns wherever he pleased, but he, too, suffered severe losses and paid with many brave men. Morgan defended himself and confronted him often with his army, causing grievous casualties. Warfare and knightly combat include defeat and victory, such is the way of war, with losses and gains [370] driving the fighting ever on. I suspect that Morgan did much the same and in turn destroyed Rivalin's castles and towns, depriving him of his people and property and imposing his will. This brought him little gain, though, as Rivalin time and again inflicted heavy losses [380] to the point that Morgan could no longer defend himself, with his only recourse being retreat into his strongest and best citadels.

---

4. This may have originally referred to Lothian (Lat. *Lodonesia*), a region in southeastern Scotland, which would be appropriate for the originally Pictish hero, but not for a continental version known to the Anglo-Norman audience for which Thomas wrote. Gottfried's comment on the veracity of Thomas's geography may be a reaction against Eilhart's version, which introduces Rivalin as the lord of Lohnois, and he may also be polemicizing against Wolfram von Eschenbach, who in his *Parzival* mentions a Rifalin von Lohenis (73,14).

5. Most young men of the nobility were knighted around age eighteen, although there is some variation. William Marshal, for example, was knighted in 1166, at the age of nineteen or twenty.

Rivalin besieged these and stormed them as often as possible. He drove the enemy behind their gates, [390] while he paraded his troops before them in tournaments and chivalric contests. Finally he gained the upper hand and, pillaging and burning, devastated the land. Morgan was prepared to parley and with great effort achieved a truce. They agreed on a peace to last a year, [400] secured with hostages and oaths as was the custom.[6] Rivalin thereupon returned home with his troops, filled with power and satisfaction. His generosity rewarded them and made them all rich, and he allowed them happily to return to their homes, much to his own honor.

Since Canel had been so successful [410] it didn't take long for him to undertake another expedition, this time for pleasure. He rode out with great pomp and circumstance, as one does who is intent on gaining honor, and all the equipment and goods that he would need for an entire year were loaded onto a ship. [420] He had heard it often told how courtly and honorable the young king of Cornwall, Mark, was, and how greatly his honor increased. He ruled both Cornwall and England. Cornwall was his by birthright, but the situation with England was as follows. He had ruled it since [430] the Saxons from Gales[7] had driven out the Britons. They remained there as lords and gave the land its name. What had once been called Britain was named England by those who came from Gales. After they had conquered the land and divided it up amongst themselves, they all wanted to become little kings [440] and independent lords, but this turned out to be their downfall. They began to fight and kill each other until they finally put themselves and their lands under Mark's protection. From that time on the land served him so faithfully that no kingdom since has served a king better. [450] The story also tells us that in all the neighboring lands that knew of his reputation, no king was more respected than he was. This was Rivalin's destination. He intended to stay there with him for a year and to learn from him the virtues of character and the new knighthood[8] and to perfect his own manners. [460] His noble

---

6. It was common practice to exchange young sons or daughters of the high nobility with the enemy as hostages, whose safety was only guaranteed if the terms of the agreement were kept.
7. Most sources agree that the first wave of Anglo-Saxon settlement was completed around 450 CE. This of course would place the time of the story back into the Migration Age, an anachronism that would not necessarily have troubled the reader of the early thirteenth century. The name Gales could refer to Wales but could also stand for all the lands once occupied by the Britons, or *Walas*. The assumption that the Saxons, as the new occupiers of the Briton lands, or Gales, then transferred the name to England, is explained with some rather dubious linguistic sleight of hand. In one spelling, E(n) – gal – lant, the attempt is made to show the connection. It is also possible that Gales and England are not etymologically connected, as the text only says that England was named by those who came from Gales, not that they named it after Gales.
8. The manuscripts and editions diverge in their reading of *niwan* (only, except) or *niuwe* (new) in line 458. Mss. H and M read *niwan*, and this is followed by Ranke/Krohn and

heart told him one thing: if he appreciated the customs of a foreign land, he could improve his own behavior and be appreciated in turn.

With this intent he set out. He entrusted his people and his lands to his marshal,[9] a noble from the land whom he knew to be loyal named Rual *le trés loyal*.[10] [470] Rivalin then set out to cross the sea with twelve companions. He had no need of more than this, he had all that he needed.[11] When he arrived off of Cornwall, he heard while still at sea that the renowned Mark was in Tintagel, and to there he set a course. [480] He landed and, much to his delight, found him there. He outfitted himself and his men splendidly, as was to be expected, and when he arrived at court, Mark, a man of great courtesy, welcomed him and all his men most courteously. Rivalin was received with honors, [490] the likes of which had never before at any other time or place been extended to him so graciously. He was enthralled with thoughts of these manners at court and often thought to himself, "Surely God himself has brought me to these people. My good fortune continues to favor me. [500] Everything that I heard tell about Mark's virtues is on display here. His life is refined and proper." He shared with Mark the reasons that he had come.

When Mark heard his story and his intentions, he said, "You are welcome in God's name. My life and property, all that I own, these are at your disposal."

Canelengres was well pleased with the court, [510] and the court was well pleased with him. Poor and rich alike were fond of him and held him in high esteem. Never before had a guest been so beloved, and he was well-deserving. Rivalin, full of virtue, was always at their service with person, property, and pleasant demeanor. [520] He lived in this fashion, admired, without want, and secured daily by his conduct and virtue, up until the time of Mark's festival. Mark's will and wish insured the celebration would be well attended, and whenever he sent out his messengers the chivalry [530] of the kingdom of England quickly assembled every year in Cornwall. The knights would bring with them a multitude of lovely ladies and all kinds of beautiful things.[12]

Marold/Schröder. Haug/Scholz, however, use manuscripts FWNERSP to support a variant of *niuwe* (i.e., *niwe* or *nuwe*) arguing that the context would allow for a reading that Mark and his court represent the "new," or courtly form of knighthood, something that Rivalin seeks to experience and learn from. This translation agrees with the latter view.

9. The court position of marshal was, by the end of the twelfth century, one of the four main court appointments, the others being seneschal, cupbearer, and chamberlain. The marshal was responsible for military command and matters of logistics and lodging.

10. From the Old French *li foitenant*, or "the most trustworthy."

11. Setting out with a small band of warriors was still considered to be typical of the heroic warrior's quest for adventure.

12. The connection between women and "other beautiful things" is intentional, as women were often used as decorative figures in the public display of wealth and power in order to enhance a court's reputation for beauty and joy.

The festivities were fixed and finalized for the four weeks [540] from the beginning to the end of sweet, flowering May.[13] Very near Tintagel they gathered in what was the most beautiful meadow that anyone has ever set eyes on, before or since. Fair, lovely summer had made it the object of its loving attention. The little birds of the forest [550] that please the ear, flowers, grass, foliage, and blossoms, everything that soothes the eye and brings joy to noble hearts, all this was there in abundance in that summer meadow. Everything one could wish that May might provide was present: sun and shade; a linden tree near a fountain; and soft, light breezes [560] that gently blew toward Mark's company. The radiant flowers laughed out from the dew-moistened grass. May's friend, the green grass, had clothed itself in a wonderful summer garment of flowers that was reflected in the eyes of the dear guests. The sweet flowering trees [570] smiled down at each of them, and their hearts and sentiments responded to the verdant merriment with playful eyes that smiled back in return. The soothing birdsong, sweet and splendid, refreshed both ears and spirits as it filled the hills and dales. [580] The uplifting nightingale, that lovely, sweet little bird, may its sweetness live on always, called out from among the blossoms with such exuberance that many a noble heart was touched with joy and ardor.[14]

The company joyfully pitched tents on the green meadow [590] as it suited each of them. As everyone was intent on joy, so they were situated. The rich rested luxuriously, the courtly with courtliness, some covered by silk, others covered by flowers. The linden tree was roof enough, many used green boughs as their pavilion's crown. [600] Neither the residents nor the guests had ever been so wonderfully accommodated as they were here. As customary at such festivities, there was an abundance of food and costly attire, whatever each person had chosen to wear. In addition, Mark treated them so generously and splendidly [610] that they all enjoyed themselves and were happy.

So the festival began, and whoever among the enthusiastic wanted to experience even more was not disappointed. One could watch whatever one wanted to watch. Some went to gaze at the ladies,[15] others went to view the dancing. Some watched the equestrian games, [620] others the jousting.[16]

---

13. This Pentecostal festival is common throughout Arthurian literature, and Mark here follows in King Arthur's footsteps.

14. This classic *locus amoenus* passage, with descriptions of nature's openness, joy, and beauty, sets the stage for the protagonists and the readers in the expectation of what is to follow, and what is naturally reflected in noble hearts: love.

15. This pastime of watching ladies was apparently something of a sport for noble men, as witnessed in a poem by Hartmann von Aue, wherein he expresses a reluctance to join his friends in this entertainment (MF XXII/XV,1: 1–4; L 216,29–32).

16. These chivalrous games were quite varied. The first, or *bûhurdieren*, was a mass parade of riders with one side often chasing the other, and was meant to show off equestrian skills. It was something akin to modern polo, in that it was exclusive to the wealthy and was meant as

Whatever tickled one's fancy, there was plenty to be had. All those in their youth vied with one another for the joys of the festival.

Noble Mark, courtly and keen, had one particular wonder with him aside from the beauty of those ladies [630] that surrounded him, namely his sister Blancheflor. She was a young woman more beautiful than had ever been seen there or anywhere else. We hear it said of her beauty that any man alive who saw her with his own eyes would forever after love [640] womankind and excellence all the more.

This blessed vision made some men there on the meadow bold and brave and noble hearts jubilant. There in the glade were many other beautiful ladies, each of whom could have been a powerful queen, based on her beauty. They, too, brought passion and joy [650] to all who were there and made many a heart joyful. Then the equestrian games began with both the court retainers and the guests. The worthiest and most talented rode from all over to join in. Noble Mark was there along with his companion Rivalin, not to mention the rest of his company, who were also intent [660] on accomplishing deeds to be recounted and praised. On display were many horses covered expansively with precious materials and silks. Some covers were white as snow, others yellow, plum, red, green, and blue. Still others could be seen that were made of the finest silks [670] and fashioned, colored, and festooned in a variety of ways. The company of knights wore splendid outfits that were perfectly tailored and fitted. The summer also wanted to demonstrate that it was Mark's ally, and so there were many beautiful garlands of flowers to be seen in the crowds, [680] worn as a tribute to him.

In this lovely fullness of summer the knights began their games, with various companies entangled in the melee. They drove each other back and forth so often that the contest ended up where dear Blancheflor, that wonder of wonders, and many other beautiful ladies [690] were seated as spectators. The knights were riding so expertly, even imperiously, that people were riveted by the spectacle. Whatever they accomplished, though, the courtly Rivalin without a doubt surpassed them all on that day and in that place. The ladies took special notice, [700] remarking that no one else in the throng rode so skillfully and chivalrously. They praised everything he did.

"Look," they said, "at that brilliant young man there, how brilliantly he manages everything he does! How perfect his body is, [710] and how shapely his long legs. How his shield is always fixed in place. How the lance rests in

---

much as a demonstration of horsemanship as it was an actual game. Jousting, or *justieren*, on the other hand, was a contest of one knight riding against another, with armor and blunted lances. The tourney, or *tjostieren*, involved one team squaring off against another, with the use of swords included, meant as a mock game of war and valuable in the practice it afforded warriors on horseback in combat skills. As a result of the use of real weapons, the results were occasionally fatal.

his hand. How well his clothes fit. How he holds his head and wears his hair. How exquisite his every move. How brilliant he is. Whoever has her pleasure with him, what a lucky woman."[17]

[720] Noble Blancheflor heard everything they said. She, too, held him in high esteem in her own heart, regardless of what the others did. She had feelings for him, he had won her heart, he by rights carried scepter and crown in her heart's kingdom. [730] She kept it all properly secret and hidden from the rest.

When the contest had finally ended and all the knights had dispersed, each to where his desires led him, it just so happened[18] that Rivalin rode by where beautiful Blancheflor was sitting. [740] He guided his horse a bit closer, and as he looked into her eyes he said to her most tenderly, "*Ah, Dieu vous sauve, la belle.*"[19]

"*Merci,*" replied the young woman, and added most modestly, "may God the Almighty, who makes all hearts glad, gladden your heart and mind. And although I am much beholden to you, [750] I reserve the right to take up a matter of concern with you."

"Oh, my dear, what have I done?" responded courtly Rivalin.

She said, "You've caused me distress on behalf of the very best friend I've ever had."

"My God," he thought to himself, "what is she talking about? What have I ever done to upset her? [760] What is she accusing me of?" He thought that perhaps he might have unknowingly injured one or the other member of her family in the tournament, thereby causing her sorrow and anger.

No, the friend of whom she spoke was her heart, wherein she felt an uneasiness on his account. [770] This was the friend of whom she spoke, but of whom he knew nothing.

He spoke to her affectionately in his most courteous manner, "Dearest, I don't want you to harbor any hatred or ill will toward me. If what you say against me is true, then judge me for yourself. Whatever you command, I will do."

The lovely woman said, [780] "I don't hate you all too much on account of this affair, but I also don't love you for it. I will take some time to consider how you can compensate me for what you have done to me."

---

17. Gottfried characterizes the ladies' praise as gushing, with the constant repetition of *wie* (how), an effect that punctuates the action being described in staccato-like fashion. The sexual overtones are obvious.

18. The original *âventiure* can imply both chance as well as destiny, and so the line could also mean "it was meant to be."

19. Gottfried's Old French speech is here rendered in modern French, following Haug/ Scholz's (2011/2012) example, in order to retain the flavor of the dual-language nature of German-speaking courts around 1200, where French was still the "courtly" language. Rivalin's greeting translates: "God bless [or protect] you, lovely woman," from the Latin *Deus te salvet.*

He bowed down to her and wanted to be off, but the beautiful woman sighed quietly and spoke from her heart, "Oh, dear friend, may God bless you."[20]

[790] This was the moment when they first started to have feelings for one another. Canelengres turned away, lost in thought. He thought hard about what was bothering Blancheflor and what she meant. He thought about her greeting and what she said, her sigh, her blessing, and her demeanor. He considered all of this [800] and thought that her sigh and her kind farewell might be signs of love. He finally came to the conclusion that these two things could only have been caused by love. This aroused his imagination so much that it raced back to Blancheflor, seized her, and led her straightaway [810] to the land of Rivalin's heart, where she was crowned queen.[21] Yes, Blancheflor and Rivalin, king and lovely queen, they shared their hearts' kingdoms equally. Hers became Rivalin's, and his heart became hers, even though neither one of them knew [820] how the other felt. Both of them had totally and completely become one in their thoughts, and so both got what they deserved. He felt her presence in his heart with the same pain that he caused her, but since he had no assurance of her desires [830] or why she had acted as she had, out of dislike or out of love, his mind reeled with doubt and his thoughts swayed back and forth. One minute he was headed one way, and the next another, until finally he was so entangled in his thoughts [840] that he could find no way out.

Rivalin, lost in thought, was himself the perfect example of how a mind intent on love is like a free bird that, while enjoying its freedom, lands on a lime-covered branch.[22] When it notices the lime and seeks to fly off, its feet remain stuck. [850] It flaps its wings to escape, but if in doing so it touches even one small part of the branch then it is stuck and caught. It begins to fight with all its might this way and that, until it finally defeats itself and remains glued to the branch. [860] A mind that is still carefree will behave in the same way. Whenever someone is engaged in reveries of yearning, and love works its wonders with the heaviness of desire, then the one who yearns seeks

---

20. In the original text, Blancheflor uses the informal address, you (*du*), here for the first time, a sign of growing familiarity and affection.

21. This short scene of an abduction through the imagination invokes the theme of the bridal quest.

22. The use of birdlime on branches is still used (mostly illegally) as a method for hunting birds. Hunting metaphors depicting the entanglement or capture of a lover were a commonplace of classical Roman literature and often employed by Ovid (for example, *Ars Amatoria*, I, 45–48; 1982, 167). Gottfried makes ample use of hunting techniques and terminology in much the same way. Rivalin's inability to escape love projects the metaphor of a trap onto the love potion that later ensnares Tristan and Isolde.

to regain his freedom. But the sweet stickiness of love pulls him back down again. He is then so entangled that there is no escape [870] in any direction.

So it was with Rivalin. His thoughts were also entwined in the love of the queen of his heart. All this confusion misled him in a most peculiar way, since he didn't know if she was well or ill disposed toward him. He was unable to distinguish one from the other, [880] her love or her hate. He could find neither hope nor despair, neither one nor the other to cling to. Hope and despair were constantly pulling him back and forth. Hope spoke to him of love, despair of hate. Because of this swirling around he was unable to rely with any certainty on hate or love, [890] and so his thoughts were set adrift in an uncharted port. Hope drew him to land, and despair back out again. Neither one offered him firm ground, and there was no way to unite the two. When despair came along and told him that Blancheflor hated him, then he wavered and wanted only to leave, but quickly hope appeared and offered him her love and pleasant illusions, [900] and so he had to stay. He was confounded by this tug of war and didn't know up from down anymore. The more he struggled, the more love held him fast. The harder he tried to escape, the more love pulled him back. Love persisted until hope emerged victorious. Despair was driven from the field. [910] Rivalin was secure in the knowledge that his Blancheflor loved him. His heart and all his thoughts remained fixed on her, the struggle was over.

Even after sweet Love[23] had bent his heart and mind to her will, he remained ignorant of the fact that heartfelt love was [920] such a close neighbor to sorrow. When he looked back on his fateful encounter with his Blancheflor and thought about her hair, her brow, her temples, her cheeks, her mouth, her chin, and her eyes that laughed as on a joyful Easter day,[24] then true Love, [930] that real firebrand, came and kindled her fire of yearning. This fire inflamed his heart and from then on showed him what intimate sorrow and yearning desire really were. From that moment on his life changed; he was given a new life. [940] His entire way of thinking and acting changed; he became a completely different man. Everything he started was undercut by strange behavior and recklessness. His good senses were made erratic and unstable, as if he had taken leave of them.[25] His life began to lose

---

23. I follow Haug and Scholze's (2011/2012) and Hatto's (1960) convention of capitalizing Love (*Minne*, as distinct from *liebe*) from this point on when it seems most likely to be a personification or representation of the classical goddess of love, Venus.

24. Easter Sunday is the epitome of a particularly joyous occasion or outlook, when the future is imbued with new hope. In the convention of courtly love poetry it can also serve as a metaphor for a beautiful lady.

25. Several translations read the verb as *erbeten*, which is supported by most manuscripts (e.g., Hatto: "as he had asked for"), whereas some translators, going all the way back to Grimm, use another manuscript variant, *erbiten*, in its meaning "to let go of something." This certainly seems to fit the context better than the former. See Haug/Scholz 2.291.

its vitality, [950] and his heartfelt laughter, once a commonplace, vanished completely. Silence and unhappiness were all that life had left to offer him, and all his contentment was thoroughly transformed into longing and pain.

Blancheflor, in her longing, was affected by the same yearning. She was burdened by the same pain [960] on his account as he was on hers. That aggressor, Love, had assailed her senses a bit too intensely and robbed her of her composure. She was no longer at ease with herself or the world as was her custom. Whatever joys she had possessed, [970] whatever fun she had previously enjoyed, these were now all out of place. She lived from day to day filled with the pain that lay close to her heart, but with all that she suffered she still had no idea what was wrong with her. She had never before experienced this kind of burden [980] and heartfelt care.

She often said to herself, "Oh my Lord and God, what kind of life is this? What has happened to me? I have seen many men before and never been hurt by them, but since I first saw this man, my heart has lost the calm and joy it once had. Seeing him as I did [990] has brought me all this pain. My heart, which had never before felt such an ache, has been wounded. It has changed the way I think and feel. If every woman who listens to him and sees him experiences what I have, and if this is truly his nature [1000] then beauty is wasted on him and will only harm others. But if he has gained the knowledge of some kind of magic that causes this strange marvel and this marvelous anguish, then it would be better if he were dead and no woman had to look upon him ever again. By God, how is it that I have suffered such pain and sorrow because of him? [1010] I certainly never looked at him or any other man with hostility before, or was hateful to anyone. What have I done to deserve being harmed by someone on whom I looked with kindness?

"What am I accusing this man of? He may be completely innocent. The heartfelt cares that I have [1020] on his account, God knows, are mostly caused by my own heart. I saw him among many men. How can he help it if my thoughts focused on him alone instead of all the others? I heard so many noble women praising his majestic stature and his knightly eminence [1030] and bouncing around compliments like a ball. They praised him most highly, and I saw the qualities they were admiring with my own eyes. I took everything that was praiseworthy about him into my heart. I lost my head, and my heart fell for him. Truly I was blinded [1040] by the magic that made me forget who I was. That dear man, the object of my complaints, did me no harm. It is my foolish, impulsive nature that harms me and wants my unhappiness. It wants more, more than it should want [1050] if it thought about what is appropriate and honorable. It can't see past its own willfulness where this exalted man is concerned, for whom it has fallen so completely and in such a short time.

"I believe, so help me God, if I may believe it honorably and not be afraid [1060] for my unblemished reputation, that this ache I carry here in my heart on his account can only come from love. I know this is true because I want only to be with him. Whatever this state of affairs may be, something is growing in me that wants to love this man. What I have up to now only heard about love [1070] and about women genuinely in love has pierced my own heart. This sweet love sickness that tortures so many noble hearts now resides in my own heart."

This courtly lady, full of thoughts and emotions, recognized, [1080] as do all those in love, that her friend Rivalin was meant to be the joy of her heart, her greatest consolation, and her life's fulfillment, and so she began to cast glances at him and to see him whenever she could. Whenever modesty would allow she would greet him discreetly with tender looks. With longing eyes [1090] she often watched him affectionately. When her dear friend,[26] that loving man, began to take notice, his love for her truly strengthened and gave him hope. His heart's desire was kindled, and he returned the sweet woman's looks more boldly and sweetly than he had ever before. [1100] When he had the chance he also greeted her with his gaze. When the beautiful lady recognized that he felt about her as she did about him, her greatest worry vanished. She had actually thought before that he had no feelings for her at all, but now she knew full well that his feelings for her were loving and kind, as feelings of love should be. [1110] He knew the same was true of her. Their senses had been kindled, and from then on they began to think of and love one another with their hearts. It happened to them just as the saying goes: "Where one love looks into another love's eyes, there love's flame is sure to arise."

Chapter 2: Rivalin and Blancheflor: Love and Loss

[1119] After Mark's festival had come to an end and the honored guests had all left, Rivalin received reports that one of Mark's enemies, a king, had invaded his lands with a large army. If he wasn't quickly opposed then his mounted forces would destroy everything within reach. Mark quickly called together a large host [1130] and rode out in force to repel him. He joined battle and gained the victory, killing or capturing many of the enemy, and anyone who escaped or survived could thank his lucky stars.[27] Rivalin, that worthy man, had been wounded in the side by a spear, and he was so gravely

---

26. The term *vriunt* often denotes a much more intimate relationship than our contemporary word "friend," although it would be going too far at this point to translate the term as "lover."
27. King Mark is still depicted here as a strong, active ruler, in contrast with the role he later takes on with Tristan at his side.

injured that his men quickly [1140] carried him back home to Tintagel fearing he was already half dead. Once there they prepared a bed for the man, as he was near death. Reports quickly spread that Canelengres had been mortally wounded in the battle, and a clamor of lamentation arose in the court and across the land. Whoever recognized his outstanding qualities was heartsick over his injury. [1150] They grieved that his courage, his handsome figure, his fine youth, his much praised chivalry should be lost and come to such an untimely end. His friend, King Mark, grieved exceedingly, more than he had ever grieved for anyone before. Many noble women shed tears for him, [1160] many a lady mourned him, and whoever had seen him in the past was moved by his suffering.

Regardless of how much everyone else was saddened by his affliction, it was only his Blancheflor, the chaste, the courtly, the virtuous, who with all her thoughts, her eyes, and her heart [1170] bemoaned and bewailed the pain of her heart's devotion. When she was alone and able to grieve fully, she used her hands against herself. She struck herself a thousand times where it hurt the most, there where her heart lay. This is where that beautiful woman beat herself. This is how that gentle woman tortured [1180] her young, beautiful, delicate body with such terrible violence that she would have gladly exchanged her life for any other death not caused by love.[28] She would have perished and died from this suffering had she not gained strength from faith and kept up hope that she might see him again, [1190] however that might be possible. If she could see him, then she would gladly suffer whatever happened afterward. This kept her alive until she was able to think clearly and consider how she might see him again, which her pain compelled her to do.

So it was that her thoughts hit [1200] upon a particular governess, who had always and in all ways taught her and cared for her and still watched over her now. She took her aside and went to a place where they were alone. There she began to lament as those in the same situation once did and still do. Her eyes welled up, [1210] and hot tears fell in streams upon her fair cheeks. She pressed her hands together and held them up in supplication.

"Oh miserable me," she cried. "Oh," she said, "what a miserable life! My dearest teacher, show me the loyalty which you have in such abundance. [1220] You are so caring, and all my happiness and my salvation depend on your counsel. I place my heartfelt pain in your compassionate care. If you can't help me, I will die."

"My lady, what is this pain and your woeful lament?"

"Oh dearest, do I dare reveal it to you?"

"Yes, dear lady, tell me."

---

28. The self-flagellation of grieving women is a common theme in antiquity, especially for Ovid and Virgil.

22

[1230] "This dying man, Rivalin of Parmenie, is killing me. I need to see him before he dies, if it were possible and I knew how. He will undoubtedly not recover. If you could help me with this, I would never deny you anything for the rest of my life."

The governess thought, [1240] "If I agree to such a thing, what harm could come of it? This mortally wounded man will surely die tomorrow, or soon enough. I will have safeguarded my lady's life and honor and will then be dearer to her than any other woman."

"Beloved lady," she replied, "dearest, your lament breaks my heart, [1250] and if I myself can lessen your distress in any way, then never doubt that I will. I will go there to see him and return at once. I'll find the place and see how and where he is resting and what kind of people are in attendance."

She went to that place acting as if she wanted to lament his suffering, [1260] but she secretly told him that her lady wished to see him, if he could arrange it in an appropriate and honorable way. She then returned from there with this information. She disguised the young woman as a poor beggar, hiding her beauty behind a full headdress,[29] [1270] and then took her lady by the hand to see Rivalin. He had in the meantime sent all his attendants out and was alone, having told them that he needed some time to himself. The governess said for her part that she was bringing a healer and was therefore allowed entry. [1280] She locked the door.

"Dear lady," she said, "now you may see him."

The beautiful woman went to him, and when she saw him with her own eyes, she said, "Alas, and a thousand times alas, that I was ever born. Now all is lost."

Rivalin bowed his head toward her slightly, as best as the mortally wounded man could. [1290] She hardly noticed, paying no attention as she sat there practically blind. She rested her cheek on his until both love and pain robbed her of all her strength. Her red mouth turned pale, her face lost [1300] all of its previous bright coloring, and her brilliant eyes lost their light and were overcome by the darkness of night. She lay there unconscious and unaware for a long time, her cheek against his, as if lifeless.

After she had recovered a little from her distress, [1310] she took her beloved in her arms and placed her mouth on his and hurriedly kissed him a hundred thousand times until her lips kindled his senses and love's strength. In this way love revealed itself. Her lips revived his joy, her lips gave him strength, so that he firmly and affectionately pressed the noble woman [1320] to his battered body. It didn't take long for them to give in to their desire, and

---

29. This was most likely a full wimple and chin band, the typical headdress of a married woman around the year 1200, similar in some ways to the hijab, but most likely not like the full-face veil of the niqab.

the gentle woman became pregnant with his child. He, on the other hand, nearly died from their lovemaking. If God had not saved him from his suffering, he would never have recovered. [1330] But he recuperated, as it was meant to be.

So it happened that Rivalin was healed, and Blancheflor the beautiful was now both unburdened and burdened by him with two kinds of heartache. She left one great sorrow with him and carried an even greater one away. She left the pain of her yearning behind, but what she took away with her from there was death. With love she lost sorrow, [1340] but with her child she found death. Yet however she lived on, and however she was burdened and unburdened by him with gain or with pain, she saw nothing but lovely love and a loving man. She did not yet know about her child or the death to come. Her love and her man were what she was certain of, [1350] and so she acted as do all those who are alive and in love. Her heart, her thoughts, her longing were for Rivalin only. He, too, thought of her and her love in the same way. In their thoughts they had both one love and one desire. In this way he was she and she was he; he was hers and she was his.[30] [1360] Here was Blancheflor, here was Rivalin; here was Rivalin, here was Blancheflor. Wherever they both were, there was *loyal amour*.[31] Their life was one, they spent happy times together and raised each other's spirits through mutual respect and kindness. Whenever they were able to find an appropriate moment to be together, then their physical pleasure was complete. [1370] They were at ease and without want, and they would not have traded their life for any other heavenly kingdom.[32]

This didn't last long. In their new beginning, as they lived the very best life they could imagine, messengers arrived for Rivalin. His enemy Morgan had gathered a large army against him. [1380] Given this news a ship was quickly made ready for Rivalin and all his belongings brought on board. Provisions and horses were all prepared for the voyage.

Her worries began anew when lovely Blancheflor heard the distressing news about her lover. The heartache caused her again [1390] to lose her

---

30. This is one of several examples of Gottfried's use of chiasmus, or inverted parallelism. Here it foreshadows the hallmark entanglement and inseparability of Tristan and Isolde, already demonstrated in the Prologue, ll. 128–30, as the relationship between Rivalin and Blancheflor is further tied to that of the main characters.

31. The Old French, *lêal amûr*, refers to the concept of "loyal" love found in Old French stories that emphasized the natural suitability of partners as well as their social compatibility, that is a kind of love meant to be fulfilled in marriage.

32. Manuscripts HM have *künicrîche*, or (secular) kingdom, while others write *himelrîche*, or heavenly kingdom. Ranke, along with other editors, opts for the latter reading, even though it goes against two of the main manuscripts. The latter term presents an analogy of physical bliss to heaven on earth, while also shifting the joy of physical love to the realm of mystical and spiritual ecstasy.

hearing and sight. The color of her skin took on the pallor of a corpse, and nothing escaped her mouth except for a single cry, "oh." This was all she said and nothing more. "Oh, oh" she cried on and on. "Oh, unfortunate Love and unfortunate man. How you have overwhelmed me with misery. [1400] Love, scourge of the world, when the joy you give is so short lived, when you are so unreliable, what is it that the world loves about you? I see very well that your reward is a fraud. Your ending is not as happy as you promise. You lure us with love that is short, and it turns into suffering that is long. [1410] Your seductive deception is shrouded in insincere delights that cheat all living things. I'm the perfect example. What was to be all my joy is now nothing more than mortal heartache.[33] My consolation has gone and left me behind."

In the middle of her tale of woe, her dear companion Rivalin entered [1420] with a tearful heart, wanting to take his leave.

"Lady," he said, "I remain your servant, but I am obligated to return home. May God protect you, my dear. May you be always happy and in good health."

There again she collapsed from the pain in her heart and lay as if dead in her governess's lap. [1430] When that faithful companion saw such great suffering from the love of his heart, it became his own. He took in her yearning sorrow and made it his. His color and all his strength began to drain from him. Miserable, given the dire circumstances, he sat down [1440] and could hardly wait until she regained her strength somewhat. He took her in his arms and held the unhappy woman gently against him, repeatedly kissing her cheeks, her eyes, her mouth, caressing her this way and that until she finally came to [1450] and was able to sit up on her own.

Once Blancheflor had recovered and noticed her friend, she looked at him sorrowfully. "Oh," she said, "blessed man. How much pain I have because of you. Sir, why did I have to lay eyes on you, so that I should suffer all the heartache that I bear on your account? It's all your fault. [1460] If I dared say it out loud, if you would permit me, then I would ask you to be gentler and kinder to me. My lord and companion, I have much pain from you, and above all three kinds that are fatal and irreversible. The first is that I carry a child whose birth I may not survive without God's help. The second is worse yet. [1470] When my brother, my lord, sees me in this condition and recognizes in it his own disgrace, he will have me sentenced to death and left to die miserably. The third pain is the worst of all and even worse than death. If it should happen that my brother lets me live and does not have me executed, [1480] then he will certainly disown me and take my property and honor. I will be forever

---

33. Love (*Minne*) takes on many of the characteristics of classical *Fortuna*, with her capricious and fickle nature.

disgraced and worthless. In addition I will have to raise my child without a father, even though his father is alive.

"I would never complain if I could bear the burden by myself, and if the royal family [1490] and my brother, the king, could remain untouched by my shame and with their honor intact. But if people all around spread the news that I had a child out of wedlock, then both kingdoms, Cornwall and England, will be openly humiliated, and if that should happen, [1500] then I will be seen as the reason that two lands have been brought down and weakened. I would be better off dead. You see, my lord," she said, "this is the suffering, this is the never-ending heartache that I will have to endure for the rest of my days, dying but still alive. Sir, if you cannot help, and if God does not intervene, [1510] then I can never be happy again."

"My beloved lady," he replied to her, "if you suffer because of me, I will make restitution and from now on ensure that you will suffer no pain or burden through my fault. Whatever may happen in the future, I have experienced such wonderful days with you that it would be shameful [1520] if you were to suffer any hardship on my account. My lady, I will tell you openly what is in my heart and mind. Sorrow and joy, harm and benefit, whatever else should happen to you, I will be a part of it. I will always be there, no matter how difficult it may be. I offer you a choice between two things, [1530] please consider them carefully. Should I stay here or should I return home? You can decide for yourself. If you want me to stay to see how things go for you, then I will. If you want to return home with me, then I and all that I have will be forever yours. You have been so good to me here [1540] that I must repay it in every way I can. Whatever you are thinking, my lady, let me know. I want whatever you want."

"Thanks to you, my lord," she replied. "May God reward your speech and your proposal, and may I always find my place at your feet. [1550] My love and lord, you know very well that I can't stay here. I can't hide the fear that I have for my child. If I could somehow just run away and hide, that would be the best solution for me given the circumstances. Dearest lord, please help me."

"My lady," he replied, "then do as I tell you. When I go down to the ship tonight, [1560] make sure that you have already boarded without being seen. I will have taken my leave, and I will then see you among my retinue. Do this—this is how it must be."

After saying this Rivalin went to Mark and told him the reports that he had received concerning his people and his lands. [1570] He immediately took his leave from him and went to the court. They all cried loudly for Rivalin in a way that he had never heard before nor since. He received many farewells and hopes that God might protect his honor and his life. When it began to get dark, he boarded his ship [1580] and had the rest of his gear brought onboard. There he saw his lady, the beautiful Blancheflor, and the ship immediately cast off and got underway.

When Rivalin landed and heard of the great destruction that Morgan had accomplished with overwhelming force, he sent for his marshal. [1590] His loyalty was beyond doubt, and Rivalin had placed in him all his hopes to safeguard the honor of his people and lands. His name was Rual *le trés loyal*,[34] he was a treasure of honor and faithfulness, and he never wavered in his loyalty. He reported to Rivalin, since he was well informed, [1600] how desperate the situation was for the land.

"However," he said, "now that you have returned to us in time to give all of us support, since God has sent you home, everything will turn out alright, and we may yet recover fully. We can be confident and forget our fears."

Rivalin then told him about his romantic encounter [1610] with Blancheflor, and Rual was truly happy. "I can clearly see, Lord," he said, "that your honor grows in every way. Your position and reputation, your joy and your bliss, these all rise as does the sun. You wouldn't be able to gain a higher standing on earth through any other woman than her. [1620] Given that, Lord, please take my advice. If she has done well by you, then you should allow her to reap the benefits. Once we have finished with this business and the danger that is so hard upon us has been averted, then declare a magnificent and costly festival. There, in front of witnesses and supporters, you should publicly take her to be your wife. [1630] I especially counsel you first to declare your matrimonial vows in church, where priests and lay people can witness the marriage according to Christian tradition. This will ensure blessings for the both of you, and you will truly know then that your bond in honor and wealth will grow ever stronger."

This is indeed what occurred. It happened that Rivalin brought all this to pass, [1640] and after he had taken her to be his wife, he handed her over to the trustworthy *Foitenant's* care. He brought her to Canoel, that very castle that gave his lord, as I read, the name Canelengres. Canel comes from Canoel.[35] His own wife was in this same castle, [1650] and she was a woman who dedicated her mind and body in feminine constancy to courtly conduct. He put Blancheflor in his wife's care there and made sure that she was comfortable, as befitted her rank.

Rual returned to his lord, and both were in complete agreement concerning the nature of the threat they faced. [1660] They sent word out across the land and gathered their knights. They directed all of their resources and forces

---

34. This is Rûal *li foitenant*, Rivalin's regent, first named in l. 469.

35. Gottfried may be using some etymological sleight of hand here, as was not uncommon throughout the Middle Ages. The name Canoel, the town and castle, may come from the town of Canuel in Brittany or Canoel in Cornwall. The name Canelengres goes back to Thomas, who names Rivalin Kanoël-angrès or Kanelangrès.

toward a counteroffensive and rode out against Morgan. Morgan and his troops were waiting for them and confronted Rivalin in a hard-fought battle. [1670] How many brave warriors were brought down and killed! There was no holding back. How many men faced danger, and how many lay wounded or dead on both sides! In this murderous battle was lost that unfortunate man whom all the world should grieve, if sorrowful mourning [1680] after death were of any use. Brave Canelengres, who had never once wavered one inch from the spirit of chivalry or the virtues of nobility, lay there grievously fallen. In the middle of the fight his men were able with difficulty to reach him and carry him away. With great mourning they took him from there [1690] and buried a man who took not more and not less than all of their honor with him to his grave. If I told you more of their agony and the grief that each of them expressed, what good would it do? It would be pointless. They had all died along with him. Dead was their honor and wealth [1700] and all the inspiration that should give good people happiness and a blessed life.

This is what happened, it can't be changed. Brave Rivalin is dead. There is nothing more to be done than what should by rights be done for any dead man. There really is no way around it. They ought to and must let him go. [1710] God in heaven, who never yet forgot a noble heart, will care for him.

We should instead speak of what was happening with Blancheflor. May you, God almighty, keep us from ever feeling what was in her heart the moment this beautiful lady heard the terrible news. I have no doubt whatsoever [1720] that if a woman ever experienced mortal heartache on account of a beloved man, then this is also what she felt in her heart. It was filled with deadly pain. She showed all the world that his death had pierced her heart, but her eyes never filled with tears throughout this pain. Dear God almighty, how was it that there were no tears? [1730] Her heart had turned to stone. There was no life left in it except the living love and the enduring pain that waged a lively fight to end her life. Didn't she grieve for her lord with lamentations? No, she did not. She could not speak from that moment on, and her lament expired on her lips. Her tongue, her mouth, her heart, her thoughts, [1740] all these had died. The beautiful lady said not a word of lament, she spoke neither "oh" nor "woe." She fell to the ground and lay there in agony until the fourth day, more pitiable than any woman ever. She tossed and turned and contorted her body this way and that and kept on until she had painfully given birth to a son. [1750] You see, the son survived, and she lay dead.

Part 1.2

Chapter 3: Tristan's Childhood

[1751] **O**h woe this vision and this sight,
whereafter such a painful plight
an even greater painful plight
comes into such plain sight.[1]

The people, whose honor depended on Rivalin and whom he attended with great honor as long as God willed it, their pain was unfortunately all too great, [1760] greater even than any other pain. All their solace and strength, their accomplishments and all their chivalry, their honor and all their status, this was all at an end. His death may have been laudable, but hers was pitiable. As detrimental as the damage done to people and lands was that resulted from their lord's death, [1770] it was not as lamentable as the sight of the agonizing demise and pitiable death of that precious woman. Her misery and her distress should be mourned by the fortunate, and whoever has found or hopes to find inspiration in a woman should reflect on how easy it is [1780] for everything to turn out badly even for good people, how easy it is for joy and well-being to turn to suffering. So he should pray to God to have mercy on this innocent woman, that his grace and power might aid and comfort her. Now we turn to tell of the child that had no father or mother, [1790] and what God intended for him.

[1791] **R**ue and constant loyalty,
with a friend's death renewed should be,
so then that friend renewed will be.
This is the greatest loyalty.

Some grieve for a friend and remain faithful to him after death: this is the highest reward and the crown of faithfulness. With this same crown [1800] were crowned, as I read, the marshal and his blessed wife, who were united in loyalty and body before God and the world. They gave witness to both the world and God by embracing faithfulness according to God's law.

---

1. The first pain (*leid*) is Rivalin's death, the second, even more disturbing death is Blanche-flor's. A man could find an honorable death in war, but a woman's death giving birth to a child, brought on first through love, was in every way cruel and unjust.

They remained faithful without fail [1810] until their dying day. If anyone on earth could become a king or queen through loyalty, then indeed it could have been them. I can vouchsafe this for both of them in how he lived and how she acted. After Blancheflor, their lady, died and Rivalin was buried, [1820] the future of the surviving orphaned child seemed at first in doubt but soon took a turn for the better. The marshal and the marshaline[2] took the little orphan and concealed his whereabouts from public view. They said and directed others to say that their lady had carried a child, and that it had died along with her. [1830] This threefold tragedy only increased the mourning throughout the land. The people's lamentations were ever increasing, first that Rivalin was dead, next that Blancheflor had perished, and finally that their child, who was to be their consolation, had perished as well.

Along with all these troubles, their extreme fear [1840] of Morgan was as disconcerting as their lord's death. This is the greatest suffering in the world, when people are threatened day and night by their mortal enemy. This is a suffering that is at once close to home and like a living death. In the midst of all this misery of those still living, Blancheflor was buried. [1850] At her gravesite there was great mourning and lamentation. You may rest assured that the grief was overwhelming, but I don't want to upset your ears with tales of woe, since the ears dislike it whenever there is too much talk of grief. There is nothing so good [1860] that it doesn't suffer when overdone.[3] So let us leave this long lament and concentrate on telling about the orphaned child who is the subject of this story.

[1865] Such worldly affairs
oft turn to cares,
but then from cares
return to fair affairs.

Remember that in times of trouble, someone who is bold should concentrate [1870] on how to make things better, however things may turn out. As long as he has life, he should live among the living and see to his own will to live. This is what Marshal *Foitenant* did. He had reason to worry, and so in the midst of these difficulties he thought about the harm done to the land,

---

2. A grammatical construct that in the original is created by making the masculine noun feminine, based here on the analogous forms in English for margrave and margravine or burgrave and burgravine. This form is attested only with Gottfried.

3. This may be Gottfried's way of criticizing some of his contemporaries, especially Wolfram von Eschenbach, who was well known for his elaborate circumlocutions.

and about his own mortality. Unable to mount a successful defense [1880] and challenge the enemy openly, he was forced to resort to a more pragmatic solution. He promptly spoke with the nobility in his lord's realm and convinced them to seek peace. They had no other choice than to sue for peace and to yield, and they gave up their property and lives to Morgan's mercy. [1890] The terrible violence that had occurred on both sides was prudently set aside, and so they were able to save their people and their lands.

Loyal Marshal *Foitenant* returned home and spoke with his cherished wife. He told her in no uncertain terms that she was to take to her bed as a woman expecting a child. [1900] At the appropriate time she should insist that she had given birth to a son, who was actually to become their lord. The blessed marshaline, the noble and faithful, the uncorrupted Florete, the epitome of feminine honor and a gem of true goodness, needed little admonishment, [1910] since this increased her own honor. She prepared herself both mentally and physically to properly mimic the pains of childbirth. She commanded that her rooms and her household be made ready for the secretive delivery. Since she well knew how to act in this situation, she took up her simulated complaints [1920] and pretended to be in considerable distress both emotionally and physically, just like a woman who is about to give birth and is prepared for the labor that lies ahead.

The baby was placed secretly in her arms, and no one knew the truth except for her midwife. [1930] The news spread quickly that the noble marshaline had delivered a son. It really was true in a way. She lay in bed with a son who would show her filial loyalty until both their dying day. This dear child showed her, sweet child that it was, the same kind of devotion that any child should show its mother. [1940] This was right and proper, because she also bestowed all her attention on him with a maternal love that was as real as if she had carried him in her own womb. We hear the story say that it had not happened before nor has it since that a man and a woman ever raised their lord with such love. [1950] Later in this story we will recognize how much fatherly concern and how much distress the faithful marshal would endure on his account.

When the good marshaline had supposedly recuperated after six weeks, as it is decreed for women, she was to go to church with her son, [1960] the one I have told you about. So she took him in her own arms and carried him tenderly, as she would, to the house of God. Having received her *post-partum* benediction, she returned along with her splendid retinue after giving an offering,[4] and a holy baptism was prepared for the little child. [1970] He would be christened in God's name, so that no matter what might happen to

---

4. Women were prohibited from entering a church after childbirth for forty days (see Leviticus 12:2–4). The ritual of "churching" (*înleite*) then formalized the reintroduction of the woman

him in the future he would be a Christian. Once the priest had everything prepared, he asked according to the custom at baptism what the child's name was to be. The courtly marshaline [1980] went quietly to her husband and asked him what he wanted to name him. The marshal was silent for a long time. He thought long and hard what name would be appropriate given his circumstances, considering the child's fortunes from the beginning, as he had been told, [1990] and how things had transpired up until then.

"You see, my lady" he said, "as I heard from his father how things had gone with his Blancheflor, and how she had devoted herself to him with so much sadness, how in sadness she became pregnant, and how in sadness she gave birth, we shall call him Tristan."

Now *triste* means sadness. [2000] The child was named Tristan based on this story, and so he was promptly baptized. His name, Tristan, came from *triste*. The name suited him and was right for him in every way. We can confirm this from the story. We see how sad it was when his mother gave birth. We see how soon he was burdened with difficulty [2010] and troubles. We see how he was given a sad life to live. We see how his sad death, which brought all his heartache to an end, surpassed all other deaths. It was a sadness of the most bitter kind. Whoever has read this story will easily recognize that his name [2020] was appropriate to his life. He was a man befitting his name, and his name fit who he was: Tristan.[5]

Whoever would like to know what motivated *Foitenant* to have it reported that the child Tristan had died along with his dead mother during childbirth, we can explain it this way. [2030] It was done out of loyalty. The loyal man did it because he feared Morgan's enmity. If Morgan had known about the child, he would have killed him either through treachery or force, thereby eliminating the country's heir. This is why that loyal man claimed the orphan as his own and raised him so properly. [2040] Everyone should want God's grace for him as a reward. His treatment of the orphan certainly made him deserving.

After the child had been baptized and dedicated to God according to Christian rite, the most honorable marshaline took the dear child back into her personal care. She wanted to make sure at all times that his well-being [2050] was safeguarded. His tender mother was determined in her gentle way

---

into the church community (*benedictio ad introducendam mulierem in ecclesiam*, see Leviticus 12:6–8).

5. Names were often considered to be inextricably linked to a person's heritage as well as fate. The concept of *praesagium nominis*, or the prophetic nature of a name, is evident here with the use of speculative etymology; that is, Gottfried follows the French tradition by linking the name, appropriately enough, with the word describing sadness (in adjective, not noun form). The name is most likely Welsh, originally from the Brittonic *Drust*. Tristan is later given the cognomen *trûraere*, or "sad one."

to make certain that he never bruised so much as a toe. After she had hovered over him for seven years, and when he was able to express himself well and behave appropriately, [2060] his father the marshal gave him into the care of an educated man.[6] With him he was sent to travel to foreign lands to learn other languages. He was also to begin immediately with book learning, and this was to be his most important study.

This was his first farewell to a carefree life.[7] [2070] He was attended by constraints and cares that had up to this time been kept from him and were unknown to him. In the flower of his youth, when nothing but happiness should bloom, as he was about to embark on the rest of his life with joy, his happiest days ended. Just as his joy was about to blossom, [2080] the frost of worries took hold of him, as it harms other young lives, and withered away his life's blood of happiness. Just as he was beginning to enjoy his carefree years, all his freedoms vanished. The stress of book learning was the start of his worries, but as he began the task he gave it all his attention and devotion [2090] and so read more books in less time than any other child before or since.

Along with these two main areas of study, that is books and languages, he spent much of his time playing various stringed instruments. He spent so much of his energy in this endeavor, at all times of the day and night, that he became a real prodigy. [2100] So he learned all manner of things, today this, tomorrow that, one year well, the next year even better. Along with all this he also learned how to ride skillfully with shield and lance, to guide the horse correctly on both of its flanks, spur it on, turn, give it free rein, [2110] and direct it with pressure on the sides, properly and according to the techniques of knighthood. This was a common pleasure of his: to fight well, spar strongly, run swiftly, jump far, and throw a spear. All of this he did with enthusiasm. We also hear the story tell that he learned to track and hunt better than anyone else, [2120] whoever it may be, and he knew how to play many different kinds of courtly games. In addition to all this, his physical appearance was more handsome than any man born of a woman. Everything he did was outstanding, both as it was intended and as it was done. However,

---

6. The age of seven was considered to be appropriate throughout the Middle Ages as the time of separation of boys from their nurses and mothers. It was the age at which boys could be sent to a monastic or cathedral school to learn Latin and begin the study of the seven liberal arts. They could be pledged to monasteries as novices, although this practice declined throughout the medieval period, or sent to a male relative for tutelage in the skills of warfare and courtly behavior. Tristan's education abroad would seem to be less common and probably reserved for those with the financial means that such travel would require. Hartmann von Aue's character Gregorius, also an orphan, enters a monastic school at age six.

7. It would have to be inferred by a knowledgeable reader that Tristan's second loss of freedom would come in the form of his captivity in the chains of Love.

this good fortune was undermined by continual troubles, as I read, [2130] because he was also blessed with suffering.[8]

When he turned fourteen[9] he was recalled home by the marshal and advised to travel extensively in order to learn about the people and the land and become familiar with the customs of the country. The praiseworthy man did this so laudably [2140] that at the time there was no other young man in all the kingdom who lived as honorably as Tristan. All the world looked upon him with friendship and affection, as it well should for someone whose attention is focused only on virtue and who scorns all dishonor.

Chapter 4: Abduction[10]

[2149] In these times it so happened that a lone merchant ship came across the sea from Norway to the land of Parmenie. It made land at Canoel and anchored in front of the same castle where the marshal resided along with his young lord, Tristan. [2160] As soon as the foreign merchants had set out their wares, it quickly became known at the court what could be bought there. There were reports that they had falcons as well as other fine birds of prey for sale, all to Tristan's misfortune. There was so much talk that two of the marshal's sons, [2170] because young men are attracted by such things, decided they would fetch Tristan, who they thought was their brother, and go see their father. They wanted to ask him if he would buy them some birds for Tristan's sake. It would have been difficult for Rual [2180] to refuse anything his precious Tristan wanted. He cherished him and treated him better than anyone else in the realm or at court. He was not as attentive with his own children. This was how he showed the world the complete loyalty that he kept, [2190] and how much virtue and honor were his.

He got up right away and took his son Tristan by the hand, as loving fathers do. His other sons came along, and many attendants from the court, either out of obligation or for fun, accompanied them down to the ship. Whatever people liked and wanted to have [2200] was there in abundance:

---

8. Gottfried employs an oxymoron to describe Tristan's condition: *arbeitsaelic*, literally "blessed with hardship" or "happiness and suffering." This single word exemplifies Gottfried's message of the inseparability of love and pain, life and death.

9. It was common in antiquity and the Middle Ages to divide human development into periods of seven years, so that the age of fourteen would typically signal the beginning of a new stage in a young person's life. Here Tristan begins the phase of learning how to rule by getting to know his own land and people.

10. The following episode takes much of its plot from the story of Apollonius of Tyre, where in some versions the hero is shipwrecked and becomes a tutor to a princess who falls in love with him.

jewelry, silks, costly clothes, there was more than enough of all these things. There were also handsome birds of prey: peregrine falcons in abundance, merlins, sparrowhawks, goshawks that have mewed, and red-feathered eyasses.[11] There were plenty of each for sale, [2210] and some falcons and merlins were purchased for Tristan. His (supposed) brothers also received things because of Tristan, and all three of them got whatever they wanted.

After they had been given everything they desired and it was time to go home, it happened [2220] that Tristan saw a chess board hanging in the ship. The squares and the edges were very beautifully decorated and a fine example of craftsmanship. Next to it hung chess pieces made of ivory and carved by a master's hand.[12] Tristan, talented in all things, could not take his eyes off of it.

[2230] "Cheers," he started, "honorable merchants, God be with you. Tell me, do you know how to play chess?" he asked in their own language.

They took a closer look at the young man once he began speaking their language, which almost no one knew there. They took notice of the boy's appearance [2240] and came to the conclusion that they had never seen a young man so handsome and well-mannered.

"Yes," said one of them, "my friend, there are plenty among us who know how to play this game. If you would like to try it out, that is certainly possible. Come on, I'll challenge you."

Tristan replied, "You're on!" and the two of them sat down to a game.

[2250] The marshal said, "Tristan, I want to head home now. If you want, you can stay here, but my other sons are coming with me. Your teacher will stay here and watch out for you."

So the marshal left with all of his attendants, leaving Tristan alone with his teacher, who was in charge of him. [2260] I can truly tell you about him, based on what the story tells us, that a squire had never before been more

---

11. Hunting with birds, or falconry, was a hallmark of the medieval nobility. The expense and effort necessary to train birds of prey to hunt on command could only be afforded by very wealthy landowners. The sport was not practiced by Greeks or Romans in antiquity and so most likely came to medieval Europe from the East, possibly introduced by the Huns in the fifth century. Frederick II of Hohenstaufen (1194–1250), Holy Roman Emperor, was acknowledged as a great authority in the Middle Ages, and he wrote a book on the subject titled *De arte venandi cum avibus* (*The Art of Hunting with Birds*) that detailed his extensive knowledge of the subject.

12. Chess was a popular pastime among the medieval nobility since the eleventh century. Originating in India, it was most likely introduced to Europe through interaction and trade with Muslim cultures throughout the Mediterranean, especially in southern Italy and Sicily. The game became especially popular in northern Europe during the period of the Crusader States in the Levant, starting around 1100. Examples of carved ivory or bone figures are common throughout this time, the most famous perhaps being the walrus ivory chessmen found on Lewis in the Outer Hebrides in 1831, dated to the late twelfth century, and possibly originating in Norway.

graced by courtly character or noble temperament. His name was Curvenal.[13]
He was a man of many talents and could teach anyone to acquire these same
talents.

[2270] The gifted and well-mannered young man, Tristan, sat down and
played so well and elegantly that all the foreigners observed him closely, thinking to themselves that they had never seen such a young man as this, blessed
with so many skills. Whatever aptitude he demonstrated there [2280] in eti-
quette or game play seemed to them nothing in comparison to the fact that
a child could speak so many languages. They just flowed out of his mouth in
a way that they had never witnessed anywhere else they had been. Courteous
as he was, [2290] he was able to sprinkle his conversation with civilities and
technical chess terms. He knew many of these and how to use them, and so he
adorned his play for them. He could also sing beautifully, *chançons* and artful
melodies, *refloits* and *estampies*.[14] He so regularly and masterfully employed
these courtly forms that the merchants all came to the same conclusion:
[2300] if they could conspire to steal him away with them, they would be
able to make considerable use of him and increase their own prestige as well.
They didn't hesitate but ordered their oarsmen to take up their positions.
They weighed anchor without raising any suspicion and then got underway
and sailed off. [2310] It was done so quietly that neither Tristan nor Curvenal
noticed anything until they had already been taken several leagues from land.
These two were so engrossed in their game that they thought of nothing else.
Once Tristan had won the game, [2320] he looked around and saw what had
happened. You have never seen a mother's child more upset, and he jumped
up to face them.

"No!" he exclaimed. "Noble merchants, for God's sake, what are you
doing with me? Tell me where you're taking me!"

---

13. Curvenal's name, although originally Celtic, is probably related in the French tradition
to the Old French word *governer*, which means to educate or train. Curvenal is identified as
a *knappe*, or squire, which implies a higher social status as opposed to *kneht*, which over time
became more and more identified with the free peasantry, although still present in our English
"knight." Tristan is himself identified as a *knappe* (l. 3914) by Mark's courtiers in response to
Rual's question if there is a child at court that matches Tristan's description.

14. As can be seen from the French names, these song types were borrowed from the French
styles that were fashionable at German courts at the end of the twelfth century. The *chançons*,
MHG *schanzûn*, were vernacular poems put to music primarily performed by an individual
singing the melody. A *refloit*, Old French *refroit*, is a kind of refrain or round. It is possibly
linked to the *chançons* as a kind of chorus would be to a series of verses. These terms appear
again in l. 8074 and l. 17,372. Finally, MHG *stampenîe*, Old French *estampie*, is a form associated with troubadour courtly love lyrics but could also designate a complex instrumental piece,
often played on a fiddle (see Okken, 1996, 2.1015–17). It is named once more, l. 8058, as
part of Isolde's repertoire.

"As you see, my dear friend," said one of them, "no one can change things now. [2330] You will have to come with us, so behave yourself and don't take it so hard."

Poor Tristan complained so bitterly that his companion Curvenal shed tears with him and cried out, causing the ship's crew to become agitated and angry. [2340] They placed Curvenal in a small boat, gave him an oar for the journey and a little something to eat for his hunger. They said that he was free to go wherever he chose, but Tristan would have to stay with them. After saying this, they sailed off and left him adrift there, [2350] alone with his fears.

Curvenal drifted on the open sea. He had much to agonize over. He agonized over the great suffering that he knew Tristan felt. He agonized over his own dire situation. He was afraid that he would die, since he didn't know how to handle a boat, something he had never even tried before. He cried out in his solitude: [2360] "Oh God almighty, what can I do? I have never been so afraid. I'm out here all alone, and I don't know how to steer a boat. God almighty, protect me and guide me on my journey. With your grace I will do what I have never done before. Take me away from here!" He took hold of the oar [2370] and sailed off in God's name. In a short time he arrived back home, as God willed, and reported what had happened.

The marshal and his blessed wife both broke out in a grief-stricken lament that could not have been greater had they seen Tristan dead with their own eyes. [2380] Both of them, in their shared grief, went down to the shore with their entire court and cried for their lost child. Many faithful voices were raised to God that he might come to his aid. There was a great clamor of mourning, some grieved one way, some another, [2390] but when it was evening and time to go, the various laments were unified. They had only one shared refrain, and so they all called out the same verses wherever they were:

"*Beau Tristant, courtois Tristant, ton corps, ta vie à Dieu je recommande!*[15] May your fine body and fair life [2400] be given today into God's care!"

In the meantime the Norwegians carried him off, and, after considering every contingency they thought that they had him completely in their power. Yet he who orders all things and sets them right again had other plans. The winds, the sea, and all the elements [2410] bow down in fear to his command. As he willed it and commanded it, a storm arose on the sea and presented such a danger that all the crew together were not able to maintain control.[16] They had to let their ship drift wherever the violent winds blew

---

15. Gottfried usually translates, or in this case paraphrases, the Old French of longer phrases for his readers, which could either indicate that most readers did not know French or that Gottfried is showing off the fact that he does and that he is following his French source, Thomas.

16. This storm episode and the notion that God is angry with the crew share many similarities with the biblical version of Jonah's story (Jonah 1:1–16), where Jonah is thrown into the sea as the cause of the storm.

it, and they lost all hope in saving their own limbs and lives. [2420] They had all given in to that poor navigator called Fortune,[17] and left it to chance whether or not they would survive. There was nothing else they could do except allow themselves to be carried by the waves up to the heavens and then back down again as if to hell. [2430] The heaving waves drove them upwards, then downwards, now this way, then back again. None of them could stay on their feet for a moment. This went on for a full eight days and nights, and they were close to losing all their strength and their minds.

[2440] One of them then said, "My lords, may God be with me, it seems to me that God's will has put our lives in danger. That we are barely alive in this raging storm can only come from our sins and treachery in kidnapping Tristan and taking him from his friends and family."

[2450] "Yes," they all said as one. "Certainly it is just as you say."

So they conferred and agreed that if the waves and the winds were calmed enough so that they could reach land, they would gladly give him his freedom to go wherever he wanted. As soon as it was agreed and they were all of one mind, [2460] the hazards of their voyage immediately eased. Wind and waves moderated and then abated, the seas were calm, and the sun shone as it had before. Then they wasted no time. The wind had driven them over the eight days toward the land of Cornwall, [2470] and when they were close enough to shore to see land, they made for an anchorage. They took Tristan, put him ashore, and gave him some bread and a part of their provisions. "Friend," they said, "may God protect and watch over you." [2480] They all wished him well and returned quickly to their ship.

So what did Tristan do, Tristan in his exile?[18] Well, he just sat there and cried. Children only know how to cry when something bad happens to them. The inconsolable castaway folded his hands and prayed to God. [2490] "Oh God almighty," he said, "as great as you are in your mercy, so great is your goodness. Dearest God, I beseech you to keep me in your mercy and goodness, since you saw fit that I should be kidnapped. Show me the way to a place where I can be among people. [2500] I look all around me and don't see a single living thing. I'm afraid of this great wild place. Wherever I look, it seems to me that I'm at the end of the world. Wherever I turn, I see only desolate land, deserted wilderness, rough cliffs, and rough seas. [2510] I am terribly afraid. I mostly fear that wherever I turn I will be devoured by wolves and wild animals, and the day is quickly turning to night. Whatever I do, if I don't leave this place things will

---

17. *Âventiure* is personified here and might indicate the Norwegians' lack of faith or it might simply refer to *Fortuna* as God's instrument.

18. The term used here, *ellende* (l. 2483 and again l. 2487), can at this time mean either exile or the suffering caused by being a stranger in a foreign land. There is a possible play on words here in that, unbeknownst to Tristan, he has actually come ashore in his mother's (and uncle's) land.

turn out badly. If I don't leave soon, [2520] I'll have to spend the night in the forest, and then all will be lost. I see lots of high cliffs and mountains all around me. I'll try to climb one of them, if I'm able, to see while there's still daylight if there isn't some sort of dwelling nearby or far away. There I might find people [2530] who will take me in and help me survive in some way."

So he got up and left that place. He was wearing a tunic and a marvelously woven cloak made of rich silken material. It was made by Saracens,[19] [2540] who had in their foreign and heathen fashion excellently embroidered and interlaced it with fine thread. It was also well fitted to his handsome body, and no man or woman had ever tailored more princely garments than these. In addition, the story tells us that the material was greener than the grass in May [2550] and was lined with a white ermine that could not have been whiter. He got up and, with tears and great unhappiness, went on his way, since there was little choice in the matter. He lifted up his tunic a little higher under his belt, rolled his cloak together [2560] and, throwing it over his shoulder, took off into the wilderness through forest and fields. There were no roads or paths except for what he could make himself, and he had to use his hands and feet to clear the way and climb higher. He climbed up the mountain over under-growth and rocks [2570] until he reached the top. There by chance he found an overgrown and narrow forest path, which he followed down the other side into the valley below in hopes of finding a proper road. In a short time he reached a main thoroughfare that was wide and heavily traveled. [2580]

He sat down along the road to rest, and cried. His thoughts turned to friends and family and to the land where he knew the people. This caused him great sorrow and pain, and he fervently lifted his head to heaven and began again to complain to God about his misfortune.

"God," he said, "gracious Lord, [2590] how is it that my father and mother have been lost to me? If only I hadn't played that damned chess game, something I will never do again. Sparrowhawks, falcons, merlins—may they be cursed by God. They took away my father, and it was because of them that I lost my family and companions. [2600] Everyone who wanted only happiness for me is now downcast and sad because of me. Oh, dear mother, I know well how you are torturing yourself with grief. Father, your heart is full of pain. I know that both of you are weighed down with sorrow. Oh dear Lord, if only I could be sure [2610] that you both knew that I am still alive and well, that would be a great gift from God for you and also for me. I know very well that you will never be happy again unless, God willing, you find out that I'm still alive. Consoler of the afflicted, God almighty, please make it so."

---

19. The term *Saraceni* entered the Latin vocabulary by the third century CE as a loan word from Arabic. By the Middle Ages it came to represent both Arabic-speaking peoples and Muslims generally throughout northern Africa, parts of southern Europe, and the Levant.

[2620] While he was sitting there lamenting as I have described, he saw two old pilgrims in the distance walking toward him. Sworn to God, they were advanced in years and had long beards and hair, as true children of God and wayfarers often do. These pilgrims [2630] had hooded cloaks made of linen and were otherwise dressed appropriately as pilgrims. On the outside of their clothes they had sewn on seashells and other emblems from far away, and each one had a pilgrim's staff in his hand. Their hats and pants also fit their vocation. [2640] These same servants of God wore linen trousers that came down almost to their ankles and were secured to their legs, but their feet and ankles were unprotected from scrapes and bumps. They also wore palm fronds on their back as a religious sign of penitence.[20] [2650] They were just then engaged in reading their prayers and psalms and other good works.

When Tristan saw them he was frightened and said to himself, "Merciful Lord, how can I save myself? These two men who are coming this way, if they've seen me they may well try to seize me."

[2660] As they came closer, he recognized their vocation based on their staffs and clothing, and he quickly realized what they were and began to take heart. His spirits were lifted a bit, and he spoke fully from the heart. "Praise to you, my Lord! These are righteous people, and I have no need to be afraid of them."

[2670] Soon thereafter they saw the boy sitting there ahead of them. As they advanced toward him, he jumped up and courteously approached them, his graceful hands folded in front of him. Now the two men began to look at him more closely and noticed his fine manners. They went up to him amiably and greeted him kindly [2680] with this gracious greeting, "*Dieu te sauve, bel ami!*[21] Dear friend, whoever you are, may God protect you."

Tristan bowed before the old men and replied, "Oh, *Dieu bénisse si sainte compagnie!* May God with all his might bless such a holy communion."

The two of them said to him, [2690] "Dear young man, where do you come from, and who brought you to this place?"

Tristan was cautious and clever beyond his years, and so he started to tell them a fabulous story. "Blessed lords," he said to them, "I was born in this land, and I and some other people were to ride today to hunt in this forest.

---

20. The typical pilgrim's gear consisted of staff, hat, and satchel. This was not unique to pilgrims, however, and so the further identifying characteristics of the shell and palm fronds made recognition easier. Pilgrims were granted extra protection by the Church and secular authorities, and so proper identification was important. The seashell was associated with the pilgrimage to Santiago de Compostela, whereas palms would have indicated a journey to Jerusalem. Other signs sewn on a pilgrim's cloak might include small tokens made of lead that represented certain saints or pilgrimage sites.

21. Virtually the same greeting as Rivalin first gave to Blancheflor (l. 743), except that here the pilgrims address Tristan informally, as would be suitable for a child.

[2700] Somehow, I'm not sure how, I lost the other hunters and the hounds. Those who knew the forest paths fared better than I did, but then I got off of the path and then completely lost my way. So I ended up on a treacherous trail that led me down into a ravine. I couldn't hold my horse, it just wanted to rush down the hill. [2710] Finally the horse and I both ended up falling down in a heap. I couldn't get back into my stirrups quickly enough, and it ripped the reins from my hands and ran into the woods. So I came to this small path that led me here, and now I have no idea where I am or where I should go. [2720] Good sirs, please tell me where you are going."

"Friend," they answered, "if our Lord wills it, we hope to make it all the way to the town of Tintagel tonight." Tristan asked them kindly if he could go along with them. "Dear child, yes of course," answered the pilgrims. [2730] "If that's where you want to go, then come along."

Tristan went along with them, and they began to talk about all sorts of things. Well-mannered Tristan was careful about what he said, and whatever they asked him he said just enough to answer the question. He was so measured [2740] in his speech and demeanor that the wise old men thought it a great blessing. They observed his behavior and his manners all the more closely, along with his attractive appearance. The clothes he wore were especially noteworthy because of their richness [2750] and magnificent materials. They thought to themselves, "Oh gracious God almighty, who is this child and where does he come from? His manners are impeccable." They went along and continued to observe closely everything he did, something that kept them occupied for about the length of a mile.

Chapter 5: The Hunt

[2759] Now it happened shortly thereafter that the hounds of Mark of Cornwall, his uncle, had driven a great stag to the road nearby, so the story tells us in truth. There it was run down and stood at bay, totally exhausted by the speed of the chase. [2770] In the meantime the huntsmen had arrived with a great commotion, blowing their horns for the kill.

When Tristan saw that they had brought it to bay, he said to the pilgrims in his clever way, "My lords, these are the hounds, the stag, and these the people that I lost today. Now I have found them. [2780] These are my companions. With your permission, I will go to them."

"Child," they said, "God bless you. Go in peace."

"Thank you, and may God bless you and keep you," replied fair Tristan. He bowed to them and made his way to where the stag was.

After the stag had been killed, the master of the hunt [2790] stretched out the animal on all fours to dress it like one would a wild boar. "What, master,

"Quarry? *Dieu nous bénisse!*"[25] they all said. "What is that? It would be easier for us to understand Arabic. What is 'quarry,' young man? Don't explain it to us in words but, whatever it is, show us so that we can see it with our own eyes. Please do this as a courtesy to us."

[2970] Tristan was glad to do so. He took the windpipe, I mean everything that is attached to the heart, and cut it loose. He cut the heart out from the top toward the pointed end and took it in his hands. He divided it with a cross cut into four pieces and threw them onto the hide. [2980] Then he returned to the rest of the pluck and separated the milt and the lungs. This took care of the pluck, and everything was lying on the hide. He cut off the gorge and pluckstring at the top of the ribcage and then cut off the head with the antlers at the neck and had it carried to where the breast was.

"Come here quickly!" he said to them. [2990] "Take the backbone away. If there is anyone who is poor and can make use of it, then give him this backbone, or do whatever you normally do with it. Then I can perform the quarry." The whole crowd came closer to admire his skill.

Tristan asked them now to bring what he had them prepare for him. [3000] Everything was spread out there, fixed and prepared as he had previously told them. The four quarters of the heart lay on the four sides of the hide, spread out on the hide according to proper huntsman custom. He cut up the milt and lungs, then the entrails and the gut [3010] and everything else that the hounds would get into small pieces as was fitting, spreading them all out on the hide. Then he began to call the dogs loudly with a "*ça ça ça*," and they all quickly came running and devoured their meal.

"You see," said the linguist, "this is called 'quarry' [3020] at home in Parmenie. I'll tell you why. It is called 'quarry' because everything that the hounds get is laid out on the *cuir*. Hunters derived and formed the name quarry from *cuir*, and so quarry comes from *cuir*. It was invented [3030] for the sake of the dogs, and it is a useful custom. What is laid out for them is tasty because of the blood, and it fleshes the hounds. Now take a look at this excoriation, this is all there is to see. You can decide what you think of it."

"Good Lord," they all said. "What do you mean, young man? [3040] We can easily see that this technique was created to benefit the scent hounds and the pack."[26]

Then skilled Tristan replied, "Go ahead and take away the hide, there's nothing more I can do with it, and please be assured that, if I could have served you better, I would have gladly done so. Everyone should now go and cut a stick [3050] and put your pieces on them. Carry the head by hand and

---

25. "God bless us."
26. This refers to certain dog types, specifically the *Bracke*, or German hound, a smaller breed that hunts primarily through scent.

present your gifts to the court according to courtly ritual. In this way you add to your reputation as courtiers. I'm sure you know how to present a stag. Present it properly!"

The master of the hunt and his men were again amazed [3060] that the young man was able, in such detail and expertise, to demonstrate so many different hunting customs, and that he knew so much about these techniques.

"See here," they said, "young man, the wonderful distinctions that you make and have demonstrated for us are so extensive, that if we don't see them to the end, [3070] we won't be able to make sense of what you have done up to now."

Quickly bringing up a horse, they asked him if he would be so kind as to ride to court with them in his artful manner. He could let them see his country's customs up to the end.

Tristan replied, "That's easy to do. Take the stag and let's go." [3080] He mounted up and rode along with them.

As they were riding together, something they had eagerly anticipated, each of them began to think about what country Tristan might come from and how he had come to be there. They would gladly have known his background and his heritage. [3090] Clever Tristan realized this and began to make up another story. What he said was in no way typical for a child, and he spoke most thoughtfully.

"There is a land that lies across from Brittany called Parmenie. My father is a merchant there [3100] and lives a good life according to his station, what I mean is, as a merchant should. You should also know that he is wealthier in honorable character than he is in goods and property. He made sure that I was taught whatever I needed to know. We often had merchants from foreign kingdoms visit us. [3110] I learned a great deal about their languages and customs, and my desire to visit foreign kingdoms grew ever greater. I wanted to learn more about unknown people and strange lands, and I thought about it day in and day out, until I left my father [3120] and sailed off with some merchants. This is how I arrived here in this country. Now you know the whole story, although I don't know if it will satisfy you."

"Ah, young man," they all said, "you were motivated by noble intent. The unfamiliar is of benefit to many and teaches many different qualities. Dear companion, young man, blessed [3130] by God is the land where a merchant was able to raise such a virtuous child. All the kings of today could not have raised a child better. Now dear young man, tell us this, by what name did your honorable father call you?"

"Tristan," he said. "My name is Tristan."

"*Dieu nous assiste,*"[27] replied one of them. "By God, why did he name you that? You would have been better named [3140] *jeunesse belle et riante*, or

---

27. "May God help us."

beautiful, smiling youth." So they rode along in conversation, each talking in his own way. They were completely engrossed by this young man, and each one of the group asked whatever he wanted to know.

It didn't take long before Tristan could see the castle. [3150] He broke off some twigs from a linden tree to make two wreaths. One he wore himself, and the other one he made somewhat larger and gave it to the master of the hunt.

"Ah," he exclaimed, "my dear master, what castle is that? It looks to be a royal fortress."

The master responded, "That is Tintagel."

"Tintagel? Ah, what a fortress! [3160] *Dieu te garde*,[28] Tintagel, and all of your inhabitants."

"Bless you, young man," said all of his companions. "May you always be blessed and happy, and may your future be as bright as we pray."

They came to the castle gate, and Tristan halted. "Dear lords," he said to them, [3170] "since I am a stranger here, I don't even know your names. Please pair up and ride by twos in the order of the stag's presentation. First come the antlers, then the breast, the ribs after the shoulders and forequarters, and then make sure that the haunch and hindquarters [3180] follow the ribcage. After that pay attention that the final pieces are the quarry and the 'forks.' This is proper huntsman style. Don't be in too much of a hurry, but ride well spaced one after the other. My master and I, his attendant, we will ride alongside each other, if that's alright and you approve."

[3190] "Yes, dear young man," they all said, "as you want it done, so do we."

"Done!" he said. "Now please loan me a horn that is the right size for me, and finally watch out for one more thing. When I blow the horn, listen carefully and then echo what I have played."

The master said to him, "Dear friend, blow the horn and do as you think right, [3200] and those who are here will all follow your lead."

"*A la bonne heure*," said the young man. "With luck, so shall it be." They gave him a small high-pitched horn, and he said, "Onward! *Allez, en avant!*"

They rode on in formation, in columns of two, as directed. When the entire troop had entered, [3210] Tristan took his little horn and blew it so brilliantly and expertly that those who were riding with him were overjoyed and could hardly wait to follow him. They all took their horns and blew his tune most pleasingly along with him. He showed them how it was done, [3220] and they followed his melody perfectly. The castle was filled with sound.

The king and all the court listened to the strange hunting fanfare and were shocked and alarmed, as they had never before heard anything like it

---

28. "God be with you."

at court. [3230] By now the troop had reached the palace gate, and many members of the court had run outside on account of the horn blowing. They all wondered at the meaning of this clamor. Famed Mark himself came out to see what was going on, followed by numerous courtiers. [3240] When Tristan caught sight of the king, he was attracted to him more than all the rest. His heart selected him because they were of the same blood: nature drew Tristan to him.[29] He fixed his eyes on him, greeted him pleasantly, and then took up another strange horn fanfare. [3250] He blew so vigorously that no one could follow him anymore. This soon came to a close, and the well-mannered outcast put down his horn and was silent.

He graciously bowed down to the king and said with much kindness, as he was well able, "*Dieu sauve le roi et sa maisnie!* [3260] May God in his goodness preserve the king and his court."

Mark, who was well intentioned, along with his entire household thanked the young man honorably and generously, as it should be for the talented. "Ah," they all said together, both great and small, "*Dieu donne une douce fortune* [3270] *à cette douce créature!* May God grant such a charming being a charmed life."

The king looked at the youth and called for the huntsman. "Tell me," he asked, "who is this young man who is so lyrical in his speech?"[30]

"Ah, Lord, he is from Parmenie and is so wonderfully courteous and so completely educated [3280] as I have never before seen in a child. He says his name is Tristan and that his father is a merchant."

"I don't believe it. How could a merchant ever have devoted so much time to him with all his business? Would he have spent his leisure with him when he had so much work?"

"Ah, Lord, he is so accomplished. [3290] Look at this new artistic virtuosity. Coming to court as we did just now is something we learned entirely from him. Listen to this marvelous scheme: just as the stag is shaped, that is how it is presented at court. When was a technique ever more clever? As you see, the head goes first, then the breast comes right after, shoulders and forequarters, then all the rest. [3300] Never before has this been presented at court so exquisitely. See here, have you ever seen this kind of *fourchie*? I never before heard of such a technique among huntsmen. In addition he showed us how to excoriate the stag. I think so highly of this method that whenever I go hunting in the future I will never again just [3310] cut up a hart or hind into four pieces."

---

29. This is based on the medieval belief that a familial relationship through blood causes a natural affinity, expressed in an emotional connection to the heart.

30. Gottfried (l. 3276) says much the same of Heinrich von Veldeke in his discourse on poets (l. 4729).

of their proper senses. All kinds of thoughts and emotions were conjured up. Many of them thought, "Ah, blessed is the merchant [3600] to whom such a son was born."

His white fingers adroitly flew across the strings and sent the notes out far and wide so that the entire palace resounded with them. The eyes were also not overlooked, and many there watched his hands and were entranced.

When the lay had come to an end, [3610] the king directed that he should be asked to play another song.

"*Trés volontier,*"³⁹ replied Tristan. He briskly began to play a touching lay, *de la courtoise Tisbé*⁴⁰ from the ancient city of Babylon.⁴¹ He played this so beautifully and [3620] so expertly let the notes reverberate clearly that the harpist was amazed. At the right moment the talented young man pleasingly and skillfully introduced vocal lyrics. He sang the tunes in Breton and Welsh, Latin, and French, so sweetly [3630] that no one knew which was more beautiful or praiseworthy, his harp playing or his singing. His performance started a conversation about his virtuosity, and they all said that they had never before seen such artistry in all the kingdom.

[3640] Here and there people said, "Ah, what kind of young man is this? Whom do we have here as our companion? All the other young people we have here can't compare with our Tristan."

After Tristan had finished his song, Mark said, "Tristan, come here. Whoever taught you all this, [3650] may he be honored by God, and you along with him. That was magnificent! I would be pleased to hear your songs before bedtime, if you're also not able to sleep. That would do us both good."

"Yes, Lord, of course."

"Tell me, do you know how to play other stringed instruments?"

"No, Lord," he replied.

"Really? [3660] Tell me truthfully, Tristan, if you have any affection for me."

"Lord," said Tristan quickly, "you don't need to urge me so to answer, I would have answered in any case. I have to confess, and since you want to know, Lord, that I have tried to play all kinds of stringed instruments, but I can't play any of them so well that I couldn't do better. [3670] I didn't have lessons for all that long. Actually, I stayed at it off and on for less than seven years, maybe a little more, and that's the truth. In Parmenie I learned to play the fiddle and the symphonia. The harp and rote I learned in Wales from two

---

39. "Very gladly."
40. "About the courtly Thisbe." This lay, not otherwise known, must be based on a story originally told by Ovid in his *Metamorphoses, Book IV*, about Pyramus and Thisbe, two lovers who remained inseparable even in death.
41. This is a reference to Baghdad.

Welsh masters. [3680] I also had teachers from Britain,[42] from the town of Lud, for the lyre and sambjut."[43]

"What is a sambjut, dear fellow?"

"That's the best stringed instrument I know of."

"See here," said the rest of the household, "God has blessed this young man with his grace for a truly promising life."

Mark had more questions. [3690] "Tristan, I heard you before singing in Breton and Welsh, in good Latin and French. Do you know how to speak these languages?"

"Yes, Lord, fairly well."

A crowd of people then gathered around, and whoever knew one of the languages from a neighboring land put Tristan to the test, some this way, some that. [3700] He replied most courteously to what all of them said, Norwegians, Irish, Germans, Scots, and Danes. Many hearts longed for Tristan's talents, many wanted to be like him. Many a heart's desire spoke to him with sympathy and warmth. [3710] "Ah, Tristan, if only I could be like you. Tristan, you know how to live a good life. Tristan, you have all the skills that anyone could have in all the world." They continued to express amazement as they talked. "Listen," said one. "Just listen," said another. "All the world should listen to this. A fourteen-year-old youth [3720] knows every art form there is."

The king said, "Tristan, listen to me. You have everything I could desire. You know how to do everything I like to do: hunting, languages, playing stringed instruments. I want us to be companions, you mine and I yours. During the day we can go hunting, in the evening we can stay at home and occupy ourselves with courtly entertainment, [3730] playing the harp or fiddle and singing. You can do these so well, do this for me. I know a pastime that I can play with you, something your heart will also certainly desire.

---

42. Lud could refer to London, in which case *Britûnoise* (l. 3680) would refer to teachers from Britain. The etymology in this case for London is fanciful, going back to a legendary King Lud. Gottfried refers twice to London as *Lunders* (l. 15,302; l. 15,309), but also once more as *Lût* (l. 8068) along the Thames. A place in Brittany would seem to better fit the context, but no such place named Lud has been identified.

43. All of these instruments can be identified by name except for the sambjut, which is mentioned only by Gottfried. Given that it is also unknown by Mark, it may simply be a fanciful name for a nonexistent instrument; that is, Tristan is joking with his host. The fiddle refers to types of the instrument of the same name today that are stringed and played with a bow. The symphonia was most likely a kind of hurdy-gurdy. The harp existed in different sizes and forms as it does today as a plucked and strummed stringed instrument, and the rote or rotta is related to the Welsh crwth (pronounced krooth), a stringed instrument similar to the fiddle but somewhat square in shape that has been revived in Wales by a few performers. The lyre is known from antiquity, and although similar to a harp, was played with a plectrum or sometimes a bow.

"A boy?" he replied abruptly. "I don't know anything about a boy. There is a squire here in the household who is to be knighted. The king is tremendously fond of him, based on the fact that he is very artistic and has many skills and courtly abilities. [3920] He's a strong young man with curly hair and an elegant manner. He's a foreigner, and this is who we call Tristan here."

"Now sir," asked Rual, "do you belong to the court here?"

"Yes."

"Sir, by your honor, please do me one more small favor, as you would be doing something very good thereby. [3930] Please tell him that there is a poor man here who would like to see him and speak with him. You can also tell him that I am from his country."

So he told Tristan that a fellow countryman was there. Tristan immediately returned to that spot, and as soon as he laid eyes on him said, "May our Lord [3940] be forever praised, father, that I might see you again!"

This was his greeting at first, but then he ran to him laughing and kissed the loyal man, as a child should his father. This was all as it should be. He was his father, and he his child. All those fathers who are living now, and all those who went before us, [3950] none of them was more fatherly toward Tristan than was Rual. Yes, Tristan embraced his father then and there, and with him his mother, his family, vassals, and all the friends he ever had. He spoke from the heart, "Ah, my dear, loyal father, tell me if my precious mother and my brothers are still alive."

[3960] "I don't know, dear son," he replied, "but they were still living when I saw them last. They were very concerned about you. What has happened to them since I can't tell you. I haven't seen anyone I know for a very long time now. I also haven't been home since that cursed moment [3970] that took you away from me."

"Ah," he said, "my dearest father, what is the meaning of this? What happened to your handsome appearance?"

"My son, this I've lost on your account."

"Then I will be the one to give it back to you."

"Son, if only we could live to see that day."

"Father, come with me to the court."

"No, my son, I can't go there with you. You can see that I don't look respectable."

[3980] "On the contrary, father," he replied, "this has to happen. The king, my lord, must see you."

Rual, that noble and respectable man, thought it over. "I'm not so concerned about my lack of clothes. Even if I appear before the king like this, he'll be happy to see me when I tell him that his nephew stands before him. [3990] When I tell him from the start everything that I've done, he'll see how beautiful the clothes I'm wearing really are."

Tristan took him by the hand. Rual's clothes and his appearance were what they had to be. He had a small, miserable tunic that was worn and torn, with holes here and there, which he wore without a cloak. [4000] What the noble man wore under his tunic was as poor as could be, threadbare and soiled. His hair on his head and face was unkempt and as matted as a wild man's. The praiseworthy man also had completely bare feet and legs. [4010] Finally, he was dreadfully weather-beaten, as anyone would be who is subjected to hunger, frost, sun, and wind and loses his fair complexion because of it. This is how he appeared before Mark, who looked at him closely.

Mark said to Tristan, "Tell me, Tristan, who is this man?"

"My father, Lord," he answered.

"Is that right?"

"Yes, my lord."

[4020] "Then he is welcome here," said the honorable man.

Rual gave him a courtly bow. Then a company of knights came running up, and along with them the entire courtly entourage. They all proclaimed, "*Sire, sire, Dieu vous sauve!*"[45]

You should know that Rual, as uncourtly [4030] as his appearance was, was nevertheless entirely noble in his stature and comportment. He was noble in the way he carried himself, his limbs and torso were massive, his arms and legs were long, his movements graceful and aristocratic. Everything about him physically was well proportioned. [4040] He was not too old or too young, but rather in the best age, when maturity and youth both lend life their best qualities. He was the equal of any emperor in his true dignity. His voice boomed out like a horn, his speech was clear and articulate. People saw him standing in this noble company with noble grace. [4050] He had always acted in this way.

A great murmur arose among the knights and barons as they talked back and forth. "So," they all said, "is that him? Is that the courtly merchant whom Tristan, his son, has been bragging about? We've been told over and over again about his merits, [4060] so why does he come to court like this?"

This is how they spoke. The king had him taken to an inner room and outfitted with magnificent clothes, and Tristan made sure that he was bathed and dressed. A small hat was at hand, which he put on his head, [4070] and it fit him better than any other man. Given his noble expression, his appearance was impressive. Tristan affectionately took him by the hand, as was his custom, and led him back to see Mark.

Now everyone was greatly impressed by him. They all said to each other, "Look how quickly noble clothing [4080] has made the man worthy of praise. The clothes suit the merchant perfectly, and there is nobility in him as well.

---

45. "Lord, lord, may God protect you."

Who knows, he might be a man of great character, at least he carries himself so, truth be told. See how he walks with authority, how he moves so elegantly in these noble robes. [4090] See how his nobility is mirrored by Tristan. How could a merchant have raised a child so well if it had not come from his own noble heart?"[46]

In the meantime water had been passed around for hand washing, and the king arrived at the head table. He had his guest, Rual, seated at his table and made sure that he was served courteously, [4100] as a man of the court ought to be served. "Tristan," he said, "come here and take care of your father."

I know for a fact that this is what happened. Every honor and amenity that he could provide, he did so gladly. Noble Rual ate with gusto, and he was overjoyed with Tristan. [4110] Tristan served him during the entire meal, but just seeing Tristan was all the respite he needed. As they were getting up from the table, the king engaged his guest in conversation, asking him all sorts of things about his country and his journey. During his questioning, the knights listened closely [4120] to Rual's story.

"Lord," he said, "it is true that it has been nearly three and a half years since I left my country. Wherever I went, I asked only for news concerning the purpose of my travels, and that eventually led me here."

"What purpose was that?"

"Tristan. The one standing here. In truth, Lord, God has granted me other children, [4130] and I am as devoted to them as one should be to one's children. I have three sons, and if I had stayed with them then one or the other of the three would by now have become a knight. If I had suffered half the worry for the three that I suffered for Tristan's sake, even though he is not my real son, [4140] it would have been more than enough."

"Not your real son?" interjected the king. "Tell me, what does that mean? He must be your son, as he himself says."

"No, Lord, he is not mine at all, but rather I am his liege man."

Tristan looked at him in shock.

The king continued, "But tell me, what compelled you to suffer such hardship, [4150] leaving your wife and children for such a long time, as you have said, if he is not your son?"

"Lord, God and I alone know why."

"Friend, then enlighten me as well." said noble Mark. "This is truly amazing."

---

46. Okken (1.211, n. 4092–94) reads this "literally," as he says, to mean that only a man of noble lineage, and not a bourgeois merchant, could have raised a child in such a noble fashion. No other translator follows this logic, though, as it goes against the text, *ûz edelem herzen* (l. 4094) and Gottfried's intent to express the notion of an inner nobility, as reflected in the Prologue several times (l. 47; l. 170; l. 216; l. 233).

"If I knew," said that loyal man, "that I might do so without regret and that [4160] it was my place to speak of it here, Lord, I could tell a marvelous tale about everything that happened, and the circumstances surrounding Tristan, who is standing here."

The entourage, Mark and his baronage, all responded together, [4170] "Tell us, blessed and loyal man: Who is Tristan?"

Noble Rual replied, "It happened some time ago, as you and all who were here at the time know. My lord, Rivalin, whose retainer I was and would still be if God willed that he were still alive, often heard tell [4180] of your excellence and so put his people and his land in my care. He came here to this land to make your acquaintance and then became a member of your household. You also know what happened to beautiful Blancheflor, and how she became his lover, [4190] and that she ran away with him. When they arrived back home they were wed. This took place in my own home, and I and many others witnessed it. He then handed her over to my care. From that moment on I cared for her in every way to the best of my abilities. At the time he and his kin and retainers were hurriedly preparing [4200] for a military campaign throughout his realm. With them he took to the field and was killed, as you have certainly heard. Once this became known and the beautiful lady heard what had happened, the deadly pain pierced her heart so deeply [4210] that Tristan here, whom she was carrying at the time, was born under difficult circumstances. She herself died as a result."

With this the loyal man felt a deep pain he could not hide. He sat down and cried like a child. All the others were affected by the story as well, [4220] and their eyes filled with tears. Noble King Mark felt an overwhelming sadness in his heart that poured out of him, as tears ran from his eyes and moistened his cheeks and clothes. For Tristan the story was emotionally painful for the simple reason [4230] that in that loyal man he lost his father as well as the dream of having a father.[47]

So Rual the Loyal, disheartened though he was, sat there and told those gathered there about the poor child, how much he paid heed to his care after his mother had given birth; how he had him [4240] secretly hidden away;

---

47. Tristan lost *vater unde vaterwân* (l. 4231), literally a father and the belief in or hope for a father. Translators have struggled with this latter term, which occurs once more (l. 4372) when Tristan laments the loss of two fathers. Hatto translates the first occurrence as "and the belief that he had a father" (1960, 99), and the second as "and the one I never saw" (1960, 101). Haug/Scholz (2011/2012) translate "and at the same time could not have hoped for another [father]" (und zugleich auf keinen andern hoffen konnte); and "father and hope for a father" (Vater und Hoffnung auf einen Vater). Hatto therefore interprets the term *vaterwân* to relate to the past and Tristan's mistaken belief that Rual was his father, whereas Haug/Scholz and others see it as a reference to what had been up to this point a hope for or belief in his reunion with his "father" Rual.

how he had the story spread among common people that he had died along with his mother; how he had commanded his wife, as I told you before, to take to her bed as if she were pregnant, and at the appropriate time tell everyone [4250] that she had had a baby; how she went with him to church, and how he was baptized there; why he was named Tristan; how he sent him abroad and how he made sure that he was taught all kinds of skills, both technical and linguistic; how he left him in the ship and how he was kidnapped; [4260] and finally how he arrived in their country after much hardship.

He sat there and told the whole story from beginning to end. Mark was crying, Rual cried, and everyone else cried, too. Tristan alone was unable to weep because of what he had just heard. The whole report simply overwhelmed him. [4270] Whatever tragedies Rual, that loyal man, told those assembled there about the lovers, Canel and Blancheflor, all of this mattered little compared to the singular loyalty that Rual demonstrated to them after their death and to their child, as you have already heard. [4280] This was for those assembled the greatest loyalty that any man had ever shown his lord.

Once the story came to an end, Mark said to his guest, "Sir, is this story true?"

Noble Rual placed a ring in his hand. "Sire," he replied, "with this token you may confirm my speech and my story."

[4290] Mark, noble and sincere, took the ring and inspected it. The deep sadness he had felt was renewed. "Ah," he said, "my dear sister, I gave you this ring, as my father gave it to me when he was dying. I must believe your story. Tristan, come here and kiss me. [4300] In truth, as long as you and I shall live, I will be your adoptive father. Blancheflor, your mother, and your father Canel, may God have mercy on their souls and grant them both eternal life together. Since it has transpired that you were left to me by my dear sister, [4310] my dear Lord [Christ] willing, I can now be happy always." He then said to his guest, "My dear friend, so tell me, who are you and what is your name?"

"Rual, Sire."

"Rual?"

"Yes."

Mark remembered now that he had long ago heard much about him, how wise and how honorable [4320] and how faithful he was. He said, "Rual *le foitenant*."

"Yes, Sire, that is what I am called."

Noble Mark went to him, kissed him, and welcomed him graciously according to his rank. The nobility then followed and kissed him one after the other. It was wonderful how they embraced him [4330] and courteously saluted him.

"Welcome, Rual the Honorable! You are a marvel among men."

Rual was welcome there. The king took him by the hand and escorted him away. He most kindly sat him down next to him, and they began again to tell stories. They talked about all sorts of things, [4340] and also of Tristan and Blancheflor, of all their adventures, what Canel and Morgan had inflicted on each other, and how it had all come to an end. Soon the conversation turned to Mark, who told Rual how Tristan had arrived with such self-assurance, [4350] and how he had told them some story about his father being a merchant.

Rual looked at Tristan and said, "My son, I did indeed conduct 'business' for a long time and under difficult conditions, until I was destitute, all for you.[48] Fortunately all this has now come to a happy end. [4360] For that I will always lift up my hands to God."

Tristan said, "I understand, but this turn of events will bring happiness later rather than sooner. I am, as I have just heard, part of a strange tale. I hear my father say that my father was killed long ago, and with this he is also lost to me. [4370] After having gained two fathers, now I have none. Ah, both father and the hope of having a father are lost. When I said that my father was found, at that moment I lost two: him and the father I never knew."

The noble marshal replied, "What is this, dear Tristan? [4380] Don't say these things, they're not true. My arrival has made you all the more noble than you thought to be, and from now on you will be all the more honored. You still have two fathers just like before: my lord here and myself. He is your father, just as I am. Take my advice and you will be the equal of kings. [4390] Stop this talk and do this instead: ask my lord, your uncle, to help you return home and make you a knight. You can take care of your own affairs from now on. My lords, please speak up so that my lord the king will agree."

They all spoke as one, "Sire, this is quite correct. [4400] Tristan is strong and a man full grown."[49]

The king said, "Tristan, my nephew, speak. What are your thoughts on this? Do you want me to do this?"

"My dear lord, I will tell you what I think. If I had sufficient wealth to become a knight as I would wish, that is, if I need not be ashamed of being called a knight, [4410] or if chivalry need not be ashamed of me and chivalric honor not suffer on my account, then I would gladly be a knight. I would discipline my carefree youth and turn my attention to worldly honor. Chivalry, as people say, must begin already in childhood, [4420] or it will rarely grow strong. I have spent little of my youth practicing honor and excellence, and that is surely a mistake I regret. One thing I have known for a long time

---

48. Gottfried allows Rual a moment of high irony in his comment on the "business" of searching for Tristan, where we might say he literally "lost his shirt."
49. Tristan is most likely around eighteen or nineteen years old at this time.

is that leisure and knightly renown are contradictions and work against each other. [4430] I have read it for myself that honor requires physical sacrifice.[50] Leisure is the death of honor when it becomes the everyday focus of youth. You should know in truth, if I had known a year ago or more about my circumstances, I would not have waited this long. [4440] But now that so much time has been wasted, I need to make up for lost time. I have what it takes in terms of strength and determination. May God help me find the means to follow through on my intentions."

Mark replied, "Dear nephew, decide for yourself how to proceed, and think of yourself as king and lord over all of Cornwall.[51] [4450] Your father Rual is here, and he is completely loyal to you. He will be your advisor and counselor, so that whatever you desire shall come to pass. Tristan, dear nephew, don't think that you are without means. Parmenie belongs to you and will be your demesne[52] for as long as I and your father Rual are alive. [4460] I will support you as well. My lands, my people, and everything I have, dear nephew, are at your disposal. If you want to turn your heart to rule and honor, and if you have the resolve, as I have heard you say, then make abundant use of what I have. Cornwall will provide you with an income and my crown lands will pay you tribute. [4470] If you want the world's praise, then you need to be magnanimous. I will give you great wealth. You see, you will have an emperor's estate, so don't underestimate your own worth. If you have the determination that you need, as you have told me, I will quickly recognize it. If I see that you have the ambition to rule, [4480] then you and your aspirations will always have my full support. Tintagel will always be your resource and your security. Should you outdo me in generosity, and if I fail to follow up with support, then I deserve to lose all that I have in Cornwall."[53]

---

50. The chivalric concept of *arebeit* (hardship, self-denial, suffering) is central to the code of knighthood, especially in the works of Hartmann von Aue, for example in *Erec*, where the hero squanders his honor by spending his days in leisure and in bed with his wife, Eneid. The term for this leisure, and therefore the antonym to *arbeit*, is *verligen*.

51. Translations vary here considerably. Hatto translates the original *ob du künic wesen soltest / und hêrre über allez Curnewal* (ll. 4448–49) as "if you were a king, and lord over all of Cornwall" (1960, 102). Krohn (1980) has much the same. Haug/Scholz (2011/2012) translate in the sense of "considering that you could someday become king and lord of all of Cornwall" (im Blick darauf, daß Du einmal König und Herr über ganz Cornwall werden könntest); Knecht (2004a) translates "as if you were meant to be king and lord of all Cornwall" (wenn du zum König und Herrn über ganz Kurnewal bestimmt wärst). My translation relates the text to the context of what follows, which is to say that Mark is offering him the wealth and means of the kingdom in the present, not the future.

52. Gottfried uses the term *eigen* (l. 4458). This term can denote property possessed through vassalage or, as in this case, land that is inherited outright and free from obligations.

53. Mark's speech is based on the virtue of *milte*, or generosity, that is central to all good rulers. The ruling nobility maintains loyalty and service through the reciprocity of sharing the wealth that accrues from their landownership.

All those present bowed. [4490] Everyone who heard this conversation was in complete agreement, and they praised and honored the king with loud acclaim. "King Mark," they all exclaimed, "your speech is noble and honors the crown. Your tongue, your heart, and your hand, may they always rule this land! Long live the King of Cornwall!" [4500] Lord Rual, the loyal marshal, and his young lord, Tristan, generously took up their work, as the king had encouraged them and as they thought appropriate.

I wonder how these two worked together as father and son. Someone will ask us, since maturity and youth [4510] are seldom in agreement on values—youth is oblivious to wealth while a mature man seeks to hang on to it—how the two of them could make decisions with each one getting what he wanted and deserved, so that Rual could control spending while [4520] Tristan had enough to pursue his ambitions. I will answer this promptly and honestly. Rual and Tristan were so much of one mind that neither would recommend something, whether for ill or good, unless the other wanted it as well. Rual, who recognized good character, [4530] had faith in Tristan and took his youth into account. Tristan, on the other hand, yielded to Rual's experience. This would lead them to a common goal, each one wanting the same thing, and so they were in agreement with regard to their desires and intent. In this way, maturity and youth [4540] came together for a common good. High spirits were tempered by reason.[54] They maintained between them Tristan's necessary ambition and Rual's control of resources, so that neither one infringed on the rights of the other. Rual and Tristan embarked thoughtfully on their undertaking, as it seemed right to them. [4550] Within thirty days they had purchased armor and clothing, enough for the thirty knights who would become courtly Tristan's companions-in-arms.[55]

Whoever asks me about their wardrobe, or their wardrobe's value, and how it was all brought together, I will in short order tell him what the story says.[56] [4560] If I don't tell it correctly, then he can correct me and tell it better himself. Their clothes were conceived and fashioned by four kinds of Excellence,[57] each worthy of its office. The first was Ambition; the next was great Wealth; the third was Discernment, [4570] which stitched the first two

---

54. Rual apparently did not have the same effect on his young lord Rivalin, and so this might be seen as a commentary on the importance of balancing reason and ambition, something Rivalin was not able to do (see ll. 290–318).

55. It was common in the late twelfth and thirteenth centuries to knight entire groups of young men, who would then swear fealty to the young noble who was being knighted and groomed for rule.

56. This does not come from any source known to us.

57. Gottfried's term, *rîcheit* (l. 4564), has a broad range of meanings, but here the four "Excellences" bring to mind the concept of the four cardinal virtues of Antiquity: prudence, courage, temperance, and justice (*prudentia, fortitudo, temperantia, iustitia*). Hatto translates this term as "Splendours" (1960, 104).

choose my words very carefully. They should be adorned as I would want them to be [4850] in other people's stories and as I value in another poet's work.

So now I don't know how to start. My mouth and my mind refuse to come to my aid, and what words I had have been taken right out of my mouth. I don't know what to do. [4860] I could do something I have never done before. For the first time I will offer my plea and prayer with my heart and hands to Helicon,[73] to that nine-fold throne from which the fountainheads flow, that source of the gifts of language and mind. [4870] The master and his nine mistresses, Apollo and the nine muses, sirens for the ears, they watch over these gifts there at court, distributing and sharing their blessing with the world as they see fit. They give the streams of imagination in good measure to many, and they could not honorably refuse me just a drop. [4880] If I can acquire just one drop, then I can maintain my reputation, the reputation one maintains with poetry. This same, single drop should suffice to straighten out, that is to guide and form both mouth and mind, which have failed me to this point. It will put my words [4890] into the glowing crucible of poetic inspiration and therein forge them into a rare wonder, as perfect as any gold from Arabia.

These goddesses of grace, of the true Helicon,[74] the uppermost throne, the source of all the words [4900] that sound in our ears and bring laughter into our hearts, that make language translucent like a precious jewel, may they hear my voice and my prayer above in their heavenly choirs,[75] just as I have petitioned.

Now let's say that all this has been done, that I have been granted everything [4910] I want in the way of words; that I have a full supply of all this to make my words pleasing to every ear; that I provide shade to every heart with the linden's evergreen leaves; that I proceed evenly with my art, so that with every step I clear and sweep the path; that I leave not even the smallest speck of dust along the road, [4920] but remove it; and that my art walks only on clover and bright flowers. Still I should focus my mind, what little of it I have, on staying away from, as much as I can, what has led so many others astray in their search. In truth, I must avoid exactly this.

Even if I were to turn all my attention [4930] to chivalric equipment, as God knows so many others have done, and if I were to describe to you

---

73. The previously mentioned font of Pegasus (the Hippocrene) is located on Mount Helicon, as is another spring (the Aganippe) that was sacred to the nine Muses and where their cult was located.

74. Here Gottfried seems to switch from Greek mythology to the one, true Christian Heaven (*wâren Elicônes*; l. 4897).

75. Christian tradition has it that there are nine orders of angels in the heavenly choirs.

how Vulcan,[76] that wise and famous, able craftsman, admirably and masterfully fashioned with his own hands Tristan's hauberk, sword and chausses and other armor parts that are needed by a knight;[77] [4940] how he conceived and shaped the boar on his shield, an animal never lacking in daring; how he forged a helmet for him, attaching at the crest a fiery arrow as a sign of love's pain; how he manufactured both of these, perfect and astonishing in every detail;[78] [4950] and how my Lady Cassandra, that wise Trojan, employed all her skills and knowledge to create and prepare Tristan's clothing so expertly as only she could, (I read [4960] that the gods in heaven had enchanted her spirit with faerie dust), even then, how could any of this be more impressive than how I prepared Tristan's companions for the ceremony of knighthood before?

With your approval, my idea, and it is a good one, is as follows: take Ambition and Wealth and add to these two devices Discernment and Sophistication. [4970] These four can accomplish together more than anyone else. Yes, Vulcan and Cassandra themselves were never better able to outfit knights than these four.

Continuation of Chapter 7

Since these four Excellences are able to prepare such a magnificent ceremony, we command the four to take our friend Tristan [4980] by the hand and prepare this worthy man for us, since no one can do it better, with the furnishings and form that have already been so well provided to his mounted companions. In this manner may Tristan be led to court and to the field,[79] [4990] ornately and expensively equipped, as are his companions. I'm thinking mainly of the clothing sewn by human hands, not the attire that is innate and originates in the halls of the heart, which people call noble spirit. This gives a man his poise and ennobles body and person. His companions were outfitted differently than their lord in this sense. [5000] God only knows, Tristan,

---

76. Vulcan and his wife Venus are also mentioned in Heinrich von Veldeke's *Eneit*. Vulcan made the armor for both Aeneas and his opponent Turnus.

77. The hauberk is a shirt made of chainmail that could reach down to the knees. The chausse is the corresponding leg and foot armor, also originally of mail, before plate armor was introduced in the fourteenth century.

78. Heraldry, and especially heraldic symbols on helmet and shield, developed around the middle of the twelfth century and had become fairly standard even for the lower nobility by 1210.

79. The term used here, *ze ringe* (l. 4987), could mean an assembly (in the form of a ring) or a field of martial exercise or combat. See l. 5056.

confident and hungry for honor, wore extraordinary clothing, adorned far beyond the norm where poise and conduct are concerned. He surpassed all of them when it came to a pleasant disposition and excellent character. As for the clothing sewn by human hands, there was no difference. [5010] The worthy captain wore the same as everyone else.

So the self-assured lord of Parmenie and all his retinue went together to the church, listened to Mass, and received their blessing as they merited. Mark turned his attention to his nephew Tristan [5020] and bestowed on him his sword and spurs.

"You see," he said, "Tristan, nephew mine, now that your sword has been sanctified[80] and you have been made a knight, attend to chivalric values, and also to yourself, to who you are. Your birth into nobility, be mindful of this. Be humble and be honest; [5030] be truthful and disciplined; be always charitable toward the poor, always self-assured toward the rich; take care of and respect yourself; honor and cherish all women; be magnanimous and loyal, and keep these things always new. By my honor I declare that neither gold nor rich furs are suited to lance and shield [5040] better than loyalty and generosity."

He then presented him with his shield, kissed him, and said, "Nephew, now go, and may God in his might protect you in your knighthood. Be always courteous, be always joyful!"

Tristan then in turn bestowed on his companions, just as his uncle had done, sword, spurs, and shield. [5050] Humility, loyalty, and generosity, on these he gave all of them clear instruction. Then without delay they went to compete in war games and riding, at least that's what I imagine. How they rode out on the fields, how they used their lances, how many of these were shattered, let the boys [5060] who gathered them all up report on this. I can't acclaim these contests the way a herald can, but I am willing to offer them one service, namely that I wish them an increase in their honor in every way and that God grant them in their knighthood a knightly life.

---

80. Since the eleventh century the knight's sword was blessed by the Church. The knight was then instructed to protect the Church, widows, orphans, and all servants of God, as well as to protect against the cruelty of heathens (see Okken, 1996, 1.297, n. 5012–24).

Part 1.3

Chapter 8: Return to Parmenie

[5069] Then if anyone alive did constant pain
along with constant joy maintain,
so did Tristan always constant pain
along with constant joy maintain.

What I want to tell you is this. His fate was to have a full measure of both grief and happiness. He was more than successful at everything he undertook, but grief remained a constant companion to happiness, [5080] as much as the two are counterparts. So the two were opposed, constant happiness and relentless grief, partners in this one man.

"In the name of God, explain this! Tristan has just been knighted and has found complete happiness in his knightly renown. Let us hear what kind of grief intruded on his happiness."

[5090] God knows, there is one thing that has always troubled every heart, including his. His father had been killed, as he heard Rual tell, and this pained him deeply. So then bad and good, happiness and misfortune, love and grief, all these were firmly bound together in his heart.

[5099] It's generally agreed, you see,
that someone young can often be
more keen on hate, it's plain to see,
than any older man might be.

Over all of Tristan's renown, grief and hidden hardship hovered constantly. Although unseen by others, the fact that Rivalin was dead and Morgan still alive left him no peace. This grief burdened him with great cares. [5110] Careworn Tristan and his faithful advisor, the blessed *Foitenant*, who took his name from faithfulness, promptly fitted out a splendid ship with rich provisions that left nothing to be desired. Then they appeared before Mark.

Tristan said, "My dear lord, [5120] I seek your blessing to return to Parmenie. As you advised, I want to find out what the situation is concerning the people and lands which are mine, as you said."

The king replied, "Nephew, so be it. As much as I hate to be without you, I will grant your wish. Go home to Parmenie, [5130] you and your comrades, and if you need more knights, then take as many as you think proper. Take horses, silver and gold, and whatever else you think you might need, and whomever you retain, reward him well as a brother-in-arms, so that he will gladly remain in your service [5140] and stand by you in loyalty. My dear nephew, act and live as your father, faithful Rual, instructs you. He stands here with great loyalty and honor and has watched out for you until now. If God grants that you obtain justice and are able to settle your dispute with success and honor, [5150] then you should come back. Come back to me.

"One thing I will promise and undertake for you. You have my hand in good faith that I will equally divide my property and lands with you, and if you are fortunate enough to outlive me, then everything will belong to you. For your sake I resolve [5160] to remain without a wife as long as I live. Nephew, you have heard my wish and my intent. If you hold me dear as I do you, if you care about me as I do you, then God knows that we will live out our days together in joy. I give you permission to go. May the Virgin's son keep you, [5170] and may you be mindful of your affairs and your honor."

Without further delay, Tristan and his companion Rual, along with their company, sailed from Cornwall home to Parmenie.

[5177] **O**f all this would you hear me tell
how all these lords were welcomed well,
then I will say what I've heard tell
how all of them were welcomed well.

It was their commander, faithful, reliable Rual, who first set foot on land. He courteously removed his hat and cloak and then, laughing, ran back to Tristan. He kissed him and said, "My lord, may you be welcomed by God, your country, and me! [5190] Look, Lord, do you see this beautiful country along the shore? There are strong towns, strong fortifications, and many marvelous castles. You see, your father Canel left you all this. Since you are brave and thoughtful, whatever your eye sees here will never be lost to you. I will be the guarantor of that."

[5200] After making this speech he turned with a full and joyful heart to welcome each of the knights. He greeted and welcomed them splendidly with his kind words and then escorted them to Canoel. The towns and castles in the entire land, once given over by Rivalin [5210] to Rual's care, were now given over to Tristan as loyalty demanded. Along with these

Rual relinquished his own property, which had been handed down to him through the generations.[1]

What more is there to be said about this? Rual had means and honor. With these he offered his lord support, [5220] and with him all his people, as one does who has means and honor. The diligence and effort that he kindly devoted to them for their own benefit alone had never been seen before.

What now? How could this have happened to me? I've jumbled everything up. What was I thinking? [5230] The noble marshaline, the pure and constant one, my lady Florete, how could I have left her out? That was not very courtly at all. I repent and will make it up to the sweet lady, the courtly, the noble, the nobly minded, the distinguished, and the best. [5240] I well know that she did not welcome her guests with words alone. Sincere intentions preceded everything she said, and her heart flew to meet them as if it had wings. Her sentiment and words were completely in agreement. I'm sure that they both overflowed with friendliness [5250] as she greeted the guests. The blessed Florete, what joy filled her heart for her lord and child, the same child that is the subject of this story. Of course, I mean her son Tristan. I know this to be true based on the illustrious lady's many virtues and qualities of which I have read. [5260] That these were not a few she demonstrated as a woman can best. She provided her child and his companions with all the honor and amenities that knights have ever received.[2]

Following this the lords and nobility of Parmenie, [5270] those with authority over towns and castles, were called together. Once they had all arrived in Canoel and saw and heard the truth about Tristan, as the story tells us and as you have now heard for yourself, a thousand welcomes flew out of every mouth. [5280] The people and the realm began to awaken from a long period of suffering and gave themselves over to joy, in wonderfully wonderful ways. Each of them received his fief, his people, and lands from his lord Tristan's own hand. They all swore fealty and became his vassals.

At the same time Tristan had a secret pain hidden in his heart caused by Morgan. This pain never left him, morning or night. He sought counsel from

---

1. It was customary under feudal law to give over personal property to one's lord in the expectation that it would be returned as a fief in exchange for fealty and service.

2. Some editions (Bechstein [1869/1870], Marold [1906], and Golther [1888]) and translations that follow them (Knecht [2004a], Ertzdorff et al. [1979], Kramer [1966], and Hertz [1877]) add six lines after l. 5266, although they are not included in manuscripts HMBE. This has led to additional confusion concerning the line numbering across editions. Ranke's edition does not include these lines, and his numbering system is used here (as well as in the Haug/Scholz [2011/2012] and Krohn [1980] editions and translations). Ranke's (1949) line 5267 now equals Bechstein's and Marold's line 5271 (Ranke's numbering was already two more, since the changes at l. 235). The six additional lines are: "I know one thing very well, something that I could not know better, concerning courtly Curvenal. Tristan could not have been more welcome to him, of that I have no doubt."

his kin and vassals and said that he wanted to travel to Brittany to receive his fiefdom from his enemy's own hand, [5300] so as to make a more rightful claim to his father's lands. This is what he said and did. He rode from Parmenie along with his troop of companions, well prepared and armed, as a man should be who is seriously intent on danger.

When Tristan arrived in Brittany [5310] he heard by chance, and it was verified as true, that Duke Morgan was hunting in the forests. He ordered the knights to arm themselves quickly and put on their hauberks and other armor under their tunics, so that not a single ring of mail would show from beneath their clothes. [5320] This is what happened, this is what was done. Over all this each man wore his hooded cloak, and then they mounted their horses. Straightaway they ordered their baggage train back to the rear, with instructions to stop for no one. The knights were then divided into companies, and the larger troop was sent back [5330] to guard the train as it moved along the road. After this was done, those who remained with Tristan totaled about thirty knights, and those who turned back numbered about sixty or more.

It didn't take long for Tristan to catch sight of some dogs and huntsmen. He asked them for information about [5340] where the duke was located, and they told him straightaway. He immediately set off in pursuit and quickly discovered many Breton knights inside a forested expanse. There were pavilions and tents set up in a meadow, with greenery and bright flowers scattered all around. [5350] They had their hounds and birds of prey close at hand and greeted Tristan and his company courteously according to the custom at court. They also informed him that their lord Morgan had ridden into a nearby wood. Tristan immediately gave chase and found Morgan there [5360] along with many Breton knights mounted on their Castilian palfreys.[3] They trotted up to meet them, and Morgan greeted the strangers most hospitably, as it is proper to greet strangers, since he knew nothing of their intentions, and his people did the same, each one running up to greet them.

[5370] After all the commotion of greeting had died down, Tristan said to Morgan, "Sir, I have come on account of my fief, and I require that you grant it to me here and now, and that you not deny me what I should have by rights. In this you would be acting courteously and properly."

Morgan replied, "Sir, tell me [5380] where you come from or who you are."

Tristan in turn responded to him, "I was born in Parmenie and my father's name was Rivalin. Sir, I am his heir, and my name is Tristan."

Morgan said, "You come to me with totally irrelevant declarations. It would have been better for you to keep silent than to utter them. [5390]

---

3. Horses bred in Spain, especially Andalusia and Castile, were a mix of Arabian and indigenous breeds and were prized for their size and strength.

There's not much I need to say. If you should receive anything from me, then you would promptly have it. There would be no reason to deny you if you were a man deserving of the honor you so desire. But we all know too well, this is known in every land, how Blancheflor [5400] fled her country with your father, what became of her honor, and how the love affair ended."

"Love affair? What do you mean by that?"

"I don't need to elaborate, I think the phrase speaks for itself."

"Sir," said Tristan, "I take issue with what you have said. Do you mean to say that I was born out of wedlock [5410] and have therefore lost my right to my fiefdom?"

"Indeed, good sir squire,[4] this is what I and many others think."

"What you say is vile," said Tristan. "I think it is suitable and appropriate, that when a man does another man wrong, he should speak to him with consideration and respect. [5420] If you had any respect or consideration for everything you've done to me, then you would have spared me any new hurt or rekindling of old guilt. You killed my father. You seem to think that this pain alone is insufficient. You say that my mother who bore me did so illegitimately.[5] [5430] So help me God almighty! I know for certain that many noble men, whom I won't name here, placed their folded hands in mine.[6] If they had recognized the failing of which you accuse me, not one of them would have put his hands in mine. They know the truth, namely that my father Rivalin [5440] married my mother before his demise. If I should need to demonstrate and prove this in combat with you, then I will gladly do so."

"Enough!" replied Morgan. "Go to hell! What do you mean by proof? You would never be allowed to fight a man of noble birth."[7]

"We'll see about that," said Tristan. [5450] He drew his sword and charged. He struck him from top to bottom, splitting both his skull and brain in two, all the way through to his tongue. He then stuck his sword straight into his

---

4. Morgan addresses Tristan as *knecht*, not *ritter or herre*, an insult to his age and station.

5. The claim is that Tristan was conceived out of wedlock. The adverb used is *kebeslîche*, related to *kebse*, meaning concubine or even prostitute. This is the same accusation made by Kriemhild against Brunhild in the *Nibelungenlied*. Kriemhild claims that Brunhild first slept with Siegfried and not her husband Gunther, therefore throwing doubt on the legitimacy of her marriage to Gunther, because her virginity had not been taken by her husband but by Siegfried instead. Even though this was not true, the accusation was enough to cause the cataclysm of events that ended in the destruction of the Nibelungen.

6. This was the gesture of fealty.

7. Morgan not only asserts that Tristan was born illegitimately (i.e., that his parents were not properly married before his conception), but he also claims therefore that Tristan has no rights to claim for himself a noble birth, and with that the right to trial by combat.

heart. This confirmed the truth in the old saying, "Debts may linger, but they don't spoil."[8]

Morgan's guard, [5460] the valiant Bretons, were unable to protect him there or come to his aid quickly enough to save him from death. All of them, though, armed themselves as well as they could. Soon enough there was a great many of them and these men, although taken by surprise, confronted their enemy with courage. [5470] Very few thought about their own safety or protection but instead charged in formation and with their strength drove them out of the forest into the open fields. There was a great noise with much screaming and crying. Morgan's death rose up in a multitude of cries as if it had wings. [5480] The sad news soared up to castles and out into the countryside. Throughout the realm there arose a single cry of grief, "*Ah! notre seigneur, il est mort!*[9] What will now become of this land? You excellent warriors, come out of your towns and fortresses and repay these foreigners for the pain they have inflicted on us."

[5490] They assailed those who were hard pressed with constant attacks but found that the foreigners were at all times full of fight. Tristan's forces defended themselves again and again, turning in closed formation and causing many casualties, but they had to continue their retreat in the direction of their main body. [5500] They joined their main force and set up defenses on a fortified hill where they spent the night. During the night the realm's forces grew so strong and organized that they were able to attack the hated foreigners as soon as it was dawn. They struck down many of them [5510] and often broke into their formation with spears and swords, which did not remain intact for long. In fact, spears and swords didn't remain intact for long at all and were often broken as they set upon the company. But the small troop was so tenacious in its defense that they caused a great many casualties [5520] whenever their formation was assaulted. The formations on both sides took casualties throughout the battle. They took and gave losses, and many men suffered. The battle continued until the defending force began to weaken as it grew smaller and the other side grew larger. [5530] The attackers grew stronger throughout the day, both in their position and their numbers, so that they were able before nightfall to encircle the foreigners inside a moat. There the foreigners were able to defend themselves and survive the night. The company was cornered and surrounded by the opposing host as if a wall had been thrown up.

---

8. This saying was known in Latin since about 1100 (*noxa iacens crescit, nec enim dilata putrescit*). This is the first evidence of this saying in German (see Okken, 1996, 1.310, n. 5458).
9. "Oh, our lord, he is dead!"

[5540] "How were the beleaguered foreigners, Tristan and his men, able to handle this situation?"

I will tell you what happened to them, how their troubles were ended, how they escaped from there and claimed victory over their enemies.

Tristan had left his own country, as he was advised to do by his counselor Rual, in order to receive his fief [5550] and then return as quickly as possible. Since that time, blessed Rual worried constantly about how Tristan was managing, although he hadn't advised that Morgan be harmed. He mustered a hundred knights and set out for Tristan along the exact same road. [5560] It didn't take very long for him to reach Brittany, and there he promptly found out what had happened. Based on reports from around the country he resumed his journey to where the Bretons were ensconced. When they approached and were able to see the enemy, no one in their company [5570] disgraced himself, either by staying behind or falling out. They all charged forward in formation with banners flying and with a great cry coming up from the troops, "*Chevalier! Parmenie! Parmenie! Chevalier!*"[10] Banner followed banner [5580] through the enemy camp, causing destruction and chaos. They drove the Bretons through their tents with deadly blows. When those who were encircled recognized the banners of their own country and heard their battle cry, they broke out of their narrow space into the open. Tristan continued to push the attack, [5590] causing a great deal of damage to the local force. Capturing and killing, striking and stabbing, they charged through the enemy, whose morale was broken by the constant cry in both companies of "*Chevalier! Parmenie!*" on each flank. [5600] They were left helpless, unable to defend themselves, to attack, or undertake any other kind of action except to hide or retreat, to flee toward some castle or forest. The battle broke up into small skirmishes, and flight was the only defense left that could save them from certain death.

After this defeat [of the Bretons], [5610] the knights [of Parmenie] dismounted and set up camp. They had the comrades who lay dead on the battlefield buried and the wounded put on litters. Then they returned home. Tristan was able in this way to grant [5620] himself fief and independent territory[11] by his own hand. He was both lord and vassal of a man who had never granted the same to his father.[12] This is how he recovered and restored

---

10. "Knights! Parmenie!" These words are then repeated in reverse. They do not constitute a phrase but instead serve as exclamations and shouts of encouragement.

11. The phrase *sîn lêhen und sîn sunderlant* (l. 5619) probably refers to one and the same land, but not to Parmenie. The designation *sunderlant* refers to some geographically separate territory that was originally Rivalin's fiefdom, which he had from Morgan.

12. The meaning of this line is in some dispute. The original *er was von dem hêrre unde man, von dem sîn vater nie niht gewan* (ll. 5621–22) raises the problem of to whom *von dem* refers. Knecht offers: "He was lord and vassal of a son that was never born to his father" (und war

all that he wanted.[13] He recovered his property and restored his own peace of mind. His wrong had turned to right, his troubled mind had been eased, and he now had possession [5630] of his father's birthright and all his land without challenge, so that no one else at that time had any claim on his lands whatsoever.

His mind turned back to Cornwall, to the charge and advice his uncle had given him when he left, but he did not want to turn his thoughts away from Rual, [5640] who, out of fatherly devotion, had done so much for him. His affection was equally strong for Rual and Mark. These two occupied all his thoughts, alternating from one to the other and back again.

Now a virtuous man might ask, "How can Tristan, a virtuous man, act [5650] so that he does right by both of them and rewards each as he should?"

Each one of you knows quite well that he can only choose to leave one and stay with the other.

"What do you think? What will happen?"

If he returns to Cornwall, he will damage Parmenie's honor and distinction. [5660] Rual's joy and hope will be ruined, along with all the wealth[14] that should endow his happiness. If he stays, however, then he rejects higher honors as well as Mark's counsel, on which all his honor depends.

"How can he make the right choice?"

[5670] By God, he has to go back! We should grant him that much. If things are going to take a turn toward goodness and happiness, he must enrich himself in honor and grow in ambition. He should strive for and aspire to every honor, and if good fortune bestows this on him, then it does so rightly. [5680] It is all that he desires.

Tristan was intelligent, and so he intelligently came to the conclusion that he would split himself in half for his fathers, as if with a sword. He cut himself in two as precisely and smoothly as an egg and gave each of them [5690] the part that he knew was best for him. For anyone who has never heard what parts a man is made of, I will tell him how this division was accomplished. No one has any doubt that two things make up a man, by that I mean his person and his property. These two beget a noble mind and great worldly honor.

---

somit Herr und Vasall eines Sohnes, der seinem Vater nie geboren wurde). Spiewok (1994) translates: "He was his own vassal, as his father had never been" (Er war sein eigener Lehens-mann—wie es sein Vater nie gewesen). Others refer the pronoun back to Morgan, such as Hatto: "He was now both lord and vassal of one from whom his father had never acquired a thing" (1960, 118–19), with a footnote that reads "Rivalin had despoiled Morgan in war but apparently not acquired a sovereign title to the fief for which he owed allegiance."

13. Gottfried emphasizes that Tristan won his land in this way (*sus*), but conspicuously does not make any mention of honor (*êre*). This is most likely intentionally ironic and critical. There was certainly little honor to be won by ambushing Morgan and slicing him in two before he could defend himself. Refer back to Mark's instructions (l. 5149).

14. MHG *guot* (l. 5662) can mean both goodness and wealth, as in line 5674.

[5700] When someone separates the two, first wealth turns to poverty and then a person is shown no respect and is therefore no longer worthy of being called a person. The man becomes a half of himself even with a whole body. The same is true for women. Whether man or woman, property and person must stay together [5710] to make a whole person. If they are separated, then both become worthless.

Tristan pondered these things often and untiringly and then came to a clever decision. He had excellent horses and noble clothing delivered, along with fine dishes and other provisions generally needed for festivities. [5720] He organized a festival and sent out invitations to the nobility throughout the realm, to those who had the most authority and power. They did what would be expected of supporters and friends and came as they had been asked. Tristan finished all of his preparations and then made two of his father Rual's sons knights, [5730] because he intended that they later become Rual's heirs. Whatever else he was able to do for their renown and honor with his wealth, he did so night and day as sincerely and willingly as if they were his own children. The two of them became knights along with twelve companions, [5740] one of which was Curvenal, that courtly man. Tristan, virtuous as always, took his brothers by the hand and in his courtliness escorted them from there. His family and vassals, and everyone else who was reasonable and astute as a result of their intellect or experience or both, [5750] were all invited to assemble at court.

Now, dear sirs, they are all here. Tristan stood up in front of them and said, "All you lords, whom I am at all times ready to serve in loyalty and sincerity as well as I am able, [5760] my kin and my dear vassals, from whose grace I have whatever God has bestowed on me in honor, with your help I have achieved everything that my heart desired. As much as I am thankful to God, I also know full well that it was your resolve that made it a reality. What more can I say to you? [5770] In this short time you have conferred on me your esteem and blessing in so many ways that I have no doubt that this world would first have to come to an end before you would ever oppose me in any way. Allies and vassals, and all of those who are here by virtue of my request or your own goodness, [5780] please don't take offense at what I am about to say.

"I proclaim and say to you all, just as my father Rual, who is standing here, saw and heard for himself, that my uncle placed his lands in my hands and intends to remain unmarried so that I may be his heir. [5790] He requires that I live with him wherever he may reside or wherever he may travel. Now I have come to a decision that I support with all my heart and mind. I will respect his bidding and return to him. The income and property rights that I have in this realm here, these I grant my father Rual as his fief, so that, [5800] should things go badly for me in Cornwall, whether I perish or live, these lands will remain his feudal inheritance. His sons, who are standing here, as well as his other children, those who stand to inherit from him, will all have these rights. My vassals and my liegemen and the feudal rights over all these lands, [5810] these I will keep myself for the rest of my life."

A great hue and cry went up from all the knights. They all despaired, their confidence and their hopes disappeared.

"Ah, lord," they all said, "it would have been better for us if we had never seen you. This would have prevented the suffering [5820] that you have now inflicted on us. Lord, our hopes and dreams were placed in you that we would have something to live for because of you. Now sadly all our lives, which we imagined as full of joy, are dead and buried if you leave us here. Lord, you have increased our suffering, not diminished it. [5830] Our fortune had risen a bit but now has fallen again."

I know this as surely as death is certain: as fervent as their complaint and as great as their sadness was on hearing this, Rual, who benefitted and gained great advantage from this both in honor and wealth, [5840] was more upset than anyone else. God only knows that he never received a fief with such sorrow as the one he received there.

After Rual and his children had been enfeoffed and were established as heirs by their lord, Tristan put his people and lands in God's hands and left the country. [5850] Curveval, his teacher, went along with Tristan. Was the grief and sadness that Rual, his men, and all the people felt for their dear lord short lived? One thing I know for sure: Parmenie was full of grief and lament, [5860] and the grief was genuine. The marshaline Florete, who was loyal and honorable, suffered greatly, which is understandable for a woman who lived a life as granted her by God and filled with womanly honor.

Chapter 9: Morold

[5867] **W**hy should I go on with this? After Tristan, now without his lands, had returned to Cornwall he heard a report that concerned him a great deal. Morold, who had a strong army, had come from Ireland threatening force and demanding that Mark surrender the income of both his lands, Cornwall and England. This income was arranged as follows. There was a king in Ireland, [5880] as I have read in the sources and as the story correctly recounts, whose name was Gurmun the Bold.[15] He was born in Africa, where his father was a king. When his father died he inherited the land along with

---

15. There is a historical figure from the Migration Age (c. 350–550 CE) who forms the basis for this story. Gormund was a Germanic prince of the Vandals and son of Geiserich in northern Africa who briefly established his own kingdom in Ireland, supposedly with the permission of the eastern Roman emperor Zeno, as presented here. He was defeated by the Frankish king Chlodwig, and his tribe was supposedly settled in southern England around Hastings.

his brother, who was also designated as heir. Gurmun was so power hungry and ambitious, [5890] however, that he did not want to share property with anyone. His aspiration to become a lord in his own right was all consuming, and so he began to seek and select the strongest and most courageous men, those who were acknowledged by all as completely reliable in battle, both knights and sergeants. These he recruited for his cause with money [5900] or prospects of chivalric deeds.

At the appropriate time he left all of his land to his brother and then departed immediately. He received from the legendary and mighty Romans permission and the right to claim for himself anything he could conquer by force, [5910] while turning over certain rights and title to them. Without delay he traveled with a large army over land and sea until he came to Ireland, where he conquered the land and forced the inhabitants against their will to acknowledge him as their lord and king. [5920] They were obliged at all times to make war and help in conquering neighboring lands, and in this way he also brought Cornwall and England under his control. Mark was still a boy at the time and too young to defend himself, so he lost his kingdom [5930] and became tributary to Gurmun.

It was also to Gurmun's advantage, and it gave him strength and renown, that he had wed Morold's sister, and because of this he was feared by all. Morold was a duke there with ambitions of possessing lands somewhere. He was daring, owned land and large amounts of other property, [5940] had great physical strength and courage, and he was Gurmun's champion.

I will tell you exactly how the payments that were sent to Ireland from all these countries were arranged. In the first year they delivered 300 marks[16] in bronze and nothing more. The second year the payment was in silver, the third year in gold. [5950] In the fourth year, mighty Morold came from Ireland prepared for single combat or war. Barons and other nobles from Cornwall and England were ordered to appear before him, and in his presence they picked lots as to who would provide their children as hostages. They had to be old enough to serve [5960] and be handsome and refined, so that they would be suitable for court. There were to be no girls, only boys, and there should be thirty from each of the two lands.[17] The only way to avoid this disgrace was through single combat or declared war. [5970] They were unable to

---

Gottfried's source could possibly have been Wace's *Roman de Brut* (see Okken, 1996, 1.319–321, n. 5878–30).

16. The mark was a common weight throughout the Middle Ages, although its value varied considerably. A rough average would be about 200–250 grams, or about half a pound, or 8 ounces. In gold this would, of course, have been a very large payment, equivalent today to more than four million dollars.

17. The comment that there should be no girls is certainly a reaction against the Eilhart version, which makes prostitutes out of the female hostages in Ireland (Thomas, 1978, 53).

defend their rights through open warfare since their lands' strength had been crippled. On the other hand Morold was so strong, so ruthless, and so cruel that not a single man, once he looked him in the eye, dared risk his life any more than would a woman.

Once the tribute [5980] was on its way to Ireland, in the fifth year at the time of the summer solstice both lands were required to send ambassadors to Rome who were worthy of such a mission. They were to heed the commands and directives that the mighty senate sent out [5990] to each land subject to Rome. Laws were proclaimed every year, and they were instructed in how to govern according to Roman law and right, and how to conduct their judicial courts. They had to act as they were commanded. The tribute and gifts [6000] were submitted by the two lands each fifth year to almighty Rome, their overlord. In no way did they offer her these honors because of the law or God, but only because of Gurmun's demands.

Now we return to our story. Tristan had heard about Cornwall's burden, [6010] and he already knew about the conditions of the tribute payments, but now every day wherever he rode from one town or castle to another he heard people complaining about the country's disgrace and agony. When he returned to the court at Tintagel, [6020] you should know that he heard such an expression of grief in the alleys and streets that he was deeply moved. The news that Tristan had arrived quickly made its way to Mark and the rest of the court, and they were all glad. I mean glad, though, inasmuch as they could be happy given their grief. [6030] The very best men who could be found in all of Cornwall had at the time already arrived at court, to their shame, as you have just heard. The nobility of the land was there to draw lots for their children's ruin.

Tristan found them all on bended knee in prayer, [6040] each one praying unashamedly and openly, with tear-filled eyes and his own private anguish in body and heart, that God in his goodness would protect and safeguard his honor and his child. Tristan came upon them as they were praying. [6050]

"How was he received?"

I can tell you that quite easily. Tristan was greeted by the household and others, and even Mark, and this is the truth, not nearly as well as would have been the case had they not been in such distress.

Tristan took little notice of this, however, [6060] and boldly went up to where the lots were being drawn, where Morold and Mark were seated. "My lords," he said, "all of you, to address you all together, those who have come here to draw lots and sell your honor: Are you not ashamed of the dishonor that you bring to this land? As courageous as you are at other times [6070] and places, you should by rights increase your honor and renown and that of your country. You have instead placed your freedom at your enemies' feet and in their hands with this shameful tribute. Your noble children, [6080] who should be your joy, your happiness, and your life, you have and continue to give up as vassals into bondage, yet you are unable to explain who is forcing you to do this, or what it is that compels you, except for single combat and a single man. There is no other justification.

"Among all of you [6090] there is not one who will risk his life for victory or death against just one man. If you should die, well then it's true that a quick death and this long miserable life mean very different things in heaven and on earth. If you should win [6100] and conquer injustice, then you will forever have God's reward there and honor here. Since fathers live on in their children, they should be willing to give up their lives for them, as God wills it. It is against God's will to give up your children's freedom to serfdom, to turn them into serfs, [6110] while you live in freedom. If I can give you some advice for a life lived both according to God's will and honor, then I strongly urge you to choose a man wherever he can be found among your peers, someone skilled in fighting and willing to leave it to fate whether he lives or dies. [6120] All of you should then pray to God that the Holy Spirit grant him luck and honor, and that his fear of Morold's size and strength may not be too great. He should trust in God, who never abandoned a man on the side of justice. Meet in council now [6130] and decide quickly how you will defend yourselves against this dishonor and free yourselves from this man. No longer should you disgrace your nobility and your honor."

"Ah, sir," they all said, "this man is different. No one can withstand him."

Tristan replied, "Don't say that! By God, consider this. [6140] You are all as nobly born as kings and emperors, and still you want to sell your children, who are as nobly born as you, and turn them into serfs? Should you fail to find someone to fight this man because of your suffering [6150] and the misery in this land and for justice in God's name, and if you leave it to up to God and me, then my lords, I will wager my youth and my life for God and take up the fight on your behalf. [6160] May God grant you a fortunate outcome and restore justice. If the fight ends badly for me, then your cause will not suffer. If I die in the duel, then your suffering will not end or change, be diminished or increased. Things will by rights be as they were before. [6170] If, on the other hand, it turns out well, then it will be by God's will, and you should thank no one except God. The one whom I will face, so I have often heard, is an experienced and battle-hardened knight with confidence and strength. My own confidence and strength are still developing, [6180] and my own knighthood is not as excellent as we might need. In this fight, however, I have two aids to victory, namely God and a just cause, and they will join me in battle. I also have great determination, which is always helpful in combat. If these three support me, [6190] though inexperienced as I am, then I am hopeful that I will prevail against one man."

"Lord," said the entire assembly of knights, "may God's holy might, which created all the world, repay you for the help, advice, and encouragement that you have given us all. Lord, let us tell you where we stand. [6200] Our council will be of little use. If our prayers had been answered to the same degree that our appeals were made every time this situation arose, then our problem would not be unresolved today. We have discussed our misfortune more than once here in Cornwall. We have often talked about it but have never found [6210] among us anyone who would not rather give up his son into serfdom than lose his own life fighting this devil."

"How can you talk that way?" said Tristan. "Many things have happened in the past, and it has often been demonstrated that injustice and pride have been brought low by a weaker opponent.[18] That could well happen again [6220] if someone dared to try."

Morold listened to all of this and was displeased that Tristan spoke so boldly of combat even though he looked like a child. His heart was full of anger toward him.

Tristan nonetheless continued to speak, "My lords all, tell me what you want me to do."

"Sir," they all replied, [6230] "if the hope that you have given us could be fulfilled, then that would be our wish."

"Is this your decision?" he asked. "Since it has taken this long, and it is now up to me, then with God's help I will endeavor to see if God will grant you [6240] deliverance through me and if I might have fortune on my side."

At this point Mark tried to dissuade him with various arguments, hoping to convince him to drop the matter for his sake. No, by God, he would not. He could not be swayed by commands or pleas [6250] to let it be on Mark's account.

Instead Tristan walked up to where Morold was seated and addressed him as follows. "Lord," he said, "tell me in God's name, what do you want?"

"My friend," Morold replied without hesitation, "why do you ask? You know well enough what I am here to demand and what I want."

"All of you, my lords, my lord the king and his vassals, listen to me," [6260] said clever Tristan. "My Lord Morold, you are correct, I know full well and recognize how things stand. It is a reality, regardless how shameful, that no one can deny. The tribute has been sent for some time from here and also from England to Ireland without just cause. Over time this has been accomplished [6270] through intimidation and violence. Castles and towns across these lands have been destroyed, and the people have been persecuted until they were crushed by violence and injustice. The brave knights who were left

---

18. The standard example in story form for the Middle Ages was the defeat of Goliath by David (see 1 Samuel 17).

[6280] had to submit to everything required of them. They feared death and were unable in their condition to do anything else. This is the great injustice that has been perpetrated since that time and that you still see today.

"It is long overdue [6290] that they defend themselves in battle against this great injury, now that these two lands are greatly restored. The population of residents and foreigners has increased, as have towns and fortifications, wealth and renown. We shall now have restitution for what was taken from us. Our survival will from now on be secured by force. [6300] If we are ever to recover fully, then we will have to assert ourselves in battle and in war. We have a good many inhabitants, in fact both lands are full of people. We should get back what has been taken from us by force our entire lives. We will appear on the enemy's own shores as soon as God is willing. [6310] Whatever they have taken from us, be it little or much, if my counsel should prevail then they will have to give it back to us, all of it down to the last link of chainmail. Our brass may yet turn into red gold. Stranger things have happened in this world. [6320] These lords' noble children who have been sent into slavery may yet be set free, as impossible as that may seem at the moment. May God grant that I achieve this! I ask it in his name that I may with my own hands [6330] plant the battle banners in Ireland along with my countrymen, and that I may conquer their country and their lands."

Morold answered, "Sir Tristan, I think it would be better for you if you were somewhat less ambitious in this matter and this cause. Whatever is said here won't make us abandon what we by rights should have." [6340] He then walked up to Mark and said, "King Mark, speak now so that all of you, those assembled here to deal with me concerning your children, may hear what you have decided. Is it your will and do you all agree with what your spokesman, Sir Tristan, has stated here?"

[6350] [Mark replied,] "Yes, lord, what he has said and done, this is our common view, our will, and our intent."

Morold said, "You are hereby breaking your oath of fealty with my lord and with me, as well as all of the agreements that have been made between us up to now."

Tristan politely responded, "No, sir, you are not correct in this. [6360] It is malicious to accuse someone of breaking his fealty. No one here is breaking his oath of loyalty. A sworn agreement was concluded between all of you, and this will remain in place. Every year the agreed upon tribute is to be readily delivered from Cornwall and England to Ireland, [6370] unless they resist in single combat or open warfare. If they are prepared to satisfy their oath of fealty through tribute or combat, then they will have done right by you. Sir, consider this. Take counsel and then tell me what you would prefer, [6380] that is which of these two you want: single combat or war. From now on and in the future, you can rest assured that we are ready, and that lance and sword

by women's hands to create a marvelous appearance.[21] Ah, when he put it on, how handsome and admirable he looked. It was a sight to behold.

But I don't want to draw this out too long. It would take far too long if I were to recount every detail, as I should. One thing you should know, though. [6570] The man conferred on the coat more in praise and honor than the coat ever granted the man. As noble and praiseworthy as the surcoat was, it hardly matched the worthiness of the one who wore it. Mark strapped a sword around him that was to be his life and his heart, [6580] and it saved him from Morold and many others since. It hung at his side perfectly and fit his stride so well that it did not swing around but stayed properly in place.[22] A helmet was brought that looked like a crystal, unblemished and hard, [6590] the most attractive and best that any knight has ever worn. I don't think that any better had ever come to Cornwall. The crest was an arrow, a symbol of love, the love that was to express itself in him, even though that was still a long time away.

Mark placed the helmet on him and said, [6600] "Ah, nephew, I cry out bitterly to God that I ever saw you. I will renounce everything that brings a man joy if anything should happen to you."

A shield was brought, crafted with great care by a skilled hand. It was entirely silver white so as to match [6610] the helmet and chainmail and was so highly burnished and flawless that it gave the appearance of a new mirror. Masterfully etched in the shield was a boar, finished in coal black sable. His uncle armed him with this as well. It suited that exceptional man and nestled snuggly against his side, [6620] then and in the future, as if it were joined to him. Once Tristan, praiseworthy, handsome, and youthful, had taken the shield in hand the four pieces of equipment, the helmet and hauberk, the shield and chausses, all shone brilliantly. They reflected each other as if the armorer had designed all four [6630] to enhance the beauty of the others, as each was enhanced by them. Their brilliance could not have been better matched.

Now we come to that completely new marvel hidden within and underneath the armor, to the harm and dismay of his enemies. Was it insignificant [6640] in comparison to the exceptional masterpiece that could be seen on the outside? I know it as clear as day: as great as the exterior appeared, the inner figure was even better formed and more masterful, and the knight more perfect than the exterior. The interior work of art was fashioned [6650] most worthily in form and spirit. Ah, how magnificently the creator's wisdom was

---

21. This refers to the technique of tablet weaving, or *Brettchenweben* in German.

22. This remark about the sword's fit could have two meanings: "the sword was so well balanced that it always honed in on its mark," or, as here, "it hung so well that it did not sway up or down while walking."

apparent. His chest, his arms, and his legs were imposing and powerful, well-shaped and noble. The iron armor fit him splendidly and admirably.

His horse was held at the ready by a squire. [6660] Not even in Spain had a more superb animal ever been bred. It was not too thin anywhere, but its chest and quarters were sizeable and sturdy, both flanks were strong, and it was ideal in every sense. Its feet and legs were well made to their purpose, [6670] the hooves were rounded, the legs slender and straight like an animal in the wild. It was also stout and sturdy. In front of the saddle and the chest everything was well proportioned, as it should be with a horse. It was covered with a white blanket, bright and clear as day, to match the armor. [6680] It was long and sumptuous and hung down almost to the horse's knees.

Once Tristan had been admirably armed for the fight according to custom and the manner of chivalry, those who were able to judge both men and weapons unanimously agreed [6690] that both, weapons and man, had never before presented such a striking image. As impressive as this picture was, it was even more remarkable once he mounted his horse and took hold of his lance. The portrait was marvelous. Seated there, this knight was exemplary above and below the saddle. Arms and shoulders [6700] were broad and strong. He knew exactly how to sit in the saddle properly. His handsome legs extended alongside the horse's shoulders, straight and well-proportioned like staves. There they stood, the horse, the man, they both complemented each other as if the two [6710] had been born and grown up as one single being. Tristan's seat and position on the horse were elegant and solid at the same time. As fine as his posture was to behold, however, it was the spirit on the inside that was pure and good. In fact, never before [6720] had a helmet crowned such dignified character and uncorrupted nature.

In the meantime the two fighters had been informed that they were to fight on a small island[23] in the sea, so close to the shore and the crowd that what happened on the island could be easily seen. It was also agreed that no one would set foot there aside from the two men [6730] until the fight was over. This command was fully honored. Two small boats were brought for the two fighters, each one large enough to carry a horse and an armed man. When the boats were ready Morold stepped into one of them, took hold of the tiller, [6740] and sailed to the other shore. When he landed on the island he pulled his boat up onto the beach and was soon mounted on his horse. He seized his lance and galloped from one end of the island to the other at full

---

23. In French epics of the twelfth century it was common to hold these fights on an island. It allowed for a more controlled environment, focused the action in a small space, and of course prevented one of the fighters from escaping. Chrétien de Troyes names the island *l'Isle saint Sanson* (l. 1249) in his *Erec et Enide*. This could be a place named St. Samson, St. Sansom, or St. Sanson, none of which has been identified (see Krohn, 1980, 3.87, note on l. 6723).

almost killed him. Flesh and bone were exposed under the mail and hauberk, and the blood gushed out [6930] all over the sand.

"What now?" cried Morold. "Do you yield? This will show you that no one should support the wrong cause. Your illegitimate grievance has been exposed here. You have to consider, if you want to live, how things look for you. Truthfully, Tristan, this wound will certainly be the death of you. Unless I alone prevent it, [6940] there is no man or woman alive who can save you. You have been wounded by a sword that carries a deadly poison. There is no doctor or medical skill that can save you from ruin except for my sister, Isolde, the queen of Ireland. She knows all manner of plants and the power of herbs [6950] and is a master healer. Only she and no one else knows the cure. If she doesn't help you, you are lost. If you are willing to submit to me and accept my right of tribute, then my sister the queen will heal you herself. I will share with you whatever I have in goodwill, [6960] and I won't deny you anything you want."

Tristan said, "I will not renounce my claim and my honor for your sister's sake or for your sake. I came with the freedom of two lands in my hands, and this I will bring home again or else suffer great harm, even death. [6970] This single wound has not forced me to give it all up, and the battle between us is by no means decided. The question of tribute will result in your death or mine. There is no other way."

With this he renewed his attacks. Now some people might certainly ask, and I would join them, [6980] where have God and Justice gone, who were Tristan's fellow combatants? I'm astonished that they don't want to help him. They really have been stragglers, and their squadron and their side have been harmed as a result. If they don't come quickly then it will be too late. May they make haste! [6990] Here two are up against four and fighting for their lives. They are left with only doubt and despair. If they are to be saved, then it will have to be done quickly.

God and Justice rode into the fray for the cause, to save their side and defeat their enemies. [7000] Now the troops had been squared up again, four against four, squadron against squadron. When Tristan became aware that his fellow combatants had joined him, his determination and courage grew. These reinforcements lent him heart and strength. He set spurs to his horse [7010] and charged at such a wild gallop, driven by his fury, that his horse collided violently with his opponent. Morold and his horse tumbled to the ground together. After he collected himself a bit from the fall and attempted to remount, Tristan was on the spot, [7020] striking his helmet so hard that it flew off his head. Now Morold rushed at him, slicing off his horse's leg despite the covering. It collapsed under him, and all he could do was leap to the side.

Morold, skilled as he was, threw his shield onto his back, [7030] something experience had taught him. He reached down with his free hand and grabbed his helmet. He cleverly thought out a way to get back on his horse, put his helmet on, and renew the attack against Tristan. Once he had grabbed his helmet, he ran to his horse. [7040] Just as he came up close enough to take hold of the reins and put his left foot in the stirrup, grasping the saddle with his other hand, Tristan caught up with him. He struck him on the pommel of the saddle, cutting off the right hand that held his sword. Both fell into the sand along with his mail gauntlet. [7050] Even before they hit the ground, Tristan gave him another stroke to the top of his head, right on the coif.[26] The blow sank so deep into his head that when he pulled the blade back a piece of it remained stuck in his skull. This was later to be the cause of much grief and great danger for Tristan, [7060] in fact it almost cost him his life.

Morold and his desperate troop, having lost all its strength and ability to defend itself, tumbled and collapsed in a heap. "What now, what now?" cried Tristan. "God be with you, Morold, tell me, are you aware of how things stand? It seems to me that you've received quite a wound, I think that things look bleak. [7070] Whatever happens with my own wound, you might benefit from some herbs as well. You would need everything that your sister Isolde knows about medicine to be cured. God, who is just and steadfast, and God's unwavering law have judged your wrong and allowed my just cause to triumph. May he protect me always. [7080] Pride has been destroyed!" He walked up next to him, gripped his sword with both hands, and struck off his opponent's head right through the mail coif.

He returned to the beach where he found Morold's boat, got in and immediately returned to the assembled crowd on the other shore. [7090] There by the sea he heard sounds of great joy and great lament. The joy and lament I will explain to you. For those to whom his victory brought salvation, it was an auspicious day that brought great joy. They clapped their hands, they praised God with their voices, they sang great songs of victory to heaven. [7100] To the foreigners, however, the hated people from Ireland who had been sent there, the day brought great sorrow. They cried out in lament as much as the others sang. They wrung and contorted their hands in grief. Those grieving strangers, the lamenting Irish, [7110] were heading mournfully back to their ships when Tristan approached them and caught up with them on the shore.

He said, "My lords, cross over and collect the rights to tribute that you see over there on the island. Take him back to your lord and tell him that my uncle, King Mark, and his lands [7120] send him this present along with a message. If it is his will, and if he wishes to send emissaries here for this kind of tribute, then we will never let them return with empty hands. We will send

---

26. This could be either an arming cap made of leather or, in this case more likely the chain-mail hood of the hauberk, which was pulled over the head and worn under the helmet.

them back with honorable deeds such as this, [7130] however difficult it may be."

While he was saying all this, he covered the blood and his wound from the foreigners with his shield, something that would later save his life, since they all returned home without being any the wiser. They promptly left and went over to the island, [7140] where instead of their lord they found a mangled body, which they took with them.

When they had arrived back home they took up the horrible gift they had been given, I mean all three pieces, and put them together so that nothing would be lost. [7150] They carried them to their lord and told him, as I just said, exactly what they were to convey. It seems to me, and I imagine it's not hard to imagine, that King Gurmun the Bold was depressed and full of grief. He had every reason to be. With this one man he lost daring and determination, hope and strength, [7160] and the knightly prowess of many men. The wheel that carried his honor and that Morold had freely spun in neighboring lands had now turned.[27] The queen, his sister, was even more affected by grief, sorrow, and lamentation. She and her daughter Isolde[28] abused themselves in many ways. [7170] As you know all too well, women grieve excessively when sorrow strikes their heart. They gazed upon the dead man only to increase their suffering, so that their heartfelt pain was all the greater. They kissed the head and the hand that had previously conquered people and lands for them, [7180] as I said before. They examined the wound on the head from top to bottom with painful thoroughness. The astute and learned queen discovered the metal fragment. She asked for a small pair of forceps to reach in and extract the splinter. [7190] She and her daughter examined it with sorrow and pain, and together they put the piece in a small container. This same fragment was later to prove extremely dangerous for Tristan.

Well, Lord Morold is dead. If I were to say much more about their suffering and lament, what good would it do? [7200] We would not be any better off. Who could manage to do justice to all their pain anyway? Morold was buried just like any other man. Gurmun, in his grief, quickly sent out

---

27. The figure of the Wheel of Fortune (Lat. *rota fortunae*), initially derived from the zodiac, was made widely known to the Middle Ages first by Boethius, and then by wandering poets such as those found in the *Carmina Burana*. It applied especially to kings and the mighty and represented *Fortuna*'s all-inclusive power.

28. Gottfried maintains that both women share the same name, Isolde, the queen and the princess, Morold's niece. Other sources vary the names slightly (the Norse version has Ísodd and Ísönd). Here, the young Isolde is clearly drawn into her mother's circle during this "autopsy," and so the suspicion of black arts, poison, and magic which falls on the mother can be applied to the daughter as well. Queen Isolde's medical expertise is clearly evident in the following scene, as her daughter is instructed in the clinical aspects of examining and preparing a corpse.

an order throughout the kingdom of Ireland to keep close watch and that whoever arrived there from Cornwall [7210] should be put to death, men and women alike. This edict and sentence was so strictly enforced that no one from Cornwall could travel there at any time [7220] without losing his life, even if he offered to pay a ransom. Over time many innocent people were killed without cause, since Morold had died by rights. He relied only on his own strength and not on God, and in all his battles he flaunted violence and pride, [7230] which finally brought about his downfall.

Chapter 11: Tantris

[7231] So let me start where I left off. When Tristan arrived on the shore, without his horse and lance, thousands of people came up to greet him, some on horseback, some on foot, and they welcomed him with great joy. The king and his entire kingdom had never before experienced such a happy day, [7240] we can be sure of that. He had single-handedly resurrected great honor for them, and their hardship and suffering were all put to rest. They complained about the wounds he suffered and were very sorry, but thinking that he [7250] would quickly recover from his injuries didn't give it much more thought. They escorted him in their midst toward the palace, where they quickly took off his armor and provided for his well-being and comfort just as he or others thought best. They called for doctors throughout the land and towns, for the best that could be found.

[7260] "What happened?"

Those who were called employed all of their medical skills on his behalf.

"What was the result? Did it help?"

He didn't improve at all. Their combined knowledge of medicine did not benefit him in any way. The poison was of such a kind that they were unable [7270] to get it out of the wound. It eventually spread throughout his body, which turned a terrible color and made him virtually unrecognizable. In addition there was such a terrible smell emanating from the wound that life became unbearable for him, and his own body disgusted him. His greatest hardship, though, [7280] was constantly seeing that he was a burden to his former friends.

What Morold had told him became more and more apparent. He had often heard how beautiful and accomplished his sister Isolde was. There was even a saying that had spread over all the neighboring lands [7290] where her name was known: "Isolde wise, Isolde bright, she glimmers like the dawn's red light." Careworn Tristan had long considered and knew well that if he was going to be healed then it could only come from her skills, that is, from the one who had these abilities, the all-knowing queen. [7300] He didn't know, however, how to make this happen. He began to think it over, and since he would die in any case he could just as well take a chance on life or death as remain in this fatal condition. So he decided, despite everything, to undertake the journey and let everything go according to God's will, [7310] that he might be cured if it was meant to be.

He called for his uncle and told him everything that had happened, including what he had kept secret. He informed him of his intentions, from one friend to another, and what he wanted to do based on what Morold had said. Mark was both pleased and not pleased, but if adversity is unavoidable, then we should accept it as best we can. [7320] If faced with two evils, we should choose the lesser of the two. This is a useful adage. So the two were in accord about everything and how it should all be prepared, which is then how it was done. They would keep his voyage to Ireland a secret and tell everyone [7330] that he had gone to Salerno[29] to be cured. After this had been decided, they called for Curvenal and told him right away what they had planned. Curvenal agreed and said that he wanted to go with him, to die with him or be saved.

As evening was approaching [7340] a bark and a skiff were prepared for their voyage, with full provisions of rations, food items, and other necessities. Amidst much sorrow, poor Tristan[30] was secretly carried on board so that no one knew what was happening, [7350] except for those who had been summoned. Tristan insisted that his uncle Mark take charge of all his people and property and make sure that nothing fell into anyone else's hands until reliable reports arrived concerning his situation. He called for his harp, [7360] which was the only thing he took with him.

Then they weighed anchor and put to sea. Tristan and Curvenal sailed with only eight other men, who had all pledged their lives and sworn to God that they would never deviate from the orders given by these two. [7370] Once they had sailed off, Mark watched Tristan go, and I'm certain that his happiness and well-being vanished as well. The parting affected him to the core of his being, even though all would end in joy and happiness for both of them. When the people heard how ill Tristan was [7380] and that he had traveled to Salerno to be cured, their sorrow could not have been greater even if he had been their own child. Since his suffering had resulted from his service to them, it hurt them all the more.

---

29. The university in Salerno (*schola medica Salernitana*) was famous throughout the Middle Ages as a center for healing and medicine on account of the medical knowledge accumulated by nearby Arabic and Byzantine scholars and doctors. The ailing hero of Hartmann's *Arme Heinrich* travels to Salerno to seek a cure for his leprosy.

30. Gottfried calls his hero *der arme Tristan* (l. 7345), possibly continuing the reference to Hartmann's *arme Heinrich* beyond his reference to Salerno.

Tristan, overtaxing his condition and strength,[31] [7390] traveled day and night in the direction of Ireland in the capable hands of the ship's captain. As the ship began to approach Ireland and they could see land, Tristan ordered the helmsman to set course for the capital, Dublin.[32] [7400] He knew that the wise queen was living there. The helmsman hastened toward his destination, and when he was close enough to see the town and recognize it, he said to Tristan, "Look, sir, I see the town. What is your command?"

Tristan replied, "We will drop anchor [7410] and stay here for the evening and part of the night."

They dropped anchor and stayed there for the evening. During the night he ordered them to sail closer to the town, and when this had been accomplished they took up a position about half a mile from the town. [7420] Tristan then told them to give him the shabbiest robe they could find in the bark. After he had put it on, he ordered them to carry him from the bark into the small skiff. He also had his harp brought to him, along with enough to eat for three or four days. [7430] This was all quickly done according to his wishes.

He asked that Curvenal come to him along with the ship's crew and said, "Curvenal, my friend, take command of this bark and the crew and take good care of them for me at all times. When you have returned, pay them handsomely [7440] so that they keep our secret and tell no one else. Return home straightaway, and greet my uncle and tell him that I am still alive, and that with God's grace I may still live and be cured. He should not worry about me. Tell him [7450] that I will return within the year if I am cured, and if my plan is successful then he will hear of it soon enough. Tell the court and the people of the realm that I died of my wounds during the voyage. Don't let my own retinue, those whom I still have, leave. Make sure they wait for me [7460] for as long as I have told you.

"If it should happen within a year's time that I am unsuccessful, then you can assume the worst. Let God care for my soul and you take care of yourselves. Now take my people, return home to Parmenie, [7470] and stay with Rual, my dear father. Tell him for me that he should reward you with his loyalty in place of mine, and he should make things as comfortable and good for you as he can. Tell him also that he should grant me just one wish, and

---

31. Translations differ of the phrase *über state und über maht* (l. 7389). Haug/Scholz (2011/2012) and Hatto (1960) take *über* to refer to Tristan's state of being, as in overtaxed. Hatto: "taxed to the utmost of his strength and resources, Tristan sailed on" (1960, 140), others refer back to the verb *vuor* as in "sail" or "journey." Krohn (1980): "Tristan sailed in the meantime with great strength" (Tristan segelte indessen mit äußerster Kraft); Knecht: "Tristan sailed . . . with the best wind and full strength" (Tristan segelte . . . mit bestem Wind und aller Macht).
32. Dublin became the English capital of Ireland in 1172.

thank and reward those who have served me up until now [7480] according to their service.

"My dear people," he said then, "with this I put you in God's hands. Be on your way and let me drift here. I can only ask for God's mercy. It's high time that you leave and save yourselves, it's almost daybreak."

[7490] Amidst much sorrow and much lament they returned home, crying as they left him adrift on the desolate sea. Never had a parting been so painful. Any loyal man who ever gained a loyal friend and knows how he should be appreciated understands very well how sad Curvenal was. [7500] As unhappy as he was in heart and mind, he nevertheless went on his way.

Tristan was left completely alone. He drifted here and there, in grief and in misery until daylight. When the people of Dublin spotted the pilotless boat out on the water, [7510] they sent some men to take a look at the skiff, and a search party set out immediately. Approaching, they saw no one but heard the pleasant and alluring sound of a harp. Singing along with the harp was a man's voice so charming [7520] that they thought this must be some kind of strange and wonderful reception. They were glued to the spot as long as he played and sang, but their enjoyment lasted only a short time. The music that he played and sang was not true, because it did not come from his heart. [7530] This is in the nature of music. It is difficult to play for long if your heart is not in it. Even though it is often heard, it isn't truly music if played without heart and feeling. Tristan's youthfulness motivated him [7540] to play and sing just to pass the time, but it was still a painful agony for the tormented man. When he stopped playing, the other boat came closer. They tied up to the skiff and all vied to have a look inside.

Once they spotted him and saw how miserable he looked, [7550] they were shocked that he was still able to play and sing so wonderfully. They greeted him with words and gestures as a man who had earned a friendly greeting, and they asked Tristan to tell them what had happened to him.

"I will tell you this," said Tristan. [7560] "I was a courtly minstrel,[33] well versed in everything that is courtly: when to speak, when to keep silent, how to play the lyre and vielle,[34] the harp and the rote, telling jokes and making fun, I knew how to do all this as well as anyone in my trade. I made a good living at it [7570] until I was overcome by greed and wanted more than was my due. I took up trading, which was to be my ruin. I teamed up with a wealthy merchant, and together we loaded a ship at home in Spain with all

---

33. The Middle High German term is *höfscher spilman* (l.7560). This was the designation for a peripatetic musician and entertainer who performed at courts throughout Europe. Some achieved fame, or notoriety, and were well compensated, others had an existence more akin to begging.

34. This is the French term for a medieval fiddle with a somewhat longer and deeper body than the modern violin, with three to five strings.

sorts of merchandise, [7580] planning to sail to Britain. Out on the open sea we were attacked by pirates who took every last thing we had. They murdered my business partner and everyone else on board. The fact that I was the only one who survived with this wound that I received can be attributed to my harp. All of them could see, [7590] as I told them myself, that I was a professional minstrel. I pleaded with them to let me have this small skiff and enough to eat to survive until now. Since then I have drifted on the sea in agony and great suffering a full forty days and forty nights, wherever the winds [7600] and the untamed waves drove me, first here and then there. So I have no idea where I am, and what's more, I don't know where I should go. May our Lord reward you, gentlemen, if you could be so kind as to help me find other people."

"Friend," replied the men, "your pleasant voice and your music will be of advantage to you here. [7610] You don't need to remain adrift, without hope and assistance. Whatever brought you here, whether God or the waves or the wind, we will take you to people."

This they did. They towed him and his skiff into town, as he had asked them to do. They tied up the boat at the pier and said, "See, minstrel, [7620] take a look at that castle and this beautiful town next to it. Do you know what town this is?"

"No, sirs, I do not know what it is."

"We will tell you. You are in Dublin, in Ireland."

"Praise be to the Savior that I am back among people. Someone here will take pity on me [7630] and help me in some way."

The men then left and started to talk with others about his case, causing much astonishment. They related what a marvelous encounter they had with a man of whom they would not have expected such a thing. [7640] They explained exactly what happened. When they had come closer, they heard the pleasing sound of a harp, and along with the harp there was singing. God himself would have enjoyed such music in his heavenly choirs. They went on to say that he was a poor victim, a fatally wounded minstrel.

[7650] "Take a look, you can see that he'll be dead by tomorrow, or even today. Even with all this suffering, he still has such a positive attitude. You couldn't find a bigger heart in any kingdom, someone who would take so little notice of such great misfortune."

The citizens came [7660] and spoke with Tristan, asking him about this and that. He repeated the same thing to each one that he had previously said to the rescue party. Then they asked him to play the harp for them, and so he focused all his attention on their request and put his whole heart into it. His only desire was to make them fond of him [7670] through his hands and his voice. This is what he intended, and this is what he did. When the poor minstrel started to play his harp and sing in such an exquisite manner, in spite of his condition, everyone took pity on him. They had the poor man carried from his skiff [7680] and requested that a doctor take him into his house. Whatever he might need, he should do his best to help him and make him comfortable at their cost. This was done and this is what happened, but when the doctor brought him home and began to treat him, employing all his [7690] skill and knowledge, nothing could help him. This became known all over the town of Dublin, and a crowd of people was constantly coming and going, lamenting his misfortune.

In the meantime a priest came to see him and heard how well he could play and sing. [7700] He himself was skilled and talented in many art forms. He could play various stringed instruments well and also knew many foreign languages. In fact, he had devoted much time and energy to mastering courtly skills. He was the queen's tutor and part of her household. [7710] Since her childhood he had instructed her in several different subjects, and she had learned many rare arts from him as well. He also tutored her daughter Isolde, an exceptional young woman,[35] known in all the world and the subject of this story. [7720] She was the queen's only child, and she had directed all her efforts to teaching her since she was old enough to learn. The court priest was also responsible for her education. He instructed her constantly in reading books and playing instruments. Now that he recognized in Tristan such virtuosity and talent, [7730] he felt genuinely sorry for his hardship and without further delay went to see the queen. He told her that there was a minstrel in town who suffered greatly and was mortally afflicted, and also that there had never been a man born of a woman who was as artistically talented as he was [7740] or had such a spirited heart.

"Ah," he said, "noble queen, it would be wonderful if we could think of a way to bring him to a place where you could inconspicuously come to witness such a miracle. He is a dying man who plays the harp and sings with such passion and musicality, [7750] even though there is no relief or help for his condition. He can't be cured. His doctor, a master, who has treated him until now has released him from his care, since there is nothing more that he can do for him."

"Look," said the queen. "I will tell the servants, [7760] provided he can tolerate being carried and moved, that they should bring him here to us to see if there isn't something that could help him in his condition or possibly cure him."

This was done and this is what happened. When the queen saw what shape he was in, [7770] his wound and its discoloration, she recognized the poison.

---

35. The terms *maget* and *kint* are both translated here as "young woman," rather than the outdated "maiden" or "girl." Isolde is clearly in her teens and of an age to be married, which in the Middle Ages was generally between fourteen and eighteen years of age for women.

"Ah, poor minstrel," she said, "you have been poisoned."

"I don't know," replied Tristan quickly. "I don't understand what it is, but none of the medical treatments have helped. I don't know what else to do but trust in God [7780] and live as long as I have left to live. Whoever takes pity on me, given my desperate situation, may God reward him. I urgently need help, since I am practically dead already."

The wise woman said to him, "Minstrel, tell me, what is your name?"

"Lady, my name is Tantris."[36]

"Tantris, you can trust me. I can cure you. [7790] Take heart and be of good cheer. I will be your doctor."

"Bless you, dear queen. May your voice never fade, your heart never stop, your wisdom live forever to help the helpless, may your name be honored around the world!"[37]

"Tantris," said the queen, [7800] "if your condition permits, if you are not too weak, which would not be surprising, then I would like to hear you play the harp. You are very good at it, or so I have heard."

"Lady, please don't worry about that. My misfortune cannot stop me from doing anything with pleasure if it would serve you."

His harp was brought to him, [7810] and the young queen[38] was also invited. She was the signet's impression of love, with which his heart was later sealed and closed to all the world except to her. Beautiful Isolde arrived and paid close attention to Tristan as he sat there and played the harp. [7820] He played better than he had ever played before, given his hope that his misfortune was coming to an end. He sang and played for them not as someone near death but with the liveliness of someone full of life. He did everything so well, both the playing and the singing, [7830] that in a short time he had gained the admiration of all of them, and everything took a turn for the better. While he was playing, however, whether there or elsewhere, his wound smelled and gave off such a foul odor that no one could stand to be in his presence for even an hour.

The queen then spoke, [7840] "Tantris, if it comes to pass that this stench leaves you and people can be around you again, then this young woman, Isolde, shall be given over to your tutelage. She has been devoted to her studies in books and stringed instruments, and she is quite accomplished given the time [7850] that she has dedicated to these. If you possess knowledge and skills unknown to her tutor or me, then teach her for my sake. As a reward

---

36. Aside from being an obvious play on the name Tristan, this form in French could also mean *tant ris* ("laughing a lot"). This would in some way make the name doubly ironic.

37. Tristan addresses the queen informally (*du*).

38. The title queen could be used generically in a royal house to include a princess, who was at least potentially also a future queen.

at court, [8040] that Isolde would be called to the great hall by her father. She entertained him and those who were gathered there with her extensive knowledge of courtly arts and fine manners. Whatever she did to please her father also pleased others, whether of low or high standing. She was to all of them [8050] a feast for the eyes, a delight for the ears and heart, a delight that was equally tangible and invisible. Isolde, precious and pristine, could sing and write and perform poetry, in fact whatever others enjoyed was to her just a game. She fiddled the *estampies*, lays, and unfamiliar melodies, [8060] so that the French style of Sens and St. Denis could not have been more striking.[41] She had a large repertoire of these. To great acclaim she played the lyre and harp from both sides, with hands as white as ermine. Neither in Lud nor in Thames[42] have ladies' hands [8070] strummed strings lovelier than did Isolde, *la douce, la belle*. She sang her *pastourelles*, her *rotruenge* and her *rondeau, chansons, refloit*, and *folate* well and even better than well.[43] Many a heart was filled with thoughts of yearning by her, many began to reflect on and consider all manner of things. [8080] Because of her they thought of wonderful things, which happens, as you well know, when one sees such a wonder of beauty and talent as was Isolde.

With whom can I compare her, this beauty, this blessing, other than the Sirens, who draw ships to them with lodestones?[44] [8090] In the same way, it seems to me, Isolde drew many hearts and thoughts to her, even those who considered themselves immune to longing and suffering. Desire and a ship without an anchor, these two are a good analogy. Either is seldom on a safe course but mostly in unsure ports, [8100] rocking up and down, swaying to and fro. This is how aimless longing and unanchored feelings of love drift about, just like a ship without an anchor. Clever Isolde, the wise and lovely

---

41. Little is known about a specific musical style in either of these clerical schools.

42. Lud is most likely London, see l. 3680. Thames seems here to be either a town or other location, see l. 15,348 and l. 15,426, where the Bishop of Thames speaks at the assembly in London.

43. Most of these terms have been discussed previously, see footnote to ll. 2293–95. The *pastourelle* is a form that seems not to have found its way into the German repertoire. It is a classical dialogue form in which a man attempts to seduce a shepherdess, which gives the genre its name. In the end, the man may win the "debate" or not. The form was especially popular in northern France at the end of the twelfth century but was also at home in the south, as witnessed in an example by Marcabru from around 1140 (*L'autrier jost'una sebissa*). The word *folate* is only found in Gottfried, and its Old French form, which might have been *folet*, is not attested (see Okken, 1996, 2.1042, for further speculation on its meaning).

44. In antiquity Sirens and magnets were not connected, that is to say they were two different kinds of attraction, one audible, and the other invisible. Here, the island of the Sirens seems to be co-located with a magnetic mountain. An alternate translation could be: "the Sirens, who along with the magnetic mountain, pull" as in two separate but unrelated examples of the power to attract.

young queen, likewise drew out thoughts from many a heart's vault, [8110] just as the lodestone attracts ships along with the Sirens' singing. Publicly and in secret, through ears and eyes, she sang herself into many hearts. Her audible song, which she performed in various venues, involved her delightful singing and the gentle sound of the strings, which clearly and openly [8120] resounded through the domain of the ears down into the heart. Her silent song, however, was her breathtaking beauty. This music of the soul[45] inaudibly stole into many noble hearts through the windows of the eyes, pervading them with a magic that captured their thoughts [8130] and bound them with longing and suffering.

Beautiful Isolde had taken Tristan's teaching to another level. Her disposition was delightful, her manners and her behavior beyond reproach. She could play instruments beautifully and knew other fine arts. She could compose song texts and melodies, [8140] her verses were refined, and she knew how to read and write well.

By now Tristan had recovered and was completely healed, and a healthy coloring had returned to his entire body. He feared the entire time that someone at court or in the countryside would recognize him, and so he was constantly thinking about [8150] how he could properly take his leave and end this worrying. He knew very well that if he should try, neither of the two queens would let him go, but he thought about how his life was in danger all the time. He went to the queen [8160] and spoke eloquently, as always.

He knelt down before her and said, "My Lady, for the kindness and care and aid that you have conferred on me, may God compensate you in the eternal Kingdom. You have treated me so kindly and well [8170] that God should forever reward you, and I shall be at your service all my life. Although only a poor man, wherever I find myself I will sing your praises. Blessed queen, I would like to ask your leave to return to my homeland. My circumstances are such that I can no longer remain here."

[8180] The lady laughed at him and replied, "Your sugar-coated words won't work. I will not give you leave to depart. You won't be allowed to go before an entire year has passed."

"No, noble queen, please take into account that this is a matter of holy matrimony and heartfelt love. At home I have a wife, [8190] whom I love as much as my own life. I'm sure that she believes and is quite certain that I must by now be dead. This is my fear and my distress, that if she is given to another

---

45. This term, *muotgedoene* (l. 8124), is found only in Gottfried. It can also be circumscribed as a "sound" or "song" of emotional intensity, or desire, yearning, intent, will, and other aspects of *muot*, here broadly characterized by "soul," as in an emotional quality found in music, for example.

man then my solace and my life and all my happiness, my only hope, will be destroyed. I will never again be happy."

[8200] "Truly," said the wise woman, "Tantris, this is a legally compelling reason. The bond of matrimony should not be broken by anyone of good will. May God bless you both, your wife and you. As much as I hate to be without you, I will relinquish you for God's sake. I give you leave to go, and I remain well-disposed and devoted to you. [8210] I and my daughter Isolde will give you two marks of red gold for your journey and your sustenance. You may collect them from Isolde."

The poor outsider folded both of his hands, both as a real and figurative gesture, before each of the queens, the mother and her daughter.

[8220] "For both of you," he said, "I pray that God grant you mercy and honor."

He stayed there not a moment longer but sailed to England, and from England directly on to Cornwall.

Chapter 12: The Bridal Quest

[8226] When his uncle Mark and the citizens heard that he had returned completely healed, everyone in all the kingdom was exceedingly glad and their hearts were overjoyed. His friend, the king, asked him what had happened, and he told him the story from beginning to end as best he could. They were amazed and began to make jokes, [8240] and finally everyone broke out in laughter about his journey to Ireland and the fact that his enemy had cured him so well with her own hands, along with all the other tricks that he played on them. They said that they had never heard the likes of such an amazing story. After all this, and after they had finished [8250] laughing about his cure and his journey, they asked eagerly about the young woman, Isolde.

"Isolde," he replied, "is a young woman that surpasses everything that anyone in the world says about beauty. Brilliant Isolde is a young woman with a demeanor and presence more pleasant and exceptional than any child or woman [8260] ever born of a mother. Isolde, pure and bright, is purer than Arabian gold. I thought I knew everything from the books that I have read praising Aurora's daughter and child, the legendary Tyntarides,[46] that she combined the whole of female beauty [8270] in a single blossom. I have since given up that fiction; Isolde took this fantasy away from me. I can never again believe that the sun rises in Mycenae. Perfect beauty did not dawn in Greece,

---

46. This refers to the legendary Helen of Troy, the classical example of the pinnacle of feminine beauty. Helen's nickname is taken from her stepfather Tyndareus, although actually Helen is the daughter of Leda, not Aurora.

it has dawned here. Every man need look in his thoughts only to Ireland. His eyes will be thrilled [8280] to see how the new sun follows the reddish dawn, one Isolde after the other Isolde, and shines from Dublin into every heart. This brilliant wonder illuminates every land. Everything that is said to commend women, what stories say in praise of them, all of it is nothing in comparison. [8290] Whoever looks into Isolde's eyes, his heart and soul will be purified just as gold is purified by fire. It makes life worth living! She does not make other women less beautiful, as some are wont to say [of their ladies].[47] Her beauty beautifies, she refines and crowns the very name 'woman' for all. [8300] No one need be ashamed because of her."

After Tristan had said everything he knew about his lady, the charming beauty of Ireland, all those assembled there took the account to heart and were refreshed in spirit by this portrayal, just as the dew in May refreshes the flowers. All were enchanted.

[8310] Tristan confidently took up his former life again. He had been given a second chance at life, he was a man born again. Actually, his life had only just begun. He was happy and joyful. The king and the court were well disposed toward him until vile envy, that cursed disruptor [8320] which never really rests, raised its head among them and began to darken the thoughts and actions of the nobles at court. They envied the renown and prominence that the court and the entire realm had bestowed on him. They started spreading ugly rumors about him, [8330] including talk that he was a sorcerer. What he had accomplished before, how he had defeated their enemy Morold, how he was cured in Ireland, they began to say among themselves that it had all been done through sorcery.

"Look," they all said, "think about it and then tell us, how could he have defeated the mighty Morold? [8340] How did he fool Isolde, the wise queen, his archenemy, into taking such good care of him until he was finally healed by her? Think about how incredible that is, and then listen to this. How can this impostor blind everyone around him and achieve everything that he sets his mind to?"

[8350] Those who regularly advised Mark came up with a plan to pester him day and night and urgently suggest that he take a wife, someone who would provide him with an heir, a daughter or a son.

Mark said, "God has granted us a worthy heir. [8360] May God grant that he live a long life! As long as Tristan is alive, have no doubt, there will be no queen or lady here at court."

This only increased their hatred and jealousy of Tristan, and it began to show. [8370] They could no longer hide their feelings and threatened him

---

47. This could possibly refer to a poem of Reinmar's (MF XXI/X,1; L 159,1) wherein the poet praises his lady by declaring that she has checkmated all other women with her beauty.

with gestures and words, so that he feared an attempt on his life. He was constantly worried that sometime, somehow they would hatch a plan to kill him. He asked his uncle Mark [8380] to consider his fears and his peril for God's sake and to give in to the nobles' request, otherwise he had no way of knowing whether his death was imminent.[48]

His uncle, noble and upright, said, "Tristan, dear nephew, be still, I will never agree to this. I have no desire for an heir other than you. [8390] You need not fear for life or limb, I can protect you. Their envy and hatred, by God, how does this hurt you? Hatred and envy must be endured by any reputable man. His renown increases the whole time that he is envied. Fame and jealousy go together [8400] like a mother and her child. Fame is always pregnant and gives birth to hate and envy. Who is hated more than a fortunate man? The happiness that never encountered hatred is poor and weak indeed.

> [8407] "Live and always strive to be
> someday without hostility,
> yet you will see you cannot be
> set free from all hostility.[49]

"If you don't want to be hated by wicked people, then sing their tune and become wicked like them. Then they won't hate you. Tristan, whatever others do, always strive to be of noble character. Consider thoughtfully what will be to your advantage and enhance your honor. [8420] And please stop advising me to do something that would be to your disadvantage. Whatever is being said around here, I will not listen to them, or to you either."

"Lord, then allow me to leave the court. I am incapable of defending myself. If I continue to be surrounded by this hate, then I cannot succeed. Instead of ruling [8430] every kingdom there is in fear, I would rather be forever without lands altogether."

When Mark saw that he was serious, he asked him to be quiet and said, "Nephew, as much as I would like to be steadfast and loyal to you, you are making it impossible. Whatever may happen after this, I wash my hands of it. [8440] I am always prepared to do whatever I can to help you. Tell me, what do you want me to do?"

"Call together your council of nobles, those who have been pressing you in this matter, and find out what each one of them thinks. Ask them what they think is appropriate, so that you can find out what they want and so come to an honorable decision."

---

48. These fears of court intrigue show that Tristan has taken on the role of a cleric or courtier rather than the warrior and knight who so ably defended himself against Morold.
49. Although not marked by an initial in the manuscripts, these four lines stand out due to their alternating rhyme scheme (ABAB): *daz – haz – daz - haz.*

[8450] It was quickly arranged that they should all come together, and just as quickly they arrived at a consensus that could have only one outcome: Tristan's death. Provided it could be arranged, beautiful Isolde would make a most suitable wife for Mark in terms of lineage, character, and beauty, and this is what they unanimously recommended. They all came before Mark, and one of them, the most articulate, [8460] expressed their united will and desire.

"Lord," he said, "we agree on the following. Beautiful Isolde of Ireland, as is known in every land that neighbors us and them, is a young woman who has been blessed by feminine excellence in every quality that it can bestow. [8470] As you yourself have often heard it said of her, she is perfect and complete in conduct and appearance. If she became your wife and our lady, we could find nowhere in this world a better woman."

The king replied, "Sir, that remains to be seen. Even if I wanted her, [8480] how could this be possible? You have to take into account how it has been between us and them for quite some time now. The people there hate us. Gurmun despises me, for good reason, and I him. Who could foster such a great friendship between us?"

"Lord," they all said, [8490] "it happens often that two countries harm each other. Still they should try to find a resolution, and their children should be reconciled. Out of terrible circumstances can come a great friendship. If you would consider it, you might still live to see the day [8500] when Ireland is yours. Ireland is ruled by just three persons, the king and the queen, and Isolde as the sole heir, since she is their only child."

Mark answered them, "Tristan has caused me to reflect on her a great deal. I've been thinking about her often since he sang her praises to me. [8510] All this reflection has let her take hold of me, more than any other, and if she can't be mine then I don't want to marry any other woman in the world. This I swear to God and myself." He swore this oath not because he had changed his mind. [8520] Swearing it was a ploy, because he thought that it would never get that far.

The king's counselor responded, "Sire, if you were to charge my lord Tristan, who stands here and who knows the court, with taking your proposal to them, then everything would work out as planned and be brought to a successful conclusion. [8530] He is wise and thoughtful and lucky in all things. He can guarantee success. He knows their language well, and he always accomplishes whatever he sets out to do."

"Your counsel is hateful," said Mark. "Your intent is clearly aimed at causing Tristan harm and putting him at risk. He faced death once already for you and your heirs, [8540] and now you want to see him dead a second time. No, my lords of Cornwall, you will have to go there yourselves. Don't ever again advise me to have him do this."

"Lord," said Tristan, "they aren't wrong in what they say. It could be the right solution, if you agree. I would be more daring [8550] and more willing than any other man. It is also the right thing for me to do. I am well qualified for this, and there is no one who could make this proposal better than I can. You can order them all to accompany me on this journey and so guarantee your enterprise and your honor."

"No. You should never again fall into their hands, [8560] now that God has delivered you safely back to us."

"Lord, it must be so. Should they all die or survive, my fate is tied to them. I want them to see for themselves if it is my fault that the country has no heir. Command them to make ready. I will captain the ship and take the helm myself for the journey [8570] to blessed Ireland, back to Dublin, back to the brilliant sun that brings such joy to so many hearts. Who knows if this beauty will be ours? Sire, if beautiful Isolde were to become yours, then there would be little harm done if the rest of us were all dead."

When Mark's counselors heard how the plan had unfolded, [8580] they regretted the outcome more than anything before in their lives. But now it was decided and had to be. Tristan had the king's secretary select twenty brave knights from the court, the most reliable in battle, and from the countryside and among foreigners he chose another sixty as paid recruits. [8590] From the council he took twenty nobles, who were not paid. This made for a company of exactly one hundred, not one more, and these Tristan took overseas with him. This was his contingent, and they took provisions and clothing and other supplies with them so that this many people [8600] had never before been better outfitted for a voyage.

People can read [elsewhere] about Tristan that there was a swallow that flew from Cornwall to Ireland.[50] It took a lady's hair there to build its nest and brought it back across the sea. I don't know how it knew to do that. Did a swallow ever build its nest in such a toilsome manner? [8610] Given that it had so much building material in its own land, why would it fly abroad to a foreign country for these things? My God, this is where the tale tells lies, and the story makes no sense. It's also nonsense to say that Tristan and his company just sailed out into the ocean blue, not knowing [8620] how long it would take or where he was going, and not even who he was looking for. In what books did whoever had this written and read unearth this?[51] All of them

---

50. This is a direct criticism of Eilhart's version (although Eilhart has two swallows), along with other so-called common or primitive versions of the story that include fantastic and "illogical" elements such as this.

51. Translations of this sentence vary. Hatto has: "What old score was he settling with the book" (1960, 155). The crux is the verb form *rach* from *rechen* (l. 8622), which can either mean "to gather together by hand" or "to avenge, settle a score." Krohn (1980) writes: "What did he gather together out of the books" (Was hat der sich bloß aus den Büchern zusammengesucht);

together, the king who sent them out, his royal council, and the ambassadors would have been fools and idiots if they had gone on a bridal quest this way.

Now Tristan was on his way, [8630] and he and his company sailed directly to their destination. Some of them were gripped by fear, I mean the barons, the twenty companions from the Cornish council. They were filled with dread and worry and already thought themselves dead men. They cursed [8640] in their hearts and with their voices the hour they came up with the idea of going to Ireland. They had no counsel to give themselves concerning their own survival. They spoke of this, then of that, but they had no ideas that made any sense or that could even rightly be called counsel. This was really no great surprise. [8650] One way or another, there was only one of two things that could save their lives: luck or deceit. Deception was hard to come by, and no one thought they had much luck either. They were lacking in both.

Still, some of them said, [8660] "Wisdom and skill are things that this man has in spades. If God grants us good fortune, then we might still survive along with him. If only he would rein in his blind recklessness. Of this he has too much. He's too brazen and too daring, and he doesn't consider the consequences of what he does. He doesn't give a damn about us [8670] or his own life, and yet our best chances still lie with his good fortune. His cunning might point the way for us to save our own necks."

When they arrived in Ireland they came close to shore near Wexford,[52] where they had been told the king was staying. [8680] Tristan gave the command to drop anchor, far enough from the port that they were out of missile range. The nobles asked him for God's sake to tell them what his plan was for accomplishing this bridal quest, since their lives depended on it. They thought it would be a good idea [8690] if he told them what he had in mind.

Tristan said, "Stay put and be sure that none of you goes out where you can be seen. All of you should remain hidden. Only the crew and sailors should scout out the situation from the bridge, the rest of you can't be outside. Be quiet and go below decks. [8700] I will stay out front, since I know the local language. The citizens of the town will soon be coming with questions and suspicions. I will have to tell them whatever lies I can think up today. Stay below decks, because if they become aware of you then we will have trouble, [8710] and the entire country will be against us. While I'm away tomorrow, riding out early to try my luck, to succeed or fail, Curvenal and anyone else

---

Haug/Scholz (2011/2012) have: "What made him . . . so misuse the story" (Was brachte den . . . dazu, die Erzählung so zu mißhandeln); Knecht (2004a): "What did the poor book ever do to him that he abused it so" (was hatte dem . . . das arme Buch zuleide getan, dass er es so misshandelte).

52. Wexford, about 130 kilometers south of Dublin on Ireland's east coast, was founded around 800 by the Norse and captured by the Anglo-Normans in 1169. Much of the twelfth-century wall and fortifications remain today.

Chapter 13: The Dragon

[8897] Tristan had secured his own safety, but no one yet knew what he was planning. You will now be told so that you don't lose interest in the story. The story at this point tells about a dragon that was in the realm. This cursed devil had overpowered the people and the land with such great destruction that the king had sworn an oath [8910] and royal pledge that whoever killed the dragon would have his daughter, provided he was of noble birth and a knight. This declaration and the woman's beauty together caused untold thousands to lose their lives, who had come to fight but met their end instead. The whole country was talking about nothing else, [8920] and so Tristan heard about it as well. This alone gave him the courage to make the journey in the first place. This was his greatest hope; in fact it was his only hope.

"Enough already, let's move on!"

The next day in the morning he armed himself fully, as a man does to prepare himself for danger. He mounted a powerful horse [8930] and had a heavy and sturdy lance handed to him, the strongest and best that could be found on the ship. Then he promptly got underway and rode over fields and across open lands. He had to take several winding paths through rugged country, and as the day progressed he hurried on [8940] to the valley of Anferginan, where the dragon dwelled, according to the French source.[54] In the distance he could see four armed men fleeing at a gallop (they were riding just a bit faster than a canter) across the fields and scrubland, one of whom was the king's seneschal.[55] [8950] He was, no, he wanted to be the young queen's *ami*,[56] although she was completely against such a notion. Whenever someone rode out to challenge fate and test his manhood, the seneschal was always at hand, but only so that people would say that they saw him there, too, when someone rode out on a quest. [8960] There was no other point to it, since every time he saw the dragon he bravely advanced to the rear.

Tristan could tell from the little fleeing troop that the dragon was somewhere in the vicinity, so he quickly rode on in that direction until he saw to his eyes' horror the terrifying dragon. [8970] It blew a whirlwind of fire and smoke out of its mouth like some spawn of the devil, then turned and came at Tristan. He lowered his lance, spurred the horse forward, and charged with such ferocity that he lodged the lance in its throat, breaking its jaws in the

---

54. A compound in Old French with *enfer* (cave) and possibly *guigner* (to observe, spy). The word used for the source is *geste*, pointing to a French source, presumably Thomas.

55. The office of seneschal or steward is one of the four main royal court appointments, along with marshal, cupbearer, and chamberlain. The seneschal was responsible for domestic logistics and labor.

56. "Friend," or in this case, "lover."

114

process and penetrating all the way through to the heart. [8980] He ran into the dragon so violently with his horse that the horse was killed on the spot, and he was barely able to get out from under it. The dragon then turned its attention to the horse with fire and fury until the monster had swallowed it all the way up to the saddle. But the dragon was sorely wounded by the lance [8990] and turned away from the horse to retreat into a rocky ravine. Tristan, its foe, stayed hard on its trail. The mortally wounded dragon crawled on in great pain and filled the forest with a terrible roar, burning down brush and tearing trees out of the ground. [9000] It continued for some time until, overcome by pain, it slithered under a stone ledge.

Tristan drew his sword, thinking that the battle was over, but no, it was just about to get much more terrifying than before. As dangerous as it was, Tristan continued to attack the dragon, [9010] but the dragon fought back against the man and put him in such grave danger that he thought he was as good as dead. It kept him off balance and denied him virtually any opportunity to attack or defend himself. There was a great army fighting alongside. It brought with it smoke and steam and its other compatriots: [9020] blows and flames, teeth and claws, honed to cut and slash and sharper than a razor. With these it drove Tristan back and forth in a perilous zigzagging between trees and bushes. Tristan had to find cover and concealment as best he could, [9030] since his attacks had been ineffective. He tried to defend himself, but the shield he was holding had been burned to cinders as the dragon attacked with fire. He barely survived. This didn't last long, though, as the murderous serpent soon [9040] began to tire. The lance had taken its toll, and it lay down again and coiled up in pain. Without hesitation Tristan charged forward and drove the sword next to the lance straight into its heart, all the way up to the hilt. The cursed fiend let out a roar [9050] from its abominable gullet so grisly and gruesome as if heaven and earth had come crashing down. This death-cry echoed throughout the land and horrified Tristan.

With the dragon lying there, he saw that it was dead, and after much effort he opened its jaw [9060] and cut the tongue out of its throat with his sword. He took as much as he wanted and then stuffed it under his chainmail. Finally he closed up the mouth again and took off for the backwoods where he thought to hide and rest up during the day. Once he was restored to full strength, [9070] he would find his way back to his compatriots during the night. But he was overheated, both from exertion and also from the dragon fire, and he was so exhausted that he was barely able to stay alive. He saw a shimmering pond, it was small and fairly shallow [9080] and fed by a cool little brook that flowed over a rock face. He threw himself into it, fully armed as he was, and sank all the way down to the bottom, with only his mouth still above water. There he stayed the rest of the day and night. The foul tongue that he was holding drained him of all his strength, and the fumes that came over him completely robbed him [9090] of all color and strength so that he was unable to extricate himself until the queen finally pulled him out.

The seneschal, as I said before, who wanted to be the blessed woman's lover and knight, began to conjure up big ideas once he heard the dragon's roar that boomed [9100] over field and forest with such terror and intensity. He put two and two together and figured out what had happened. He thought to himself, "The dragon must certainly be dead, or very near so, and I might be able to turn things my way with some careful planning."

He slipped away from the other three, carefully made his way down into the valley and then rode [9110] to where the bellowing had come from. When he got to Tristan's horse, he stopped short and took a break. He stayed there for a while and looked all around with care and trepidation. The short ride had already filled him with fear and terror, but he eventually continued on, frightened and dispirited, without any real plan. [9120] He went in the direction where he saw that the brush and grass had been scorched, and in a short time before even realizing it ran straight into the dragon, which lay right in front of him. The seneschal was terrified to the core, so much so that he almost fell off his horse, [9130] because he had come so close. He quickly regained some self-control but then turned the horse about so sharply that both of them fell down in a heap. When he got up again, I mean, off the ground, he couldn't even think straight for all his fright, [9140] not even to get back on his horse. The pitiful seneschal just left it there and fled on foot, but since no one followed him he stopped and slowly tiptoed back. He picked up his lance, took the horse by the reins, led it to a tree stump, and then got back on.[57] [9150] He ignored his previous losses and, riding up to a safe distance, took another look at the dragon to see whether it was alive or not.

When he saw that it was dead, he said, "Saved, by God's will! This is a fortunate turn of events.[58] It's my luck that I've arrived at just the right time."

[9160] He lowered his lance, dropped the reins, and spurred his horse on into a full charge, with a battle cry to match:

> "*Chevalier de la demoiselle!*
> *Ma blonde Isot, ma belle!*"[59]

He stabbed the dragon with such force that the sturdy wooden shaft flew right out of his hands. [9170] That he stopped the fight right then was only

---

57. Aside from being short on courage, Gottfried allows himself a joke at the cost of the seneschal's lack of physical stature.

58. This is an ironic play on the double meaning of the term *aventiure*, in that his luck is that he has not found an adventure to test his luck or skill.

59. "[I am a] Knight of the young lady! My fair Isolde, my lovely!"

because he had another idea. He thought, "What if he is still alive, whoever killed the dragon, then everything I've done here will be for nothing."

He turned around and rode off, searching here and there in hopes of finding someone [9180] who would be so tired or injured that he might be able to fight him. He could then kill him and bury him somewhere. But after he found no one, he thought, "Well, Lord, let it be. If he's alive or not, I'm the first one here, no one can dispute that. [9190] I have such important and well-regarded relatives and vassals that whoever disputes this would lose in any case."

He spurred his horse again and hurried back to his adversary, where he dismounted. He rejoined the battle at the same place where he had previously broken it off. With the sword he carried [9200] he stabbed and struck the enemy over and over again until he had hacked it completely to pieces. He tried many times to cut through the neck, as he would have gladly chopped off its head, but it was so hard and thick that he gave up. He broke his lance on a tree trunk and then stuck the front half into the dragon's mouth, [9210] as if it had been done in a joust.

Then he mounted his Castilian again and joyfully rode back to Wexford. He ordered that four horses and a wagon be sent out to bring back the head, and he told everyone the story of what he had accomplished and what dangers [9220] and difficult trials he had suffered.

"Yes, gentlemen, all of you," he exclaimed, "lend me your ears, behold and see the marvel that a courageous man with unrelenting determination can accomplish for the sake of love. It is a miracle and amazes even me that I was able to survive the peril I was in, [9230] and I'm certain that I would not have survived had I been weak like that other man. I don't know who he was, a fortune hunter,[60] someone on a quest, he arrived to his own undoing before I did, and there he met his end. God was not with him. [9240] Horse and man both were devoured and are dead. Half the horse is still there, chewed up and scorched. But why should I bore you with that? I risked more in all this than any other man ever did for the sake of a woman."

He called all of his supporters to gather around him and went with them to see the dragon. He showed them all the wonder [9250] and asked them explicitly to testify to the facts they had all witnessed. He took the head back with him and then called for his family and vassals to join him, after which he ran to see the king to remind him of his pledge. The country was then called together for a judicial assembly in Wexford. [9260] Messengers were sent out across the realm, I mean, to call the nobility together. All of them prepared themselves as the court had commanded.

---

60. MHG *aventiuraere*, or adventurer, fortune seeker.

The news soon reached the ladies at the court. The agony and distress they all suffered as a result had never before been seen in ladies. The sweet young woman, beautiful Isolde, [9270] was devastated to the core. She had never experienced such a painful day.

Isolde, her mother, spoke to her, "Don't, my beautiful daughter, don't. It's alright. Don't let this dishearten you. Whether it's true or false, we will figure out a way to contest it. God will save us from this. Don't cry, my daughter. [9280] Your bright eyes should never turn red on account of such a trivial affair."

"Oh, mother," cried the beautiful young woman, "dear lady, do not dishonor yourself or your lineage. Before I consent, I will plunge a knife into my heart. Before he has his way with me, I will take my own life. [9290] He will never make Isolde his wife or lady unless I'm already dead."

"No, my beautiful daughter, do not fear. Whatever he or anyone else says about this, it's all meaningless. Even if all the world had sworn it, he will never become your husband."

As night approached the sage queen consulted [9300] her magical arts with regard to her daughter's dilemma. She was incredibly skilled in these arts, so much so that she saw in a dream that events had not transpired as people were saying.

As soon as it was day she called out to Isolde, "Ah, dear daughter, are you awake?"

"Yes," she replied, "my lady, dear mother."

[9310] "You can stop worrying. I have good news for you. He did not slay the dragon, instead it was some foreigner, here seeking his luck, who killed it. Hurry, we have to get there soon to see for ourselves. Brangane, get up quietly and tell Paranis to saddle the horses. [9320] The four of us will ride out, I and my daughter, you and he. He should bring the horses here as quickly as possible, to the back door that leads out through the orchard to the open field."

After everything had been prepared the group mounted up and rode to where they had heard [9330] that the dragon had been killed. They found the horse and began to examine and inspect the saddlery. They came to the conclusion that they had never seen such horse tack in Ireland, and they all agreed that whoever was brought there by that horse [9340] must have killed the dragon. They rode on and then came upon the serpent. This devil's companion was so monstrous and massive that the radiant trio of ladies turned white as a sheet for fear when they saw it.

The mother said to her daughter, "Oh, now I'm certain [9350] that the seneschal would never have dared to face it. We can leave all our cares behind. Indeed, my daughter Isolde, I have a strong feeling that this man, dead or alive, is hidden near here somewhere. That's what my intuition tells me. If you agree, then we should look around [9360] to discover if God sees fit that

118

we should find him here somewhere. With him we can overcome the boundless heartache that has afflicted us like death."

They quickly discussed it, and then all four of them rode out in different
directions, one searching here, the other there. Now it happened, as fate
would have it, [9370] that the young queen Isolde was the first to catch a
glimpse of her life and her death, her joy and her suffering. His helmet spar-
kled brightly and that gave the foreigner away. Once she saw the helmet, she
turned around and called out to her mother, "Lady, hurry, come over here!
[9380] I see something shining over there, I don't know what it is, it looks like
a helmet. I think I've found him!"

"Truly," said the mother then, "it seems to me that you're right. God is on
our side. I think that we've found the one we're looking for." They called to
the other two to come to them, [9390] and then all four rode to that spot.

When they approached him and saw him lying there, they all thought he
was dead. "He's dead!" said both Isoldes, "Our hope is lost. The seneschal
murdered him and carried him to this swamp."

All four dismounted [9400] and quickly pulled him out of the pond onto
dry land. They took off his helmet and removed his chainmail coif. Wise
Isolde took a look at him and saw that he was still alive but hanging on by a
thread. "He's alive," she said, "that much is certain. Hurry, take off his armor!
[9410] If I'm lucky and he's not mortally wounded, then things might still
turn out for the best."

As all three of the beautiful women, that radiant company, began to take
off the stranger's armor with their pale white hands, they discovered the
tongue. "Wait, look at this," said the queen. [9420] "What is this, what could
it be? Brangane, dear niece, say something."

"It's a tongue, I think."

"You're right, Brangane. I think it belongs to the dragon. Our fortune is
on the rise. Dearest daughter, beautiful Isolde, I'm as sure as death that we
are on the right track. [9430] It was the tongue that took all his strength and
his senses."

They took off all his armor and were happy not to find any injuries or
wounds. The wise and learned queen gave him theriac,[61] in fact so much that
he began to sweat.

[9440] "This man will survive," she said. "The vapors that went out from
the tongue will quickly dissipate, and then he'll be able to speak and see."
That is exactly what happened. He lay there only a short while longer until
he sat up and looked around.

---

61. Theriac or treacle was a common medieval remedy, homeopathic in nature and most
typically made from honey, herbs, opium poppy, and viper's flesh.

When he saw the angelic trio and became aware of who was there, he said to himself, [9450] "Oh merciful Lord God, you have not forsaken me. I am surrounded by three lights, the most brilliant in all the world, the joy and consolation of many hearts and the delight of many eyes. Isolde, the bright sun, and her mother Isolde, the blissful dawn, and proud Brangane, [9460] as beautiful as the full moon."

He then found some strength and spoke haltingly in a barely audible voice, "Who are you, and where am I?"

"Ah, sir knight, you can speak. Talk! We will help you in your time of need," said the learned Isolde.

"Yes, dear lady, blessed woman, I don't know how my body and all my strength so quickly [9470] faded and then completely abandoned me."

The young Isolde looked at him and said, "This is Tantris, the minstrel, if ever I saw him before."

The other two said, "It seems to us just so."

The wise queen asked, "Are you Tantris?"

"Yes, lady."

"Then tell us," said the wise woman, "where did you come from [9480] and what are you doing here?"

"Most blessed of all women, I am not strong enough yet to tell you my story properly. Please for God's sake have me carried somewhere where someone can care for me today and tonight, [9490] and when I'm strong enough again, I will do and say whatever you want."

So they took Tristan, all four of them, lifted him onto a horse, and together led him away. They surreptitiously brought him into the castle through the secret entrance, so that [9500] no one had the slightest inkling of their excursion. Then they helped him and cared for him. There was no trace left behind of the tongue, which I mentioned before, or his armor or anything else of his, since they took everything with them, all his equipment along with the man himself.

As the next day dawned, the wise queen came to him. "Now Tantris," she said, "tell me [9510] everything, for the sake of what I did for you once and now again. I have healed you twice and am as kindly disposed and dedicated to you as surely you are to your wife. When did you arrive in Ireland? How did you slay the dragon?"

"Lady, I will gladly tell you. I arrived just a short time ago, it's been three days since [9520] I and other merchants came to this port by ship. Then a gang of bandits descended on us, I don't know what set them off. They would have taken our goods and our lives, if I hadn't prevented it by paying a bribe. Our situation is this: we often have to travel to and become familiar with foreign lands. [9530] We don't know whom we can trust and are often victims of violence. So I know it can be advantageous if I can in some way be well known in other lands. If people recognize you in other lands, then a merchant can become rich. You see, lady, this is what I was thinking, [9540] and I had for a long time known about the story with the serpent. I killed it only because I thought it would help me gain safe conduct and the good will of the people."

"Safe conduct and good will," said Isolde. "These are guaranteed to you with honor till the day you die. You came here to benefit yourself and us. [9550] Now think of your fondest wish. It will be yours, I promise you in my lord's name and in mine."

"With thanks, my lady, I commend my ship and myself into your faithful hands. Please see that I do not regret entrusting you with wealth and health."

"No, in truth, Tantris, you don't have to worry [9560] about your life and your wealth ever again, by my loyalty and my honor. See here, take my hand as a pledge that never again will you suffer here in Ireland as long as I live. But please don't refuse me one request. Give me counsel regarding a matter on which my honor and all my happiness depend."

[9570] She told him what I have already said, namely how the seneschal boasted about his deed; how persistently and urgently he made his claim for Isolde; and how he demanded trial by combat to prove his lies if anyone took issue with him and wanted to dispute the claim.

"Blessed lady," answered Tristan, [9580] "You need not worry yourself about this. You have now twice, with God's help, given me back my health and my life. By rights both will stand with you in this contest and in all your troubles, as long as I am able."

"May God reward you, dear Tantris. I have complete confidence in you and want to say this to you. [9590] If the unimaginable were still to happen, then both of us, I and Isolde, would already be among the living dead."

"No, dear lady, do not say that. Since I am under your protection, and my life and all that I have are safeguarded and insured by your honor, dear lady, you can rest assured. Help me get back my strength, [9600] and I will take care of this by myself. Tell me, lady, do you know where the tongue is that you found with me, or was it left behind?"

"No, absolutely not, I have it here with everything else that belongs to you. My daughter, beautiful Isolde, and I brought everything along."

"This will help our cause," said Tristan. "Now, blessed queen, [9610] don't worry about a thing. Help me regain my strength, and everything will turn out alright."

Both queens took him into their care equally, and whatever seemed to them to be beneficial to his health and well-being was their primary concern. [9620] In the meantime his companions on the ship were in great distress. Most of them were afraid that they would never make it back alive. No one thought they would survive, given that they had not heard anything from him for two days. They had also heard the dragon's great roar, and there were lots of rumors [9630] that a knight had lost his life and that half his horse was still lying there.

His friends thought to themselves, "Who else could that be if not Tristan? There can be little doubt that he would have come back by now if death had not taken him."

They all agreed to send Curvenal out to take a look at the horse. [9640] This he did. Curvenal rode out, and once he found the horse recognized it. He rode on a bit farther and promptly came upon the dragon. Finding nothing that belonged to Tristan, neither clothing nor armor, he fell into great despair.

"Ah," he thought, "Lord Tristan, are you alive or are you dead? [9650] Oh," he said, "Isolde, oh, that your fame and your name ever found their way to Cornwall. Were your beauty and nobility meant to injure one of the greatest men ever distinguished by the lance, who appreciated you all too much?"

He returned to the ship crying and lamenting [9660] and reported everything he had seen. His report was displeasing to many, but not to all of them. The same sorrowful tale was not sorrowful to all. Some of them were quite satisfied, but you could see that many of them took it very hard. [9670] This was certainly most of them. So their intentions and desires were divided between good and evil. Given this split, the divided ship fell to grumbling and murmuring. The twenty barons were not sorry about the uncertain state of affairs as it was reported to them. They thought it was reason enough [9680] to leave and not wait any longer. They made their case, I mean just these twenty, and suggested to the others that they leave that night. Others counseled that they should stay until they had more information about what happened to him. So they were at odds with each other, [9690] some wanted to go, others wanted to stay. Finally it was decided, since his death was not certain or apparent, that they should stay in order to find out more, at least for another two days. The barons were not happy.

In the meantime the day [9700] of the assembly in Wexford had arrived, which Gurmun had proclaimed and on which he would decide the case of his daughter and the seneschal. Gurmun's neighbors, his vassals and his clan, all those he had called together as a council for the assembly were promptly present. He took them aside [9710] and urgently sought their advice, as someone concerned for nothing less than his honor. In addition he asked his dear wife, the queen, for her counsel. She was very dear to him, because he had in her one woman with two special gifts, the very best that a man [9720] can find in a dear wife: beauty and wisdom. These she had in such abundance that she was well loved by him indeed. The blessed queen, beautiful and wise, was there by his side. Her husband the king took her aside from the rest of the council.

"What do you advise?" he asked. "Tell me. This case weighs on me like the grave."

[9730] "Don't worry," she responded. "Everything will turn out fine for us. I have everything under control."

"How? Tell me as well, my dearest. Then I can be cheerful about this, too."

"Our seneschal, you see, did not kill the dragon as he claims. And I know who did. I can even prove it if I need to. So have no fear. [9740] Go back to your assembly and tell them all that once you have heard and seen the seneschal's truthful testimony you will gladly fulfill the pledge that you made to the country. Tell them all to go with you and take their seats in the court. Don't worry, let the seneschal plead his case [9750] and say whatever he wants to say. When it is time, I'll be there along with Isolde. When you call on me, then I will speak for both of us, and for Isolde. But enough talk for now. Let me go get Isolde, and we'll be right back."

She went to get her daughter, and the king went back into the great hall. [9760] He took his seat in the court, as did much of the baronage, the lords of the realm. There was also a great and splendid assemblage of knighthood, not so much to honor the king but more because they wanted to see what was going to happen, given all the gossip across the country. [9770] They were all curious.

The two blessed Isoldes, as they entered the great hall together, greeted and welcomed each of the lords one after the other. In the midst of all this there was much conversation and deliberation, speeches and opinions were voiced concerning how divine the two appeared. [9780] Even so, more people were talking about the seneschal's success than about the ladies.

They said or were thinking, "Just imagine, everyone, if this unlucky man, on whom fortune never shone, should get this blessed maiden, then he will be the luckiest man [9790] ever to have gained such fortune from a woman."

The two then came before the king, who rose in their presence and kindly offered them seats by his side.

"Now," said the king, "Seneschal, speak. What is your claim and your petition?"

"Very well, your Majesty," he said. "Lord, in my case I petition that you not break with the royal customs of this land. [9800] If you remember, you said and pledged, both with promises and an oath, that any knight who killed this serpent with his own hands would receive your daughter Isolde as a reward. This oath cost many men their lives, but this was of little concern to me, because I loved this woman. [9810] So I put my life in greater danger than any other man, until I finally succeeded in killing it. This should be sufficient evidence: here is the head, take a good look at it. I have brought it as proof. Now you should honor your pledge. The word and oath of a king must be truthful and reliable."

[9820] "Seneschal," said the queen, "whoever wants to receive a reward as precious as my daughter Isolde without having earned it goes too far."

"What?" said the seneschal. "My lady, you wrong me. Why do you speak out of turn? My lord, you must make the final decision, and you can well speak for yourself. Please speak and answer me."

[9830] The king said, "Lady, you shall speak for yourself, for Isolde, and for me."

"With thanks, my lord, I will do so," replied the queen. "Seneschal, your love is honest and good, and you have a brave heart. You are worthy of a good wife. But when someone aims for such a great prize without having earned it, [9840] in truth, this is too much. You have claimed for yourself an act of manly courage in which you played no part, as I have heard."

"My lady, I don't know what you're talking about. I have the evidence right here."

"You have brought a head that any other man could have brought just as easily, I mean if he wanted [9850] to lay claim to Isolde. But she can't be had with such a paltry gesture."

"Certainly not!" said young Isolde. "I could never be had with such a minor exploit."

"Ah, dear lady and young queen," replied the seneschal, "you speak harshly in my case with regard [9860] to the hazards that I have suffered so often on account of your love."

"It is to your credit that you love me," said Isolde, "but I was never devoted or committed to you, nor will I ever be."

"Yes," he said, "I can see that you are just like any other women. You are all created and predisposed [9870] always to think that bad is good and good is bad. This is a characteristic common to all of you. Everything is always the reverse for you. Everyone who is stupid is wise, and the wise are all stupid. What is straight becomes crooked, and the crooked is again straight. You have all the wrong things tied to your leash.[62] [9880] You love what hates you, and you hate what loves you. How is it that you are fashioned to love contradictions so much, a fact so often evident? The one who wants you, you don't want, but you want the one who wants you not at all. Of all the board games, yours is the most confusing. [9890] A man is devoid of reason if he ever risks his life for a woman without assurances. But this is not how things work. Whatever you or my lady says, things will be handled differently here or the oath to me will be broken."

---

62. This is part of a hunting metaphor. The *seil* (l. 9879) is the long line used to control hounds as they track their game.

The queen responded, "Seneschal, your reasoning is clear and clever, [9900] that is, if reason is judged by cleverness. It seems as if all this had been thought out by women in the privacy of their chambers. Moreover you have presented this reasoning exactly as a ladies' knight should. You are all too well acquainted with the qualities of women, in fact you've gone too far in this, and it has robbed you of the qualities of manhood.[63] You also love [9910] the opposites of things too much, and it seems to me that this does not bother you in the least. You have hitched this same female trait to your own wagon. You love what hates you, you want something that does not want you. This is the game we women play. Why are you playing the same game? By God, you're a man, leave the feminine to us, [9920] it doesn't suit you. Stick to the ways of men and love what loves you back, want what wants you as well. This game can be won. You tell us constantly that you want Isolde, but she doesn't want you. This is how she is, who can change that? She leaves untouched [9930] what she could easily have. She could care less about anyone who wants her. In this you are the first among many. She takes after me. I myself never liked you much either. I know that Isolde feels the same way, she has this from me. All your love is lost on her. The beautiful, the pure, [9940] she would be very ordinary indeed if she wanted every man who wanted her.

"Seneschal, as you have said, my lord should uphold his oath to you. Be careful, though, that you keep up with your stories and claims and don't lose track of some of them along the way. Stay focused on your goals! [9950] I have heard it said that another man killed the dragon. Consider carefully what you have to say to that."

"Who is he?"

"I know him very well, and I can bring him here if I need to."

"Lady, there is no one who would dare take up this case and dishonor me with lies. But should he give me the opportunity for justice, [9960] then I will risk life and limb as determined by the court, man to man, before I withdraw an inch."

"I find this praiseworthy," said the queen, "and I myself will stand as warrant and ensure that you get your wish. I will bring the man who killed the dragon here to do battle three days from now, [9970] but not a day sooner."

The king said, "Let it be so."

The nobles all said the same. "Seneschal, it will be done; this is only a short postponement. Come here and assent to the trial by combat, and my lady please do the same."

---

63. Gottfried's critique of the *vrouwen ritter* (l. 9905) seems to be aimed more broadly at those *minnesinger* who praise high ladies in hopes of attaining the unattainable. Hartmann von Aue levels a similar critique at his compatriots when he says that he would rather have a woman who wants him as well (MF XXII/XV,2: 5–8; L 217, 2–5).

The king took their pledges and securities [9980] that the duel would take place in three days, and that was the end of the proceeding.

Chapter 14: The Splinter

[9983] The ladies both left and took their minstrel into their care. All their efforts were kindly directed to accomplishing only one thing: helping him in any way possible. He was quickly revived and regained his healthy glow. Isolde looked at him again and again, paying special attention to his looks and his movements. She secretly observed his hands and face, his arms and legs, and these made plain what he was trying to hide.[64] [10,000] She looked him over from top to bottom. Whatever young women like to see in a man, she saw enough of him that she liked very well and thought about it admiringly.

When the beautiful and gracious woman inspected and observed how well-endowed his features were and with what bearing he presented himself, her heart secretly said, "God almighty, worker of wonders, [10,010] if anything that you have ever done or will do or have made here on earth can be imperfect, then there is something imperfect here. This impressive man, to whom you have given such a splendid physical appearance, has to wander from one realm to another in order to provide for himself. [10,020] It would only be right that some realm or land that is worthy of him should serve him instead. The world is a strange place where so many kingdoms are ruled by weaklings, yet he has been given none.[65] Someone with such a noble physique and such character should have wealth and honor. [10,030] He has been sorely wronged. Lord God, you have given him a life that does not suit his looks." She contemplated these matters over and over again.

By now her mother had told her father everything about the merchant from the very beginning, as you have heard for yourself, the whole story and what happened, and that he only wanted [10,040] to be guaranteed safe conduct in the future should he find himself in the kingdom again. All this she told him in confidence from beginning to end.

The young woman had in the meantime instructed her squire Paranis to polish Tristan's armor and weapons and restore them to their white gleam, [10,050] and to look after all of his other things with care and attention. Once this had been done it was all nicely laid out and neatly stacked. The

---

64. That is, his outer beauty revealed his inner nobility and high birth. Isolde believes that he is of noble birth and therefore could not be a mere minstrel. Function should follow form, as Isolde thinks to herself, not the other way around.

65. This seems to be a stinging critique by Gottfried of contemporary rulers, but it certainly applies to Mark as well, who has become little more than a figurehead at this point in the story.

young woman went in secret to look at everything in detail. By chance it happened that Isolde discovered what would torment her heart [10,060] a second time. Her heart was drawn to it, her eyes were fixed on where the armor lay. I don't know what made her do it, but she lifted up the sword, curious and inquiring as young women and children are, and just as, God only knows, plenty of men are as well. [10,070] She pulled it out of its scabbard and, examining every last inch of it, she discovered the chip and inspected it at length. Then she thought to herself, "May God have mercy on me. I think I have the piece that fits into this space. I must find out if this is true."

[10,080] She brought the splinter and placed it in the gap. The cursed piece fit perfectly into the space as if they were one, which in fact they had been two years ago. Her heart turned to ice as she remembered the old injustice. Her coloring turned both deadly pale and fiery red [10,090] from the anger and pain. "Oh," she said, "unfortunate Isolde, someone help! Who brought this cursed weapon here from Cornwall? My uncle was killed with it, and the man who killed him was named Tristan. Who gave it to this minstrel named Tantris?"

[10,100] She started then to consider the two names and reflected on their sounds. "Ah, Lord," she said to herself, "these names trouble me. I don't know what it is about them, but they sound so much alike. Tantris and Tristan: there must be some mysterious connection."

Then she started [10,110] to turn the names around in her mouth, considering the letters that made up both. She discovered that they were the same for one as for the other. She then divided them up into their syllables, turned them around, and so found the clue to the names and the solution to the mystery. [10,120] Forward she read 'Tris-tan,' in reverse she read 'Tan-tris.' Now she was sure about the name.[66]

"Well, well," said the beautiful woman, "if this is how it is, then it was my heart that first uncovered this lie and this deceit. It was clear to me the whole time since I've been observing him, since I pondered his appearance and bearing [10,130] and everything else about him in my heart, that he had to be of noble birth. Who else besides him could have accomplished all this, coming from Cornwall to his mortal enemies? And we cured him twice? Cured?! There is no saving him now! This sword will be the death of him. Now hurry, avenge your pain, Isolde! [10,140] If he is killed with the sword that he used to kill your uncle, then my vengeance will be complete."

She took the sword in her hands and ran to stand over Tristan, who was seated in his bath. "So," she said, "are you Tristan?"

---

66. Gottfried likes to play with anagrams, and there are others throughout the story. This particular feature of reversing the syllables of the name is most likely not in Thomas, at least it is not in the Norse *Saga*.

Brangane replied to her, "My dear lady, follow my advice, both you and young Isolde. As sure as I am of my own mortality, I know [10,490] that it is difficult for you to overcome your old suffering in your hearts, but at least give him the guarantee that his life is not in danger. He could then more easily say something on his own behalf."

The ladies said, "So shall it be."

They told him to stand, and once they had given him assurances all four of them sat down. [10,500] Tristan came back to his news. "You see," he said, "noble queen, if you are willing to enter into an amicable relationship with me, then I can assure you, without any thought of deception, that within two days your dear daughter will be betrothed to a noble king. He is well suited to be her husband, he is handsome and generous, [10,510] a noble knight born to lance and shield. He is descended from kings and in addition is even more powerful than your father."

"Truly," replied the queen, "if I could trust your proposal, then I would agree to do what is necessary."

"Lady," said Tristan, [10,520] "I can promptly provide you with guarantees, and if I can't produce them right away after we have reconciled, then you may release me from your protection and do with me what you will."

The wise queen spoke, "Brangane, speak, what is your advice, what do you think?"

"I think his proposal is a good one, and I advise you to take him up on it. Put all your doubts aside, [10,530] both of you rise and give him the kiss of peace, and even though I am not a queen, I want to be a part of this reconciliation. Morold was my relative, too, even though I am not high born."[71] All three of them kissed him, although young Isolde was very reluctant to do so.

Once the reconciliation was complete, Tristan addressed the women again. "God in his goodness knows [10,540] I have never been so happy as I am right now. I risked all the perils that might threaten me in the hope that I might gain your favor, something that is no longer a possibility but a certainty. You can forget all your cares. [10,550] I came from Cornwall to Ireland to benefit you and your honor. Since my first voyage when I was healed here, I have sung your praises and your honor to my lord, Mark. I did so until finally he turned his thoughts to you so fervently that he came to a decision, although reluctantly at first. I will tell you why. [10,560] First he feared your enmity, and second he wanted to remain without a wife for my sake, so that I might be his heir after his death. I counseled him against this until he finally gave in. So the two of us agreed between us that I would undertake this voyage. This is why I came to Ireland, [10,570] this is why I killed the dragon.

---

71. Brangane's familial relationship to the royal family is never fully clarified, although the younger Isolde refers to her as her *niftel*, which can mean "cousin" or "niece."

Since you graciously went to such great efforts on my behalf, my young lady will become ruler and queen of Cornwall and England. Now you know the reasons for my journey, blessed company, blessed trio. But please, all this must be kept secret."

[10,580] "Now tell me," said the queen, "shouldn't I tell the king and suggest a general amnesty to him? Would that be wrong of me?"

"No, my lady," Tristan replied, "by rights he should know about this, but please make sure that I'm not harmed because of any of this."

"No, sir, you need not fear, nothing is going to happen."

[10,590] The women then retired to their chambers and wondered about his good fortune and success in all his endeavors. They talked about his intelligence, the mother from one perspective, Brangane from another.

"Just listen, mother," said her daughter, "to the strange way I found out [10,600] that his name was Tristan. After I recognized the sword, I thought about the names 'Tantris' and 'Tristan.' Once I started thinking about them, it seemed to me that the two had something in common. Then I started to consider them more closely and discovered that the letters [10,610] used for both of them were the same. However I read them, they came out either 'Tantris' or 'Tristan.' Either way was correct. Now, mother, separate the name 'Tantris' into a 'tan' and a 'tris' and then say the 'tris' before the 'tan' [10,620] and you have 'Tristan.' But if you say the 'tan' before the 'tris' then you have 'Tantris.'"

The mother made the sign of the cross. "May God bless me," she said. "However did you get such an idea?"

As the three of them were discussing these various matters the queen sent for the king, who came right away. [10,630] "Sire," she said, "listen closely. We ask that you grant us a favor, something that's very important to all three of us. If you do so, it will benefit all of us."

"I will grant what I am able. Whatever you want, it shall be done."

"Are you leaving it up to me then?" asked the noble queen.

"Yes, whatever you want, you shall have it."

"Thank you, sire, that will suffice. [10,640] Sire, the man who killed my brother, Tristan, I have him here. You should grant him your friendship and your mercy. His business is of such a nature that a reconciliation is appropriate."

The king replied, "Truly, I leave this decision completely up to you. It concerns you more than it does me. Morold was your brother [10,650] and so more closely related to you than to me. If you want to drop the matter, then I will do the same, if you wish."

She told the king Tristan's story exactly as he had told it to her. The king was well pleased with the account and said to her, "Just be sure he does so in good faith."

The queen then sent [10,660] Brangane to get Tristan, and when Tristan entered he threw himself at the king's feet. "Mercy, your Majesty!" he exclaimed.

"Rise, Sir Tristan. Come here and kiss me," said Gurmun. "As much as I dislike it, I will put aside this hostility, since the ladies have done so already."

"Sire," Tristan asked, [10,670] "are my lord and both his lands also included in this reconciliation?"

"Yes, sir," replied Gurmun without hesitation.

Once the reconciliation was complete, the queen took Tristan by the hand and sat him next to her daughter. She asked him to tell the king his story in detail from the beginning, how everything had transpired, [10,680] about the dragon and about King Mark's proposal. So he recounted it once again to the end.

The king said, "Sir Tristan, how can I be sure that this story is true?"

"Quite easily, lord. I have all of my king's barons here. Tell me what guarantees you want, and I will provide them. It will be done [10,690] even if only one of them is left."

With this the king departed, and the women and Tristan stayed behind. Tristan turned to Paranis and said, "My friend, go down to the port. There is a ship at anchor there. Quietly go aboard and ask who among them is named Curvenal. [10,700] Tell him quickly and in secrecy that he should come to see his lord. Don't tell anyone else anything and then bring him here discreetly, like the courteous fellow that you are."

Now dear sirs, this is exactly what Paranis did. He quietly brought him back, and no one was the wiser. When they entered the private chambers and appeared before the ladies, he was greeted by the queen, [10,710] but no one else. They took no notice of him because he did not appear to be a knight. When Curvenal saw that Tristan was happy and left unharmed in the company of these women, he said in French, "*Ha, beau doux sire,*[72] in God's name, how could you stay happily hidden away [10,720] here in this heavenly paradise while leaving us to worry? We thought everything was lost. Up until now I would have sworn that you were dead. What grief you have caused us! Your ship and your crew just today swore and still believe that you are dead. [10,730] It was with great difficulty that they stayed until last night, and they were all agreed that they would set sail this evening."

"On the contrary," said the noble queen, "he lives and is healthy and cheerful."

Tristan answered him in Breton. "Curvenal," he said, "return quickly and tell them that all is well, [10,740] and that I will accomplish everything we set out to do."

---

72. "Ah, good, sweet lord."

He then told him in detail, at least as best he could, how favorable things stood. After he had reported on his good fortune and his difficulties, he said, "Now, go back down and tell the barons and the knights as well [10,750] that each of them should get ready tomorrow morning, dressed in the best clothes they have, and await my messenger. When I send him, they should ride here to me at court. I will also send someone to you tomorrow morning to whom you should give the chest, [10,760] where I keep all of my valuables, along with my most elegant outfit. You should also dress to impress, as a courtly knight should." Curvenal bowed and turned to go.

Brangane spoke, "Who is that man? He spoke about these rooms as if they were a heavenly paradise. Is he a knight or a servant?"

[10,770] "Lady, whatever you may think of him, he is a knight and my liegeman, and you may rest assured that there is no one under the sun with a more virtuous heart."

"Ah, may he be forever blessed," said both queens, and Brangane agreed, given her courtliness and good manners.

When Curvenal arrived at the ship [10,780] he reported everything just as he had been instructed. He told them what he had been told and also how he had found Tristan. They all reacted as if they had been dead and were now resurrected. They were all extremely happy, but many of them were happier about the peace between the countries [10,790] than about Tristan's increased honor. The envious barons started murmuring and grumbling as before. Given this great accomplishment, they returned to accusing Tristan of all sorts of sorcery, and each one of them said, "Think about how incredible it is, the miracles this man can perform. [10,800] Good God, how is it possible that this man can accomplish whatever he sets out to do?"

Chapter 15: The Trial

[10,803] The day of the trial had arrived. A great many of the nobility and commoners were gathered there before the king in the great hall. A lively discussion was underway among the knights, and they wondered who would do battle with the seneschal for the young Isolde. The question was tossed back and forth, but there was no one among them who knew anything about this. In the meantime Tristan's chest and clothing had arrived, and he took out three belts for the ladies, [10,820] and neither empress nor queen had ever received any better. The chest was filled to the rim with headbands, brooches, purses, and rings, all of which were so precious that no one could have imagined anything more costly. Nothing was removed [10,830] except what Tristan took out for himself, including a belt that fit him splendidly, a headband, and a small clasp that seemed suitable to him.

"You beauties, all three of you," he said, "this chest and its contents, take them and do what you want with them."

After this bestowal he departed. [10,840] He put on his clothes and made every effort to outfit himself in the style that was proper for a proud knight. Everything fit him superbly. When he returned to the ladies, they began to scrutinize him, freely using their imagination. [10,850] He seemed to all three of them to be handsome and distinguished. The three gracious women all thought to themselves, "Truly, this man is the epitome of masculinity. His clothes and his shape bring out his manliness and are so well matched that his overall appearance is complete."

[10,860] Tristan had by then called his companions together, and they had come and taken a seat together in the hall. Everyone there stared at the magnificent clothes they were wearing. Many of them said that never before had so many men all worn [10,870] such uniformly splendid clothing. The fact that they were all silent and did not speak with the locals was only because they could not speak their language.[73]

The king sent a courier to the queen telling her to come to the court along with her daughter. "Isolde," she said, "it's time, let's go. [10,880] Sir Tristan, you should stay here. I will send for you in a minute. Then you can take Brangane by the hand, and the two of you will follow us."

"Gladly, your Majesty."

Queen Isolde then arrived, that joyful Dawn, leading her Sun by the hand, that wonder of Ireland, brilliant young Isolde. [10,890] She walked at Dawn's side, serene and stately, following her lead and keeping step. She made a charming picture: tall, slender, well rounded, and formed in her dress as if Love had carved herself a feathered pet, as Desire's ultimate objective, beyond which no other desire exists.[74] [10,900] She wore a gown and cape made of

---

73. Gottfried's explanation runs directly counter to what is reported in Eilhart's version, namely that Tristan tells the barons to remain silent until he arrives, thereby demonstrating his authority over the group. Gottfried opts for the more logical explanation.

74. The word *vederspil* (literally a feathered play thing or pastime) has often been discussed as it is related to courtly love (*minne*) and courtly women (*vrouwe*). The term is used clearly to denote trained birds of prey in l. 2167 and l. 2203, when Tristan is kidnapped. In l. 5350, Morold's men are using birds for hunting. This is also the case in l. 13,100 when Tristan hunts with a bird for entertainment. Then in l. 10,897 and l. 11,985 the term refers to Isolde as Love's tamed bird of prey. The analogy between these birds of prey and hunting and a lady and love are based on several concepts: the woman is courtly and thereby "tamed" to be entertaining; the birds are beautiful and expensive, they require a high degree of attention and dedication. Later in ll. 10,994–99, Isolde is compared to a falcon, a hawk, and a parakeet or parrot. Here the prominent features of comparison seem to be Isolde's beauty, refinement, self-assuredness, and alertness.

dazzling brocade and tailored in the French style.[75] The gown was cut with a narrow waist and accented with a silk belt that was snug and set perfectly on her hips. She and the gown were made as one. It was form fitting [10,910] and clung to her shape, and it was not loose anywhere but shaped her from top to bottom. It was draped at her feet at just the right length, as each of you would think proper.

The cape was costly and lined completely with white ermine, [10,920] with the bands aligned in waves along the edge. It was not too short or too long, and flowing down it neither touched the ground nor rode up too high. In the front it was trimmed with sable, neither too narrow nor too broad, as if cut by Temperance herself, dappled in black and gray. These colors were interspersed in such a way [10,930] that neither one overpowered the other. The sable followed the ermine along the entire hem, which gave it a pleasing effect. Instead of a clasp it had a small chain of white pearls, around which the beautiful woman hooked her left thumb. [10,940] Her right hand reached lower, where, as you well know, the mantle is supposed to stay closed, which she managed to accomplish fashionably with two fingers. Below that it fell open again and was draped in such a way that this and that, I mean the lining and the brocade, were both visible, and you could see the inside and the outside [10,950] as well as what was hidden even further within: the image that Love had shaped so beautifully in body and spirit. Both of these, the sculpting and the stitching, had never before worked so well together and created so perfect a living image. Stolen glances flew all around like driven snow. [10,960] I think that Isolde must have robbed many a man of his senses.

She wore a golden headband in her hair that was fittingly delicate and made with great artistry. It was studded with jewels and precious stones, radiant despite their size and the best in all the land. [10,970] Emeralds and hyacinth, sapphires and chalcedony were all set all around so exquisitely that no goldsmith had ever set gemstones better or with greater skill. Gold shone on gold, the diadem and Isolde competed with each other. [10,980] Her hair was so like gold that no one, regardless of how perceptive he was, could have said there was a band there if he had not seen the stones. Isolde walked next to Isolde, the daughter next to her mother, happy and carefree. Her steps and her stride [10,990] were measured, neither too long nor too short, but just right. Her bearing was upright and confident, like a sparrow hawk, and as sleek as a parakeet. Her eyes scanned the surroundings like a falcon on its perch. She took it all in, not too tentatively, but not too boldly either. [11,000] Her eyes scouted about calmly

---

75. The French fashion at the time was known for particularly tight-fitting and shape-revealing clothing.

and quietly, in such a gracious manner that everyone's own eyes deemed the two reflections to be a wonder and a joy. The joy-bestowing Sun shone its light all around, she delighted everyone in the hall as she glided alongside her mother. [11,010] Both of them were graciously busy, each in her own way, speaking words of greeting and nodding silently. Their actions were determined and intentional, as one greeted and the other nodded, the mother spoke, the daughter was silent. They acted in complete harmony, [11,020] this was their main goal.

Once Isolde and Isolde, the Sun and the Dawn, had taken their seats next to the king, the seneschal looked all around and asked here and there where the ladies' champion was. No one had an answer for him. [11,030] He gathered his clansmen around him, there were a great many, and then proceeded to make his appearance before the king. He presented himself to the judicial court. "Now, lords," he said, "I am here and demand trial by combat. Where is the good knight who thinks that he can challenge my honor? I have here my supporters and vassals. [11,040] My claim is well founded, and if you apply the law of the land as it should be, then I will secure my rights. I do not fear authority, as long as you alone wield it."[76]

"Seneschal," said the queen, "if this combat is inevitable, then I am at a loss as to what to do. I am completely unprepared for this. Should you, however, agree to renounce your claim [11,050] and agree to release Isolde and let her go free, Seneschal, then this would benefit both you and her."

"Free?" replied the other. "Dear Lady, would you so easily give up a game that is already won? Whatever you say, I think I will [11,060] profitably and honorably emerge the winner of this game. I would have wasted considerable effort if I were to give up now. Lady, I make my claim on your daughter, and that is my final word. You say you know the man who killed the dragon, so produce him now, and let us stop this talk."

"Seneschal," said the queen, [11,070] "I understand. It must be done. I will act to defend my own interests."

She beckoned Paranis to her side and instructed him, "Go and bring him here."

They all looked at each other, knights and barons, and a great murmur arose with questions and speculation about who the champion was, but no one knew. [11,080] At this moment proud Brangane entered with gliding steps, the beautiful full Moon, and at her side she led her companion, Tristan. Proud and refined, she escorted him courteously, pleasing beyond measure in

---

76. The phrase *ir entuot ez danne al eine* (l. 11,044) has been translated variously. Hatto: "unless you alone employ it" (1960, 186); Krohn (1960): "as long as you alone employ it" (solange Ihr alleine sie ausübt); Haug/Scholz (2011/2012): "unless you employ it" (es sei denn, daß Ihr sie ausübt); Knecht (2004a): "except from you" (außer von Euch).

appearance and bearing, confident and sovereign. [11,090] Her companion walked confidently at her side. Everything about him was also praiseworthy and admirable, in every quality that distinguishes a knight. He had everything that should be praised in a knight. His physique and his clothing were in splendid harmony, [11,100] and both together formed the perfect knight. He was wearing clothing made of unusually fine silk, woven with gold thread, both exotic and admirable. These were not like clothes normally given out at court, and the gold that was interwoven in the material was not of the normal court variety either. The silk material was hardly visible. [11,110] It was so covered in gold, practically drenched in gold, that the material itself was barely detectable. Over this lay a netting with small pearls, with the mesh about a hand's breadth wide, through which the brocade shone as if it were on fire. [11,120] It was lined inside with a silk material that was more radiant than violets and just as richly purple in color as the blue Iris. This silk's folds were creased as one with brocade, just as a lining should be. The robe fit the praiseworthy man admirably well and just as he wished. [11,130] On his head he wore a gleaming work of art, a wonderful gold circlet that shone as brightly as a candle. Its jewels shone like stars, there were topazes and sardonyxes, chrysolites and rubies. It was bright and iridescent and gave a shimmer to his entire head and hair.

[11,140] This is how he entered, formidable and self-confident. His bearing was commanding and noble, his appearance truly impressive, and everything about him was larger than life. They made room for him as he entered the great hall, and his companions from Cornwall now recognized him [11,150] and happily ran up to greet and welcome him and Brangane as they came in together. They took both of them by the hand, him and her, and escorted them with great pomp to the throne. The king and the queen [11,160] made their courtliness manifest as they stood to greet him. Tristan bowed to all three, after which the three also acknowledged his companions in such a chivalrous manner as nobles would expect.

The entire company of knights then crowded around and greeted the guests, [11,170] although no one knew why they were there. The foreigners began to recognize the family and kin that had been sent from Cornwall to Ireland as tribute payment. Many a man ran to his family and kin with tears in his eyes, and there was much joy and lament that I won't describe further. The king took Tristan by the hand [11,180] as he appeared before him, as well as his companion, I mean him and Brangane, and sat them next to him, making sure that Tristan sat directly at his side. The two brilliant queens sat on the other side of him. The knights and barons, Tristan's companions, sat below on the ground level, [11,190] but in such a way that each of them could see the judicial court and everything that was happening.

There arose then a great murmur and much discussion among the people about Tristan. I know full well that there in the hall fountains of praise soon began to spout and cascade out of many a man [11,200] with regard to everything about him. They praised him in many regards and in many ways. Many of them were saying, "Where did God ever create a man who better embodied all that is knighthood? How suited he is to fighting and to making war. [11,210] How amazingly well fitting are the clothes he wears. Never before in Ireland have we seen such clothes fit for an emperor, and his companions are clothed with royal splendor. Truly, whoever he is, he is highborn in spirit and wealth." Many other similar things were said. For the seneschal it was all like pouring vinegar in his eyes, [11,220] and that's the truth.

Then the call went out for quiet in the hall. Everyone complied, and once that had happened and everyone was quiet, the king said, "Seneschal, speak, what do you claim to have done?"

"Lord, I killed the dragon."

The foreigner then arose and hastily exclaimed, "Sir, you did not!"

"Sir, I did! [11,230] I can prove it right here and now."

"How can you prove it?" asked Tristan.

"As you see, this is the head that I took from there."

"My lord king," replied Tristan, "if he wants to provide the head as proof, then command that it be examined inside. If the tongue is found there, then I will withdraw my claim and not prosecute the matter any further."

[11,240] They opened the dragon's mouth and found nothing. Tristan then commanded them to bring the tongue. It was brought in, and Tristan said, "My lords, look and see if this is the dragon's."

They all agreed with him and all together proclaimed it so, with the exception of the seneschal, who still wanted to deny it [11,250] but didn't know exactly how to proceed. The villain's mouth and tongue, his voice and thoughts began to falter and sputter, and he could neither speak nor stay silent. He didn't know what to do.

"My lords, all of you," said Tristan, "consider what a miracle that must have been, and how it must have happened. [11,260] Once I had killed the dragon and without much effort cut the tongue out of its lifeless mouth and carried it off, he came along and killed it again."

All of the nobles said, "There is little honor to be gained from boastfulness. Whatever anyone says or claims, all of us know [11,270] that the only correct conclusion must be that whoever came first and cut out the tongue must have also killed the dragon." Everyone immediately agreed.

As soon as the impostor had been exposed and the truthful foreigner had convinced the court, Tristan said, "Your Majesty, now I remind you of your promise. [11,280] I have a right to your daughter."

The king replied, "Sir, I agree, as you have kept your promise to me."

140

"No, Sire," said the imposter, "for God's sake, don't say that. Whatever just happened here, there must surely be treachery involved. This could only have been accomplished with deceit. Before I allow my honor to be stolen unjustly, [11,290] it must be taken from me in combat. Lord, I insist on trial by combat."

"Seneschal," said wise Isolde, "your objections are without merit. Against whom do you claim the right to combat? This man has no interest in fighting. With Isolde he has won everything he wanted. He would have to be more gullible than a child [11,300] if he were to fight you over nothing."

"Why not, dear lady?" said Tristan. "Before he says that we are compelling him to give up his honor unjustly, I would rather fight him. Your Majesties, speak out and command him to go and arm himself immediately. He should prepare himself, as will I."

Once the seneschal realized [11,310] that they were about to agree to a duel, he took his relatives and vassals outside to speak with them and receive their counsel. They thought that the whole affair was so undignified that he received little support. Their unanimous and immediate response was this: "Seneschal, your claims [11,320] were without foundation from the outset, and now they have come to an unhappy conclusion. What are you doing? If you want to fight a duel in an unjust cause, then it will ultimately cost you your life. What else can we say? There is no honor in this matter. If you were to lose your life in addition to your honor, [11,330] then the harm done would be all the greater. We all think, and we agree that your opponent in this duel looks to be a courageous man in a fight. If you challenge him, it will certainly mean your death. Since you were betrayed by the devil's counsel and have lost your honor, you should at least save your own life. Consider if there isn't someone [11,340] who might find a way out of this dishonesty and fraud."

Then the impostor said, "How do you think I should do that?"

"Our advice is short and to the point. Go back inside and say that your supporters have told you to renounce your claim and that you will have nothing more to do with the matter."

This is what the seneschal did. [11,350] He went back into the hall and told them that his relatives and vassals had talked him out of it, and that he agreed to retract his challenge.

"Seneschal," said the queen, "I never thought I would live to see the day when you would give up on a game already won!"

The hall resounded with similar sarcasm and ridicule. [11,360] The poor seneschal was their violin and their rote.[77] They kicked him around with

---

77. Unlike our saying "they played him like a fiddle," which refers to clever manipulation, this seems to indicate that ridiculing someone is as much a form of entertainment as playing an instrument or playing with a ball.

insults like a ball, until derision finally gave way to jeers and laughter, and so in the end the impostor was publicly disgraced.[78]

Chapter 16: The Love Potion

[11,367] After this whole affair had been concluded, the king told his country's nobles in the hall, his knights and barons, that this was Tristan. He told them the story, as he had been told, of why he came to Ireland and how Tristan, along with Mark's nobles, had promised to provide guarantees with regard to all the points that Gurmun had stipulated. [11,380] The Irish nobility was very happy with this news. The nobles said that reconciliation was agreeable and proper, and that the long enmity between the two was causing more harm the longer it lasted. The king then asked Tristan to endorse the agreement [11,390] as he had promised. Tristan did exactly that. He and his lord's men swore together that Isolde should receive Cornwall as her dowry and that she would be queen over all of England. With this Gurmun put Isolde's hand in Tristan's, [11,400] her enemy. I say "enemy" because she still hated him at that time.

Tristan took her by the hand and said, "King and Lord of Ireland, my lady and I appeal to you, for her sake and also mine, that the knights and boys who were sent here as tribute from Cornwall and England [11,410] and who are now by rights under my lady's authority as queen of these lands, might be set free for her sake."

"Very well," replied the king, "let it be so. They shall all go home with you with my blessing."

This news made many people very happy. Tristan ordered that another ship be hired along with his, [11,420] which would be reserved for him and Isolde and others as he saw fit. As this ship was being made ready, Tristan made his own preparations for the journey. The exiles were summoned wherever they could be found, whether at the court or out in the countryside.

While Tristan [11,430] and his companions got themselves ready, Isolde the wise queen crafted a love potion in a small glass bottle.[79] It was so artfully

---

78. In the French prose *Tristan* the seneschal is actually executed, a comment on how serious the loss of honor from lying to the court and the king really was.

79. The preparation of poisons and potions such as this was illegal and could lead to accusations of witchcraft, and this long before the witch hunts and persecutions of the late Middle Ages. Queen Isolde is here clearly identified as a master of the dark arts, not just herbal and medicinal healing, and the epithet *wise* here indicates more than just learned and wise. Her secretive instructions to Brangane indicate the nefarious nature of the potion, its production, and distribution.

formulated and prepared and was so potent that whoever drank it with someone else [11,440] would love that other person more than anything whether he wanted to or not, and the other person would love only him in return. They would be united in one death and one life, one sorrow and one joy.

The wise queen took the potion and whispered to Brangane, "Brangane," she said, "my niece, don't be saddened by what I'm going to say to you. You will be going with my daughter, [11,450] so prepare yourself for this and listen carefully to what I am going to tell you. Take this bottle with this drink and safeguard it above all else. Make sure that absolutely no one else knows about it and take every precaution to ensure that no one drinks from it. Make sure of one thing: [11,460] when Isolde and Mark are united in love, serve them this drink as if it were wine and have them drink all of it together. Make certain that no one else drinks with them, that's crucial, or that you drink with them. This is a love potion, remember that. I give my precious Isolde [11,470] over to your care. She means the world to me, and we entrust ourselves to you, as you value your soul. That's all I need to say."

"Dear Lady," said Brangane, "if both of you wish it, then I will gladly go with her, and I will protect her and her honor in any way I can."

[11,480] Tristan took his leave from his people, and they all left Wexford full of joy. Out of love for Isolde, the king and queen and all the court escorted her down to the harbor. That dazzling and delightful woman was not yet Tristan's love and future heartbreak. [11,490] She was at his side, crying the entire time. Her father and mother both spent what little time they had with their own laments. Many eyes shed tears and turned red. Isolde moved many a pained heart and was the cause of [11,500] much hidden sadness. They all had to cry over Isolde, the joy and light of their eyes, and many hearts and eyes wept, some openly, some secretly. Now when the one and the other Isolde, the Sun and its Dawn, along with the Full Moon, [11,510] the beautiful Brangane, had to part, the one from the other two, there you could see real sorrow and pain. That faithful company was separated with much grief, and Isolde kissed both of them lovingly and often. When the people of Cornwall [11,520] and the ladies' Irish attendants had all said their goodbyes, they boarded the ships. Tristan went aboard last. That fair young queen, the flower of Ireland, Isolde, took him by the hand in her sadness and deep unhappiness. Both of them bowed in reverence toward the shore and asked for God's blessing [11,530] on the people and the country. They weighed anchor and as they sailed away raised their voices and sang, repeating, "We travel in God's name,"[80] and then set sail.

---

80. This is a pilgrim song whose roots go back to a melody of the twelfth century. Although the text is only known to us in a collection from 1567, it should be assumed that Gottfried is referring here to the first line of a contemporary song (see Okken, 1996, 2.1043, n. 11,534).

As soon as the woman and the man, Isolde and Tristan, had both drunk the potion,[83] [11,710] that great agitator appeared, Love, that besieger of all hearts. She stole her way into both of their hearts, and before they were even aware of it she had raised her banner of victory and had them both in her power.[84] They who were previously two and separate became one and the same. The two of them would no longer and never again repulse each other. [11,720] Isolde's hatred had vanished. Love, that peacemaker, had cleansed their hearts of hatred and united them, and each one saw the other clearly as in a mirror. They both shared one heart, her sorrow was his pain, his pain was her sorrow. [11,730] They were both united in love and in sorrow but kept this fact hidden from each other out of doubt and shame. She was ashamed, so was he. She doubted him, he doubted her. Although their hearts' desire was blindly united in one will, the first step was difficult for both of them. [11,740] They kept their desires secret.

When Tristan felt the stirring of love he first thought only of loyalty and honor and wanted only to turn away. "Stop," he thought to himself, "let it be, Tristan, get hold of yourself, pay no attention to it." But his heart always wanted to go to her. He waged war against his will, [11,750] one desire fought another. He wanted to go, he wanted to stay. The prisoner often tried to escape his chains, and for a long time he did not waver, but the loyal man was hard pressed by two different agonies. Whenever he looked into her eyes, dearest Love [11,760] would begin to torture his heart and his thoughts. Then he reflected on Honor, which took him away again. But Love, his fated sovereign,[85] would return, and he had no choice but to obey her. Loyalty and Honor were hard task masters, but Love was even tougher. [11,770] She

---

83. Gentry (1988, 262) presents a footnote concerning the love potion with reference to and a translation of the first four lines of a poem by Heinrich von Veldeke (MF XI/IV, 1–4; L 58,35–38): "Whether he wanted to or not, Tristrant / had to be faithful to the queen, / for a potion forced him to do so / more than the power of love." This poem is earlier than Gottfried's text.

84. Siege terminology in matters of love is common, but the allusion here is to ending a siege through treachery, as demonstrated during the First Crusade in the siege of Antioch in 1097–1098. After eight months of siege, during which two relieving Muslim armies were defeated, the city finally fell in June 1098, when an Armenian guard gave over the Tower of the Two Sisters to Bohemond's forces, and the entire city except for the citadel was quickly taken.

85. MHG *erbvogetîn* is an unusual term and unique to Gottfried. The word *voget* in the masculine form was a title of authority, usually with regard to protection of people and property, from the Latin *advocatus*. Twice Gottfried gives Tristan this title with regard to Parmenie (l. 5013) and again as Tristan takes up the cause against Morold (l. 6348). The other two instances of the word in the feminine form refer to *Minne* as the advocate or overlord of Tristan and Isolde (l. 11,765; l. 12,000). The prefix *erb-* is trickier, and can refer to heritage or inheritance. Hatto translates: "liege lord" (1960, 196); Haug/Scholz (2011/2012): "his lady that he inherited from his parents" (seine von den Eltern ererbte Herrin); Krohn (1980): "his heir-lady" (seine Erbherrin), with a note (3.119 on l. 11,765) that explains his "inheritance" of Love as his lord,

hurt him with an even greater pain and punished him more than Loyalty and Honor combined. His heart looked at Isolde with laughter, while at the same time he averted his eyes, but when he couldn't see her at all, that was his greatest agony.

He always thought about ways to escape, as a prisoner does, [11,780] and often said to himself: "Go one way or the other, but direct this desire, this love and longing to some other purpose." But the chains were still there. When he looked into his heart and mind for some sign of change, the only things he found there were Isolde and love.

The same was true for Isolde. [11,790] She tried in vain, but her life was also unbearable. When she sensed the quagmire of spellbinding love and knew that her thoughts were mired in it, she tried to escape. She wanted only to get to shore and get away, but she remained stuck like glue, and she was pulled down further and further. [11,800] The beautiful woman resisted with all her might and fought with every step, she didn't want to give in. She tried all sorts of ways, using her feet and hands she twisted and turned but sank only deeper. Her hands and feet slipped down into the blind sweetness of man and love. [11,810] Her thoughts were trapped and unable to strike out on any road, bridge, or path for more than a few feet without running into love. Whatever Isolde thought of, whatever thoughts came to her, they were not about this or that, but only about love and Tristan.

All of this took place in secret. [11,820] Her heart and her eyes worked against each other. Modesty turned her eyes away from him, Love pulled her heart toward him. These battling contingents, woman and man, Love and Modesty, completely bewildered her. The woman wanted the man but turned her eyes from him. Modesty wanted Love, [11,830] but no one was the wiser. What was the point? Modesty and women, so all the world agrees, are all too fleeting. They bloom only a short while and offer only short-lived resistance. Isolde gave up the fight and accepted her fate. Defeated, she quickly surrendered her body and her thoughts [11,840] to the man and to Love. She began to watch him secretly, her bright eyes and thoughts now totally in accord. In secret her heart and her eyes lovingly ensnared him.

The man looked at her gently and caringly. [11,850] He began to weaken as well, since Love would not release him. Man and woman gazed at each other at all hours of the day, at least when it could be done with decency. The lovers both thought that the other was much more beautiful than before. This is Love's right, it is her law, it holds true this year as it did last, [11,860] and it will as long as there is affection. It is true for all who love that they appreciate each other more as affection grows, as it brings forth a flowering and

---

because she had already been his parents' ruler; Knecht (2004a): "his inherited ruler" (seine angestammte Herrschaft).

proliferation of loving things. Fruitful Love makes everything more beautiful than it was. This is the seed she carries [11,870] and the reason she never dies.

> She appears more lovely than at first,
> and this makes Love in merit first.
> If Love seemed always as at first,
> then Love's law would not be first.

Chapter 17: The Confession

[11,875] The ships weighed anchor and set out again happily, unaware that Love had brought two hearts among them off course. The two of them were lost in their thoughts, encumbered with the pains of love that work such miracles. Honey turns to gall, sweetness turns sour, dew drops burn, softness hurts, hearts become heartless, and all the world is turned upside down. [11,890] Tristan and Isolde suffered greatly and were oppressed by an untiring and strange cruelty. They could find no rest or relief unless they saw each other, but when they saw each other they were even more discomfited, because between the two of them [11,900] neither one could be satisfied. Shyness and modesty were the cause, and these took away all their joy. Whenever they could secretly look at each other with eyes held fast, their hearts and thoughts reflected in the color of their faces. Love, that artist, thought it unsatisfactory [11,910] that she was hidden and carried secretly in noble hearts. She wanted to make her power known to all. This was evident in both of them in several ways. Their coloring was never the same for very long, it never lasted. It went from white to red, from red to white, [11,920] however Love painted them. Each of them could recognize, as one does with such signs, that something like love was present in the other's thoughts.

So they started treating each other lovingly and looked for a time and opportunity to talk privately. [11,930] Love and its two poachers would frequently lay snares and nets, set up blinds and ambushes for each other with their questions and answers.[86] They talked about everything. Isolde would start as most young women do, and she approached her love and her *ami* in a roundabout way, from a distance. [11,940] She began by telling him how it all started: how he arrived in Dublin in a little boat, alone and wounded; how her mother took him in and how she healed him; what happened then, how she learned to write all sorts of things under his tutelage, including Latin and how to play stringed instruments. [11,950] She talked about a lot of

---

86. Love as huntress is a frequent allegorical figure. The function of questions as traps later returns when Mark attempts to ensnare Isolde with his interrogations (ll. 13,675 ff).

other things, like telling him how brave he was, and also about the dragon, and how she had recognized him twice, in the pond and in the bath. The talk went back and forth, she would tell him something and he would do likewise.

"Ah,"[87] said Isolde, "the one time I had a real chance [11,960] to kill you in the bath, my God, why didn't I do it? If I had known then what I know now, it surely would have meant your death."

"Why, beautiful Isolde?" he asked. "What's got into you? What do you know now?"

"What I know is what concerns me. Whatever I see is what hurts me. The sky and the sea are a burden to me, my whole life depresses me."

[11,970] She leaned on him, supported by her elbow. This was the first sign of her boldness. Her bright eyes inconspicuously filled with tears, her heart overflowed, her sweet lips swelled, her head bowed low. Her friend started to wrap his arms around her, [11,980] not too formally or too closely, but more like an acquaintance. He said gently and softly, "Ah, beautiful, sweet thing, tell me. What's wrong, why are you sad?"

Isolde, Love's feathered pet, answered, "*Lameir* is my anguish, *lameir* is what oppresses me, *lameir* is what causes me pain."

Since she repeated the word *lameir* over and over, [11,990] he thought long and hard about what the word meant. He remembered that *l'ameir* meant love, *l'amer* meant bitter, and *la mer* meant the sea. [88] There seemed to be many meanings. Out of the three, he ignored the one and thought about the other two. He left out "love," [12,000] their sovereign, their hope, their desire, and asked only about "sea" and "bitter."

"I believe, beautiful Isolde" he said, "that your suffering is the sea and bitterness. You taste the sea and the wind, and I think that these two must be bitter for you."

"No, sir, no. What are you saying? Neither one of them is a problem for me, I don't taste the air or the sea. [12,010] *L'ameir* is the only thing that pains me."

Once he had considered the word thoroughly, he understood it to mean love. He whispered to her, "In truth, my fair lady, it is the same with me. *L'ameir* and you, you both are my anguish. Dear Isolde, you are the lady of my heart. You alone and your love have taken and turned my thoughts upside down. [12,020] I have been so sorely driven off course that I can't find my

---

87. This line (11,958) marks the corresponding beginning of the Carlisle fragment of Thomas. The similarity in terms of content between the fragment and Gottfried's text is remarkably close, although the French fragment of only 154 lines is equivalent to a corresponding 721 lines in Gottfried's text (to l. 12,678).

88. This word play originated in Latin and was well known in French literature as well. It can be found in Chrétien's *Cligés* (ll. 546–57), and Gottfried takes it directly from Thomas's *Tristran* (Carlisle ll. 33–35).

Interlogue: A Call for Change (12,187–430)[1]

[12,187] As little as I myself have been burdened with the joys of suffering in my time, that is, the kind of heartache deep inside that hurts in such a pleasurable way, my instinct tells me, and I believe I can trust it, that the two lovers felt pleasure and relief once they were rid of their Watcher, Love's true menace and enemy. [12,200] I have thought a lot about the two of them, and I think about them still today and always will. Whenever I imagine love and sighs of yearning and reflect in my heart on their nature, then my own Yearning grows, and my brother-in-arms, Aspiration, soars as if he would rise up to the heavens. Whenever I think about [12,210] all the wonderful things that could be found in love if only one knew where to look, how much joy love could give if only it were practiced faithfully, then words cannot express[2] how near my heart is to bursting.

I feel sorry for love with all my heart, because most everyone [12,220] holds on to love, but no one does right by it. We all have the right intent—we want to experience love. But it's not love when we mislead each other. We take the wrong approach to the whole matter. We sow seeds of henbane[3] and then expect [12,230] lilies and roses to grow. Certainly that's not how it works. We have to reap what we sow and harvest what the seed produces. We have to cut and mow the same thing we planted. We cultivate love with bitter thoughts, with falsehood and deceit [12,240] and then want to enjoy the pleasures of body and heart. But love only yields what was planted: pain and bad, rotten fruit and malice. When we have regrets, when our heart aches and then destroys us, we accuse love and blame it for something [12,250] of which it is innocent. We sow falsehood and harvest disgrace and sorrow. If the sorrow pains us greatly, then we should consider this first. If we sow better seed we will reap the same.

---

1. This excurse is not found in Thomas (i.e., in the Carlisle fragment, or the Norse *Saga*). It falls in what has been calculated as the exact middle point of the text, assuming that Gottfried would have completed his work as he envisioned in his grand plan.

2. The original text of l. 12,216, *groezer danne setmunt* (manuscript F) or *sefremunt* (manuscript H) seems to be corrupted, as *sefremunt or setmunt* cannot be explained. The scribes also seem not to have understood the word and so offered their own emendations. Krohn (1980), Ranke (1949), Marold/Schröder (2004a), and Spiewok (1989) have: *groezer danne Setmunt* and so stay with manuscript F. Haug/Scholz (2011/2012) suggest *græzer, dan ie seite munt*, based on manuscript O's reading of *seite myn munt*, along with Okken's (1996) suggestions (1.491), or literally "greater than any mouth could ever say." This is the basis for the present translation as it seems plausible and makes the most sense given the context.

3. This refers to *Hyoscyamus niger*, or "stinking nightshade," a poisonous plant with psychoactive properties.

Those of us who are engaged in the world, whether for good or bad, my how we [12,260] squander and throw away our time in the name of love.[4] In return we only get the same effort that we put into it, more failure and misfortune. We don't find the good that we all want; it eludes us instead. [12,270] This good is steadfast friendship.[5] It never fails to comfort us, it offers roses along with thorns, relief along with strife. In such a friendship, joy can always be found hidden among cares, and in the end it yields joy as often as sorrow. Yet almost no one finds this steadfast friendship, such poor gardeners are we.

It is certainly true what people say: [12,280] "Love has been hounded and hunted to the ends of the earth." All we have left of it is the word itself, only the name remains, and it has been undone, abused and misused[6] to the point that Love, all worn out, is ashamed of her own name and loathes the very word. Love is embarrassed of and a burden to herself here on earth. [12,290] Disgraced and pitiful, she creeps from house to house begging,[7] lugging a shameful patchwork sack, in which she carries her loot and plunder, offering to others what she denies herself. And we create the market for these goods! We treat Love outrageously and then claim that we are not to blame. [12,300] Love, the queen of hearts, free and incomparable, is now for sale, but her domination has come at a price.[8] We set glass into a gold ring and even fool ourselves with it. Someone is a particularly poor swindler if he lies to a friend in such a way [12,310] that he ends up deceiving himself. We are false lovers. We deceive Love. Our days are misspent, and we almost never turn our suffering into a happy ending. How we waste our lives without love and without goodness.

But we are encouraged by something that doesn't even involve us. [12,320] If someone has some nice story about matters of the heart to tell, if we tell stories about people who lived hundreds of years ago, that warms our hearts. We

---

4. This echoes the Prologue, ll. 82–92.

5. The phrase *staete vriundes muot* (l. 12,269) appears only here in Gottfried's text. The phrase can refer to an affectionate friendship or a faithful, romantic love.

6. Gottfried heightens the affect with two neologisms: *verwortet und vernamet* (l. 12,285), literally "over-worded and over-named."

7. The image of a begging *Minne* could well be taken from Hartmann von Aue's *Iwein* (ll. 1557 ff), where it is borrowed from Chrétien's *Yvain*.

8. The translation of this line is in doubt. The original lines, *wie habe wir unser hêrschaft / an ir gemachet zinshaft* (ll. 12,305–6) can mean either: we have to pay *Minne*, or she has to pay us. Haug/Scholz (2011/2012) opt for: "How we have had to pay for her reign" (Wie haben wir für ihre Botmäßigkeit bezahlen müssen); Krohn (1980): "How we have forced her to pay us tribute" (Wie haben wir sie gezwungen, uns tributpflichtig zu sein); Knecht (2004a): "Oh, how we have made ourselves bound to pay tribute to our ruler" (Ach, wie haben wir uns unsere Herrin tributpflichtig gemacht); Hatto: "What shameful dues our dominion has extorted from her!" (1960, 203).

are so taken in by all this that there is hardly anyone, if he is faithful and true and without deceit toward his love, [12,330] who wouldn't want to create for himself this kind of happiness in his own heart. But the one thing that makes it all possible is sadly trampled underfoot. This is heartfelt loyalty, which offers itself to us in vain. We look away and [12,340] shamefully knock down this tender thing. We have disgracefully trampled it to the ground. If we were willing to search for it, we wouldn't even know where to start. As valuable and rewarding as loyalty is between lovers, why don't we appreciate it? One look, one tender glance [12,350] can in truth relieve a hundred thousand pains in body and soul. One kiss from a beloved's lips, rising up from the bottom of the heart, oh how that could end all yearning and heartache.

I know for sure that Tristan and Isolde, impatient as they were, [12,360] relieved their mutual pain and sadness and claimed their desire's reward. That craving that constrains all thoughts was gone. They had plenty of what lovers long for as soon as they had the opportunity. When it was time, [12,370] they faithfully gave and took tribute and tax for themselves and Love. They were completely contented during the voyage and the journey, and now that modesty was gone, they enjoyed their intimacy fully and completely, which was both wise and sensible. [12,380] Those who hide their feelings from each other after having revealed them, whose modesty returns as they retreat from love, end up robbing themselves. The more they hide from each other, the more they deprive themselves and mix love with pain. Our two lovers hid nothing from each other. [12,390] With words and with looks they shared confidences.

They spent the voyage in total bliss, but it was not perfect, because they were afraid of what was to come. They feared what then actually did happen, what robbed them of their joy and brought them terrible suffering. [12,400] The problem was that beautiful Isolde had been given to a man she did not want. And then there was another problem that burdened them. That was Isolde's lost virginity. They were concerned about this and were both distraught. Still, this problem was easy to bear, since they were able to satisfy their passion [12,410] with each other over and over again.

Once they were close enough to Cornwall to see the coastline, they all rejoiced. All of them were happy except Tristan and Isolde. For them their arrival meant only fear and peril. If they could have had their way, [12,420] they would have wanted never to see land again. Fear for their honor began to weigh on their hearts. They had no idea what they should do, or how they could hide Isolde's lost virginity from the king. But even as inexperienced as young lovers are in their youth, [12,430] the young woman came up with a plan.

Part 2.1

Chapter 18: Brangane the Pure

[12,431] So when Love comes to find
it's played by those of youthful mind,
then in this youth we're sure to find
that wiles and tricks will come to mind.[1]

[12,435] Leaving the long and short of it aside, and as young as she was, Isolde came up with a way to cheat as best she could under the circumstances. She could think of nothing else except to ask Brangane to lie down quietly next to Mark in their first night and please him. There was no better way to hide the facts from him, she was beautiful and still a virgin. This is how Love teaches upright minds to engage in falsehood, [12,450] even though they really shouldn't know how to be deceitful and dishonest. This is what the lovers did. They asked Brangane over and over again, as long as it took until they had her promise that she would do it, although she made the promise with grave reservations. [12,460] She turned red and then white not just once on account of this request, which upset her a great deal. It really was an exceptional request.

"Dear lady," said Brangane, "your mother, my lady and blessed queen, ordered me to protect you. I should have protected you [12,470] from this calamity during this cursed journey. Now my carelessness has caused you shame and suffering. I suppose I can't complain then if now I have to bear the shame along with you. It would be right and just if I had to bear it alone if it would spare you. Dear Lord, how could you abandon me so?"

[12,480] Isolde then spoke to Brangane, "My proud niece, tell me, what do you mean, what's bothering you? I don't understand what you're complaining about."

"Lady, I threw a glass bottle overboard the other day."

---

1. There are differing translations of this last line (*witze unde liste finden*, l. 12,434), the difference centered on whether or not *witze* and *list* are positive or negative qualities. The negative readings include Hatto: "cunning and guile" (1960, 205); Haug/Scholz (2011/2012): "wiliness and guile" (Schläue und Hinterlist); the more positive are Krohn (1980): "reason and cleverness" (Verstand und Klugheit); Knecht (2004a): "reason and shrewdness" (Verstand und Schlauheit). The same two words are used again in l. 12,437. The context would seem to convey a more negative meaning, although excused by their young age and inexperience.

"Yes, you did. Why is that a problem?"

"Oh dear," she said, "that bottle and the concoction in it will be the death of you both."[2]

[12,490] "Why is that, cousin?" asked Isolde. "How is that possible?"

"It just is." Brangane then told both of them the story from beginning to end.

"It's in God's hands," said Tristan. "Whether it means death or life, I have been gently poisoned. I don't know how the other death will be, but this death is agreeable. If my wonderful Isolde should [12,500] forever be my death, then I would do whatever I could to die forever."

[12,503] Let all speech come to an end.
If love is what we do intend,
then it cannot there come to an end,
but that we too must pain intend.

[12,507] Soothing as love may be for us, we always need to think of honor as well. [12,510] Those who want to enjoy nothing but the body's cravings will ruin their honor. As much as Tristan enjoyed the life he had, still his honor drew him away from it. Most important to him was his own loyalty, which urged him to bring Mark's wife to him. These two, faithfulness and honor, [12,520] now constrained his heart and mind, even though they had formerly been vanquished when Tristan favored Love. These then, previously defeated, could now claim victory over Love.

Tristan sent two small boats with messengers ahead and had them report to Mark [12,530] what had happened with regard to the beautiful lady from Ireland. Mark quickly sent out a call to everyone he could reach, and immediately a thousand couriers went out to gather the knights of the realm. Foreigners and locals alike were received in great numbers. Mark received the two, who were to bestow on him the best and the worst [12,540] that he was to experience in life, as well as any man receives what he holds most dear in all the world. Mark commanded that all barons of the realm be told to appear at court in eighteen days in a manner befitting the celebration of his nuptials.

[12,550] This was all accomplished, and everyone appeared in great luxury. Many a magnificent company of knights and ladies came to see the brilliant Isolde, their eyes' delight. She was constantly being held up as a marvel, and everyone said the same thing. "*Isot, Isot la blonde,* [12,560] *merveille de tout*

---

2. These lines (12,487–89) are taken directly from Thomas in a later section (Fragment Douce ll. 1221–26; Haug/Scholz [2011/2012] ll. 2493–98) and echo Brangane's speech l. 11,705.

le monde.[3] Isolde is peerless in all the world. It is true what people say about this blessed maiden. She gives the world joy as does the sun. Never before has a realm gained such a marvelous young woman."

Once she was married, her rights [12,570] according to the law were secured. Cornwall and England were placed under her authority, and Tristan was named as heir should they remain without issue. She was paid homage and was then to retire at night with her husband Mark. She and Brangane and Tristan [12,580] had already gone to great lengths to inspect and prepare the place as they made their plans. There was only the four of them in Mark's chambers, the king and the three of them. Mark then lay down in bed. Brangane wore the queen's nightclothes, [12,590] since they had already exchanged clothes between them. Tristan led Brangane to her dreadful martyrdom, and her lady, Isolde, put out the lights, after which Mark pulled Brangane toward him. I don't know how she liked his advances, but she endured it in silence and made not a sound. [12,600] Whatever games he played with her, she played along and returned a value worth brass and gold, just as he wanted it. I am also fairly certain that it has never before been the case that such beautiful brass was paid in place of the golden debt due on the wedding night.[4] [12,610] I would be willing to bet my life that since the time of Adam there has never been minted a more noble counterfeit,[5] nor a more convincing imitation placed into a man's bed.

The entire time they were in bed together playing their games, Isolde was consumed by fear and trepidation. She thought to herself, [12,620] "God almighty, protect me and help me, so that my dear cousin stays true to me. If she plays these games in bed too long and too often, I'm afraid she might get to like it and not stop until daylight. Then all of us will be ridiculed and there will be a great outcry."

But no, Brangane's thoughts and intentions [12,630] were pure and good. After she had done what she was supposed to for Isolde and had paid her debt, she slipped out of bed. Isolde was immediately at hand and sat on the bed as if she were the same person. At that point, the king called for wine. By doing this he was following an old custom [12,640] that was practiced at the time. When someone had been with a virgin and taken her virginity, then wine was served and both would partake equally. This custom was also followed here. His nephew Tristan brought a light and wine, [12,650] and the king and the queen both drank. Some stories even say that it was the same

---

3. "Isolde, Isolde the fair, the wonder of all the world."
4. Gottfried uses the term *bettgeld* (l. 12,609). This word is found only here and represents a metaphor for the payment to be made by the woman on the wedding night. There is no evidence that any actual payment was involved.
5. The distinction is one that comes from counterfeiting coins, that is, determining the difference between real and imitation gold. Bronze was used in counterfeit coins to mimic gold.

potion that had caused Tristan and Isolde to fall victim to their heartache and torment. But that's not true, because there was nothing left of that potion. Brangane had thrown it into the sea.[6]

Once they had finished observing this custom and had drunk accordingly, young Queen Isolde [12,660] lay down with her lord and king with considerable anxiety and a hidden emotional pain in her heart. He took up his sport again and clutched her close to him. He thought women were all alike, and this one was soon just as agreeable. The one was like the other to him, [12,670] and he found brass and gold in both of them. The two women also paid their dues to him in one way or another so that he was completely unaware of anything untoward.[7]

Isolde was deeply loved and cherished by her lord Mark and praised and honored by the people and the realm. [12,680] People were witness to such courtly refinement and grace in her that anyone who could applauded her with praise and honor. At the same time, she and her *ami* had their own form of amusement at all times of day and night, because no one suspected anything. No one, woman or man, [12,690] thought that anything inappropriate was going on. She was in Tristan's safekeeping at all times and places, and so she could live the way she wanted.

Isolde started to consider her situation. Since no one knew about her secret and her deception except for Brangane, if she were out of the way, [12,700] then she wouldn't have to worry about her reputation any more. She was terribly worried and afraid that Brangane, if she had fallen in love with Mark, might tell him about her shameful plot and how everything had been arranged. The apprehensive queen [12,710] in this way revealed that people fear shame and derision more than God. She had two squires called who were foreigners from England. She demanded that they swear oath upon oath of unwavering loyalty and commanded them on pain of death to obey and execute all her commands [12,720] and to keep everything secret. Then she informed them of her murderous intent.

"Listen closely to what I say. I will hand over a young woman to you. Take her and the three of you ride secretly and swiftly out into the forest

---

6. It is difficult to say whether this is a direct criticism of Thomas or of other versions. The Carlisle fragment does not give us any incontrovertible evidence in this regard. There we can only read that Mark drinks *le vin*. In the Norse *Saga* Mark drinks the remainder of the love potion, thus creating a true lover's triangle of supernatural character. Eilhart excuses Tristrant in this episode, while not making any mention of the wine: "it was not disloyalty, for it was done against his will: the fatal potion was to blame" (Thomas, 1978, 80). It seems in any case that Gottfried is intent on both making the reader aware of the consistency of Gottfried's own narrative logic and not using the potion as a metaphor for Mark's love, or infatuation, with Isolde.

7. End (l. 12,678) of the Carlisle Fragment of Thomas's *Tristran*.

somewhere, close by or far away, [12,730] whatever you think best, as long as no one lives nearby. Then cut off her head. Remember everything she says, and then report back to me whatever she said. And bring me her tongue.[8] You can rest assured that I will arrange it in some way that by tomorrow both of you [12,740] will be made knights and given great wealth. I will grant you fiefdoms and support you for as long as I live." The plan was agreed to by all.

Isolde then called for Brangane. "Brangane," she said, "look at me. Do I look pale to you? I don't know what's wrong with me, I have a terrible headache. Please go out and gather some herbs. [12,750] We have to find some kind of cure, otherwise I might not survive."

Faithful Brangane replied, "Lady, your suffering concerns me greatly. There's no need to ask again, just send me out to where I can find something that will help you."

[12,760] "Look, there are two squires right here. Ride with them, and they will show you the way."

"I will gladly do so, my lady."

She mounted up and rode out with them. When they had arrived in the forest where they could find as many roots, herbs, and grasses as needed, Brangane wanted to stop, but they took her farther to a desolate and remote area. [12,770] Once they had gone far enough away from open land, they took the noble woman, faithful and blameless, down from her horse and with sorrow and grief drew their swords. Brangane was so terrified that she fell to the ground and lay there for a long time. [12,780] Her heart quivered and her entire body was trembling.

She looked up in terror and cried, "Sirs, have mercy! My God, what are you doing?"

"You must die."

"But why? Tell me!"

One of them said, "What did you do to anger the queen? She ordered us to kill you. It must be done. Our mutual lady, Isolde, decided [12,790] that you must die."

Brangane clasped her hands together and through her tears said, "Sir, no, for the sake of decency and in God's name, please wait and let me live long enough to explain. Then please kill me quickly. Tell my lady, and be assured yourselves, that I never [12,800] did anything to hurt her or anything that I could have known would make her angry. There is just one thing, but I can't believe it's the reason. When the two of us left Ireland, we took along two items of clothing that we had both picked out for each other. We sorted them from the rest of the wardrobe, [12,810] and took them along on the voyage.

---

8. This is an addition of Gottfried's. Eilhart has the liver, others nothing.

They were two nightshirts as white as snow.[9] While we were crossing the sea on our journey here, she was so overheated by the sun that she couldn't stand to wear anything else during that time except for that one pure white shirt. She loved to wear that shirt. [12,820] As she wore it over and over again, it became soiled. I had my shirt stowed away in my wardrobe, folded up in a clean white cloth and kept safe there. After my lady arrived here and was married to the king, she was to sleep with him, [12,830] but her shirt was not as attractive as it should have been or as she wanted it, and so I loaned her mine. The one fault I'm guilty of is that at first I resisted.

"If that's not what she's angry about, then as God is my witness, I never at any time disobeyed her request or command. [12,840] The both of you, in God's name, please send her my greetings as they are appropriate from a lady in waiting to her mistress. And may God in his mercy keep and protect her honor, her health, and her life.[10] I forgive her for causing my death, and I place my soul in God's hands. My life is now at your disposal."

The two men [12,850] looked at each other miserably and took pity on the innocent woman and her tears. They were sorry and regretted that they had sworn to commit this murder. Since they could find nothing about her or discover any reason that she deserved [12,860] to die, they discussed it between themselves and agreed that regardless of what might happen to them, they would let her live. They tied the loyal woman high up in a tree so that she would not be eaten by wolves until they returned. They cut out the tongue [12,870] of one of their hunting dogs and rode away. The two men reported to Isolde, who had instigated the murderous plan, that they had killed Brangane, although it pained them to do so. They both told her that they had brought her tongue.

Isolde said, "So tell me, what did the girl say to you?"

[12,880] They told her everything that she had said to them, all of it from beginning to end, holding nothing back.

"Fine," she said, "but didn't she say anything else?"

"No, my lady."

Isolde then cried out, "Oh, what terrible news! How could you have committed such a murder? Both of you will hang for it!"

"My God," they said, [12,890] "is this how things stand now? Lady Isolde, this is outrageous. You are the one who pleaded and insisted and forced us to kill her."

---

9. The white shirt is a metaphor for virginity, and the use of this symbolism is already present in Eilhart's version. Brangane's "shirt" was safely hidden away, Isolde's had become soiled.

10. There is some question as to whether or not Brangane is sincere in this, but as she prepares for (saintly) martyrdom it is entirely conceivable that innocent Brangane remains faithful to Isolde and prays for the one who has sentenced her to death.

"I don't know anything about such a request. I gave my attendant over to your safekeeping for you to protect along the way, so that she could bring me [12,900] what I needed to get well. You will have to return her to me or both of you will lose your lives. You cowardly murderers will both hang or be burned at the stake!"

"Surely, my lady," they both responded immediately, "your attitude and meaning are not honest or honorable, and what you say changes every minute. [12,910] My lady, please stop your threats. Before we lose our lives, we will give her back to you as pretty and healthy as ever."

Isolde broke down in tears and said, "Don't lie to me anymore. Is Brangane alive or is she dead?"

"You confuse us, Isolde, but she is still alive."

"Oh dear, bring her back to me [12,920] and I will fulfill the promises I made to you earlier."

"Lady Isolde, it will be done."

Isolde kept one of them behind. The other rode back to where he had left Brangane and brought her back to her lady, Isolde. When she appeared before Isolde, Isolde took her into her arms and kissed her cheeks and mouth [12,930] again and again. She gave the men twenty marks each for the promise that they would keep the whole affair a secret.

Queen Isolde had found Brangane to be faithful and unwavering, even in the face of death. Her heart was completely without fault [12,940] and, tested by fire, had been found to be as pure as gold.[11] Brangane and Isolde were from then on so loyal and loving in their hearts and minds that there was nothing that could drive them apart. They were happy to be always together. Brangane was content at court, [12,950] and the court was full of praise for her. She was kind to everyone and bore no one a grudge, whether openly or in in private, and she was always at hand with advice for both the king and the queen. There was nothing that happened behind closed doors that Brangane did not know about.

She was especially attentive in her service to Isolde [12,960] and served her in any way that she wanted with regard to Tristan, her *ami*. They were able

---

11. The purification by fire refers to Proverbs 17:3, "The crucible for silver and the furnace for gold, but the Lord tests the heart." The question arises as to whether or not this was truly supposed to be a test of Brangane's loyalty, or if Isolde had a change of heart and changed her story. The syntax of the passage is not without its difficulties, and various translators have either put Isolde as the instigator of the test or made the passage passive. Hatto (likewise Krohn, Kühn): "Now that Queen Isolde . . . had smelted her in the crucible and refined her like gold" (1960, 211); whereas Knecht (2004a) translates: "Her [Brangane's] intentions were pure and without falsehood, smelted in the furnace and purified like gold" (Rein und ohne Falsch war ihr Sinn, im Tiegel geschmolzen und geläutert wie Gold); likewise Spiewok (1994): "after Brangane had like gold been purified in the furnace by the flames" (nachdem Brangaene also gleichsam wie Gold im Tiegel von der Flamme geläutert worden).

to do this so quietly that no one had the slightest suspicion. Their behavior, their speech, their conversations, and any other kind of interaction were all perfectly inconspicuous. No one had any idea. They were carefree and happy, [12,970] just as two lovers, able to find the time and opportunity whenever it pleases them, should be. They were *amie* and *ami* at all times and at every opportunity, always on the hunt for love. During the day they would often exchange intimate glances in the midst of a crowd of people. [12,980] With these meaningful glances they communicated what they were thinking and shared everything that lovers love. They did this day and night and without the least concern. They shared everything in word and deed, coming and going, whether sitting or standing, completely in the open. [12,990] Their public discourse, which was wonderfully clever, was at various times interlaced with subtle meaning. Their conversations were woven through with the language of love as with a golden thread.

No one thought their words or their conduct had the slightest thing to do with love [13,000] but put them off instead to the close kinship between Mark and Tristan, of which everyone was aware. This kinship provided cover for a great deal and let them play their games of love. Love overindulged in its sport by fooling many who had no idea how things really stood with regard to their love, which between them was flawless and complete. [13,010] Their thoughts, their feelings, all were in accord. Yes met yes, no met no, but yes and no, no and yes, that did not exist. There was nothing to divide them, both were the same. So the two passed the time tenderly, sometimes this way, sometimes that. [13,020] Sometimes they were happy, sometimes unhappy, as Love will have it between lovers. Love engenders hearts that are carefree and yet suffer, that are happy yet also distressed and pained.

When Tristan and his lady Isolde could not satisfy their desires, they suffered. One way or another [13,030] they were sad or happy. It was also unavoidable that anger reared its head, but I mean the kind of anger without malice.[12] If someone were to claim that anger was misplaced among lovers, then I would reply with conviction that he had never truly been in love. This is, in fact, the very nature of Love. [13,040] This is how she enflames the lovers and ignites their passions. Even if anger can be hurtful, lovers are soon reconciled by their devotion, love is renewed, and they are more devoted to each other than ever before. Just how their anger is first kindled and how they are then reconciled, this you have heard often enough. Lovers who are often

---

12. The theme of love and anger can be found in Ovid and other classical writers. In his *Amores*, II, 19 (1982, 135), Ovid speaks of the importance of rekindling the flame of love through temporary rejection. As in other cases, Gottfried seems led by a saying from Publilius Syrus (fl 85–43 BCE): "The lovers' anger is the renewal of love" (Amantium ira amoris integratio est; Maxim 37). Similar ideas can be found in Andreas Cappellanus's *Rules for Love* (2, 21, and 28).

[13,050] together and want to be together can easily suspect that someone else is more loved and closer than they are. They take the smallest doubt and start a huge fight, take the smallest concern but soon kiss and make up. This is the way it is, and we should allow them this. [13,060] Love is enriched in this way, it is made new again, and its devotion is refueled. Love grows poor and old, it cools off and turns cold if its flames are absent. If anger goes away, then Love can't rejuvenate itself. If friends have some small disagreement, [13,070] then devotion is always there, fresh and new again, to reconcile them. A quarrel renews fidelity and refines love like gold.

In this way Tristan and Isolde spent their time in love and in pain. Love and pain were constantly in flux, but I mean love without heart-rending pain. They did not yet know [13,080] the kind of heartache, the kind of misfortune that pierces the heart. They covered up their affair, anxiously keeping their secret strictly to themselves, and did so for quite a long time. They were both full of confidence and optimism, and their hearts felt carefree and happy. Isolde the queen [13,090] was loved by everyone in the realm, and the same was true of Tristan. He was celebrated and esteemed and greatly feared in all the kingdom.

Chapter 19: Gandin the Rote Player[13]

[13,097] Tristan was ambitious and spent much of his time in the earnest pursuit of his knightly duties. His leisure time was spent with falconry, and he went hunting whenever he had time. In those days a ship arrived in Cornwall, in Mark's port city, and with it a knight who was a noble baron from Ireland named Gandin. He was courteous, handsome, and wealthy, [13,110] and so strong and well-built that all of Ireland talked about his manly deeds. He appeared at Mark's court elegantly dressed as a knight, with gallant manners, but all by himself and without a shield or lance. On his back he had slung a small rote, [13,120] which was decorated with gold and gemstones and strung with superb strings.[14] After he had dismounted, he entered the great hall and greeted, as was proper, Mark and Isolde. He had on different

---

13. There has been considerable speculation on the meaning of this short story and the role it plays in furthering the plot. It seems to belong to older Tristan material. It is not included by Eilhart but is included in the Norse *Saga*. It certainly denigrates Mark as ruler, husband, and knight and correspondingly elevates Tristan to the status of Isolde's protector as well as lover. The story has certain illogical elements and is more along the lines of fantasy than Gottfried claims for his own tale.

14. This is the same Welsh instrument mentioned l. 3677 and again l. 7565 by Tristan, along with the harp. It is also called a crwth, rotta, or crowd, from Latin *chorus* or *crotta*.

occasions and at different times been Isolde's champion and secret admirer, [13,130] and he had come to Cornwall from Ireland just for her sake.[15]

She recognized him right away, and the well-mannered queen greeted him, "*Dieu vous bénisse, messire Gandin.*"[16]

"*Merci,*" replied Gandin, "*belle Isolt*, in Gandin's eyes you are as beautiful, no, more beautiful than gold."

Isolde then told the king under her breath who this was. [13,140] The king thought it very strange, as did everyone else, that he carried a rote on his back. Everyone had something to say about it. Mark did his best to honor him, for the sake of his own reputation and because Isolde asked him to. [13,150] She asked him to show him honor especially because he was a countryman of hers. Mark was certainly willing to do so, had him seated at his side, and asked him all sorts of things about his people and his country, the ladies and life at court. As food was being served and members of the household were washing their hands, [13,160] the water bowl came to him. He had been repeatedly asked to put aside his instrument, the rote, but no one could persuade him to do so. The king and queen let it go, but many thought his behavior uncourtly and improper. What was more, [13,170] some of them began to laugh and make jokes. The Knight of the Rote, this lord with his object of shame, paid them no attention. He was seated next to the king for the meal and drank and ate as he pleased.

After the tables had been cleared away, he arose and went [13,180] to sit with Mark's retainers. They kept him company and entertained him with all sorts of stories from court. Courteous King Mark, rich in all virtues, asked him in front of everyone if they might hear him play, assuming he could.

[13,190] The guest said, "My lord, I will not unless I first know the stakes."

"Sir, what do you mean by that? If you want something of mine, then you shall have it. Let us hear your artistry, and I will give you whatever you want."

"Done!" said the nobleman from Ireland.

He played a melody for them that was pleasant enough, [13,200] and the king asked him right away to play another. The swindler laughed to himself and then said, "The reward inspires me to play whatever you like."

He played the next one twice as well. After the second song was done, Gandin went to stand before the king with his rote in his hands. [13,210] "Now my lord," he said, "I remind you of the promise you made to me."[17]

---

15. Gandin undertakes this adventure as a Minnesinger or Troubadour. He expressly denies himself the martial trappings of a knight and so hopes to win Isolde through his own cleverness and artistry rather than strength, although he is prepared to fight for his rights if denied.
16. "May God protect you, my lord Gandin." "Thank you, beautiful Isolde."
17. The motif of the so-called rash boon, or blind promise (in German, "blanko Versprechen"), is not uncommon in Celtic and Arthurian literature. Numerous archetypes exist in biblical as well as Greek and Roman literature, such as Herod's promise to his daughter

The king replied, "Yes, I gladly remember my promise. Tell me, what do you want?"

"Isolde," he said. "Give her to me."

"My friend," he said, "whatever you want is yours, except for her. That will never happen."

"By my faith, lord," said Gandin, "I don't want anything else, large or small, [13,220] I want only Isolde."

The king answered, "Truly, that won't happen."

"My lord, so you refuse to keep your word? If it is determined that you are untrustworthy, then you will henceforth be unable to be king in any land. Let the king's law be read aloud. If it is not written there, [13,230] then I withdraw my demands. If you or anyone else claims that you did not make this promise to me, then I will prosecute my rights against you or him, as determined by the court. I will stake my life in combat if I am denied my rights. Whomever you choose, or you yourself, [13,240] will ride with me onto the field. I will prove at the appropriate time that beautiful Isolde belongs to me."

The king looked all around him to see if there was anyone who would dare to face this man. There was not one who would risk his life, and Mark was also not inclined [13,250] to fight for Isolde. Gandin was so strong, unyielding, and daring that no one wanted to fight him.

At the time, my lord Tristan had ridden out into the forest to go hunting. He would never have returned to court from the forest so quickly had he not heard the dreadful news along the way [13,260] that Isolde had been handed over to Gandin. It was all true, that is in fact what happened. Gandin had taken her, as she cried miserably and protested, from the court down to the harbor. At the harbor he had erected a wonderfully rich and impressive pavilion, which he entered with the queen [13,270] to wait for the tide to come back in. His ship was stuck on the sand and would need the tide to raise it up again.

In the meantime Tristan had returned and heard the story about the rote in greater detail. He immediately got on his horse and, taking his harp with him, [13,280] raced down to the harbor. When he got close, he shrewdly went up to a group of trees and tied his horse to a branch. He left his sword

---

(Mark 6:21–28) or in Ovid's *Metamorphoses* (detailed in Okken, 1996, 1.511–12). The medieval context juxtaposes the king's roles as warrior, judge, and patron of the arts. In a courtly context, the king no longer takes up arms personally, and so the defense of his judgments, or in this case an exaggerated promise or commitment, must be left to others. The king, in his desire to appear both magnanimous and discerning in his artistic tastes, ends up appearing rash, foolish, and weak, as he is unable to prioritize defending his kingdom and his queen over his patronage of a joyful court.

there as well.[18] He then ran the rest of the way with his harp to the pavilion, where he found the baron, and seated with him in his arms [13,290] was poor Isolde, wretched and sobbing. He was doing his best to console her, but to no effect. Then she saw the man with the harp.

Gandin greeted him and said, "*Dieu te protége, beau harpeur.*"[19]

"*Merci, noble chevalier.* Sir," he went on, [13,300] "I got here as fast as I could. I was told that you are from Ireland. Lord, so am I. As a man of honor, please bring me back to Ireland with you."

The man from Ireland promptly answered, "My friend, I promise you I will. First sit down and play something for me on your harp. If you can console my lady [13,310] and get her to stop crying, I will give you the best robe that can be found here in my pavilion."[20]

"I agree, my lord," said Tristan. "I'm confident that she will dry her tears, unless, that is, she won't stop crying regardless of who is playing."

He started to play [13,320] his harp, and the charming melody he performed crept into Isolde's heart. She was so lost in thought that she stopped crying, and her *ami* was all she could think about. As the song came to an end, the tide had finished raising the ship and it was afloat again. The crew shouted down [13,330] from the ship to the strand, "My lord, my lord, get on board. If Sir Tristan should arrive while you're still on dry land, there'll be trouble. The people and realm obey him, and they say that he's so fearless, daring, and brave [13,340] that he could make things difficult for you."

Gandin didn't like what he was hearing and replied heatedly, "God strike me down if I board any earlier today on that account. Dear friend, play the Lay of Dido[21] for me. You play the harp so well, I really do appreciate it. [13,350] Play it well for my lady. As thanks I will take you away from here with us and give you that robe I promised, the very best one I have."

Tristan said, "Lord, it is done."

The minstrel started to play, and his playing of the harp was so captivating [13,360] that Gandin gave it his undivided attention, and he could see that Isolde was also completely absorbed in the harp's music. When the song was done, Gandin took the queen and wanted to go to his ship. By now the tide was so high that the gangway was only accessible [13,370] with a very tall horse.

---

18. Leaving his horse and sword behind is a sign that Tristan again "disguises" himself, this time as a common minstrel. He is addressed (informally) as such by Gandin.

19. "May God protect you, handsome harpist." "Thank you, noble knight."

20. This turns out to be ironically prophetic, in that a robe can also be a metaphor for a lady. Walther von der Vogelweide made use of a similar metaphor in his poem *Frouwe, ir habet ein werdez dach* (L 62,36–40): "Lady, you have wrapped yourself in a worthy cover: a pure body. I have never seen a better robe. You are a well-dressed woman."

21. The story of Dido was well known to medieval audiences, and Heinrich von Veldeke's *Eneid* would have been one of the more likely sources for a German-speaking readership.

"What do we do now?" asked Gandin. "How will my lady board?"

"You see, my lord," said the minstrel, "since I know for certain that you will take me with you, there's no need to leave whatever I have in Cornwall. I have a tall horse near here, [13,380] and I think it's tall enough to carry your lady companion safely to the ramp so that she won't get wet."

Gandin replied, "Dear minstrel, hurry and fetch your horse, and take your robe with you as well."

Tristan quickly retrieved his horse and upon returning [13,390] slung his harp on his back and said, "So, my lord from Ireland, lift your lady up to me, and I will take her to the ramp."

"No, minstrel," said Gandin. "I don't want you to touch her. I'll take her myself."

"My lord," said fair Isolde, "all of this is completely unnecessary just so that he won't touch me. [13,400] You can be sure that I won't get on board unless the minstrel takes me."

Gandin lifted her up to Tristan. "Friend," he said, "watch out for her and take her across carefully, so that I may reward you accordingly."

As soon as he had Isolde on the horse, he backed away a bit, and when Gandin saw this, [13,410] he shouted at him, "Hey, you fool! What's going on?"

"No, you've got it wrong," replied Tristan. "The fool is named Gandin. Friend, you're the one who has been fooled. What you cheated Mark out of with your rote playing has been taken back with the harp. You are a cheat, and now you've been cheated. Tristan was on your heels until he was able to get the better of you. [13,420] Friend, you give away truly rich clothing, but now I have the best of what could be found in your tent."

Tristan rode off down the path. Gandin was dismayed beyond measure and was wounded to the core on account of his loss and humiliation. He traveled back across the sea disgraced and aggrieved. [13,430] The two travel companions, Tristan and Isolde, went their own way back home. I don't want to presume that they enjoyed each other resting among the flowers somewhere along the way. I should refrain from speculation and speculating. Tristan brought Isolde back to his uncle Mark [13,440] and reproached him in the strongest terms.

"In Christ's name," he said, "if the queen truly means something to you, how could you be so stupid and give her away for a harp or rote song? The whole world will scoff at this. Who ever heard of a queen being bought with rote playing? Don't ever do this again. Watch over my lady more carefully!"[22]

---

22. The irony is great. Tristan is effectively telling Mark to protect his wife from himself, Tristan. This theme can be found in Ovid, *Amores* II, 19 (1982, 136).

Chapter 20: Mariodoc the Seneschal

[13,451] Tristan's esteem and honor grew all the more, both at court and throughout the realm, as people praised Tristan's ingenuity and intelligence. He and the queen were carefree and full of joy again, and they made each other happy whenever they could. [13,460] At the time Tristan had a friend who was a noble baron, one of the king's retainers, his first seneschal, and his name was Mariodoc. He had befriended Tristan on account of the gentle queen, since he secretly had feelings for her, [13,470] just as many men do for many women who hardly notice them. The seneschal and Tristan shared lodgings and gladly spent time together. The seneschal had the habit, since Tristan was a good story teller, of sleeping near Tristan so that they could talk. [13,480] It happened one night, after talking about this and that and sharing stories with Tristan, that he fell asleep. Tristan, who was in love, snuck out in secret to venture into the open, much to the queen's and his misfortune. [13,490] Since he was confident that no one was watching him, Misfortune laid her trap, her hounds, and her chase along the same path that he happily took to see Isolde. The path had been covered by snow that night, and the moon shone brightly and clearly. [13,500] Tristan didn't see any danger nor was he aware of any trap, and so he quickly went to the agreed-upon secret meeting place. When he entered the room, Brangane took a chess board and placed it in front of the light, but I don't know why she left the door open [13,510] when she went back to bed.

While all this was happening, the seneschal had a dream as he slept, and in it he saw a terrible wild boar that came running out of the forest. It ran to the king's court, foaming at the mouth and baring its teeth, fighting everything that got in its way. [13,520] Many of the court staff rushed up, and a good many knights were running around the boar, but there was no one bold enough to confront it. So the boar roamed throughout the castle and, coming to Mark's chamber, broke down the door. [13,530] It ransacked his bed and with his slobber soiled all the coverings that made up the king's bedding. All of Mark's men saw this, but no one did anything about it.[23]

After Mariodoc awoke he couldn't stop thinking about the dream, which had frightened him. [13,540] He called out for Tristan, wanting to tell him about his dream, but no one answered. He called out again and again and then reached over to the bed. When he found it was empty and no one was there, he suspected right away that Tristan was at some clandestine rendezvous.

---

23. Tristan's coat of arms is the black boar (on his shield at the dragon fight). The dream focuses on the main features of the current situation: Tristan's desecration of the marriage, with sexual overtones, and the court's unwillingness or inability to intervene. There is some validity to thinking that the boar symbolism for Tristan heightens the notion of a hunt and its prey.

[13,550] He had no idea, however, and would never have imagined that he had a secret relationship with the queen. He was a bit annoyed, though, that even though they were friends he hadn't shared his secret with him.

Mariodoc quickly got up, [13,560] dressed himself, and quietly tiptoed to the door. He looked out and, seeing Tristan's footprints, followed the tracks through a small orchard. The light of the moon guided him through the snow and the grounds that Tristan had crossed earlier, up to the chamber's door. [13,570] He stood at the door, frightened but suddenly suspicious because the door was open, thinking all the while about where Tristan might have gone. He considered different explanations, both good and bad. At first he thought that Tristan had come on account of some young lady of the court, but then he thought about it [13,580] and quickly came to the conclusion that he was inside with the queen. He deliberated back and forth but finally took heart and entered quietly. There was no light and no illumination from the moon either. The candle that was burning did him little good because a chessboard had been placed in front of it. [13,590] So he felt his way forward with his hands along the walls until he found their bed, where he could hear both of them and everything they were doing. He was deeply hurt and his heart was broken, because he had long loved and venerated Isolde himself. [13,600] All that now turned to hatred and pain. He had equal parts of both: hatred and pain, pain and hatred; he suffered from both. He couldn't figure out the right thing to do in this situation. Hatred and pain urged him [13,610] to act contrary to civility and tell the world right then and there what was happening, but his fear of Tristan and what he might do to him made him think better of it. So he turned around and left. He was greatly upset but went back to bed anyway.

[13,620] Shortly thereafter Tristan returned as well and quietly crept back into bed. He was silent, the other man was silent, neither one said a word, which was unusual and had never happened before. Tristan could tell that something was bothering his friend, [13,630] and he was more careful from then on with regard to what he said and what he did than he had been before. It was too late, though, since the secret was out and his affair had been discovered.

Mariodoc, who was jealous, took the king aside and told him [13,640] that rumors were being spread at court about Tristan and Isolde that people around the realm found disturbing. The king ought to pay attention and take counsel as to what he should do about it. Nothing short of his marriage and his honor was at stake. He didn't tell him, however, [13,650] that he knew the real story and the truth of the matter. Mark, the most loyal and trusting king, was naïve enough to be greatly surprised by this, and he didn't want to believe that Isolde, the north star of his joy, might act improperly. [13,660] He carried this burden in silent suffering, but he was constantly on the lookout for anything that might confirm all this. He paid close attention to what they said and how they acted, but he was unable to uncover any real evidence, [13,670] because Tristan had told Isolde about the seneschal's suspicions. Nonetheless Mark kept at it and steadfastly watched them day and night.

One night as he lay next to her and they were talking back and forth, he [13,680] shrewdly set a trap for the queen and caught her in it. "My lady," he said, "tell me, what do you think about this, what would be your advice? In the near future I'd like to go on a pilgrimage, and I might be gone quite a long time. In whose care would you want me to place you during this time?"[24]

[13,690] "My God," replied the queen, "how can you ask such a thing? In whose care would I and your people and your realm be better placed than in your nephew's hands, who can best protect our interests? Sir Tristan, your sister's son, is courageous and wise and prudent in all things."

Her answer was disconcerting and made Mark [13,700] even more suspicious. He continued to set traps for her and watched her more than ever, and he immediately told the seneschal everything he had found out.

The seneschal answered him, "Certainly, my lord, it's true. You can see from all this [13,710] that she can't keep her great love for him under wraps, and it is most unwise that you tolerate his presence here. If you love your wife and value your honor, then you should no longer put up with him."

All of this weighed heavily on Mark. The doubt and suspicion that he now felt against his nephew was like a living death for him, [13,720] even though he failed to uncover any kind of misconduct on his part.

Isolde, who had been duped, was perfectly content. She laughed and told Brangane in her joy all about her lord's pilgrimage, and also how he had asked her in whose care she wanted to be placed. [13,730]

Brangane replied, "My lady, don't lie to me and tell me, so help you God, whom did you pick?"

Isolde told her the truth, just as it had happened.

"Oh, that was foolish," said Brangane. "How could you say that? Whatever you might have said, it was a trick, I can see that now, and I know for sure [13,740] that the seneschal put him up to it. They want to test you in this way. You'll have to be more careful in the future. If he mentions it again, then say what I'm about to tell you. Speak to him like this," and she tutored her lady on how she should answer these kinds of ploys.

In the meantime, Mark suffered from [13,750] two afflictions. He was haunted by the doubts and suspicions that he harbored and could not shake. He had doubts about his dearest Isolde, and he suspected Tristan, even though he could discover no false [13,760] or disloyal behavior. His friend Tristan,

---

24. Even as queen, a woman was required to be under the protection and supervision of a man at all times.

his joy Isolde, these two were his greatest anguish. They tormented his heart and his thoughts. He suspected him and her and distrusted them both. He suffered from these two afflictions as one might expect and as would most people. Whenever he wanted [13,770] to make love to Isolde his suspicions kept him away, and then all he wanted to do was get to the bottom of it all and find out the truth. When he was unable to do so, his doubts tormented him all the more, and things remained just as before.

What can do more damage to love than doubt and suspicion? What inhibits the desires of the heart [13,780] more than doubt? You never know where it might lead. You might be certain of some misdeed that you had heard or seen and so think that you were done. But before you know it, everything changes and something else comes to light creating new doubts [13,790] and resulting in more confusion. Even though everyone does it, it really is foolish to bring doubt into love. No one can be happy in love if he doubts that love.

It is even worse to try to gain certainty about these doubts and anxieties. [13,800] Even though it might have been a great aspiration to hunt down the truth, if someone were actually to accomplish that, that is to turn doubt into certainty, it would become a source of even greater heartache. The two aforementioned afflictions that weighed so heavily on him would then seem good by comparison. If he could recapture these, [13,810] he would gladly choose doubt and suspicion over finding out the truth. As it happens, bad things only get worse until something even worse comes along, something even more hurtful, and then the original evil seems good. As much as doubt harms love, it is never so harmful as not to be greatly preferred to [13,820] proof of wrongdoing.

In any case, there is no way around all this. Love will engender doubt. Doubt is a part of love, and with it love can save itself. As long as there is doubt, there is hope. Once love knows the truth, it is lost. Love has a certain propensity [13,830] that causes the greatest bewilderment and confusion. When everything is going well, it quickly loses interest and moves on to something else. Wherever it might find cause for doubt, however, it latches on and won't let go. It sets all sorts of traps and does all it can [13,840] to uncover its own heartache rather than find the pleasure it could have instead. It was this pointless propensity that Mark followed as well. Day and night he thought of nothing else but how to alleviate his doubts and suspicions and find out the truth, [13,850] the truth that would bring him nothing but heartache.

It so happened one night that he and Mariodoc had conceived a plan together to entrap Isolde and finally expose her, [13,860] but things turned out quite differently. The snare that he set to entrap her was used instead by the queen to catch the king, her lord, thanks to Brangane's instructions. Brangane was a great help, and the two of them set one trap against the other.

The king pressed the queen [13,870] close to him and kissed her over and over again, on her eyes and mouth. "My love," he said, "nothing is as dear to me as you, and now that I have to part from you, as God is my witness, I will go out of my mind."

The queen, who was well prepared, countered his move with her own. [13,880] She turned to him with sighs and said, "Oh, dear me, oh my! Oh, I was thinking all this time that this cursed notion was just a joke. Now I hear it again and see that you are serious."

Her eyes and mouth started to cry, and she lamented her suffering [13,890] so vehemently that any doubt that gullible man might have had was removed. He would have sworn that she was being sincere. This is true of all women, and they say so themselves. There may be no bitterness or deception or falseness in them, [13,900] but they can cry about anything at the drop of a hat and as often as it suits them.[25] Isolde was weeping and sobbing.

Mark, a trusting soul, said, "My dear, tell me, what's the matter, why are you crying?"

"I can't help it," she replied. "I'm crying because I have every reason to do so. I'm a woman living in a foreign country, [13,910] and all I have is myself and the good sense that I've been given. I have completely dedicated these to you and your love, so that I cherish you alone in all my thoughts. I love no one but you, but I know for a fact that you don't care as much about me [13,920] as you pretend to or say. That you intend to go away and leave me here in this strange land leads me to the conclusion that you don't care for me very much. Because of that my heart and my mind can never again be happy."

"But why, my dearest?" he said. "You have authority over [13,930] the realm and all its people, they belong to me and to you. You are their ruler, they will obey you. Whatever you command, it will be done. While I am gone, you will be under the protection of the one who can protect you best, my nephew, noble Tristan. He is prudent and intelligent, [13,940] and he will make every effort to provide for and increase your joy and honor. I trust him, as I have every reason to. He loves you and me equally, he will act for your sake and mine."

"Sir Tristan?" replied beautiful Isolde. "Truth be told, I would rather be dead and buried [13,950] than willingly give my consent to be in his care. That groveling phony is constantly hanging around, flattering me and telling me how much I mean to him. God knows what he's really thinking and how sincere he really is. I know it well enough myself. [13,960] He killed my uncle and is afraid that I hate him for it. It is out of fear that he hangs

---

25. This is taken almost directly from Ovid, *Remedia amores*: "Don't let yourself be softened by a girl in tears—they school their eyes to weep on request" (689–91; 1982, 259). P. Syrus (1856) also says: "Women have learned to cry in pretense" (Maxim 130).

around, ingratiating himself and fawning over me in his dissembling, all the while thinking that this is how he can gain my friendship. But it won't do any good, his flattery will get him nowhere. [13,970] God knows that it's only because of you and your honor's sake, not mine, that I pretend to be friendly. Otherwise I wouldn't even give him the time of day.

"Since I can't avoid hearing and seeing him, I will continue to do so. But my heart isn't in it, [13,980] and I really don't want to. I readily admit that I have often given him my attention and looked at him and spoken to him, but dispassionately and insincerely, only because it is often said of women that they dislike their husbands' friends. This is why I frequently wasted his time [13,990] with lying eyes and disingenuous words, and I'm sure that he would have sworn that I did it all from the heart. My lord, don't let that sway you. Your nephew Tristan should not watch over me for even a day. If I might ask a favor, then I think you should care for me yourself while you are traveling, [14,000] if you agree. Wherever you go, I want to go as well, unless you forbid it or death prevents it."

This is how Isolde, beguiling as she was, duped her lord and her husband. She conned him into giving up his doubt and anger, and he would have sworn that she really meant it all. [14,010] Mark, the doubter, had found his way back to solid ground. His sweetheart had taken away doubt and suspicion from him. Everything she said and did was now just fine. The king told the seneschal right away, as accurately as he could, how she had replied and what she had said, [14,020] and that there was nothing about her that was false in any way. This pained the seneschal, and he was deeply offended, yet he continued to give him ideas and tell him how he could test Isolde once again.

During the night, after Mark had gone to bed and was chatting with Isolde as usual, he tried again[14,030] to set a trap for her with his questions, hoping to trip her up.[26] "You see," he said, "my lady and queen, I think that great difficulties lie ahead of us. Let me see for myself how well women can rule a land. My lady, I have to leave the realm, and you will stay here along with my supporters and allies. Whether family or vassal, [14,040] everyone who supports me will provide for your needs and your honor when you ask it of them. Whomever you don't like or don't want around, whether ladies or knights, just send them away. You shouldn't have to hear or see people or things [14,050] that you don't like. I don't want to hold anyone dear, be it with heart or mind, against whom you hold a grudge. That's the truth. To live a happy and carefree life, however you think best, that's what I want for you, too, and since you have such strong feelings against my nephew Tristan,

---

26. Compare the previous lines 11,930–34 in terms of hunting terminology and asking and questioning.

[14,060] I will in short order expel him from the court and the household, just as soon as I can find the right opportunity. He will need to go back to Parmenie and take care of his own affairs, for his own sake and that of his own lands."

"That is very kind of you, my lord," replied Isolde. "You speak with devotion and careful consideration. Now that I know that you readily dislike [14,070] the same things that burden my heart, then it seems to me only right that I should be considerate, as much as possible, of whatever brings your eyes pleasure and your heart joy. I will support and assist you at all times with all things that may increase your honor. Consider, my lord, what you do. [14,080] I don't think it is advisable, now or in the future, to expel your nephew from the court, as this would harm my own honor. People at court and around the realm would immediately say that I had advised you to do this out of hatred and as vengeance for the death of my uncle. [14,090] All this gossip would be unpleasant for me and would not increase your reputation either. I won't support you in maligning a friend on my account, or that anybody should be vilified or hated for my sake, if they warrant your esteem instead.

"You should also consider this. [14,100] Who will protect your two lands while you are away? A woman's hand will keep them neither well nor peaceful. Whoever desires to rule two kingdoms with justice and honor must have intelligence and courage. There is no one in these two realms, no lord if left to the task besides Sir Tristan [14,110] who could do the realm justice. Except for him there is no one who could determine what to do or not to do. If war breaks out, which can happen at any time and for which we must always be prepared, it could easily happen that we might lose. Then my lord Tristan would constantly be held up to me with malice and spite, [14,120] and everyone would be saying, 'If Tristan had been here, things would not have gone as badly as they did.' And then there would be a big commotion blaming me for his loss of favor, to their and your detriment. [14,130] My lord, it is better left undone. Reconsider your options carefully, think about one and then the other: either let me go with you or hand over the protection of the realm to Tristan. Regardless of how I might feel about him, I would rather he be here than have some other man fail us."

The king could see right away [14,140] that she was intent on advancing Tristan's honor, and so he began to have his doubts and suspicions as before. He fell ever deeper into his old bitterness and anger. Isolde reported their conversation to Brangane, telling her everything [14,150] and leaving nothing out. Brangane was very upset that she had said the things she did and that the conversation had taken this turn. She tutored her again in what she should say from then on.

That night, as the queen went to bed with her husband, she took him in her arms, embracing and kissing him, [14,160] and pressed him closely to her soft, supple breasts. She started to lay her rhetorical traps with questions and answers, saying, "My lord, tell me for my sake, have you reconsidered your decision with regard to my lord Tristan? You told me [14,170] that you would send him back to his own land on my account. If I could be sure of what you said, then I would be thankful to you now and forever more. Lord, I have complete faith in you, just as I should and must. My fear is, though, that this is all a test. If I could know for sure, [14,180] as you have explained it to me, that you really want to keep me apart from the things I dislike, then I could be sure from what you say that you love me. I've been wanting to ask this favor for a while, except that I had reservations because I know very well what I can expect from him [14,190] if I'm around him much longer.

"Now, my lord, think about this and don't decide based on my hatred for him. If he should rule the realm while you are gone, and if something should happen to you, which is not out of the question on such a journey, then he will surely take away my honor and my land. Now you recognize what he can do to me. [14,200] Think about this carefully and consider your love for me, and if you can free me from my lord Tristan, then that would be for the best. Send him home again or arrange it so that he accompanies you. Your seneschal Mariodoc can then be responsible for me. If you were in favor of taking me with you, [14,210] then I would have somebody else in charge of the realm, as long as I could be with you. Whatever you decide about the realm and about me, do as you think best. This is my wish and my desire. As long as I can be sure that I am doing your will, then what happens [14,220] with the realm and its people is inconsequential."

This is how she misled her husband until she had him to the point again where he abandoned his doubts and suspicions about her intentions and feelings and deemed the queen innocent of any wrongdoing. He thought that the seneschal Mariodoc, however, [14,230] was a shameless liar, even though he had told him the complete truth about her.

Chapter 21: Melot the Dwarf

[14,235] **W**hen the seneschal realized that his plan wasn't working, he tried again another way. There was a dwarf at the court who was apparently named Melot *petit* from Aquitaine,[27] and people said that he had the ability to read hidden mysteries from the night stars. I don't want to say anything

---

27. Only Gottfried includes the name Melot from those sources we have. The dwarf's name might be related to Merlin, derived from a diminutive form *Merlot*, which would mean "little

about him except what I read myself in the source. The only thing I know for sure based on the real version is that he was clever, cunning, and good with words. [14,250] He was one of the king's intimates and also had access to the private quarters. Mariodoc and he conspired to spy on Tristan and the queen whenever he visited the ladies' chambers. If Melot could help him find out the truth about their affair, [14,260] then Mark would forever reward him with wealth and honors. Day and night he employed his lies and tricks to observe their conversations and actions at all hours and soon enough discovered the love they shared. They treated each other with such tenderness [14,270] that Melot quickly had proof of their affair, and he informed Mark that they really were in love. The three of them, Melot and Mark and Mariodoc, kept at it and came up with a plan. If Tristan were expelled from the court, [14,280] they would see by their behavior what the truth of the matter was. No sooner had they agreed than they put their plan into action.

The king requested that his nephew stay away from the ladies' chambers for the good of his own reputation, and also to avoid any places where ladies spent time. [14,290] There were rumors going around the court, and they had to be careful that the king and the queen weren't disgraced and dishonored. Everything he commanded and ordered was carried out immediately. Tristan avoided all the places where women could be by themselves and never again frequented their chambers and the palace. [14,300] The household was surprised by his sudden absence and spread hurtful rumors about him. He had his fill of hearing ugly gossip. He and Isolde, both of them, spent their days with worry, sorrow, and complaint as constant companions. [14,310] They suffered twice over. Mark's suspicions made them suffer, and they suffered because they had no opportunities to be alone. Both of them began, little by little, to lose their vigor and strength. They became ever more pale, [14,320] the man lost his coloring because of the woman, the woman lost her coloring because of the man, Tristan because of Isolde, Isolde because of Tristan. Both of them were in dire straits.

I'm not the least bit surprised that they suffered together and that their pain was inseparable. Between the two of them they had only one heart and one desire. [14,330] Their shared pain, their shared happiness, their shared death, their shared life, all these were woven together as one. Whatever one of them felt, the other felt it, too. Whatever was pleasing to one promptly made the other one happy. They were completely united in suffering and happiness. Their shared heartache [14,340] was apparent in their faces and their love was unmistakably visible in their coloring. Mark could see it right away and understood that their estrangement and separation had hurt them

---

Merlin." This would certainly fit Gottfried's (and presumably Thomas's) description of Melot as knowledgeable in the arcane and magical arts (see Okken, 1996, 1.529, n. 14,240).

to the core and that, if they had known where or how, they would have tried
to see each other.

[14,350] He thought up another scheme and called the hunters to prepare themselves and the hounds immediately to go out to the forest. He told
them and let it be known around court that the hunt would last twenty days.
Whoever was interested in hunting or wanted to take part in the amusement
[14,360] should get ready. He said good-bye to the queen and encouraged
her to do whatever she pleased, to be joyful and happy at home. He privately
ordered the dwarf Melot to spy on Tristan and Isolde and their clandestine
activities. He would be sure to reward him for it. [14,370] As for himself,
Mark rode out to the forest with much ado. His hunting companion Tristan
stayed at home, having told his uncle that he was ill. The unwell huntsman
wanted to visit his own hunting grounds. He and Isolde, both of them suffering in sadness, [14,380] wanted to seize the opportunity and tried hard to
come up with a way to see each other, but they couldn't come up with a plan.

It was during this time that Brangane went to see Tristan, knowing full
well that he suffered severely [14,390] from this heartache. She complained
to him, and he to her.

"Ah, virtuous one," he said, "tell me how to get out of this dilemma. What
can poor Isolde and I do so that we don't perish? I don't know what we
should do to save ourselves."

"What advice can I give you?" the faithful woman replied. [14,400] "God
may well regret that we were ever born. All three of us have lost our happiness and our honor, we can never again be free like before. Poor Isolde! Poor
Tristan! That I ever set eyes on you. All of your hardship is my fault. [14,410]
Now I don't even have a plan, I can't think of a way to help you or be of use.
I am dead certain that a great disaster awaits you if you are watched and separated for much longer. Since there is nothing else to do, then at least take this
advice for now, I mean, [14,420] as long as you are apart from us. If you see
an opportunity, take a branch from an olive tree and whittle off some wood
chips lengthwise. Make a mark on each one with a 'T' on one end and an
'I' on the other, so that just the first letter of your names appears. [14,430]
Don't write any more than that, and then go down to the orchard. You know
the little stream that flows from the spring down to the women's apartments.
Take one of the wood chips and throw it in, then let it float down in front of
the door of our rooms. That's where unhappy Isolde and I often sit [14,440]
crying with our broken hearts. If we see a wood piece floating by, then we'll
know that you're at the spring. Wait in the shade of the olive tree and keep
watch there. The one who yearns for you will come to you, my lady, your
lover, and I will too, if it's possible and if you want me to. [14,450] Lord, the
short time that I have left to live I want to spend with the two of you, so that
I can devote my life to both of you and advise you what to do. If I could give

up a thousand of my hours for just one hour of joy for you, I would give up all my days [14,460] to diminish your misery."

"Thank you, my dear," replied Tristan. "I have no doubt whatsoever that you are loyal and honorable. The two have never been more perfectly united in one heart. Should I have any good fortune at all, then I will put it toward your happiness and honor. As bad as things are right now, [14,470] and as much as the Wheel of Fortune has turned against me, if I knew how to give up my days and hours for your happiness, I would gladly shorten my life, you can be certain of that."

He then said to her through his tears, "My dear, faithful woman!" and pressed her close to him in a warm embrace. [14,480] He kissed her eyes and her cheeks again and again in his misery. "My dear," he said, "do as your loyalty commands and take me and the yearning sufferer, blessed Isolde, under your wings. Think of the two of us, of her and me, always."

[14,490] "My lord, I do so gladly. By your leave I will go now. Do as I have told you and don't worry too much."

"May God watch over your honor and your beauty."

Brangane bowed and departed, with tears in her eyes and filled with sadness. Unhappy Tristan cut and threw the wood chips, [14,500] just as Brangane had instructed him. So it was that he and his lady Isolde found their way to the spring in the shade of the tree eight times in as many days, in secret and at opportune moments. No one was aware or saw anything. It happened one night, though, as Tristan was on his way there again, [14,510] that Melot, that cursed dwarf and tool of the devil, unfortunately saw him, I don't know how. He followed him all the way there and saw him going up to the tree and waiting there a short while before a lady came to him and ran into his arms. But he wasn't able to see [14,520] exactly who the lady was.

The next day shortly before noon, Melot snuck down the path again, this time filled with false complaints and evil lies. Coming up to Tristan, he said, "By my faith, sir, I had a difficult time coming here to you. [14,530] You are surrounded by watchers and spies and it was with some difficulty that I was able to make my way here unseen. I feel sorry for Isolde, that faithful and virtuous queen, who is now in great trouble on your account. She asked me to come here to you, [14,540] because she didn't have anyone else better suited to bring this message. She instructed me to pass on her greetings most sincerely, and to ask you urgently to go speak with her, I don't know where, but you know the place where you met her most recently. [14,550] You should go at the exact same time as usual. I don't know what she wants to warn you of. Please believe me when I say that nothing has caused me more sorrow than her pain and your suffering. Now sir, my lord Tristan, by your leave I must go. [14,560] I will convey to her whatever message you have, but I don't dare stay here any longer. If the courtiers found out that I had come here, I could suffer for it. They all say and suspect that whatever has happened between the two of you was done with my assistance. I swear to God and to the both of you that I never [14,570] had anything to do with it."

"My friend, are you delirious?" replied Tristan. "What kind of tall tale are you accusing me of? What do the courtiers suspect? What is it that my lady and I are supposed to have done? Go! Go to hell! You can be sure of this. Whatever people may think or say, if it weren't out of consideration for my own honor, [14,580] I'd make sure that you never spread rumors again at court like the ones you dreamed up here."

Melot left and immediately rode to the forest where Mark was staying. He assured him that he had finally gotten to the bottom of the true story. He told him everything exactly as it had happened there at the spring. [14,590] "You can find out the truth for yourself, my lord," said Melot, "if you like. Ride with me there tonight. I am more certain of this than anything that, however they may arrange it, they will both be there tonight, and you can see for yourself what the two of them are up to."

The king rode out with Melot to that place to lie in wait for what would break his heart. [14,600] As they arrived in the orchard around nightfall and prepared for their undertaking, neither the king nor the dwarf could find a place to hide that was suitable for their purpose. There where the spring flowed stood a medium-sized olive tree with low branches and a broad canopy. [14,610] With some effort they both climbed up the tree and sat there in silence. [28]

As it was turning night Tristan stealthily moved along the path again. Once he had come to the orchard he took his messengers in hand and put them into the flowing stream, letting them float away. As always they announced [14,620] to the yearning Isolde that her lover was there. Tristan then went beyond the stream to the grass where the olive tree cast its shadow. He stood there lost in thought, meditating on his unseen anguish. It so happened that he caught sight of Mark's and Melot's shadows, [14,630] since the moon was shining brightly through the tree. Once he had clearly discerned the two shadows, he was concerned because he realized that he had fallen into a trap.

"God almighty," he prayed to himself, "watch over Isolde and me. If she doesn't recognize the trap [14,640] by these shadows in time, then she'll run to meet me. If that happens, then we'll surely suffer harm and injury. God almighty, safeguard both of us in your mercy. Protect Isolde on her way here, guide her every step, find some way to warn the innocent of this trap and the malice [14,650] aimed at both of us, before she can say or do something that

---

28. This scene, with Mark and Melot hiding in the tree, is the most frequently depicted scene of the Tristan story in medieval art.

would lead to hateful conclusions. Dear God almighty, have mercy on her and on me. Our honor and our lives are in your hands tonight."[29]

His lady, the queen, and their mutual friend, noble Brangane, [14,660] went out into their garden of lamentation to await Tristan's messengers. There they could commiserate at all hours of the day, provided they weren't being watched. They paced back and forth in sorrow, grieving and relating their tales of woe. Soon enough Brangane saw [14,670] the messengers, the wood chips, in the stream. She waved for her lady to join her.

Isolde retrieved some and looked at them. She read 'Isolde' and read 'Tristan'. She quickly put on her hooded cloak, covered her head, and stole through the flowers and the grass to where the spring and tree were located. Once she was close enough for them [14,680] to see each other, Tristan stood completely still, something he had never done before. She had never gone to him before without him going out to meet her. Isolde now wondered and asked herself what this meant. Her heart became heavy. She lowered her head [14,690] and fearfully approached him, she was frightened the entire way. As she cautiously came a bit closer to the tree, she glimpsed the shadows of three men, even though she saw only one man there. From this and also from Tristan's behavior, she immediately recognized the trap and the danger.

[14,700] "Ah, murderous conspiracy!" she thought. "What is going on? Why have they set this ambush? My husband must surely be here somewhere, wherever he's hiding himself. I think we must have been betrayed. Protect us, my Lord! Help us get out of this with our honor intact. Lord, save him and me!" [14,710] She went on thinking, "Does Tristan know about this plot or not?" She quickly came to the conclusion that he had spotted the trap based on the way he was behaving.

She stayed some distance from him and said, "Sir Tristan, I am offended that you are so certain of my gullible nature [14,720] that you would expect me to agree to a meeting at this late hour. It would be better if you satisfied your obligations to your uncle and me, both in terms of your own loyalty and my honor, rather than request such a late meeting with all this secrecy. [14,730] So tell me, what do you want? With some trepidation I am here, but only because Brangane, after she left you today, would not stop pleading with me to come see you here and listen to your complaint. It was a grave mistake to give in to her, but she is close by. [14,740] Even though I may be secure here, threatened by evil men as I am, I would still rather lose a finger from my hand than have it become known that I was here with you tonight. People have been saying all kinds of things about you and me. They would

---

29. Although this prayer and others by Tristan or Isolde have been criticized as disingenuous, or as attempts to enlist God's help for a sinful enterprise, this prayer in particular emphasizes the couple's vulnerability and seeks God's protection in a time of danger.

all swear that we were involved [14,750] in an adulterous relationship. The entire court suspects as much. God himself knows very well how my heart feels about you. I want to make it even clearer. As God is my witness, may my sins only be forgiven according to how I have felt about you. [14,760] I swear to God that I have never had feelings for any man and have today and for all time forsworn all men in my heart except for one, the first, the one who took the rosebud of my maidenhead.[30]

"That my lord Mark would suspect me so on your account, Sir Tristan, [14,770] God knows that he does wrong by me, especially since he knows how I feel about you. Those who have been spreading rumors about me, God knows, they don't know a thing. They don't know anything about how I feel. I have shown you kindness a hundred thousand times for the sake of the love that I feel for the one whom I should love, [14,780] and not out of infidelity, as God knows all too well. It seems to me proper that I honor whomever is dear to or related to my husband Mark, whether knight or squire, and that this honors me as well. Now this is being used against me. Still I don't want to bear a grudge against you on account of all their lies. [14,790] Sir, whatever you want to say to me, say it, because I want to go. I can't stay here any longer."

"Blessed lady," said Tristan, "I have no doubt that if you could, you would say and do only what virtue and honor demand. It's the liars, those who have suspected us [14,800] and unfairly robbed us of our lord's esteem, who prevent you from doing so, even though God knows very well that we are completely innocent. Blessed and virtuous queen, please know and believe that I am completely innocent as regards you and him, and counsel my lord that he should graciously temper [14,810] his anger and hatred, which he holds against me without cause, for at least another week for the sake of his own civility. For this long may you both at least pretend to hold me in your favor. In the meantime I'll prepare everything necessary for me to leave. [14,820] If you continue to treat me this way before I leave, then the king, my lord, and you and I will all lose our honor. Our enemies will say, 'Surely, there must have been some truth to it. Just look at how Sir Tristan left under the cloud of the king's displeasure.'"

"My lord Tristan," Isolde replied, [14,830] "I would rather die than ask my lord to do something for my sake that concerns you. You know very well that for a long time now he has been upset with me because of you. If he knew or were to hear that I'm meeting you alone at this late hour [14,840] there

---

30. This part of the oath, although technically true as it is worded, plays not only on Isolde's feelings for Tristan, that is, she claims that she was never in love with any other man, but also on the fact that Tristan first took Isolde's virginity, something that was a grave crime against his lord Mark, to whom he has sworn an oath of loyalty. In a sense, these two oaths are in competition with each other.

would be no end to the scandal, and he would never again bestow his love or honor on me. In fact I don't know if he will ever do so again. I still don't know how my lord Mark came by this suspicion or who counseled him in this matter. I have never observed, [14,850] although women quickly notice such things, that you intended to dishonor me with some gesture, nor have I ever done anything dishonorable or imprudent toward you. I don't know what brought us in disrepute, but our situation is dangerous and deplorable. May God almighty consider this and provide [14,860] relief and restoration.

"Now, sir, by your leave I will be gone, and you should go as well. God knows that your burden and your hardships sadden me. I have sufficient cause to hate you, but I will refrain from this. I am sorry that you suffer on my account [14,870] through no fault of your own. For that reason I will overlook all this, and when the day comes that you must leave this land, then, lord, I pray that God protect you, and may the Queen of Heaven watch over you. If I could be certain that my counsel would carry any weight, [14,880] then I would say and do whatever seemed best to bring your petition and your message to a successful outcome. I'm afraid, though, that the king would turn it all around. Whatever may happen, however difficult it might be for me, I do recognize that you have done nothing dishonorable toward my lord and me. [14,890] Whatever the result may be, I will bring your petition forward to the best of my ability."

"Thank you, my lady," said Tristan. "Whatever reply you receive, please let me know right away. If I should become aware of something and have to leave immediately, never to see you again, regardless of what happens to me [14,900] may the heavenly host bless you, noblest queen. God knows all too well that earth and sea have never borne such a blameless woman. Lady, your soul and your body, your honor and your life, may they be forever in God's hands."

So they went their separate ways. The queen sighed and left in sadness. [14,910] She was filled with love and yearning for love, her heart, her very self was pervaded by a hidden agony. Miserable Tristan left in sorrow as well, his eyes filled with tears. Mark was despondent, sitting in the tree and racked with guilt [14,920] that he had suspected his nephew and his wife of wrongdoing. Those who had encouraged him he cursed a thousand times in thought and word. He blamed Melot the dwarf for deceiving him and falsely accusing his wife. They climbed down from the tree [14,930] and rode back to the hunt, miserable and aggrieved. Mark and Melot suffered from different kinds of grief. Melot suffered because he was accused of treachery. Mark suffered because of the suspicions of his nephew and his wife, and ultimately himself that had so burdened him [14,940] and made him the object of gossip at court and across the realm. First thing in the morning he told all of the huntsmen that they should stay there and continue the hunt, but that he would return.

"Tell me," he said, "my lady and queen, how have you been spending your time?"

"My lord, I was occupied [14,950] with unnecessary worries, but I played the harp and lyre as a diversion."

"Unnecessary worries?" asked Mark. "What kind and for what?"

Isolde smiled and said, "However it happened, it just did, and will today and every day. Melancholic, needless complaining is just what we women do. [14,960] This is how we clarify our hearts and clear our eyes. We take the smallest thing and privately make it into a big problem, only to let it go again." This is how she joked about it.

Mark paid close attention to everything she said and what it could mean. "My lady," he said, "tell me, [14,970] does someone here or do you know how Tristan is doing? I was told before I left that he was ill."

"Lord, you were told the truth," responded the queen, but she meant it in terms of love. She knew that he was ill, that he was lovesick.

The king continued, saying, [14,980] "What do you know about it, who told you?"

"I only know what I've heard and what Brangane recently told me about his illness. She saw him yesterday and asked me to report his complaint and his words to you, that is to ask you in God's name not [14,990] to impugn his honor so, and to refrain from any antagonism for the next eight days, so that he can prepare his departure. Then you can let him leave your court and the realm with honor. This he asks of both of us." She went on to recount all of the requests [15,000] that he had made at the spring, just as the king himself had overheard as they were talking.

The king said, "My lady and queen, may he who brought me to this point be forever damned! That I ever suspected Tristan is my deepest regret. Most recently I acquired proof of his innocence. [15,010] I have now gotten to the bottom of it all, and, blessed queen, if you still love me, please let us settle our differences. Whatever you want, it will be done. Take us both, me and him, and reconcile us to each other."

"My lord, I am not inclined to do so," replied the queen. "I don't want to put my efforts into this, since if I bring it about today, [15,020] then tomorrow you'll just fall back into your old suspicious ways again."

"No, surely not, my lady, never again. I will never again question his honor. As for you, my lady and queen, I will never again suspect you based on public gestures of affection alone."

He swore to all these things. Tristan was then summoned, [15,030] and their feelings of mistrust were resolved promptly and sincerely. Isolde was handed over into Tristan's care again, and he in turn cared for her every need, protecting and advising her. He alone was given authority over her and the ladies' quarters. [15,040] Tristan and his lady Isolde once again lived happily

185

[15,210] and looked at it, however, he saw blood, and then more blood, which disturbed him greatly.

"What," he said, "my lady and queen, what is this meaning of this? Where did all this blood come from?"

"My vein reopened, that's where it came from. It just now stopped bleeding again."

Focusing his attention on Tristan next, [15,220] he said jokingly, "Time to get up, Sir Tristan!" and threw the bed covers off of him. He saw blood there as well and was stunned into silence. He left him lying there and walked out of the room. All this weighed heavily on his thoughts and his mind. He thought and thought as a man does whose future looks bleak. [15,230] He had pursued his quarry only to find it broke his heart, even though he still didn't know the truth about what exactly had transpired secretly between the two of them. He had only seen the blood, and that didn't provide definitive proof of anything. His doubts and suspicions, which he had left behind, now once again held him in their sway. [15,240] Since he didn't see any footprints in the flour around the bed, he concluded that his nephew was innocent, but since he had found blood in the queen's and in Tristan's bed, he was troubled and upset. This back and forth is common with those who waver, and he didn't know what to do about his doubts. [15,250] His thoughts went this way and that, and he didn't know how to act or what to believe. He had just discovered clues to a forbidden love in his bed but not around it. In this way the truth was both apparent and yet concealed. These two aspects bewildered him. [15,260] These two, truth and lies, both seemed plausible to him and then again not at all. He didn't want them to be guilty, but he didn't want them to get away with anything either, and this caused the doubter great distress.

Mark was confused and mostly concerned [15,270] with how he might gain some clarity and put these suspicions to rest, how he could rid himself of this burden of doubt, and how he could get the court to reject its own gossip, which was constantly being circulated about his wife Isolde and his nephew Tristan. [15,280] He called for his baronage, those lords he could trust, and told them about his dilemma. He told them about how rumors had arisen at court and how he feared for his own marriage and honor. He said that he didn't believe the accusations, but that since they had become publicly known [15,290] throughout the realm, he could no longer hold the queen in favor or be intimate with her until she had publicly affirmed her innocence and marital fidelity. He then asked them all for their counsel, how he could resolve, one way or another and in an honorable manner, the doubts about her wrongdoing. [15,300]

His supporters and vassals immediately advised him to call a church council in London, in England, in order to present his concerns to the clergy and the learned prelates who were educated in canon law. It was then proclaimed that the council would be held in London [15,310] at the end of Pentecost in late May.[35] A great many clerics and lay people followed the king's summons and came together at the appointed day, as he had requested and ordered. Mark and Isolde were both in attendance, weighed down with apprehension and grief. Isolde feared [15,320] for her life and her honor. Mark was distraught that he would be robbed of joy and dignity on account of his wife Isolde.

After Mark had taken his seat at the council, he told his lords how he was troubled by shameful rumors. He beseeched them [15,330] in the name of God and their own honor to give him some support or counsel as best they could, so that he might judge and punish this wrongdoing and bring the matter to a close one way or the other. Various men then gave their thoughts on the matter in different ways, [15,340] some with bad, others with good intentions, some in one way, others in another. One of the lords who was in the assembly arose. He was advanced in knowledge and years and therefore well suited to give advice, he was noble in appearance and elderly, gray-haired, and wise.

The Bishop of Thames,[36] leaning on his crosier, said, [15,350] "My lord and king, please lend me your ears. You have gathered us all together here, all the lords of England, so that we might faithfully give you our counsel, of which you have great need. I am one of these lords. Sire, I enjoy a high rank among them, and I am advanced in years, and so I may act on my own behalf [15,360] and say what needs to be said. Everyone can speak for himself, and so, my lord, I will say what is on my mind and in my heart. If you deem my advice to be sound, then you can act on it. My lady and my lord Tristan are suspected of wrongdoing. However, as I have heard so far, [15,370] nothing has been proven nor have witnesses come forward. How then can you right this wrong with another wrong? How can you sit in judgment of your nephew and your wife, deciding over honor and life, if there is no evidence of a crime, and there may well never be any? [15,380] Some anonymous person has accused Tristan of a crime but can't prove the accusation according to the law. Similarly, some anonymous person has spread rumors about Isolde but does not have proof.

"Since the royal court is nevertheless so convinced of their wrongdoing, you should absent yourself from the queen's [15,390] bed and table until she

---

35. Pentecost was a common time for assemblies of court, and the stories surrounding King Arthur's court serve as witness to this important opportunity to bring questing knights and wayward nobles back to a central stage.

36. There is no historical figure, or even diocese, that can be associated with this figure. It is possible that Thames refers to a part of London, as Gottfried does not seem to use the name here to refer to the river.

can demonstrate her innocence to you and the realm, wherever this rumor is known and wherever it is in circulation. Unfortunately people's ears are all too open to this kind of talk, whether true or not. [15,400] Whatever comes under a cloud of suspicion will then be made out to be even worse. Whatever may be the case here, whether it is true or not, the innuendo and accusations have been so widely disseminated that your reputation has suffered, and the court has taken offence. [15,410] My lord, I advise you, and this is my counsel, to invite the queen to appear here before us, given that she has been accused of this crime, so that we may hear both your charge as well as her response, as is appropriate for this royal court."[37]

The king responded, "Sir, I agree. [15,420] Your speech and your counsel seem to me to be fitting and persuasive."

Isolde was summoned, and she came to the hall where the council was being held. After she was seated, the wise, old Bishop of Thames did as the king commanded him. He stood up and said, "Lady Isolde, noble queen, [15,430] I don't want to upset you with my speech. The king, my lord, has commanded me to speak for him, and I must obey his command. As God is my witness, I bring to light only with the greatest reluctance whatever might harm your dignity and diminish your unsullied reputation. If only I could be spared from this. [15,440] My blessed, noble queen, your lord and husband has commanded me to question you concerning a public allegation. Neither he nor I know if someone is seeking revenge, but you have been accused at court and across the realm on account of his nephew Tristan. As God wills, my lady and queen, [15,450] you should be innocent of these charges. My lord is uncertain, however, given that there is so much talk at court. My lord himself has found you to be without blame and only began to suspect you after the court started spreading rumors, not because there was any proof. This is why he has summoned you here, [15,460] so that his allies and vassals can hear for themselves how, with the aid of our best counsel, he will put an end to these rumors and lies. It seems to me that the right thing to do now would be for you to answer these allegations in the presence of everyone here."

Once she had been invited to speak, Queen Isolde, thoughtful [15,470] and intelligent, rose and said, "My lord, lord bishop, lords of the realm and of the court, of this you can be certain. Wherever I might be required to speak out against shameful accusations against my lord and me, by my faith I will do so now and always. [15,480] My lords, I am well aware that these vulgar claims have been made for the past year at court and beyond. You all know too well that no one is so accomplished as to be able to please everyone all

---

37. This is a church, that is, canonical trial, and not a civil trial, which would have adultery as its main concern. Tristan does not stand accused (see Okken, 1996, 1.551, n. 15,387–533).

the time and not be accused of something. So it doesn't surprise me [15,490] that I, too, have become the victim of gossip. It was inevitable that I would be accused of some wrongdoing, since I am a foreigner here and can't rely on friends or family for support.[38] I don't have anyone here who would take pity on my suffering. Each and every one of you, [15,500] whether rich or poor, is prepared to believe that I am crude and immodest. If I knew what to do, how to find a way to prove my innocence with your approval and according to my lord's honor, then I would gladly do so. [15,510] What do you want me to do? Whatever kind of trial I may be subjected to, I am prepared to submit myself so that all your suspicions can be dismissed, but more importantly so that my lord's honor, and mine, can be restored."

The king responded, "My lady and queen, that is how it will be. [15,520] If I can secure certainty through a trial as you have suggested, then give me assurances. Come forward and pledge that you will stand trial by hot iron, as we will determine."[39]

The queen did just that. She consented to the trial as agreed, [15,530] which would take place in six weeks in the town of Caerleon.[40] The king and his baronage now all went their separate ways as the council came to an end. Isolde was left on her own, filled with sorrow and grief. Sorrow and grief beset her greatly, as she was concerned for her honor. She was consumed by the hidden dread [15,540] that the truth would come out about her untruths and falseness. She didn't know how to deal with these two burdens, so she entrusted them both to the mercy of Christ, who is our helper in every time of need.[41] To him she handed over all her fears and troubles with prayer and fasting. [15,550] Isolde had devised a plan to deal with this situation, in the hopes of God's gallantry.[42] She wrote and then sent a letter to Tristan asking

---

38. As a foreigner, Isolde is not able to rely on the support of her family and friends to act as witnesses (see Okken, 1996, 1.564, n. 15,594–98).

39. Trial by hot iron, unlike trial by combat, was one of the trials by ordeal based on the natural elements, usually water or fire (see Okken, 1996, 1.552–53, n. 15,469–764). The Fourth Lateran Council in 1215 put an end to clerical participation in trial by ordeal.

40. The town of Caerleon, now on the outskirts of the city of Newport, southern Wales, was the site of a Roman legionary fort (Isca Augusta), and the Welsh name means "fortress of the legion." In the Middle Ages the town and its castle were seized by the Normans in 1086, both were destroyed in 1171, and the castle was rebuilt by William Marshal in 1217. Geoffrey of Monmouth (c. 1100–1155), in his *Historia Regum Britanniae* (c. 1136), made Caerleon King Arthur's capital and the seat of an archbishop.

41. Compare Hebrews 13:6: "The Lord is my helper; I will not be afraid."

42. Much has been written on the notion of God's courtliness (*höfscheit*; l. 15,552). The concept of God being courtly or as translated here, gallant, seems incongruous and even a bit blasphemous. Hartmann von Aue used the term in relation to God in his *Erec*, ll. 3460–67 (see Okken, 1996, 1.565, n. 15,552). In *Erec*, Enite is forced to act as a lowly squire and lead eight horses behind her. Assisting her in this difficult and demeaning endeavor is *Fortuna*, or

him to come to Caerleon early on the appointed day, as best he could manage. She would arrive by sea, and he should look for her at that time along the shore.

[15,560] That is exactly what happened. Tristan arrived dressed as a pilgrim. He had changed his face's coloring and look and was unrecognizable in appearance and attire. As Mark and Isolde arrived and were making their way to the shore, the queen saw and recognized him right away. When their ship landed, [15,570] Isolde commanded that the pilgrim be asked, if he had enough strength, to carry her for the love of God from the gangway to the shore, since she did not want to be carried by a knight during this time.[43]

So they all called over, [15,580] "Come closer, good man. Carry our lady onto land."

He did as they requested and, taking his lady and queen in his arms, carried her onto dry land. Isolde whispered to him hastily that when they reached the shore he should fall down with her, [15,590] whatever the consequences might be, and so he did. When he arrived at the shore and was on dry land, the pilgrim fell to the ground as if by accident, and he managed it in such a way that he ended up lying in the queen's arms at her side. Without delay her attendants rushed over in a crowd [15,600] with clubs and sticks to make the pilgrim pay.

"No, no, leave him alone," said Isolde. "The pilgrim couldn't help it, he's weak and ailing and fell by accident."

They gave her credit and honor and applauded her in their minds [15,610] because she didn't want to punish the poor man.

Isolde said, laughing, "It would be surprising, wouldn't it, if this pilgrim wanted to play a joke on me?"[44]

---

vrou Saelde, and *gotes hövescheit* (l. 3461), both hovering above her and protecting her from the hardships of controlling the horses.

43. Isolde has taken on the role of a penitent, and so along with praying and fasting she would have taken a vow to abstain from all physical contact with men. She can make an exception in the eyes of the court with an aged pilgrim who would not pose any sexual threat.

44. Translations differ on this statement by Isolde, given the somewhat confusing negative (ll. 15,613–15). The question is, would it be a surprise or not; that is, what would be unsurprising in such a person's behavior? Hatto originally translates: "'Would it be surprising if this pilgrim wanted to frolic with me?'" (1960, 246), whereas the Hatto translation edited by Gentry has changed this to: "Would it NOT be surprising if" (1988, 205). Krohn (1980) is in agreement with this version and has: "Would it now not be very surprising if this pilgrim wanted to joke with me?" (Wäre es denn jetzt nicht sehr verwunderlich, wenn dieser Pilger mit mir scherzen wollte?). The Haug/Scholz (2011/2012) translation opts for: "Would one need be surprised if this pilgrim had wanted to allow himself to play a joke on me?" (Müßte man denn überrascht sein, wenn dieser Pilger sich mit mir einen Spaß hätte erlauben wollen?). I have opted for the Gentry/Krohn interpretation. The question is whether courtly society would have found it surprising that a pilgrim (often, but not always a commoner) would use some opportunity

They all took this as an expression of her good character and upbringing. Many of them spoke of her honor and praised her highly. [15,620] Mark was witness to all this and heard what they were saying.

Isolde continued, "I don't know what will be made of all this. Every one of you can easily see that I can't swear anymore that no one except Mark has ever been embraced by me or lain at my side."

[15,630] They rode off to Caerleon laughing about the incident with the old vagabond. Many barons, clerics, and knights had already assembled there along with a great many ordinary people, and the bishops and prelates who said Mass and blessed the ordeal [15,640] had completed their preparations. The iron bar was put into the fire. Good Queen Isolde had already given away her silver and gold, her jewelry, all her horses and clothing to gain God's benevolence, so that God might not judge her for her true guilt [15,650] but restore her honor instead.[45] In the meantime she had gone to church and heard Mass with great reverence. The wise and good woman's piety was sincere. She wore a coarse hair shirt next to her skin, over that a rough woolen frock that was so short that it only went down to about a foot [15,660] above her ankles. The sleeves were rolled up to her elbows, her hands and feet were bare. Many hearts and eyes turned to her with pity, and everyone took notice of how she was dressed and how she looked. Meanwhile the reliquary had been brought in on which she would swear her oath. [15,670] Isolde was then called upon to make a plea to the charges before God and the world.[46]

Isolde placed her honor and her life in God's merciful hands. Fearfully, how could it be otherwise, she offered up her heart and her hand to the reliquary and her oath. Her heart and her hand were placed in God's care, [15,680] for his protection and security. There were plenty of people there who were malicious enough to want to dictate the queen's oath to her harm and ruin. That bitter and envious seneschal, Mariodoc, provoked them in all sorts of ways to cause her harm. [15,690] On the other hand there were many who were respectful and spoke on her behalf. The argument over her

---

to play a trick on a noble woman, or rather that a pilgrim should be assumed to be a devout person and above such shallow commoner tricks.

45. It was common for a penitent of the noble class to sell or bequeath large sums of money or property to the Church in the expectation that prayer and intercession would convince God to forgive sins or grant eternal life.

46. There has been some speculation as to whether or not actual events in Strasbourg in 1211 and 1212 are reflected in this episode. At that time more than eighty heretics, mostly Amalricans and Waldensians, were subjected by the Bishop of Strasbourg to trial by iron and subsequently burned at the stake. The Amalricans had been prosecuted the year prior in Paris in 1210, and the Waldensians had been excommunicated in 1184 and were persecuted from the late twelfth century on.

oath went back and forth, and some wished her ill and others well, as is often the case in these situations.

"My lord king," said the queen, "my oath must be worded in such a way that seems right to you, [15,700] regardless of what others say. You should decide for yourself if what I say or do will satisfy the oath completely. There are too many other suggestions. Listen to what I will swear: that no man ever enjoyed my body nor [15,710] that any man alive ever lay in my arms or at my side except for you, with the exception of one man, this I cannot deny and must recuse from my oath, whom you saw with your own eyes lying in my arms, that poor pilgrim. May the Lord and all the saints in heaven help secure my blessing and salvation [15,720] in this trial. If I have not included something, my lord, then I will change the oath according to your wishes, in any way at all."

"My lady," replied the king, "this seems to me to be sufficient, as far as I can tell. Now take the iron in your hand, and given what you have sworn to us, may God help you in your hour of need."

[15,730] "Amen," added beautiful Isolde. She picked up the iron in God's name and carried it without being burned.

It was revealed right then and there and proven to all the world that Christ, flawless as he is, can be supple like a sleeve.[47] He is accommodating and compliant, if you know how to approach him, and as obliging and considerate [15,740] as he by rights should be. He helps every heart, be it honest or deceitful. Whether the matter is serious or not, he is always whatever we want him to be. This was made evident by the example of the shrewd queen. Her deceit and her tainted oath, directed at God, saved her [15,750] and restored her honor.

She was once again loved and honored by her husband Mark and praised and applauded by people throughout the realm. Whenever the king became aware that she desired something, her wish became his command. He bestowed on her honor and wealth, [15,760] and his heart and mind were focused only on her, without any trace of distrust. His doubts and suspicions were put aside once again.

---

47. This passage has caused much handwringing on the part of scholars of Gottfried's text, given that it seems to be a commentary by Gottfried that Christ is malleable and can be "twisted" whichever way is most convenient for the wrong doer. This involves first the mistranslation of *windschaffen* (l. 15,736), which is taken from *winden*, to wind (as in to wind up or twist) and has nothing to do with the wind or being blown in the wind (Hatto still has "pliant as a windblown sleeve," 1960, 248). The imagery is rather that long sleeves could be twisted or rolled up; that is, were supple enough to accommodate a proper fit.

Chapter 23: Petitcreiu the Wonder Dog[48]

[15,765] Tristan, Isolde's confidante, having carried her at Caerleon onto the shore and having done what she asked him to do, traveled straightaway from England to Duke Gilan in South Wales. The duke was unmarried, young and powerful, free and fun loving. Tristan was welcome there, since Gilan had heard a great deal in the past about his heroic deeds and marvelous successes, and so he was [15,780] attentive to his honor, his happiness, and his comfort. When he was aware of something that might give him some joy, he made every effort to make it happen. Miserable Tristan was incessantly lost in thought and grief-stricken over his misadventure.

One day it happened, as Tristan was sitting with Gilan and reflecting on his sorrow, that he let out a sigh without realizing it. Gilan noticed this and commanded that his little dog Petitcreiu be brought to him, his heart's delight from Avalon[49] and the apple of his eye. [15,800] His command was carried out. A magnificent and costly velvet cloth, both exotic and marvelous and exactly the same measurements as the table, was spread out on the table and a small dog was placed on it. It was enchanted, as I heard it said, and had been sent to the duke from Avalon, the land of fairies, by a fairy queen [15,810] out of love and devotion. Two qualities had been artfully bestowed on it, these were its coloring and its magical effect. There is no one so eloquent or so discerning who could describe or put into words its beauty or its nature. Its coloring was infused with such a strange enchantment [15,820] that no one knew for sure what color it actually was. It was multicolored in a way that everyone who looked at its chest would say that it was whiter than snow, the backside greener than clover, one side redder than velvet, the other yellower than saffron, and the belly as blue as lapis. [15,830] Its back was a mixture of colors, so that no one color dominated any other. It was not green or red or white or black or yellow or blue, but still had a part of each, it was in short a kind of iridescent violet. If the strange creature from Avalon were looked at against the grain of its fur, [15,840] then there is no one so astute who could describe its coloring. It was confusing and constantly changing, as if there were no color there at all.

---

48. This chapter is an episodic story from the Tristan tradition, most likely inserted somewhat arbitrarily. It has little impact on the plot line as a whole. The story is taken up again by Ulrich von Türheim in his conclusion.

49. Avalon, from the Welsh meaning "apple (or fruit)" is a legendary island that figured prominently in the stories of King Arthur. As with much of Arthurian lore, it appeared first in Geoffrey of Monmouth's *Historia*. Arthur was taken to the faeric island, the home of Morgan le Fay, after his battle with Mordred to recover from his wounds. It was in a somewhat later tradition conflated with Glastonbury, where Arthur's and Guinevere's bones were purportedly found by monks from the abbey.

A golden chain hung from its neck, and on that chain hung a bell. It was so sweet and clear when it rang [15,850] that miserable Tristan sat there freed from the sorrow and sadness of his misadventure, and he forgot all about the suffering that weighed him down on Isolde's account. The ringing of the bell was so charming that anyone who heard it was released from all sorrow and care. [15,860] Tristan listened to and looked at this marvelous marvel. He inspected the dog and the bell, looking at each separately, first the dog with its strange fur, then the bell and its charming sound. Both of these astonished him, but somehow he noticed the marvelous dog [15,870] even more than the charmed sound of the bell, which rang in his ears and took away his sadness. It seemed to him to be an amazing thing that his own eyes, as sharp as they were, could be fooled into seeing all these colors but still not be able to pinpoint any one of all those he saw. [15,880] He carefully reached out with his hands to pet it. As he began to pet the dog, it seemed to Tristan that he was touching the smoothest silk from Palma, that's how soft it was. It didn't growl or bark or show any anger, regardless of how it was handled. It didn't need anything to eat or drink, [15,890] or at least so it was said.

As soon as it was carried away, Tristan's sorrow returned as strong as ever, actually it increased. He could think of nothing else except for one thing: how he could [15,900] gain possession of the little dog Petitcreiu for his lady the queen, to diminish her own sorrowful longing. He couldn't imagine a way to accomplish this, though, either with pleas or some scheme, since he knew full well that Gilan would never part with it [15,910] for all the riches in the world short of his own life. These thoughts and concerns troubled him the entire time, but he never let it show.

As it is told in the true history of Tristan's courageous deeds, there lived at that time in the land of South Wales a giant [15,920] who was aggressive and arrogant. He had a castle by the river, and his name was Urgan *le velu*.[50] Gilan and the land of South Wales were both under his authority and owed him tribute so that he would leave the people in peace and not harm them. It was reported at court that Urgan the Giant had come [15,930] and taken what he considered to be his tribute, namely cattle, sheep, and hogs, and had them all herded before him. Gilan then told his friend Tristan the story of how this tribute had been imposed on him long ago by force and deception.

"So tell me, my lord," said Tristan, [15,940] "if I could relieve you of this and help you quickly be rid of this tribute for the rest of your life, what would you give me as a reward?"

"By my faith, dear sir," replied Gilan, "I would gladly give you anything I have."

---

50. Urgan is Welsh for "hairy" or "shaggy." The French cognomen repeats essentially the same meaning.

Tristan continued and said, "My lord, if you promise me this, [15,950] then I will, in any way I can, deliver you in short order from Urgan forever, or I will die trying."

"Sir, I promise to give you whatever you want," said Gilan. "Whatever you command, it will be done." He offered his hand as his pledge.

Tristan promptly had his horse and armor brought to him [15,960] and then asked that he be shown the route that the devil's spawn would have to travel with his plunder. Tristan was shown the exact path that Urgan had taken into a dense forest, on the other side of which the giant's lands began, and where the stolen herd would have to cross a bridge. This is where the giant and his plunder arrived, [15,970] but Tristan had arrived before them and would not let the herd pass. When the accursed Urgan saw that there was a holdup at the bridge, he quickly made his way there with a very long steel rod that he carried up high over his head.

When he saw a knight in front of him in full armor, [15,980] he said to him with disdain, "My good fellow on the horse, who are you? Why don't you let me and my herd pass across the bridge? God knows, what you've done could cost you your life if you don't surrender."

The man on the horse replied without hesitation, "My good fellow, my name is Tristan. Just so you know, [15,990] you and your stick there don't scare me a bit. So be on your way then and know this for sure. You will not pass here with your loot as long as I can prevent it."

"Well," said the giant, "Sir Tristan, the one who brags about his defeat of Morold of Ireland. You participated in needless and unlawful combat [16,000] and arrogantly killed him. I'm not the same as that other Irishman either, when you lulled him with harp playing and then stole that budding beauty Isolde from him, even though he wanted to fight for her. No, no, here by the river is where I live, [16,010] and my name is Urgan *le velu*, so get out of the way!"

He took aim at Tristan and hauled back with both hands and let loose a great throw. He calculated the exact distance and direction [16,020] so as to hit Tristan and take his life, but as he was getting ready to throw the pole Tristan moved aside, although it was not enough to keep his horse from being hit in the flank and split in two.

The terrible giant let out a shout and called to Tristan, laughing, [16,030] "May God help you, Sir Tristan. Don't ride off right away, but stay awhile so that I can plead with you to let me and my property generously and honorably pass."

Tristan had landed in the grass when his horse was brought down from under him, and he turned around and ran at [16,040] Urgan with his lance, striking him in the eye and wounding him severely. The terrible giant Urgan then tried to get to where his pole had landed, but by the time he reached out for it, Tristan had already dropped his lance and dashed forward with his sword drawn. [16,050] He struck him right where he intended, hacking off his hand as he was reaching for the pole. It fell to the ground, and he then delivered a second blow to his thigh and retreated. Urgan, severely wounded, reached out with his left hand, grabbed the pole, and charged his opponent. [16,060] He chased Tristan through the trees in precarious twists and turns but was losing a great deal of blood from his wounds. The devilish fiend was afraid the loss of blood would quickly sap him of his strength and energy, [16,070] so he left his tribute and the knight standing there, picked up his hand where it had fallen, and beat a hasty retreat back to his castle.

Tristan was left alone with the stolen herd in the forest, worried that Urgan had escaped with his life. He sat down in the grass and thought things over [16,080] in his mind. Since he had no hard evidence for what he had accomplished except for the plundered tribute, he worried that all of the peril and effort he had suffered would do him no good, and that Gilan would not honor the deal the two of them had made. [16,090] So he quickly got back on the path and followed the trail of blood that Urgan had left on the ground and grass. When he arrived at the castle, he immediately tried to find out where Urgan was, but he could find neither him nor any other living soul. [16,100] The wounded man, as the story tells us, had put his severed hand on a table in the hall and had then run down the hill from the castle into the valley to find some medicinal herbs to treat his wounds. He knew that he could be healed by their powers. He had decided [16,110] that if he could connect his hand to his arm before it completely died off with a procedure he knew, then he could be healed, at least with his hand if not his eye.

That was not going to happen, though, once Tristan came and saw the hand lying there. After finding it unattended [16,120] he took it with him back the way he had come. When Urgan returned and saw that the hand was gone, he flew into a rage. He threw down the herbs and ran to chase down Tristan, who had already crossed the bridge and, realizing that he was being followed, [16,130] quickly took the hand and hid it under a tree trunk. He was still fearful of his terrible adversary since he was in no doubt that one of them would have to die, either the giant or him. He moved across the bridge, confronted him with his lance and stabbed him with it, but it shattered. [16,140] Having just been stabbed, cursed Urgan immediately struck back with his pole and lunged at him as hard as he could. If the thrust hadn't passed over his head, Tristan would never have survived, even if he had been made of stone. What allowed him to survive was the fact that Urgan was so eager to engage that he had come too close [16,150] and so aimed too high. Before the dreadful man could take another swing, Tristan feinted and stabbed him in the eye. Hard as it is to believe, he was actually able to hit his other eye as well. After this, Urgan could only strike out around him like a blind man.

[16,160] His blows came raining down in all directions, and Tristan gave way to let him go on flailing about with his left hand. It then happened that Urgan came close to the edge of the bridge, and Tristan sprinted up to him and put all his strength and force into his attack. Running up to him at full speed, [16,170] he pushed him with both hands off the bridge into the gorge below. He sent him from the heights to the depths so that the incredible hulk was smashed to pieces on the rocks.

Tristan, the fortunate victor, recovered the hand, departed, and quickly made his way to meet Duke Gilan, who was riding out to meet him. [16,180] He was distressed that Tristan had decided to engage in this combat, since he could hardly imagine that he would survive the way he did. When he saw him coming toward him, he happily said, "*Bienvenue, noble Tristan*.[51] Tell me, you lucky man, how are you? Are you alright?"

[16,190] Tristan showed him the giant's dead hand and told him everything that happened, how he had brought it all to a successful conclusion. Gilan was delighted to hear it. They rode back to the bridge and saw that it was exactly as they had been told, and that Tristan had told the truth about the vanquished man. [16,200] They all looked at Urgan in amazement and then turned back home. They happily drove the herd in front of them back into the land. What had happened was the talk of all of South Wales, and Tristan was showered with fame and praise and honors. Never before in the realm had [16,210] a man's courage been more honored in these three ways.

Once Gilan and Tristan, the fortunate victor, had returned home and started talking about their good fortune and everything that had occurred, Tristan, that marvel of a man, said to the duke, "Duke, my lord, may I remind you of your promise and the agreement [16,220] that was made between us and the assurances you gave me."

Gilan replied, "Sir, I do so very gladly. Tell me, what is it that you want? What would you like?"

"Lord Gilan, I would like for you to give me Petitcreiu."

Gilan said, "I have an even better idea."

Tristan asked, "What would that be?"

"Leave the dog with me [16,230] and take my beautiful sister and half of my belongings instead."

"No, my lord Duke Gilan, please remember your pledge. I really wouldn't take all the kingdoms and realms in the world in trade, given a choice. I killed Urgan *le velu* for Petitcreiu and nothing else."

"Sir Tristan, if you really [16,240] want this more than everything else I've offered you, then I will keep my faith and give you what you want. I don't

---

51. "Welcome, noble Tristan."

want to avail myself of falseness or tricks to resolve this. As much as it pains me, whatever you desire, it will be done."

He then commanded that the dog be brought before him and Tristan. [16,250] "You see," he said, "sir, I will tell you and swear it as well on my soul that there is nothing I have or hold so dear, aside from my honor and my life, that I would not rather give you than my dog Petitcreiu. Now take him and keep him. May you enjoy him with God's blessing. [16,260] With him you have truly taken my greatest delight and my heart's joy."

After Tristan took the little dog into his possession, he thought that Rome and all the kingdoms, all the lands and all the seas were meaningless in comparison. He had never been so happy before, [16,270] except for when he was with Isolde. He took a minstrel from Wales, who was clever and smart, into his confidence and instructed him on how he could astutely deliver the dog to Queen Isolde the Beautiful for her enjoyment. He ingeniously hid it in the Welshman's [16,280] rote[52] and wrote a letter, which he gave to him and in which he told her where and how he had obtained the dog for her sake.

Once he had been given his instructions, the minstrel started on his way and, without experiencing any mishaps along the road, eventually arrived in Tintagel and King Mark's castle. [16,290] He spoke with Brangane and handed the dog and the letter over to her, and she gave them both to Isolde. Isolde looked again and again at the marvelous marvel that was manifest in the dog. She gave the minstrel [16,300] ten marks of gold as his reward[53] and then wrote and sent a letter to Tristan reassuring him that he was in her husband Mark's favor, who had forgotten all about the previous difficulties, and that he should come quickly, as she had put everything right.

[16,310] Tristan did as he was told and returned immediately. The king and the court, the people and the realm honored him as they had before; in fact, he had never before been so honored at court, with the exception of course that Mariodoc and his friend *petit* Melot only pretended to show him respect. These two, who previously were his enemies, [16,320] bestowed something that was not really honor. What do all of you say? If people are only pretending to give respect, is that real honor or not? I would say yes and no, both are in some way present. No for those who offer it, yes for those who receive it. Both are possible with these two, [16,330] yes and no are correct. What more is there to say? It's not real honor, though.

Isolde the queen told her husband about the little dog and said that her mother, the wise queen of Ireland, had sent it, and that she had told them to

---

52. Musical instrument, see note on ll. 3680–82.
53. The mark is eight ounces, or half a pound, so this would be about eighty ounces of gold. Compare this to the twenty marks that Isolde offers the two knights to kill Brangane (ll. 12,931–32).

make a beautiful little house for it out of precious materials and gold [16,340] and crafted to be the best imaginable. On the inside was spread out a rich silk bed for it to lie on. So day and night Isolde had it with her, whether in private or in public. She got used to never letting it out of her sight wherever she was or wherever she went. [16,350] It was always led or carried in such a way that she could see it. She did it not for her own enjoyment, but rather, as the story tell us, to renew her yearning and sorrow and out of love for Tristan, who had sent it to her out of love. She had no consolation from it, she wanted no relief. When the faithful queen [16,360] first received the little dog and heard the bell ringing, she forgot her sorrow, but then immediately thought about her lover, Tristan, and how he was burdened by sadness on her account.

She thought to herself, "Oh my, and still I'm happy. How can I be so unfaithful? [16,370] How can I ever be happy knowing that he is sad because of me? He has given up his happiness and his life for me and is sad. How can I be happy without him, since I am both his sorrow and his happiness? How can I ever laugh knowing that his heart can never be at peace [16,380] unless my heart is also? He has no life other than my own. Should I live on without him in happiness when he is sad? May God in his goodness prevent that I am ever happy without him."

She broke off the bell and left only the chain around the dog's neck. [16,390] The bell lost its special quality and magical effect after that. Never again did it ring the way it had before. People say that it never again relieved heartache, no matter how much one listened. Isolde didn't care. She didn't want to be happy [16,400] but remained faithful and constant in her yearning. She had surrendered her happiness and her life to yearning for love and Tristan.

Chapter 24: Exile

[16,403] Once again Tristan and Isolde left their fears and troubles behind them, and once again they enjoyed life at court. The court also honored them more than they had ever been celebrated before, and as before they enjoyed their lord Mark's trust. [16,410] They were both very circumspect, however, and if they didn't have the opportunity to be alone, then they consoled themselves as most lovers do with the anticipation and hope of fulfilling what the heart desires. This always gives the heart a passion for life and renewed strength. [16,420] This is true friendship,[54] these are the best ideals of love and desire. Whenever one is denied what Love desires, then it is best to do

---

54. The original term, *trûtschaft* (l. 16,420), has a range of meaning, from intimate friendship to a sexual relationship between lovers. Given the context, I've chose to translate it as "true

without and take anticipation in place of fulfilment. Whenever there is passion but a lack of opportunity, then desire must be satisfied [16,430] with intent. Lovers should never want something they cannot satisfy, or else they want only their own demise. If someone wants something he cannot obtain, then the game becomes unwinnable. One should want what one can have, and then the game is won without heartache. [16,440] When opportunity forsook them, the players at love, Isolde and Tristan, replaced it with their mutual desire. This desire crept up between them in loving and kindness and never rested. Mutual love, mutual feelings, these alone were considered satisfying and pleasing. The lovers kept [16,450] their love a secret the whole time from both the court and Mark, or at least as much as their blind love, which had them in its power, allowed.

The seeds of love's suspicions are by their nature such that they take root wherever they are scattered. They are so prolific, [16,460] so fertile, and so fruitful that as long as there is some moisture in the ground they will not die, now or ever. This indefatigable suspicion began again to take root and frolic wildly around Tristan and Isolde. There was far too much nourishment from the tender gestures [16,470] which gave constant witness to their love. Whoever said it was right when he said, 'No matter how much we guard against it, they always find their way back to each other: the eye to the heart, the finger to the pain.'[55] The eyes, north stars of the heart, always look to find their treasure where the heart has turned, [16,480] and so, too, the finger and the hand repeatedly go to where it hurts. So it was with these lovers. Fear could not deter them from sowing the seeds of suspicion over and over again with their tender glances. Unfortunately, as I said before, [16,490] the heart's friend, the eye, always follows the heart's gaze, the hand always seeks out where it hurts. They often entwined their eyes and hearts for hours with their glances, and as a result they were unable to disengage from each other quickly enough, and so Mark could not ignore in them [16,500] the balsamic remedy of love. This is how he knew all about them. He kept his eyes on them at all times and so was secretly able to see the truth in their eyes and in nothing else but their faces, which were so loving, so tender, and so full of yearning that it broke his heart. [16,510] He became so angry about it and was filled with such envy and hatred that he no longer concerned himself with doubt and suspicion, as pain and anger robbed him of any measure of reason. He was driven mad by the knowledge that his dearest Isolde faithfully

---

friendship," which is to say the kind of intimacy that forms the bedrock of a loving and passionate sexual relationship.

55. Jakob Werner (1966) has collected a number of similar medieval Latin sayings, for example, "The hand is closest to illness, the eye closest to love" (Praxima languori manus est et ocellus amori), or "The right hand is with illness, the sight accompanies love" (Dextera languorem, visus comitatur amorem).

loved someone [16,520] else. Nothing in the world was more important to him than Isolde, and that never changed. As angry as he was, his dear wife remained more important to him than his own life. As much as she meant to him, though, this heavy burden and maddening agony [16,530] enraged him so that, consumed by his own anger, he forgot his affection and at that point couldn't have cared less if it was really true or not.

Blinded by this agony he called for both of them to appear at court in the great hall where his entire retinue was assembled. He spoke to Isolde publicly, [16,540] so that the entire court could hear and see, "My lady Isolde of Ireland, the people throughout the realm have long known how you and my nephew Tristan have been under grave suspicion. I have observed and tested you in many ways to see if you would moderate this foolishness for my sake. [16,550] But you will not let it be. I am not such an unsophisticated man that I don't know and can't see that your heart and your eyes are bound both publicly and privately to my nephew. You offer and show him gestures more tender than you do me. I can recognize from these gestures [16,560] that you love him more than me. No matter how closely I may have you or him watched, it makes no difference, it's all for nothing no matter what I do. I have so often separated you two that I still wonder how it is possible [16,570] that your hearts have remained united for so long. I have often interrupted your tender glances but still can't seem to prevent your love for each other, and I've let you get away with it far too long.

"Now I declare how I will make an end of it. I will no longer tolerate the shame and the pain that you have caused me [16,580] with such actions. I will tolerate this disgrace no more, from this point on. However, I don't want to punish you for this affair, as I should by rights, if I were to avenge myself. My nephew Tristan, my lady Isolde, as much as I hate to admit it, you are too dear to me that I should sentence you to death [16,590] or impose some other cruelty. Since I now recognize that the two of you will forever love each other more than me despite my own wishes, then the two of you should have each other as you wish. You don't need to stop for fear of me. Since your love is so strong, [16,600] I will from now on neither hinder nor forbid you from acting on it. Take each other by the hand and leave the court and this land. If you do something that might cause me harm, I don't want to hear about it or see it. The relationship that existed between the three of us has ended. I will let you stay together, but [16,610] I will remove myself in whatever way I can. This kind of relationship is evil, and I gladly separate myself from it. When the king knowingly has a rival in love, then he is nothing but a lowly fool. Go, both of you, in God's name, to love and live as your hearts desire. [16,620] Our relationship is over."

It then happened exactly as Mark had declared. Tristan and his lady Isolde bowed with reserved grief and restrained sorrow before the king, their mutual lord, and then the retinue. The two faithful companions took each other by the hand [16,630] and left the court. They wished their friend Brangane all the best and asked her to please stay at court until she heard how they were doing. They implored her to agree to this. Tristan took twenty marks of Isolde's gold to cover [16,640] his and her needs and expenses. In addition he was given what he wanted for the journey: his harp and his sword, his hunting crossbow and his horn. He also picked out a beautiful, sleek hunting dog named Hiudan [16,650] and led him on the leash himself. He commended his own people to God and told them to return to his father Rual, with the exception of Curvenal, whom he kept to accompany him and to whom he entrusted his harp. He himself took the crossbow, the horn, and the hound Hiudan (but not Petitcreiu).[56] [16,660] The three of them then rode away from the court. Brangane, the pure, stayed behind in sorrow and grief. The sad turn of events and the painful separation from her two best friends touched her so terribly close to her heart that it was a miracle [16,670] she didn't die of grief. The two of them also took their leave of her with great lament, whereby they were hoping that she would stay awhile in Mark's company so that she might reconcile both of them with him.

The three of them [16,680] rode out into the wilderness, through forests and over plains for two whole days. Tristan had for some time known of a cave inside a rugged mountain, which he once discovered by chance when he was hunting in the area and his path had led him there. This cave was once upon a time, [16,690] in pagan times before Corinaeus[57] and when giants ruled the land, carved out of the rugged mountain. This was to be their sanctuary whenever they wanted to be alone and make love. Wherever these caves were found, they were secured by a bronze door and consecrated to Love [16,700] with the designation *la caverne aux gents amants*, which means 'The Cave of Lovers.' The name was well suited to its nature. The story also tells us that the *caverne* was round, wide, high, and the walls were upright, white as snow, and smooth all around. There was a wonderful vaulted ceiling, with a crown sitting atop the headstone. [16,710] The crown was beautifully crafted and decorated with jewels. The floor was smooth, unblemished, and luxurious, and made of marble as green as grass. In the middle stood a bed,

---

56. This aside appears to be Gottfried's commentary. Leaving Petitcreiu behind would perhaps indicate that the couple wanted to leave one kind of world behind while embracing a more natural, self-sufficient kind of existence far from society. In this view, Petitcreiu would symbolize a world of magic, courtly habits (Isolde took Petitcreiu everywhere as her pet), and perhaps even vanity.

57. Corinaeus was a Trojan hero in Virgil's *Aeneid* and the eponymous hero of Cornwall in the Middle Ages. These traditions go back to Geoffrey of Monmouth and also Wace's *Roman de Brut* from around 1155, which relates how Brutus of Troy was the eponymous founder of Britain.

beautifully and flawlessly worked from a single crystal rock, high up on a platform. [16,720] All around it were engraved letters that told the story of how it was dedicated to the goddess Love. The ceiling of the cave had small windows cut into it to provide some light here and there.

The entrance was a bronze door, [16,730] and above it stood three linden trees,[58] but no others beyond that. From there down to the valley there were a great many trees that provided shade with their verdant canopies. On the far side stood a meadow with a spring that was a cool and bright source of water, [16,740] clearer than the sun. There also stood three linden trees above the spring that were beautiful and admirable, and they shielded the spring from rain and sun. Bright flowers and green grass made the meadow positively radiant, and these competed in their attempts to outshine each other. [16,750] At certain times of the year there was also beautiful birdsong, more beautiful than could be heard anywhere else. Eyes and ears had their pleasures, the eyes their amusement, the ears their enchantment. There was shade and sun, the air and the winds were [16,760] soft and mild. Around the mountain and the cave as far as a day's journey's distance there was nothing but barren rock and deserted wilderness. There were no paths or roads anywhere, but still the terrain was not so impassable [16,770] that Tristan and his companion couldn't get through, and so they were able to find refuge in the mountainside.

After they had settled in, they sent Curvenal back to report to the court and anywhere else it seemed important that Tristan and Isolde the Beautiful had gone back to Ireland with great sadness and travail [16,780] to tell the people throughout the land that they were innocent. He should then stay at court as Brangane directed him, assuring the sincere woman in all sincerity of their friendship and love. He was also supposed to find out [16,790] what Mark's intentions were. If he had some sinister plan to take their lives through some evil deed, Curvenal should let them know right away. Furthermore he should keep Tristan and Isolde in his thoughts and return every twenty days [16,800] to report any news that might be encouraging. What more can I tell you? He did exactly as he was told, and so Tristan and Isolde took up residence in that deserted hermitage.

There are plenty of people who are curious and wonder and ask lots of questions [16,810] about how Tristan and Isolde, the two lovers, could have found nourishment in this wilderness. I'll be happy to explain it to them to satisfy their curiosity. They looked into each other's eyes, that was their sustenance. The fruits of their glances, that was their nourishment. They had nothing else there [16,820] except for desire and love. The lovers constituted their own court and had no worries about what to eat. They carried in themselves, hidden under their clothing, the best nourishment that can be had in

---

58. The linden tree was representative of love and spring in medieval poetry.

all the world. It was always free and fresh and new. [16,830] This was perfect devotion, that is the balsam of love that comforts body and mind, that guides the heart and will. This was their best nourishment. It is really true that they had no food to eat except what stilled the heart's craving, gave the eyes their joy, [16,840] and kept the body whole. That was all they needed. At every step and at every hour, Love accompanied them and as nature's plow[59] cultivated for them everything they needed for a perfect life.

They were also unconcerned about being alone in the wilderness. [16,850] Why would they need anyone else, what would they do for them there? Together they were an even number, just one plus one. If they had admitted someone else to their even company of two, then they would have been uneven, and the unevenness would have only been a burden and a nuisance. Their company of two [16,860] was such a precious fellowship for the two of them that blessed Arthur never had a festival so grand in any of his castles that could have given them greater joy and pleasure. There was no other joy to be found in any other land that the two of them would have traded then even [16,870] for the price of a cheap ring with a glass stone. Whatever anyone could have imagined as a perfect life in any other land, they had it all right there. They wouldn't have given a penny for a better life, except to restore their honor.

What more could they want? They had a court, they had everything they needed, [16,880] everything that makes for happiness. Their loyal courtiers consisted of the green linden tree, the shade and the sun, the stream and the spring, flowers, grass, leaves, and blossoms that soothe the eyes. Their servants were the birds with their song: the small, faultless nightingale, the thrush, the blackbird, [16,890] and all the other birds of the forest, siskin and lark, all of them contended to serve them. This household served their ears and their senses all the time. Love was their festival, the pinnacle of their joy, which by its graces bestowed on them [16,900] Arthur's Round Table and

---

59. The original term, *erbepfluoc* (l. 16,842), is found only in Gottfried's text. Translators have been varied in their approach to this term. The compound noun is made up of two elements: *erbe*, or "something inherited or old," and *pfluoc*, which can mean "plow" or by extension "one's vocation or how one sustains oneself." This could then refer to some sort of vocation inherited from the past or from family, here being descriptive of a personified Love. Gottfried is clearly working on several levels of meaning, given the overall theme of sustenance and natural living versus the artificial life of the court, far removed as it is from the source of its nourishment. Hatto translates: "Love drove her ancient plow for them" (1960, 263); Gentry revises Hatto to: "Love, their source of nourishment" (1988, 222); Krohn (1980): "Love, their inherited vocation/business" (Liebe, ihr ererbtes Geschäft); Haug/Scholz (2011/2012): "Love, their inherited plow" (Liebe, ihr ererbter Pflug). The inheritance seems to indicate that Tristan and Isolde follow in Rivalin and Blancheflor's footsteps in many ways. It is also possible that there is a sexual metaphor at work, given that Tristan and Isolde nourish themselves with frequent sexual encounters (with the fairly common euphemism of "plowing" being the operative image).

his entire court a thousand times a day. What better nourishment could they have had for their wants or their needs? A man was with his woman, a woman with her man, what more did they need? They had what they required, and they were where they wanted to be.

Now there are plenty of people [16,910] who tell it differently, but I don't want to follow in their footsteps. They claim that other kinds of nourishment are needed along with this sort of delight. I don't know if that's true, but it seems to me that they had enough. If there is someone who has heard of a better nourishment in this lifetime, then he should say what he knows about it. [16,920] Once I, too, lived such a life, and it seemed to be enough to me.

Cave of Love Allegory

I hope it won't displease you, but let me explain why the cave was conceived inside the rock the way it was. It was, as I said before, round, wide, high, and with straight walls that were [16,930] white as snow, and all around smooth and even. The round interior represents the openness of love. Openness is well suited to love, which should have no rigid angles. Angles in love represent deception and deceit. Breadth and width represent the strength of love, because its strength is boundless. Height represents noble aspiration, [16,940] which climbs to the clouds and for which nothing is impossible as long as it strives upward, where virtues bring together the vault's keystone. One thing will never change. Virtues will always be bedecked with jewels and adorned with acclaim so that those of us whose ambitions are not stirred, [16,950] whose desires are suppressed and linger near the ground and neither soar up nor descend, gaze always upward. We look up to the treasure built up by their virtue as it flows down to the glory of those who soar above us in the clouds and shine down upon us. We gaze upon them in wonder. [16,960] This is how we grow our wings so that our spirits, too, can fly and aspire to virtue in their ascent.[60] The walls were white and smooth, representing perfection. Their whiteness and constant gleam should not be sullied by colors, and suspicion should find in them no irregularities. The marble floor [16,970] with its green color and solidity represents constancy. This

---

60. Richard of St. Victor (d. 1173) provides one of the best and most impressive descriptions of this "flight of souls" in his *De gratia contemplationis*: "Certainly birds spread their wings when they want to fly. Of course we will also spread the wings of our hearts through longing as we await the hour of divine revelation in every hour and at every moment" ("Certe aves, cum volare volunt, alas suas expandunt. Sic sane debemus et nos cordis nostri alas per desiderium extendere, et divinae revelationis horam, sub omni hora, immo sub omni momento exspectare"). See Okken, 1996, 1.609, n. 16,960–61.

meaning best fits its color and its smoothness. Constancy should rightly be as evergreen as grass and smooth and clear as glass. The bed of crystalline love in the middle was given exactly the right name. [16,980] The one who carved it out of crystal rightly understood its nature as a place of rest and opportunity. Love must be like a crystal: transparent and completely flawless.

On the inside of the bronze door there were two crossbars. Also on the inside was a latch with an ingenious connection to the outside through the wall, [16,990] as Tristan discovered. It could be operated by a small lever that was connected to the inside and that moved it up and down. There was no lock and no key, and I'll tell you why that is. There was no lock because anything on a door, I mean on the outside, that opens or closes it [17,000] represents falsehood. If someone enters the doors to love without being let in from the inside, then that isn't really love, but either falsehood or violence. This is why there is a bronze door, this gateway to love, so that no one can open it except through love. It is made of bronze [17,010] so that it can't be forced open by any means, not with might or strength, not by cheating or through skill, not by deception or lies. The two crossbars on the inside, these two seals of love, were installed across from each other, one on either side of the wall. One was made of cedar, [17,020] the other of ivory. Now listen to what each one represents. The cedar seal represents wisdom and understanding in love, the ivory represents modesty and purity.[61] With these two seals, with these perfect locks, Love's dwelling is secure [17,030] and falsehood and violence are kept out. The concealed lever that connects to the latch from the outside was made of tin, and the latch was made of gold, as it should be. Lever and latch, the one and the other, could not have more closely resembled their true natures. [17,040] Tin represents meditating on matters of the heart, gold represents its success. Tin and gold are appropriate here. Every man can shape his thoughts according to his will. He can focus them sharply or broaden them, keep them short or draw them out, let them roam freely or inhibit them, going one way or another, back and forth. [17,050] It's easy, just the way that tin can be bent and no harm is done. But whoever can contemplate love in the right way, then this insignificant lever made of tin can lead directly to golden success and to wonderful good fortune.

Up above in the cave there were only three small windows, [17,060] well-crafted and recessed, cut through the rock so that the sun could shine in. The first one represents integrity, the next humility, and the third moderation.[62] A

---

61. Elephants were thought to be especially chaste and modest, and so ivory came to represent these characteristics (see Okken, 1996, 1.613–14, n. 17,020). Elements were believed to embody traits inherited from their source.

62. These terms in the original Middle High German are *güete*, *diemüete*, and *zuht* (ll. 17,063–65). These are in themselves important concepts within the greater system of noble and chivalric behavior and serve to elevate honor.

tender glow laughs its way through these three windows, that is the blessed luminosity of honor, the best of all radiances, that illuminates the cave [17,070] of earthly bliss. There is also a good reason that the cave is isolated and located in such a remote and wild place. This can be a metaphor that love and its fulfillment cannot be found on the road or in open country, but rather is hidden in the wilderness, and the path to its hermitage [17,080] is arduous and difficult. The mountains all around crisscross it with difficult terrain. The paths that lead up and back again are obstructed by boulders for those of us who sacrifice ourselves, so that if we don't stick to the middle but take a wrong step, we will never make it [17,090] out alive. Whoever can be lucky enough to make it through this wilderness will be rewarded for his struggles. He will find there his heart's delight. Whatever pleases the ears and delights the eyes, all this is amply available in the wilderness. He would not want to be anywhere else. [17,100]

I know this to be true because I have been there. I, too, have been in the wilderness tracking the birds and game, the stag and doe through various forests. Still, my time was wasted because I never did finish the kill. My striving and my struggles were beset by misfortune. [17,110] At the cave I discovered the lever and the latch, and sometimes I even made it to the crystal. I often danced my way there and back again, but I never rested there. I pounded the nearby floor with my stomping, even though it's made of hard marble, [17,120] and if the green were not constantly repaired and restored, which is its greatest power, then the tracks of love would still be visible. My eyes were enchanted by the gleaming white wall, and I have often gazed up at the crown in the vault with its keystone. [17,130] My eyes couldn't get enough of the adornment up above, strewn with praise like so many stars. The light-bringing windows have often sent their rays into my heart. I discovered the cave when I was eleven years old, even though I've never been to Cornwall.[63]

Continuation of Chapter 24

The loyal retinue, [17,140] that is Tristan and his lover, divided their leisure and active time in this wilderness, that is, in the forest and fields, most

---

63. This is a tantalizing "autobiographical" note on Gottfried's part that has led to much speculation. As with most such references caution is in order, in that much can be read into such scant information. It is possibly a reference to Gottfried's early introduction to the works of Ovid, at age 11. Ovid, as discussed in the Introduction, is a major source for Gottfried in his approach both to the story of Tristan and Isolde and to his outlook on philosophical and moral matters generally.

agreeably. They spent all their time together. In the morning they made their way to the dew-covered meadow, where the flowers and the grass [17,150] were still fresh with moisture. The cool field was refreshing, and they wandered up and down conversing all the while and listening to the birds as they strolled along. Then they turned to where the cool spring bubbled up and listened to its babbling [17,160] as it streamed forth and flowed. Where it spilled out onto the meadow they sat down to rest, listening to its splashing and watching its current, which made them very happy. As the bright sun rose ever higher and the heat became oppressive, they went to the linden tree [17,170] for its cool breezes. This also gave them great joy, both in body and soul. The tree and the air delighted their eyes and their senses. The lovely linden tree sweetened the air and the shade with its leaves, the breeze in its shade was fragrant, gentle, and cool. The bench under the tree [17,180] was made of beautifully colored flowers and grass, the prettiest any linden ever had. There they sat next to each other, the two lovers, and told each other stories of longing and love about those who long ago had died from their yearnings. They spoke about and lamented what happened to Phyllis of Thrace [17,190] and poor Canace in the name of love; that the love for her brother broke Byblis's heart; and how Dido, the queen of Tyre and Sidon, came to such a pitiful end on account of her longing. They passed the time telling these kinds of stories.[64] [17,200]

When they tired of telling stories, they retreated to their hermitage and engaged in something else to entertain themselves. They played the harp and sang, wistfully and tenderly. They entertained themselves with hands and with tongues, [17,210] they played the harp and sang songs of love. They varied their marvelous game as it suited them, so that when one took up the harp, it was the other's turn to sing the melody, tenderly and wistfully. When the sounds of the harp and voice mingled [17,220] so tenderly inside, it was proof that the cave had been properly named for tender Love: *la caverne aux gents amants*. Whatever had been told before in old tales about the cave came to pass with these two. For the first time the true mistress [17,230] had her way at her game. Whatever had been done there before in the way of amusement and recreation was nothing in comparison, with a purpose that was never as clear and unblemished as was their game of love. They spent their time making love more passionately than any other couple before them. [17,240] They did only what their hearts desired.

They passed the time of day in many other ways. Sometimes they rode out when they felt like it, taking along the crossbow to hunt birds or other game in the forest, and sometimes they would go [17,250] after large game

---

64. These stories can be found in Ovid's *Heroides* and *Metamorphoses* (see Okken, 1996, 1.616, n. 17,182–99). All four stories end in the woman's suicide.

with their dog Hiudan, who hadn't yet been trained to track without barking. Tristan soon taught him to track stag and doe and other game through woods and over fields [17,260] without making any noise. This is how they spent many a day, not necessarily just to hunt, but mostly just for something to do. They used, this I know to be true, the hound and the crossbow more as a diversion and a way to enjoy themselves [17,270] rather than for getting food. Whatever they did and however they spent their time, it was only doing what they enjoyed and what they felt like at the moment.

Chapter 25: Discovery

[17,275] While all this was happening, Mark remained sad and distraught, grieving for the loss of his honor and his wife. He suffered in body and soul daily, status and wealth had no meaning for him. So around this time he rode out hunting into the very same forest, more out of melancholy than for entertainment. When they had come to the forest, the huntsmen took their hounds on the line, and when they came upon a herd [17,290] they roused them from their cover. The hounds then separated a strange stag from the herd. It had a mane like a horse, was strong and large and all bright white, with small, short antlers that had not yet grown back, as if it had just shed them.[65] [17,300] They hunted it with great energy, trying to outdo each other, until it was almost dark and they lost the scent. The stag got away and escaped back to where it had come from, namely back to the area around the *caverne*. This is where it fled and saved itself. Mark was annoyed, [17,310] the huntsmen even more so, that things had turned out this way with the stag, since it had such a strange appearance in terms of its coloring and mane. Angry as they were, they collected their hounds and made ready to spend the night to get some much-needed rest. All day Tristan and Isolde heard [17,320] the noise in the forest from the horns and hounds, and they both thought it must be Mark. They were anxious and afraid that they had been betrayed.

The next morning, still before dawn, the master of the hunt arose [17,330] and ordered his people to wait until it was light and then to follow him without delay. He took a hound on the line that seemed well suited for the task and had him follow the scent. It led him through dense growth, over rocks

---

65. This happens in the late winter and early spring after the rut and is caused by a lower testosterone level. The antlers normally grow back over the summer. Strictly speaking, this event therefore occurs outside of normal hunting season (see Okken, 1996, 1.622–24, n. 17,293–95). It is possible that the readership would have noted this and criticized Mark for seeking a diversionary stag hunt out of season. The sight of a white stag typically leads to some sort of adventure for ill or good.

and boulders, over dry plains and grasslands, [17,340] the entire way that the stag had taken the night before when it made its escape. He stayed on the trail until the terrain opened up and led him with the rising sun to Tristan's meadow and the flowing spring.[66]

On this very morning, Tristan and his playmate had taken each other by the hand [17,350] and gone out early to the dewy meadow of flowers down in the lovely valley. The lark and the nightingale started singing to salute their companions with a special hello for Tristan and Isolde. The wild birds of the forest [17,360] welcomed them most kindly in their own Latin tongue. The sweet birds all welcomed them into their midst and made a great effort to greet the two lovers. They sang their joyful tunes down from the branches in various forms. [17,370] Many a voice sang either the melody or descant[67] of their songs and refrains to bring the lovers joy. The cool spring greeted them, jumping out delightfully to meet their eyes but delighting their ears even more as it murmured its welcome to them and greeted the lovers [17,380] with its sweet whisper. The linden trees greeted them as well with their gentle breezes, pleasing them in body and soul, in sound and senses. The trees in blossom, the bright meadow, the flowers, the deep green grass, and everything else that was in bloom there smiled at them in all their glory, [17,390] as the gentle dew cooled their feet and soothed their hearts.

After they had had their fill of all this, they clambered back to their cave and agreed on what to do next. They were fearful, as it turned out with good cause, [17,400] that someone somehow could follow the hounds and find their hideaway. Tristan came up with an idea that both thought good. They went back to their bed and lay down again, with some distance between them, as a man would lie down next to a man, not a man next to a woman. [17,410] They lay down like two strangers, and then Tristan placed his sword between them.[68] He lay on one side, she on the other, and so they lay apart, each to themselves, and this is how they fell asleep.

The huntsman, whom I had mentioned earlier, the one who came to the spring, discovered their tracks in the dew [17,420] where Tristan and his lady had walked before him. He thought that these might be the tracks of the stag, so he dismounted and followed the tracks they had left for him all

---

66. This passage has much in common with Actaeon's hunt in Ovid's *Metamorphoses* (see Okken, 1996, 1.626, n. 17,327–45).

67. These musical terms (ll. 17,371–72) are presented by Gottfried in their French forms: *schantoit* and *discantoit*, *schanzûne* and *refloit*. *Chanter* meant the first voice, *discanter* the second or countervoice. The other two terms are discussed in the note to ll. 2294–95.

68. There are many similarities, especially the sword as guarantor of chastity, with the twelfth-century story of Amicus and Amelius, or Amis et Amiles (see Okken, 1996, 1.628–29, n. 17,405–16).

the way to the door of the cave. It was double barred, and so he was unable to enter. [17,430] Since the entrance was locked, he tried to find some other entry and walked around the cave until he found by chance at the top of the *caverne* one of the hidden windows. He looked inside with some trepidation and saw Love's attendants, a man and a woman. [17,440] He looked at them in amazement, and when he saw the woman he thought that never before had such a blessed being been brought into this world by a woman. He soon noticed that a naked sword lay there as well, which caused him to recoil in fear. It made him afraid [17,450] because he thought that something sinister was at work, and so in his fright he climbed down from the sides of the mountain and rode back toward the hounds.

Mark had also distanced himself from the other hunters and, following the trail, quickly rode up to him. The stalker said, "See here, [17,460] my king and lord, I have news. I have just now discovered a very strange thing."

"Tell me, what is this strange thing?"

"A *caverne* of Love."

"Where did you find it, and how?"

"My lord, right here in this wilderness."

"In this wild forest?"

"Yes."

"Is there anyone alive within?"

"Yes, my lord, [17,470] a man and a goddess are inside. They're lying on a bed and sleeping soundly. The man looks like any other man, but I doubt that his companion is human. She is more beautiful than a fairy. There can be nothing [17,480] so beautiful on earth that is made of flesh and bones. But I don't know why a sword, so superb and flawless and bare, should lie between them."

The king said, "Show me the way!"

The master of the hunt led him back through the forest to where he had dismounted. The king then dismounted and went on foot through the underbrush, [17,490] leaving the hunter where he was. Mark first came to the front door but left it and went around, up the steep rock, and according to the hunter's instructions wound his way up to where he found the little window. He looked inside, excited but nervous at the same time. [17,500] He, too, saw the two of them lying there on the crystal bed, still sleeping as before. He found them just as the huntsman had, each one turned away from the other, one on one side, the other on the other, with the naked sword between them. He recognized his nephew and his wife, and his heart, indeed his entire body, was frozen from both pain [17,510] and love. That they were sleeping apart was both hurtful and pleasing. Pleasing I mean in the sense that it gave him hope that they were innocent. Hurtful I mean in the sense that he had suspected them before.

He thought to himself, "Gracious Lord, what is the meaning of this? If something were going on between these two, [17,520] as I believed for a long time, then why are they sleeping apart? A woman should embrace her beloved and nestle close to his side. Why do these lovers lie like this?" He continued to ask himself, "Is there some meaning to this? Does it mean guilt or innocence?" But again suspicion reared its head. [17,530] "Guilt?" he asked. "Most certainly." "Guilt?" he asked. "Most certainly not."

Mark, hopelessly lost, went back and forth between the two, until the man began to doubt their love for each other. Love, the reconciler, snuck up on him, all made up and wonderfully adorned. [17,540] Her face was colored with the gold of lies, her best color.[69] 'No': this word illuminated and brightened the king's heart. The other word, the painful one, the hateful 'yes,' had totally disappeared from Mark's sight. It was completely gone, [17,550] there was no more doubt or suspicion. Golden innocence, embellished by Love, seductively steered his eyes and his senses toward the place where all his joy lay, as on an Easter Day.[70] He couldn't take his eyes off the love of his heart, Isolde, who appeared to him [17,560] more beautiful than ever before. I don't know what exertion the story is talking about that caused her to be overheated,[71] but her face and coloring were as warm and enchanting as a white and red rose as it shone up at the man. Her mouth was fiery and burned like a glowing ember. [17,570] Now I remember what exertion it was. Isolde had, as I mentioned before, wandered through the dew in the morning to reach the meadow, and that's why she still glowed.[72]

Now a small ray of sunshine streamed into the cave and fell on her cheeks, chin, and mouth. [17,580] Two beauties were playing with each other at that moment: light and light shone together as one, the sun and another sun created a joyful festival, all to Isolde's glory. Her chin, her mouth, her coloring, her skin, they were all so marvelous, so lovely, so beguiling [17,590] that Mark was entranced. He burned with a desire to kiss her. Love kindled the flames, Love inflamed the man with the woman's sensual beauty. The woman's beauty urged his senses toward her body and her love. He couldn't take his eyes off her, [17,600] he gazed at her and took in the beauty of her neck and breasts, her arms and hands, as they peeked out from her clothing and

---

69. Makeup is a metaphor for falsehood (see Okken, 1996, 1.633, n. 17,536–55).

70. See note on l. 927.

71. Haug/Scholz (2011/2012) provide an alternative translation: "I don't know *whether* my source says anything about what exertion could have overheated her so" (Ich weiß nicht, ob meine Quelle etwas dazu sagt, welche Anstrengung sie so erhitzt haben könnte), while Krohn and others are similar to Hatto: "Heaven knows of what exertions the tale romances here that might have flushed her cheeks" (1960, 272).

72. This seems to fit Gottfried's style of understated humor and exaggerated modesty when talking about sex.

glowed. She was wearing her hair down[73] and on her head a circlet made of clover. She had never seemed more desirable and alluring to her lord. When he saw how the sun was shining down through the rock [17,610] onto her face, he was afraid that it might be harmful to her complexion. So he took some grass, flowers, and leaves and blocked the window with them. He gave the beautiful woman his blessing and placed her in God's hands as he left in tears. He returned to the hounds in sadness [17,620] and called off the hunt, telling his huntsmen to return home immediately with the dogs. He did this because he didn't want anyone else to come and discover the couple.

As soon as the king had left, Isolde and Tristan awoke. They looked around [17,630] and, observing the sunlight, saw that the sun was only shining through two of the windows. They looked at the third window and were surprised that the light was blocked. Without hesitation they got up together and went outside to the top of the rock face. Leaves and flowers and grass [17,640] were what they found blocking the window. They also discovered a man's footprints in the soil above the cave and around it, the tracks coming and going. They were startled and frightened, since they thought that Mark had somehow made his way there [17,650] and discovered them. This is what they suspected, although they had no proof. Their greatest comfort, though, was the hope that whoever had seen them just then would have seen them lying apart and turned away from each other.

Chapter 26: Return and Final Separation

[17,659] The king immediately sent for his advisors and relatives from the court and throughout the realm in order to have their counsel. He told them and informed them, as I told you just now, how he had found the two of them and declared that he no longer believed Tristan and Isolde to be guilty of anything. His counselors knew right away [17,670] what his intentions were and that he had told them this because he wanted them to come back. They advised him, as all wise counselors do, to follow his heart and do what he wanted. He should send for his wife Isolde and his nephew, since he knew of nothing that would compromise his honor, [17,680] and in the future he should never pay heed to any evil gossip about them. They sent for Curvenal and appointed him messenger to the two of them, since he already knew all about their situation. The king assured Tristan and the queen of his esteem

---

73. This is a sign that she is living as an unmarried woman, outside of conventional society. Mark appears for the first time in the story in the guise of a typical love-struck knight. There is a parallel of secret discovery and voyeurism in Hartmann von Aue's *Der arme Heinrich*, when Heinrich peers through a small hole in the wall to see the maiden about to be sacrificed as a cure for his disease.

and love and said that they should return [17,690] and leave all their bad feelings toward him behind.

Curvenal went to the cave and conveyed Mark's sentiments. The two lovers were pleased by this, it made them happy, but they were more delighted for the sake of God and their honor than for anything else. [17,700] So they returned to their status at court as it was before, but they could never again be as intimate as they had been, and they didn't have the opportunities for joy as they once had. Mark and the court and household were keenly mindful of their honor, [17,710] but the two were never again carefree and unguarded. Mark, the doubter, commanded and pleaded with Tristan and Isolde for God's sake and for his own to maintain some decorum and abstain from tender and amorous glances, [17,720] and to refrain from their private and overly friendly chats. This proscription was painful for the lovers.

Mark, on the other hand, was happy. He was able to enjoy his wife Isolde again in whatever way his heart desired. It did not honor him but only satisfied his needs, since his wife gave him neither love nor sympathy, [17,730] nor any of the devotion as it was created by God.[74] She was his lady and queen only where the king could command. He thought it was all fine and cared for her just as if she really loved him. This was the heart's foolish blindness, [17,740] just as the saying goes, "Love makes people blind, both in body and in mind." It blinds both the eyes and reason, so that what both can see is what they want most not to see. This is what happened to Mark. He was dead certain and could easily see that his wife Isolde [17,750] was completely captivated by Tristan's love, in heart and mind, yet he ignored it. Whose fault was it then that he lived this way with her, so completely lacking in honor?[75] It would be wrong for anyone to accuse Isolde of deception. He was not deceived by Tristan or by her. [17,760] He could see it with his own eyes, and he knew well enough without seeing it that she didn't love him, but still he loved her.

"Dear sir, did he still have feelings for her?"

Yes, but for the same reason that many still have today: lust and desire. Whoever is plagued by these must suffer indeed. [17,770] Ah, you can still see lots of Marks and Isoldes today, if you want to know the truth, whose hearts and eyes are even more blind, or at least just as blind. Not just one but many are victims of this blindness. They don't want to know what's right in front of their eyes, because [17,780] they think it's all a lie, even though they know better and can see it plainly enough. Whose fault is this blindness?

---

74. There is a crucial distinction made here between the value of external honor, or social reputation, and honor that is also pleasing to God. The first can threaten the second, just as Walther von der Vogelweide opines in his famous poem, the First *Reichston*, on the relationship between three virtues: wealth, honor, and God's grace.

75. Dishonor is the same as dishonesty here, allowing oneself to be fooled by lust.

If we want to be fair about it, we shouldn't blame women. They incur no blame when they let men see what they do or plan to do. Wherever fault is to be found, [17,790] then it is not the woman who has deceived or misled the man, but instead it is lust that has pulled the wool over his eyes.[76] Desire deceives everywhere and all the time and clouds clear sight. Whatever people say about blindness, there is nothing that makes anyone so completely blind [17,800] as lust and desire. Even though we try to deny it, the saying is true: "Beauty is treacherous." Isolde's marvelous, bourgeoning beauty blinded Mark inside and out, in his sight and reason. He couldn't see anything in her [17,810] that he might hold against her, instead he saw only the positive. The point is this: he wanted her so much that he overlooked everything about her that caused him pain.

Surveillance (huote) *Excursus*[77]

Something that is constantly locked up inside is hard to suppress. [17,820] People want to turn their thoughts into deeds, their eyes want only to gaze at their quarry. The heart and eyes together often go hunting along the same trails that once led them to joy. Whoever wants to make this hunt more difficult for them, God knows, only makes the game more alluring.[78] The more they are deterred, [17,830] the more they want to play and the more they are determined not to quit. This is what happened with Tristan and Isolde. As soon as their pleasure and enjoyment were restrained by guardians and restricted by prohibitions, they suffered from that confinement. The mystical power of desire caused them great pain, [17,840] even more than they had suffered before, and they were now attracted and drawn to each other more than ever. The heavy burden of the hated watchers felt like a mountain of lead on their hearts. This surveillance, that cursed practice and enemy of Love, [17,850] drove them crazy. Isolde above all was injured and distressed, and Tristan's absence was like death to her. The more her husband forbade her interactions with him, the more her thoughts and mind were obsessed by him.

---

76. The original phrase *nacken vür diu ougen* (l. 17,793) literally means something like "turns his eyes to the back of his head" or "puts the back of his neck where his eyes should be."
77. The theme of *huote*, or surveillance by watchers, is a staple trope in the lyric poetry of *Minnesang* in the late twelfth and early thirteenth century. This surveillance of women by other women, or potentially men, at court served as a way to enforce the strict separation of men and women except when allowed to appear together and interact on certain public occasions.
78. Compare Maxim 393 by P. Syrus: "Desire loves nothing better than what it cannot have" (Nil magis amat cupiditas, quam quod non licet; Okken, 1996, 1.645, n. 17,827–57).

Another thing has to be said about surveillance. Wherever surveillance is employed [17,860] it produces only briars and thorns, that is to say, it creates animosity, destroys acclaim and honor, and discredits many a woman who would have preserved her honor had she been treated correctly. When women are treated unfairly their honor and good intentions suffer, that is, when they are watched they lose [17,870] all honor and good intent. Wherever it is employed surveillance is useless, because no one can stand guard over bad intentions. Well intentioned women don't need to be watched, they watch themselves, as the saying goes, and so whoever watches them nonetheless will only earn their hatred. He will harm [17,880] a woman in her person and honor to such an extent that she will never again be able to return to decency without some part of that thorn bush clinging to her. Once the prickly thorn bush has put down roots in fertile ground, it is more difficult to tear up again there [17,890] than in parched soil or elsewhere. I know for certain that a good heart will bear evil fruit after prolonged abuse[79] and will yield even more wickedness than a heart that was wicked from the start. This is true, I have read it myself.[80]

This is why a wise man, or anyone concerned about a woman's honor, [17,900] should not watch over her in her private sphere, which will only harm her good heart, except with advice and guidance, kindness and sympathy.[81] This is how he should protect her, and he should be confident in knowing that there is no better way to protect her. Whether she is good or bad, if treated unfairly too often she can easily become obstinate, [17,910] which should rather be avoided. Every dignified and self-confident man should trust his wife as he does himself, so that she will avoid impropriety out of love for him. However often you might try, it is impossible to force a woman to love you [17,920] through devious practices.[82] It will only extinguish love. Surveillance is an evil custom in matters of love. It engenders a destructive hatred that in the end ruins a woman.

---

79. A proverbial phrase similar to P. Syrus's Maxim 53: "The good will that is wounded becomes only angrier" (Bonus animus laesus gravius multo irascitur; Okken, 1996, 1.645, n. 17,891–96).
80. For Gottfried the validity of the written word is the ultimate guarantor. Books are the treasure houses of tradition and truth. Compare this to Bishop Pilgrim's order to write down the story of the *Nibelungenlied* and its aftermath (known as the *Klage*, or "Lament"): "Everything that happened was written in Latin so that it would be considered the truth by anyone who came upon it later" (ll. 4298–301). Although no Latin version is known to exist, the fact is that by 1210 the written word had surpassed eyewitness accounts and oral tradition as the guarantor of truth (Whobrey, 2018, 239).
81. See Colossians 3:19; Ephesians 5:25–29.
82. Compare P. Syrus's Maxim 18: "Love cannot be coerced, it can slip away" (Amor extorqueri non pote, elabi pote; Okken, 1996, 1.645, n. 17,917–21).

I think it would be a good idea to avoid the use of prohibitions altogether. It just incites women to scandalous conduct. People do things they would otherwise leave undone [17,930] if they weren't forbidden. God knows they're already born with briars and thorns in their nature. Women so inclined are children of their mother Eve, who broke the first commandment. Her lord God allowed her to have fruit, flowers, greenery, everything there was in Paradise, to do with [17,940] as she wanted. He forbade her only one thing on penalty of death (scholars report it was a fig), yet breaking God's commandment she broke off this fruit and lost herself and God. It is my firm conviction that Eve would never have done it if it hadn't been forbidden. [17,950] With the very first act that she committed, she established her nature by doing what was forbidden. If you think about it, Eve could have easily done without this one fruit and had as much of all the others as she wanted, but still she wanted only this one, [17,960] and with it she swallowed all her dignity.[83]

All those born in her image are Eve's children.[84] Ah, someone who has the power to prohibit, how many Eves might he still find today who would willingly lose themselves and God on account of that prohibition. And since it comes from their nature and nature is the cause, [17,970] how honorable and praiseworthy are those who are nevertheless able to avoid such conduct. A woman who is virtuous contrary to her nature, who willingly goes against her nature for the sake of her reputation, her honor, and her self, is a woman in name only, but a man in terms of character. Everything she does should be recognized, praised, and honored. When a woman puts aside her feminine nature [17,980] and heart and trades these for a masculine disposition, then the fir tree yields honey, the hemlock brings forth balsam, and nettles produce roses all over the world.[85]

What can be more ideal in a woman than when she, together with her honor, struggles against her own flesh [17,990] to do right by each, her body and her dignity? She must fight in such a way that she does justice to both, and she should show concern for each so that neither is neglected. A woman is not dignified if she ignores her honor for the sake of her body, or her body for the sake of honor, [18,000] when she can reasonably maintain both. She should hold on to both in love and in pain, however things may turn out. God knows every woman will grow in excellence the more she strives and

---

83. The original word is *êre* (l. 17,960), and so Eve is quickly contextualized in the contemporary courtly milieu as having lost her honor through desire.
84. Gottfried invents the verb *g'êvet* (l. 17,962) from the name, literally meaning "to become (an) Eve." This kind of word formation became fashionable after 1180; for example, with Walther of Chatillon (see Okken, 1996, 1.648, n. 17,962).
85. This series of *adynata*, or hyperbole to the point of impossibility, harkens back to the description of Isolde as the sun that rises in the West (see Okken, 1996, 1.650, n. 17,982–85).

struggles.[86] [18,010] Her life should be ordered and properly balanced, and her mind should be focused on balance. In doing so she enhances her life and her respectability. Self-control is noble and will enrich both body and honor. There is nothing that has yet seen the light of day that is so blessed as a woman who has committed herself and her life to order and balance [18,020] and who respects herself properly. While she respects herself it will follow that all the world will respect her in return. A woman who has contempt for her own body and is determined to hate herself, who can overcome that and still love her? Someone who disrespects her own body [18,030] and proves this to the world, what love or honor can proceed from that? Passion is satisfied as it arises, but still this meaningless act is given the most worthy of names: love. No, no, this is not love, this is its worst enemy and nothing more than shameless [18,040] licentiousness. It confers no dignity to womanhood, just as the proverb declares in truth: "Whoever is intent on loving many is not loved by any."[87] If someone is intent on being loved by everyone, then she should first love herself and show all the world how she exemplifies love. If she typifies true love, [18,050] then all the world will join her in this love.

A woman who lovingly embraces her womanhood to please society should in turn be praised and admired, crowned with garlands and daily tributes, and so increase their honor and as well as hers. Whomever she then chooses [18,060] and gives herself to completely with body and mind, with love and affection, he is lucky indeed. He was born to and is destined for a blessed life and will hold an earthly paradise in his heart. He need not worry that some briar thicket might prevent him [18,070] from reaching for the flowers or that he'll be pricked when picking roses. There will be no briars or thorns, the thistles of anger have no place there. Peace and reconciliation, like a rose, have gotten rid of all the thorns and thistles and briars. In this paradise [18,080] nothing sprouts or grows on branches or stems that isn't a delight to see. It is made completely verdant by feminine excellence. There are no fruits except faithfulness and love, honor and worldly acclaim. Ah, such a paradise of joy [18,090] and eternal spring could give a blessed man every blessing his heart desires and every delight his eyes might see. Would he have it any worse than Tristan and Isolde? Trust me, he wouldn't trade places with Tristan for a minute. Truly, when a respectable woman [18,100] pledges her honor and herself to a man, and gives both, my how she does so with all her heart; how tenderly she cares for him; how she clears his path of all briars and thorns and lovers'

---

86. The term translated as "struggles" is *arbeit* (l. 18,008). This term is often used by Hartmann von Aue (e.g., in his *Erec*) and others to denote an ethical concept of striving as its own reward. Women are judged by Gottfried in terms of male expectations, that is to say that women, like men, would increase their merit solely through the effort to better themselves.
87. Compare P. Syrus's Maxim 340: "The woman who marries many is unpleasing to many" (Mulier quae multis nubit, multis non placet; Okken, 1996, 1.653, n. 18,043–44).

quarrels; how she frees him from heartache, better than any Isolde ever did for her Tristan. [18,110] So I continue to believe that, for those who search properly, there are still plenty of Isoldes in whom they would find everything they could want to find.

Continuation of Chapter 26

[18,115] Let's get back to the matter of surveillance. As you have already heard, the lovers Tristan and Isolde were so distressed about being constantly watched, and these prohibitions were so hurtful, that they constantly looked for opportunities to meet, now more than ever. After all their misery they finally succeeded, but it brought them both only pain and fatal suffering. It was around midday and the sun was shining brightly, with their honor regrettably in the spotlight. Two kinds of heat [18,130] burned in the queen's heart and in her mind: the sun and love.[88] Passion and the midday heat competed in tormenting her. She tried to escape her feelings and the heat by devising a plan, but fell victim to it instead. She was looking around in her orchard [18,140] for an opportune moment. She searched for a shady spot, a shady place that would provide the benefits of protection, refreshment, and seclusion. As soon as she had found the right place, she ordered a luxurious bed to be set up. A cover and linens, silk and brocade, [18,150] and regal bedding were all laid out on the bed. Once the bed was prepared in the proper manner, fair Isolde lay down with just her night shirt on. She then sent her ladies in waiting away except for Brangane, and a message was dispatched to Tristan [18,160] that he should come to speak with Isolde without delay. He did exactly as Adam did. He ate the fruit that Eve offered him and with it sealed their death.

Tristan arrived, and Brangane, with dread in her heart, went inside to sit down with the other ladies of the court. She commanded the attendants to lock all the doors [18,170] and let no one in except on her orders. The doors were bolted shut, and as Brangane sat down she started to think. She was sorry that neither prohibitions nor surveillance had had an effect on her lady. While she was lost in thought, one of the attendants went out [18,180] and was standing in the doorway as the king rushed past him and impatiently asked about the queen.

Each of the ladies answered, "I think she's sleeping, my lord."

Awakened from her reverie, poor Brangane remained silent. Her head sank, and her hands and heart went limp.

---

88. The midday heat was thought to represent or even conjure a kind of demonic power (see Okken, 1996, 1.657, n. 18,126–34).

[18,190] The king continued to ask, "So tell me, where is the queen sleeping?"

They pointed him toward the orchard, and Mark immediately went out to where he found his heartbreak. He discovered his wife and his nephew arm in arm,[89] limbs intertwined, cheek to cheek and mouth to mouth. [18,200] Everything that he could see, that is, what he could see above the covers and what was sticking out of the sheets at the top, were their arms and hands, shoulders and upper body, pressed so closely together that if a likeness had been cast of bronze and gold [18,210] it could not have been joined together more closely. Tristan and the queen were sleeping soundly, I don't know what exertions came before.

Once the king saw his misfortune displayed so openly, he recognized for the first time the finality of his heartbreak. He was certain once again. [18,220] Doubt and suspicion, his old burdens, had vanished. He didn't suspect, now he knew. What he had always wanted he now had in spades. I am fairly sure, though, that he would have rather had the doubt than the certainty. What he had always strived for, namely to overcome his doubts, [18,230] now brought him a living death, and he left without saying a word.[90] He gathered his counselors and vassals together and told them that he had received a reliable report that Tristan and the queen were together, that they should go with him [18,240] to see for themselves, and if it was true that they should be tried and given justice as the law of the realm demanded.

It was just after Mark had left the bed and started to go that Tristan awoke and saw Mark as he was leaving.

[18,250] "Ah," he said, "what have you done, trustworthy Brangane! God knows, Brangane, I think that falling asleep will cost us our lives. Isolde, wake up, poor woman! Get up, queen of my heart! I fear we have been betrayed."

"Betrayed?" she said. "Sir, how is that?"

"My lord was standing right here next to us. He saw both of us, and I just saw him. [18,260] He's gone, but I am certain that this could cost me my life, and that he will bring his supporters and witnesses and have us executed. Queen of my heart, beautiful Isolde, we must part, and it must be forever. We will never again have the opportunity [18,270] for pleasure like before. Remember well the flawless love that we have enjoyed up to now and see to it that it remains so. Don't let me out of your heart. Whatever may happen,

---

89. The Cambridge Fragment of Thomas (ll. 18,196–307) begins here. For a comparison of Gottfried's text with the fragment, see Okken, 1996, 1.659, n. 2459. The fragment's 52 lines are expanded to 112 by Gottfried.

90. By rights Mark could have killed both on the spot, caught as they were *in flagrante*. One explanation as to why he didn't was that he was unarmed. The other possibility is that he is simply portrayed here as an emasculated king, with no real power, who fails even as an individual knight by being unarmed.

my heart will never let you go, Isolde will forever remain in Tristan's heart. [18,280] Take care, my dearest, that separation and distance do no injury to us. Forget me not, regardless of what adversity might come. *Douce amie, belle Isot*,[91] give me your leave and kiss me."

She drew back a bit and sighed, "My lord, our hearts and our minds have been too long, [18,290] too intimately, too closely joined together that they should ever know what forgetting means. Whether you are near or far, there will be nothing alive or living but Tristan. You are my being and my life. Sir, I have for a long time given you my body and my life. [18,300] Take care that no other woman should come between us and prevent our love and loyalty from being always constant and renewed.[92] Take this ring and let it be a reminder of our loyalty and love. [18,310] If you should ever be of a mind to love someone other than me, be reminded of how my heart stands at this moment, remember this farewell and what it means to our hearts and our very lives. Think about the difficult times that I've experienced for your sake [18,320] and let no one come closer to you than your lover, Isolde. Don't forget me for someone else. We two have shared pleasure and pain as one up to now, and we must remember that until our dying day. Sir, I don't need to persuade you further. [18,330] If Isolde and Tristan ever shared one heart and one faith, then it will be forever so, renewed yet never changing.

"I have one request. Whatever faraway land you go to, take care of yourself, you are my life. If I should lose you, then my life and yours would both be at an end. [18,340] I will care for and watch over my own self, your life, not for my sake but for yours. Your being and your life, I well know, are in my hands. We are one life and one being. Keep me always in your thoughts, your life, your Isolde. Let me find my own being in you, as you should see yourself in me. [18,350] You have our lives in your hands. Come to me and kiss me. Tristan and Isolde, you and I, we two will always be one, inseparable. Let this kiss seal our vow to remain, each of us, loyal to the other unto death, that we shall always remain one: Tristan and Isolde."

Now that her speech was sealed, [18,360] Tristan departed on his journey with grief and sorrow. His self, his other life, Isolde stayed behind with her own pain. The two lovers had never before parted with such anguish as now. In the meantime the king had returned with several of his counselors in tow. [18,370]. They came too late, however, and found only Isolde, still lying in bed lost in thought and despair.

Since the king found no one there except his Isolde, his council took him aside and said to him, "Lord, you're making a big mistake [18,380] and harming your and your wife's honor by constantly accusing her of shameful deeds

91. "Sweet friend, beautiful Isolde."
92. The Cambridge fragment of Thomas's *Tristan* ends here with l. 18,307.

secretly sent a message to Parmenie and his beloved retainers in which he told Rual's sons that he was in dire need of mounted troops and that they should demonstrate their strength and honor and come to his aid.

They sent him a company [18,790] of five hundred well-equipped knights along with a considerable supply of rations. When Tristan received news that help was on the way from his homeland, he rode out himself toward them and escorted them through the land during the night so that no one was aware of them except for those allies [18,800] who were supporting him. Half of them he placed in Kark, where he ordered them to stay concealed inside and not be drawn out by anyone who challenged them. When they could see that he and Kahedin were engaged there, they should ride out and attack head on and do their best. [18,810] He then took the other half and went back to the castle that had been provided to him. He brought them there during the night and also ordered them to conceal their strength and numbers like those in Kark.

The next day as it was growing light, Tristan collected a force [18,820] of no less than one hundred knights and left the rest in the castle. He ordered Kahedin to tell his people to keep a lookout for him, and if they saw him being pursued they should come out to support him, from there and from Kark. He then rode out to the border and pillaged and burned [18,830] the land openly wherever he knew the enemy's castles and towns to be located. Before the end of the day, the news had spread across the realm that proud Kahedin had launched a general attack. The enemy commanders, Rugier of Doleise, Nautenis of Hante, [18,840] and Rigolin of Nante[97] were taken aback by the news. They pulled all their available fighting forces together during the night and on the next day around noon, when they had assembled their forces, they rode against Kark. [18,850] They had more than four hundred knights, and their intent was to establish a siege camp there as they had done previously for longer periods.

Tristan and his comrade Kahedin were hard on their trail, and while the enemy was convinced that no one [18,860] would dare attack them right then, they charged at them from all sides. None of the enemy had expected to see an opposing force so soon, but when it became clear that the battle was inevitable, they quickly formed up. They advanced in close formation, and soon lance met lance, horse met horse, and man met man [19,870] in a violent clash that left many casualties. They dealt destruction on both sides, on the one side Tristan and Kahedin, and on the other Rugier and Rigolin. Whatever target one chose for sword or lance, it was there and easy to find. They raised a cry against each other, some with "*Chevalier* Hante, [18,880] Doleise, and Nante!" and others with "Kark and Arundel!"

---

97. Most likely the city of Nantes in Brittany. The two other names seem fictitious.

When those in the castle saw that the battle was at a tipping point, they charged out from the gates and attacked from the opposite direction. They drove them first one way, then another in a bitter fight, and it wasn't long before they had broken through in several places. [18,890] They rode into the formation, slashing all around them like wild boars among sheep. Tristan and his comrade Kahedin rushed toward the banners and the main force of the enemy. Rugier and Rigolin and Nautenis were taken prisoner, and their retainers were slaughtered. [18,900] Tristan of Parmenie and his compatriots struck the enemy riders from their horses, killing or taking them captive. When the enemy saw that further resistance was futile, every man tried to flee or save himself through some ruse. The only choices left [18,910] were flight, surrender, or death, and that decided the battle.

Once the battle had ended with the complete defeat of one side and the prisoners had been led off and properly secured, Tristan and Kahedin took all their knights and the rest of their army and led an incursion into enemy territory. [18,920] Wherever they encountered the enemy or what they owned, whether properties, towns, or castles, it fell to them immediately, and they sent the plunder and spoils directly back to Kark. After they had ravaged the enemy's borderlands, appeased their anger, and taken possession of the area, [18,930] Tristan sent his compatriots back home to Parmenie, thanking them profusely for the honor and fame that he had gained with their help. Once his people had departed, Tristan, a thoughtful counselor, advised that the prisoners be given amnesty [18,940] and as vassals take from their new lord what had once belonged to them. The duke told them that they were forgiven, and they sealed an agreement that Arundel would not suffer again as a result of their crimes and enmity. They were all then set free, the leaders and their men.

For this Tristan [18,950] was praised and honored at court and throughout the duchy. His intelligence and courage[98] were lauded at court and across the land, and the entire realm was disposed to obey his commands.

Kahedin's sister, Isolde of the White Hands, the flower of the realm, was self-assured and wise [18,960] and had gained such praise and admiration from the people that all they could do was talk about nothing else but her blessed perfection. When Tristan saw her beauty, his sorrow was revived, his old heartache renewed. She reminded him [18,970] of the other Isolde, the beauty of Ireland, and since she was also named Isolde, whenever he looked at her the name made him feel so sad and hopeless that people could see the heartache written on his face. Still he somehow loved this pain and carried it in his heart. [18,980] It seemed to him to be soothing and beneficial. He

---

98. Tristan possesses the ideal heroic traits of *sapientia et fortitudo*, or brains and brawn (see Okken, 1996, 1.679–80, n. 18,952).

loved this pain because he liked looking at her, and he liked looking at her because the sad longing he had for the fair Isolde was better than any other happiness. Isolde was his love and his sorrow. Yes, Isolde bewildered him and did him good and harm. [18,990] The more one Isolde broke his heart because of the other Isolde's name, the more he wanted to see Isolde.

Over and over he said to himself, "*Dieu de bonté*,[99] how much this name confuses me. It confuses and bewilders the truth and fiction in my mind and in my eyes. I'm in a strange quandary. [19,000] Isolde laughs and plays in my ears the entire time, but still I don't know where Isolde is. My eyes see Isolde, but still they don't see her at all. Isolde is far away, but yet she's right here with me. I'm afraid that I've been 'Isolded' once again.[100] It seems to me that Cornwall has become Arundel, [19,010] Tintagel has become Kark, and Isolde has become Isolde. When someone calls this girl by Isolde's name, I always have to think that I've found Isolde, but I know that I'm just confused. What a strange thing has happened to me. I've been wanting to see Isolde for a long time, [19,020] and now I've arrived where Isolde lives but still I'm not with Isolde, no matter how close to her I am. I see Isolde every day, but still I don't see her, that's my complaint. I have found Isolde, but not the fair one, who so pleasurably gives me pain. It is Isolde who has made me think of all these things, [19,030] who has tied my heart in knots, but it is the one from Arundel, and not Isolde *la belle*. Unfortunately, she's the one I can't see. Whatever I see that is sealed by her name, I will always love and cherish in my heart, to thank the dear name that so often gave me [19,040] joy and happiness."

Tristan often played these kinds of mind games by himself whenever he saw his soothing torment, that is, Isolde of the White Hands. She would rekindle the flames of love from the glowing embers that lay smoldering in his heart day and night. He didn't think about [19,050] warfare or deeds of chivalry anymore. His heart and his mind were only focused on love and diversion.[101] He sought to distract himself in the oddest way. He was determined to direct his love and hope for love toward the young Isolde, to force himself [19,060] to love her with the hope that he could somehow still ease his burdensome longing through her. He often looked at her with loving gazes, and in fact did this so often that she couldn't help but notice that he

---

99. "God have mercy."

100. This is a similar formation of a verb from a personal name to that previously discussed in l. 17,962 with regard to Eve.

101. Tristan turns away from the rigors of chivalry and knighthood to love (*minne*) and entertainment (*gemuotheit*). Without using exactly the same term, this sounds very much like Erec's fault (*verligen*) that causes him to force Enite to accompany him on a quest. Erec, though married to Enite, had forsaken his responsibilities both as a lord and a knight to prove himself and seek honor by spending all his time making love to Enite and enjoying the luxuries of his position.

had feelings for her. She had also been thinking about him a lot, [19,070] since she had heard and seen that he was so highly praised by all at court and across the realm. She had developed feelings for him, too. Whenever Tristan caught her eye on occasion, she returned his glances so tenderly [19,080] that he began to wonder how he might manage to relieve his heartache, and so he tried to see her whenever possible at all times of the day.

Kahedin soon caught on that they were constantly exchanging glances, [19,090] and so he would bring Tristan to see her more often than before, with the hope that he would marry her if he became fond of her and then stay there. He would have been able to bring a lasting peace to his land with Tristan present. He told his sister Isolde to seek out conversation with Tristan [19,100] and to say what he told her, but to do nothing else without his or their father's counsel. Isolde did as she was told since she wanted the same thing. So she sought out Tristan even more than before with words and gestures and everything that entangles the mind and rouses love in the heart. She turned her attention to him [19,110] in various ways and times until she, too, had kindled in him a flame, and her name, which up to that point had caused him pain, began to soothe his ears. He heard and saw Isolde much more than he actually wanted to. The same was true for Isolde, and she liked seeing him and was devoted to him. He was fond of her, she was fond of him. [19,120] They pledged to love each other and spend time together, something they did as often as it seemed appropriate.

One day Tristan was sitting around when his thoughts turned to his fated misery.[102] He thought deeply about all the many and various troubles that Isolde, the fair queen, [19,130] his second life, the key to his love, had suffered because of him, and how faithful she had remained throughout all of these misfortunes. It upset him terribly, and he was greatly distressed that he had let another woman into his heart on account of love, [19,140] or that such a thing had even crossed his mind.

Sorrowfully he said to himself, "I've been unfaithful, what am I doing? I'm dead certain that Isolde, my heart and my life, the one I've been thoughtless to, values and loves nothing more in the world than me, nor can she ever love anyone else but me, [19,150] while I love and care for a life here that has nothing to do with her. I don't know what has confused me so. What have I been doing? Tristan, faithless man that I am, I love two Isoldes and am devoted to both, while Isolde, my other life, loves only Tristan. She wants no other [19,160] Tristan than me, while I am courting another Isolde. Beware, Tristan, you are a foolish and bewildered man. Stop this blind foolishness, put aside these crazy ideas."

---

102. The original term, *erbesmerzen* (l. 19,127) comes close to describing something like original sin, inherited from his parents and imposed on him by the magic of the love potion.

This brought him to his senses again. He put aside any love or feelings that he had for the young Isolde. [19,170] He continued, however, to be so kind to her in his actions that she still thought he loved her, even though that was not true. It came to pass, as it must. Isolde caused Tristan's heart to reject Isolde, and Tristan chose to return to his predestined love. [19,180] His heart and mind were stirred again only by their old suffering, even though he still satisfied courtly niceties. When he saw that the young woman was suffering from love's longing and that it had taken hold of her, he made every effort to cheer her up. He told her charming stories, he sang to her, he wrote poetry and read it aloud, [19,190] and did whatever else entertained her. He was mindful of keeping her company and would amuse her sometimes by singing or playing a stringed instrument. Tristan wrote and composed songs and lots of different melodies for all kinds of stringed instruments that later became very popular. [19,200] At the time he also wrote the splendid "Lay of Tristan,"[103] which is loved and esteemed the world over, and will be to the end of time. It was often the case when the whole court was gathered together, that is Tristan and Isolde and Kahedin, the duke and the duchess, the ladies and lords, [19,210] that he would compose *chansons*, *rondeaux*, and pretty little courtly songs and sing this refrain to all of them:

> *"Isot m'amiée, Isot m'amie,*
> *en vous ma mort, en vous ma vie."*[104]

When he sang so intently they all thought, as they must, that he meant their Isolde, and they were all happy, [19,220] his friend Kahedin most of all. He took Tristan to see her and always sat him at her side, and she was exceedingly happy with him. She would get close to him and turn all her attention toward him, flirting with her bright eyes and her wit. [19,230] Sometimes her virgin virtue would weaken and turn its back on chastity and modesty. She would openly put her hands in his, as if she was only doing it to please Kahedin. Whatever he might have thought about it, she had her own pleasure in doing so.

[19,240] The young woman made herself attractive to Tristan by smiling and laughing, chatting and teasing, flattering him and kidding around until the fire stirred inside him a second time, and his love started to waver in both heart and mind. He had doubts [19,250] as to whether he wanted Isolde or not, and it made things more difficult that she was so nice to him. He often thought to himself, "Do I want this or not? I think I do, then I think I don't."

---

103. This could refer to a series of songs or texts, not just a single lay (see Okken, 1996, 1.688, n. 19,188–218).
104. "Isolde, my lover, Isolde, my friend, in you is my death, in you is my life."

But Constancy was on the spot, saying, "No, Sir Tristan, hold on to your loyalty to Isolde, think steadily [19,260] of loyal Isolde, who never strayed an inch from you."

This quickly reversed his thinking, and he once again fell into such misery on account of his love for Isolde, the queen of his heart, and his demeanor and behavior were so altered that wherever he went [19,270] he could do nothing but grieve. When he was with Isolde again and they began to talk, he lost all sense of himself and just sat there sighing. His hidden grief became so obvious that the entire household said his sadness and distress were on account of Isolde. [19,280] They were right, actually. Tristan's sadness and his misery were caused by Isolde. Isolde was his undoing, but not the one they were thinking of, the one with the white hands. It was Isolde *la belle*, not the one from Arundel. They all thought the same thing, though, [19,290] as did Isolde herself, although she was just fooling herself. Tristan never yearned so much for one of his Isoldes that she didn't yearn for him even more.

So the two of them spent time together with a pain they did not share. They were both yearning and both of them suffered, [19,300] but they were not united in doing so. Their love and affection were dissimilar, neither Tristan nor Isolde were on the same path to mutual love. Tristan was desperate to have another Isolde, whereas Isolde wanted no one else but Tristan. [19,310] The one with the white hands loved and had feelings only for him. Her heart and her mind were devoted to him, his misery was her anguish. Sometimes when she saw that he was very pale and heard his heartfelt sighs, she looked at him intensely and began to sigh herself. [19,320] She suffered along with him in friendship, although his suffering had nothing to do with her. His suffering was so painful for her that she suffered more for her sake than his own. The unfailing love and kindness that she showed him depressed him. He very much regretted that she had devoted herself [19,330] so hopelessly to loving him and had given her heart to him in such a lost cause.

He maintained his courteous manners, however, and was intent at all times with gallantries and stories to lift her out of her depression as best he could. [19,340] Unfortunately she had fallen into such deep despair that the more he applied himself, the more the young Isolde became enflamed from hour to hour, until Love finally overpowered her completely. She so often demonstrated her heartfelt devotion [19,350] with her gestures, words, and glances that he fell into painful doubt a third time, and the ship of his heart began to drift and was forced off course toward foolish thoughts. It wasn't surprising, God knows, given that when pleasure [19,360] constantly laughs in a man's face, it blinds his eyes and mind and tugs at his heart.

All lovers can see from this story that suffering for a long-distance love can be much more easily tolerated than being close to a love but still not really close. Yes, truly, as far as I can tell, [19,370] a man can desire a beloved love and renounce it far more easily from a distance than he can renounce one close at hand. He can forsake a distant love more easily than he can relinquish one that is nearby.[105] This is what had Tristan tied in knots. He longed for a distant love and suffered much on her account, but he neither saw nor heard her. He spurned a love nearby [19,380] whom he saw every day. The whole time he longed for the radiant, fair Isolde from Ireland and fled from the white-handed one, the proud maiden of Kark. He suffered for the one and fled from the other. In this way he lost them both. He wanted and then didn't want [19,390] Isolde and Isolde.[106] He ran from this one and sought out the other.

The young Isolde was undeterred in her longing and trust and desire for him. She wanted the one who kept his distance and chased after the one who flew away from her. It was his fault, she was the one who was betrayed. Tristan had lied to her so often with the ambiguous use [19,400] of his eyes and words that she was sure that he belonged to her in body and soul. The greatest betrayal that Tristan committed, and what led her to love him most of all was the fact that he always liked to sing:

> "*Isot m'amiée, Isot m'amie,*
> [19,410] *en vous ma mort, en vous ma vie.*"

This enticed her heart all the more and caused her love to blossom. She took these words to heart and pursued the fleeing man so intently that on the fourth attempt at love she was able to catch him in his flight and pull him toward her again. He chose her again [19,420] and fretted anxiously day and night about his life and himself.

"Ah," he thought, "Lord, how I have gone astray with love.[107] This love that torments me so, that robs me of body and mind and is such a burden, should it ever in this lifetime [19,430] become tolerable, then only with another love. I have often read and I know full well that one love affair can take away the other's hold. The Rhine's current is nowhere so strong that it can't be tamed and channeled into smaller streams [19,440] and so reduced in its force. The mighty Rhine would turn into a little stream. No fire is so powerful that it can't be divided into smaller fires, if one wanted to do so, and then it would burn only faintly.[108] This is the way it is with one who

---

105. Ovid, in his *Amores* II, 19, (1982, 135) articulates a very similar sentiment that only women who are hard to get are worth pursuing (see Okken, 1996, 1.690, n. 19,376–96).

106. His confusion is mimicked syntactically.

107. The main Thomas fragments, ll. 53–3144, begin here at l. 19,424. The overlap of the two texts is limited to Thomas ll. 53–142, or only ninety lines.

108. These examples are taken almost verbatim from Ovid's *Remedia amoris*: "Much channeling reduces the mightiest rivers; rake out the fire, and even the fiercest flame dies down" (445–47; 1982, 252).

loves, he can play the same game. [19,450] He can just as often take his own feelings and divert them into individual little channels and divide and send his desire off in various directions, until there isn't enough left to do any real harm. I can do the same thing if I divide and give away my love and affection [19,460] to many rather than just one. If I turn my thoughts to more than one love then I might still become a "Tristan" without the unhappiness.

"I'll give it a try, and if luck[109] is with me, then now is the time to start. This love and loyalty to my lady [19,470] are getting me nowhere. I'm wasting my life for her sake, and I don't see any hope of hanging on to my own health or life. I suffer this misery and agony for nothing. Ah, my gentle *amie*, dear Isolde, our life together has been irreparably torn apart. Things aren't like they used to be, [19,480] when we shared one joy, one pain, one love, one sorrow. Unfortunately things have changed. I'm miserable while you're happy. I yearn for your love with all my heart, and your heart, it seems to me, is only halfheartedly longing for me. The happiness that I've given up for you, [19,490] alas, is something that you can enjoy whenever it suits you, because you're married. Mark, your lord, and you are at home and together all the time, but I'm in a foreign country and alone. It seems to me that I won't be consoled by you anymore, and still I can't get you out of my heart. [19,500] Why did you take me away from myself, when your longing for me has disappeared and you can easily do without me? Ah, precious Queen Isolde, how much heartache I suffer for you, whereas I don't matter enough for you to even send a message inquiring about my well-being.

"Has she sent any message? Ah, what am I saying? [19,510] Where would she have sent a message to and how would she know where I am? I've been blown about too long now by uncertain winds for anyone to find me. I can't imagine how it could be done. If they look for me there, then I'm here, and if they look for me here, then I'm there. How and where can I be found? Where can they find me?

"Right here where I am. [19,520] Countries don't run away, I live in these different lands, and that's where Tristan can be found. Yes, if someone wanted to, they would just keep looking until they found me. If someone wants to find a person who travels about, then his search has no particular destination. Instead he has to endure great hardships for better or worse [19,530] to achieve his goal.[110] God knows, my lady, my life, could have secretly had people searching for me in Cornwall and England, France and Normandy, my own realm of Parmenie, or wherever else there might have been news of where her friend Tristan was.

---

109. Tristan now calls on luck (*gelücke*, l. 19,466) and not God for help.
110. This is reminiscent of Rual's search for Tristan after he had been kidnapped.

"She should have sent them out long ago [19,540] if I really meant anything to her. But she doesn't care about me, while I love and desire her more than my own body and soul. For her sake I avoid all other women and still have to do without her. I can't ask of her what would most give me [19,548] joy and a happy life on this earth."[111]

---

111. Some manuscripts (FBNP) add two lines at the end: "I will grow old with this strange lament."

Ulrich von Türheim's Continuation (c. 1230)

Prologue

A great misfortune has befallen us, and this story has reason to complain, left in dire straits as it is by the death of Master Gottfried, the one who started this book. His life's work makes his great artistry apparent. He was a great poet, and his poem imparts to us [10] a story that is inventive, coherent, and truly exemplary. No other poem can compete with its masterful use of language, as anyone who knows about such things would agree. Heartfelt is our grief that death took him before his time and that he was unable to complete this book.

Since it came to pass [20] that he was taken by death, I have decided to finish it in verse as best I can. I have repeatedly been asked by Konrad, Cupbearer of Winterstetten,[1] to do so as a favor to him. May my heart and mind serve him so [30] that he might be pleased with my service and granted the esteem of the lady of his heart. If I were to laud him and cover him with praise as he deserves, he would be celebrated so that many would be envious. Of everyone I know, no one is more generous.

Chapter 1: Nuptials[2]

[40] At some point you all must have become aware of the great difficulties that Tristan experienced, and what happened to Isolde.[3]

---

1. Konrad von Winterstetten was a Swabian nobleman in the services of the Hohenstaufen dynasty, serving kings Henry VII (1220–1235) and Konrad IV (1237–1254). He performed various high-level functions for the ruling house until his death in 1242 or 1243. His official office of *Reichsschenk*, or Imperial Cupbearer, was an honorary title but gave him direct access to the king and the court as a trusted advisor. Ulrich von Türheim, the author of this first continuation of Gottfried's *Tristan and Isolde*, does not name himself here in the Prologue and dedication but rather at the end of the poem (l. 3598). See the Introduction for more of Ulrich's biography.

2. The beginning of Ulrich's continuation corresponds roughly to line 6106 of his main source, Eilhart von Oberge's *Tristrant* (Lichtenstein, 1877; Thomas, 1978, 116). Ulrich begins his story proper with Tristan lost in thought as a direct continuation of Gottfried's end point (l. 19,548). Tristan's monologue is not part of Eilhart's text.

3. Ulrich continues the story in media res. The rather abrupt continuation is similar to that of the *Klage* to the *Nibelungenlied* (Whobrey, 2018, 192) in that the audience is explicitly presumed to have read (or heard) the previous story. This assumption is reasonable given the manuscript transmission of Ulrich's text. In seven (MHBNRPS) of the eleven complete manuscripts of *Tristan and Isolde*, Gottfried's text is immediately followed by Ulrich's. Three (FOE)

Tristan said to himself, "Tristan, listen, enough of this. Stop this offensive behavior that everyone denounces and that damns your very soul. Tristan, stop this craziness [50] and put away these thoughts that threaten your salvation and destroy your honor. Let your uncle, the praiseworthy King Mark, have his Isolde at home, and you love the one from Kark, who pursues you in vain. My heart, if you counsel me to do it, I will turn away from Isolde [60] and be reconciled with Isolde, I mean of the White Hands. Isolde, the one from Ireland, may she remain a stranger to my heart. Love has often weighed me down with her heavy burden."[4]

He told his friend [Kahedin] how he felt and what he intended to do. He said, "My dear companion, may your loyalty remain constant. [70] Remember what you asked of me for your sister Isolde's sake. You see, she bestows on me a yearning pain.[5] Day and night I think about how I can win her approval and her agreement to marry me. I want to stay here with her."

"Stay here? This is truly the best day of my life! [80] All that I have ever suffered is now resolved in joy. Tristan, I am completely at your service; what great times we will have together! Tristan, whatever it is you want and whatever I can provide, it will be done."

"May God reward you for your kind words. [90] You have my sincere gratitude. I have one request to make of you. Honor will be yours, as this is a noble request. Put in a good word with your father and mother, that will help."

"My father and mother will certainly be very happy. What greater fortune could be theirs in all the world? [100] Well then, we should go see Isolde, who is gentle, noble and pure, and in her tender years merits this blessing that you love her and have chosen her to be your bride and bind yourself to her."

"You should go. I'll stay here, and you can speak for me."

"Tell me what to say. I'll say whatever you want me to. [110] There is no service I won't perform for you."

---

of the four remaining manuscripts contain Heinrich von Freiberg's continuation (c. 1290). Ulrich's text is not extant in any manuscripts that do not contain Gottfried's work.

4. Eilhart von Oberge has no interior monologue at all, but moves straight from the battle (line 18,948 in Gottfried's text), to a discussion with Kahenis (Kahedin) about marrying his sister. Ulrich obviously takes this transition from Gottfried, then, and not Eilhart.

5. Translations of l. 72 vary, depending on the determination of the verb. Two manuscripts (MB) have the verb form *gît*, from *geben* (to give), others the form *giht*, from *jehen* (to claim, tell). Kühn (2003, 517) translates: "she confesses the pain of yearning to me" (sie gesteht mir Qual der Sehnsucht); Spiewok (1992, 19) has: "she entangles me in yearning pain" (Sie verstrickt mich in Sehnsuchtsschmerz); Kramer (1966, 491–92): "she causes me a great pain of love" (sie bereitet mir heftigen Liebesschmerz). Given the next line, the context would give preference to a reading of *gît* with a dative object, as Tristan is trying to convince Kahedin that his sister is the object of his yearning.

"Just say what I've told you, and ask Isolde, that pure maiden, to be kindly disposed toward me. I will never be free from suffering until she liberates me and releases me from care."

Kahedin hurried off to his family and found all three of them together. [120] He promptly began to speak in a formal tone, "I've come here to you today after having heard Tristan's intentions. He asks that Isolde, my sister, be given to him in marriage. He says that he would gladly stay here with us for all time. Let us thank him for his excellent service to us [130] and his knightly defense of our affairs. Where else have deeds of knighthood earned such great fame as have Tristan's? He is praised everywhere and no one is his equal."

"Bless you, you virtuous man," said the gentle duchess. "My dear son Kahedin, since you support this petition, [140] we should give Isolde, that pure maiden, to Tristan. If he stays with us here in our lands, then we will always be prosperous. Count Riol will have to serve under your banner out of fear.[6] Go and bring Tristan to us, and tell him to come quickly. As he has requested, we will give him Isolde [150] and remain beholden to him always. What has been done will remain done. I am of the opinion that until something has been seen to its conclusion, it can always still be undone. Only once it is finished can it not be undone. Go, bring Tristan. He will find all his wishes granted." Kahedin went to find Tristan, [160] who received him joyfully.

"So tell me, is it good news? I was worried that you were gone so long. Did you present them with my petition? How was it received?"

"To be honest, a petition has never been better received. Tristan, let's go then to where you will be welcome, [170] if things are still as you told me."

"Kahedin, I love her more than I could tell you before."

They left together. Tristan was well received by the host, his wife, and Isolde. Isolde was encouraged by her mother to greet Tristan and thereby stir his heart. "I will gladly do so," said Isolde. [180] "If he were to suffer at all on my account, I would gladly make amends, if I knew the appropriate penance."

The duchess then said, "Speak now, Sir Tristan. If what Kahedin told us still holds true, then we will gladly give her to you with our blessing. But you must remain here with us, as long as you shall live."

[190] "I will gladly marry Isolde and remain hers in marriage forever."

---

6. Count Riol is probably synonymous with their old enemy, Rigolin of Nante (Gottfried, l. 18,841), who was previously defeated by Tristan and his army from Parmenie. Eilhart names him Count Riole and identifies him as a vassal of King Havelin of Arundel (Duke Jovelin in Gottfried's and Ulrich's texts). According to Eilhart's account, Riole invaded Arundel after his proposal for Isolde of the White Hands was rejected. Havelin considered his own vassal unsuitable to marry his daughter. Riole was subsequently captured and held prisoner by Tristrant.

"Then I'll set a time of no more than six weeks. If I'm lying, then I put my life in your hands, and you may kill me."

"Tristan, this seems to me to be satisfactory. [520] Whatever grudge I held against you is past, and we are friends again." Isolde of the White Hands was not loved so much as to cause Tristan to think any less of the other Isolde on her account.

It so happened that they all found a place to rest among the flowers and the grass. Two tents, no more, [530] were set up on the green meadow. I think they both belonged to the duke. Wherever the others found a spot, they were made comfortable enough. There were lots of small shelters there made out of branches and greens. Then they went hunting, while some staged contests in throwing heavy rocks, while some threw javelins. [540] Others rode out together and hunted with falcons. The ladies played games of tag for fun. Whoever wanted to watch women could see many a beauty there.

Tristan and his high-spirited companion Kahedin rode out to find a stand [550] where they could shoot at deer.[15] He began to make calls by using a leaf, something he was very adept at. While they were in the forest a deer came up to them that was spotted like a magpie. They sat in their stand and forgot all about shooting. [560] The coloring is what saved the deer. It continued to come closer until it could distinguish between them and recognize the one who was to receive its message. Isn't that a most marvelous thing? It dropped a letter and a ring out of its ear into Tristan's lap. As soon as Tristan saw the sparkling gold, he recognized the ring. [570] The deer bowed before Tristan and then quickly went on its way. Tristan picked up the letter and read what was written there. If you like, I'll tell you what he read.

"Oh Tristan, *beau amis*. You have renounced your loyalty to me, poor Isolde. Tristan, have mercy on me, care-ridden Isolde. [580] Tristan, think of the great suffering that I have endured because of you. Tristan, my friend, I beg you on your honor as a knight to release me from this heartache. If helmet and shield still have meaning for you and if you want to be true to them, then act justly toward me for their sake.[16] Tristan, my reputation is still intact, but I don't know if yours hasn't been smashed to pieces. [590] I will go mad on account of your love if you don't quickly come back to me. Tristan, remember how we both lay in the cave[17] and loved each other even in peril? You denied me nothing there. Tristan, you see this is the deer that I raised in the forest. As it was being hunted, it fled to me where my tent was set up.

---

15. The following episode with the spotted, magical deer is apparently an invention of Ulrich's. It is not in Eilhart or any other sources.

16. Helmet and shield are representative *pars pro toto* of the office of knighthood.

17. This particular reference to *fossure* (l. 593) could only come from Gottfried (*fossiure*; l. 16,700 et al.), because Eilhart has the two lovers escape to a dark forest (*vinstern walde*; l. 4330, Thomas, 1978, 97).

[600] I helped the deer so that it recovered, and since then it has stayed with me for quite some time. One day I was feeling especially sad and cried for you, which everyone could see. The deer cried along with me and so demonstrated its loyalty to me. I said to myself, 'If only you could come to comfort me, I know you would.'

[610] "In the middle of this melancholy I lay down and fell asleep. Love came to me and gave me this letter, and it sent the deer to me to be my messenger. I did as she advised and sent this letter to you. Tristan, that I have to be without you hurts me deeply. I don't know what else to say. If you don't come soon, I will die. [620] Tristan, your dear Isolde sends you this prayer, may God and his mother keep you safe."

That was the end of the letter. Kahedin asked, "Tristan, what was in the letter? Tell me, if it's appropriate. I won't ask you if it isn't. Is this letter from the noble Fair Isolde?"

[630] Tristan began to blush and then turned white. His heartache had left him. Soon his color returned to normal, and he gladly answered Kahedin, who had asked so politely. He gave him the letter and said, "You can see for yourself, Kahedin, the queen, gentle Isolde sent me this letter."

[640] Then Kahedin replied, "Tristan, after I have read this, you will be fully reconciled with me. If you want to visit the queen, then you should do so right away. We should leave immediately."

"Kahedin, I'm too poor to undertake such a lover's quest."

"My father will spare no cost and prepare us properly. [650] He will give us horses and clothing and plenty of gold and silver. You can take as much as you need."

"Kahedin, that's good to hear. May God reward you for this. You have made me happy and you have acted as a loyal man, one who honors the loyalty of the loyal. We should go now and not remain here any longer. [660] You and I should ride to your father, and I will ask him to hear my request with an open mind."

"Tristan, he will say yes. Both of us will swear solemn oaths that we will remain true to him and that we will return soon. [670] I know that you are loyal and that you will not break your oath. I am well aware of your steadfastness."

They took each other's hand, and so the two companions went to see the duke together. Tristan, raised to be courteous, was not well received, but he nevertheless began to present his petition with courtesy. [680] Now listen to what the noble man did. He first thanked the duke graciously and said, "Dear lord, you have done many kind things for me, and I hope that you might do something for me now. You often made me happy, may God reward you for that. I was seldom deserving, but I serve you still and always will. [690] I ask you for one favor. I want to return to my homeland. I have a land, its name

245

Chapter 3: First Reunion: The Thornbush

[848] Tristan asked Curvenal to take charge of the preparations for the sea voyage [850] and said, "Keep this to yourself and tell no one who we are."

"Oh, my dear lord, I have for some time been acquainted with your methods and what I should do and not do. I will do what is good and avoid what is bad."

Courtly Curvenal then rode to the ships. Was he successful? Certainly, he was blessed with luck. [860] When he arrived at the coast he encountered a sailor who was completely unknown to him. When the mariner saw him coming, he spoke to him in a friendly manner, "May God welcome you as I do."

"Thanks be to God. Where do you come from, kind man, please tell me?"

"I've been underway for six days now and have come from the town of Tintagel. [870] The king and queen reside there in great joy. I saw many fair women and handsome men. I was transporting some merchants and their valuable merchandise. Now I do as do all those for hire. I wait to see if someone will come along who needs my services. I can take him here or there, [880] wherever he may want to go."

"So tell me, my dear captain, would you be prepared to go back to where you just came from? I can pay you in good sterling, with real weight and full value, as I have wealthy patrons."

"May I ask, with your permission, do you have more in your company?"

[890] "You don't need to worry about that, as long as I pay you well."

"Sir, then pay me what you will. I don't like to make demands when it comes to price. I will rely on your good will."

In the meantime Tristan came riding up and asked how things were going. "Curvenal, what have you been doing? Have you made a deal with this seafarer?"

[900] "The mariner will only take as much as I offer him."

"Curvenal, I would rather give him a thousand marks than stay here."

The mariner then cleverly responded, "My lord, you pay well. May God watch over us so that we arrive at our destination. You have relieved me of all need. I know it as surely as I am standing here [910] that this will make me a wealthy man."

"Go on then and make all the necessary preparations for our voyage. Make ready to offer your services."

"You noble knights, quickly bring everything here, the horses and all their baggage. With God's help and my assistance you will all soon arrive [920] where you want to go." So spoke the wise old captain. "Once everything has been loaded, then tell me which direction you want me to sail. I will quickly bring you there, of that I have no doubt."

Tristan then asked, "Captain, do you know Lytan? This is your destination, [930] as best you know how to get there."

"I am well acquainted with Lytan. I pay taxes there several times a year. Sir Tynas lives there, a famous hero. He is the king's seneschal and a virtuous man. He will receive us with kindness when we land there."

"Is that so?" said Tristan.

[940] "Yes, it is, lord."

"Then let's get underway!"

The captain did as he was told and weighed anchor in God's name. He quickly sailed to Lytan and arrived where Tynas was staying, who took a good look at the ship to determine where it was from and then said to the mariner, "Who are these passengers?"

[950] The mariner didn't know any of them, but the renowned Tynas recognized Tristan and said, "All are welcome here in God's name in my land. Your arrival has dispelled every unhappiness. You are welcome a thousand times over. [960] This is certainly an unexpected surprise and you've made me very happy. My heart is open to you."

"Tynas, may God reward you for this. Your wish has ever been my command. Please show me your loyalty. How is my lady, Queen Isolde? Your loyalty often helped me enjoy her love. [970] Tynas, without your loyalty I would have been lost. Tynas, Isolde, that virtuous woman, has it in her power to let me die or live. I swore an oath on her goodwill, and I don't regret doing so, that I know a woman who takes better care of my dog than the other Isolde takes care of me. [980] I never touched her, as close as I was to her. Among us is a witness, and he shall bear witness to the truth. If my lady demonstrates herself to be as I have described her, then I am saved from death. Tynas, I want to ask you, since you have often suffered on my account, to make sure that my lady will not let me down. [990] I will come early tomorrow before dawn and hide in this thornbush. Along with me will be the one to whom I swore that she was more beautiful and treated me and the dog better than another. This has enraged the other Isolde and her family. So please ask her to come and deliver me from this grave danger. Tynas, give Isolde this ring. When she sees it [1000] she will have no doubt that I have come to this land. I have made a wager for love that may cost me my honor. Help me win it. She would be sorry to lose me this way."

Tynas spoke, "I will do that. I will take this message, as you have asked me. My loyalty tells me what is good for you and what is bad."

[1010] Tynas rode off to deliver his message as he was asked. He put the gold ring on one of his fingers and rode to Tintagel. The king and queen were there, happy and carefree. Tynas entered while both of them were playing a board game. Tynas asked courteously, "My lady, queen, [1020] can I play as a third in your game?"

"If the king allows it, it's fine with me. Whatever I end up losing, no one better should have it."

Tynas sat down at the game and played along with the other two. The gold ring shone on his finger and as soon as the queen saw it, she thought to herself, "Tristan must be here!"

[1030] She quickly left the game and went to her private chambers. Tynas was sure that Queen Isolde had recognized the ring. Isolde sent for Tynas and implored him to tell her by his faith, and to hide nothing, whether Tristan had come.

[1040] "I will tell you the good news, if you promise to give me the messenger's reward."[22]

"I will give it to you gladly," said Isolde.

"Lady, Tristan is staying at my home in Lytan and sends you this ring. I believe that you know it well. He is in a very precarious situation, my lady, and will hide in the thornbush tomorrow before daybreak. [1050] Lady, believe what I say to you. He suffers great heartache. There is a spy here with him in the land who has his life in his hands."

"Tynas, what is going on with him?"

"He says, my lady, that he knows a woman who treats her dog better every day than Isolde [1060] of the White Hands treats him. You, my lady, must free him from this predicament. Appear tomorrow morning in your beauty and finery, and you will surely make him happy."

"I will do that, Tynas, so help me God. If they humiliated Tristan, then they will now be humiliated by him. I will make myself beautiful for tomorrow morning. [1070] If there is someone in the thornbush, then he will truly admit that he never heard of or saw a woman so dazzlingly beautiful. Petit-creiu, the little dog, will be so well treated that when this murderer sees it, he will think to himself, 'I must spare Tristan's life, he told me the truth.'"

[1080] Fair Isolde did not hesitate. She went to the king and embraced him gently. She said, "My dear lord, why don't we go out for some amusement for two days to the white land,[23] where we can go hunting? That would be good for our reign. We have been in Tintagel for too long now."

[1090] "My lady, whatever you want and whatever will bring you joy I will not deny you." The hunters were called. "Ride to the red land and take the hounds with you. I want to have some amusement with my household. And make sure that I find the lookouts alert, [1100] or I'll be angry."

"We will gladly comply," they said.

---

22. This is *boten geld* or *boten brôt*, the reward due an emissary before a message is delivered.
23. This name appears in Eilhart as *blanken lante* (l. 6396) and could either be a place name or descriptive of some hunting ground. Ulrich changes this a few lines later (l. 1094) to the red land for some unknown reason. There is also a *blanken walde* in Eilhart some lines later (l. 6619). Thomas, too, makes reference to *la Blanche Lande* in Brittany in his text (l. 2177).

The queen did not forget to take a bath before the journey. Why did she do this? There was never a woman more beautiful than Isolde. She was the image of beauty itself. In the morning just before daybreak, Mark told his retinue that it should get underway, [1110] and so a large contingent of the household started off. In the meantime Tristan had hidden himself in the thornbush, and they waited with anticipation until the entourage arrived. Kahedin saw them and said, "Who is that coming, Tristan? I'm afraid of them."[24]

"Calm down, you don't need to worry [1120] that they'll harm you. They are just the king's cooks."

"Tristan, who are these people? More of them are coming our way."

"Kahedin, they are various members of the king's household."

"Tristan, I hope they don't find us hiding here in the thornbush. [1130] If they find us hiding here it will be the end of us. Tristan, I'm scared. If we stay here much longer they will certainly find us."

"Kahedin, take heart and rest assured that no one will harm you. You have my word."

As the group rode by the thornbush [1140] they failed to see them, and the foreigner gained courage and soon forgot his fears, saying, "We should be fine if those I see coming act like those who just passed."

"God will certainly protect us from them," said noble Tristan. "Kahedin, my dear friend, you really don't need to be afraid. [1150] They are the king's priests carrying the sacraments."

"If your rose, Isolde the beautiful, is coming next, then I will gladly wait here until I can see her beauty for myself along with the little dog that she takes such good care of for your sake."

"Kahedin, she's not coming yet. [1160] If I am fortunate enough that the queen passes by, then it will be easy to recognize her. The love of my heart will pass by with such a large entourage that you will easily recognize it."

"Tristan, what's going to happen to us? Here comes another large group of people."

"Those are Queen Isolde's ladies in waiting. [1170] You will see many a red mouth pass by our thornbush."

The highborn and noble ladies rode by elegantly in costly and fashionable robes. Next to each lady rode a knight to keep her company. Those who were escorting the ladies spoke about various things as they were riding to the next resting place. [1180] Kahedin said, "Tristan, look, who's coming there?"

---

24. This humorous, and even mocking, dialogue has Kahedin frightened of his own shadow. It is an invention of Ulrich, as Eilhart makes no attempt to portray Kehenis in the thornbush in such a negative light.

"Here comes a great treasure of virtues. Let these young women ride by, as they are courteous and pure. Brangane and Camele are both courteous and beautiful."

They rode gracefully by the thornbush where the two of them were waiting for Isolde to arrive. [1190] Their lovely red lips spoke of various things, such as how it might happen that Tristan and the queen could be together for a while. They talked back and forth until they hit upon how it could be arranged that one could satisfy the other.

Kahedin said to Tristan, [1200] "I have just seen something, Tristan, that I have to tell you about. It is about to become daylight a second time. It seems to me that there are two suns. May God have mercy on me so that I might be able to see this brilliance that cannot be brighter and that hurts my eyes. Since God created Eve from Adam's rib, there has never been a woman [1210] as beautiful as Isolde. Tristan, you are blessed by great fortune, no one is luckier than you, you are the luckiest man alive. Isolde the Fair is a beauty and a marvel. Her beauty has the ability to give hearts both joy and pain."

Tristan was very happy indeed. [1220] Isolde came into the clearing and dismounted. The pure, gentle, gracious woman sat down on the grass, and the only people with her were her girls and Antret. He was part of her family, and so she asked him, "My dear nephew, please ride back and get my jewelry box. I think that I left it at home. [1230] Mark my words carefully. Tell the king that I'm waiting for him here." Antret was eager to do as Isolde commanded him. Isolde petted Petitcreiu again and again, while Petitcreiu happily sat in Isolde's lap. Any dog would have envied him, even his little dog house was made of gold. [1240] Fair Isolde began to caress the dog and often kissed it on the mouth. She said, "My dear little dog, when will I be able to caress and kiss your master like this?"

She then motioned to him to come out of the thornbush. How did she welcome him? Lovingly and in the best way, [1250] just as one lover greets another, kissing him passionately. "Thank God you are here, Tristan. My sorrow is at an end now that I am holding in my arms the man I love more than anything in the world. Tristan, I have to leave now. I don't dare stay any longer. Come meet me as soon as you can, [1260] you know the place where we last made love. We will risk our honor and our lives again."

"I will do it, pure, blessed woman."

"You should not cross the river. My tent is on this side, and there are no other tents nearby. I will say that I am not feeling well and need my rest."

[1270] Brangane saw in the distance that Antret, that faithless man, was approaching. Because he meant her harm,[25] Brangane said to the queen, "My

---

25. There is a question concerning the referent of the pronoun "her" in this sentence, either Brangane or the queen. Spiewok (1994) sets a comma between l. 1271 and l. 1272 and

dear lady, you must leave. Antret would gladly betray you if he could with his shameful schemes. It would be his happiest moment if he succeeded."

[1280] So the queen left. Tristan grieved but went back to where he had been hiding, and from there he could observe everything. Antret quickly approached the queen and said, "My dear lady, you don't need to wait here any longer, my lord the king is taking a different route. [1290] All of you will have a comfortable spot in the beautiful meadow."

"This is how the king treats me all the time. It seems to me that he doesn't care about me, and I will ask him in anger why he doesn't care about me. Help me get up, I will ride to him. The one I was waiting for here will certainly render me a service [1300] that will make me feel better. If my feelings were hurt, then that was caused by the king showing me disrespect. Well fine, he'll think better of it later." As women tend to be very clever, she went on to say, "My lord, King Mark, has almost sent me to my death by not doing what I asked of him. I said that I wanted to wait here. [1310] Why he told you to do otherwise I really don't know. Even though I asked him nicely, he took another route, and that makes me very unhappy.

"Antret, I don't feel well at all. If this really is the end, then may God grant that the Trinity receive me in its mercy. God, who is all knowing, understands my situation better than anyone else. [1320] He knows that no one is dearer to me than the man whom I just passionately kissed on the mouth. He has set my heart on fire so that it burns for love, and there is no one I love more. Antret, if only I were already there where I had my tent set up. I don't think that I will get there, [1330] as sick as I am. With women it can all happen very quickly that we meet our bitter end."

"My lady, please be strong. If you are feeling unwell now, friends will help you recover."

In the meantime, the queen had arrived at her accommodations. Thanks to her friends, she did recover some. When she had arrived at her pavilion, [1340] Antret took her in his arms and carried her into the tent. Isolde said, "Oh, this world can deliver a cruel end. The one who gave me life, to him I give over my body and my life, that he may have mercy on me."

The lady now lay lost in thought, thinking about joy and pain. Her heart held both [1350] joy and pain. How so both joy and pain? She was concerned for her womanly honor but also how she might arrange to bring together his Isolde and her Tristan, his loving woman, her loving man. Whoever might want to bring these two together will have to be very clever and creative.

---

translates: "Antret was approaching, who wanted to harm her [Brangane]" (der sie mit seinem Haß verfolgte). He then starts a new sentence. Kerth (1979), on the other hand, sets a period between the two lines, and so the one whom Antret means to harm, given the context and the following lines, is more logically the queen, not Brangane.

Chapter 4: Success and Failure in Love

[1360] Curvenal was both intelligent and courteous, and he brought bread and wine and a roasted chicken to those who were hiding in the thornbush, which made Kahedin angry. "Curvenal, my God, I hope that things are still alright after you've come here to see us."

Noble Tristan replied, "It is not suitable for a man [1370] constantly to show only fear. Curvenal, so tell me, since I trust you completely and truly without reservation, how are things in Lytan? How is my ship's captain doing?"

"He's as happy as can be. I paid him in gold until even he thought it was too much."

"In truth, you did well. [1380] Can I be sure that he'll wait for me?"

"He said that wherever he might be, he would always come back for you and be at your service. He is at your beck and call."

"May almighty God reward him, as I certainly will. I will make him a rich man if I can keep what is mine. [1390] Curvenal, you should go now, I don't want you to stay any longer. Avoid the main roads and take the paths through the forest. As you love me, so stay true to me. Come back to me tomorrow before daybreak, you know our meeting spot, there where the animals are kept.[26] I'll wait for you on the other side of the stream."

[1400] "I will do that," said Curvenal. "I will do whatever you command, since you, my lord, have retained me with ample rewards.[27] Your coat of arms suits me as well, since we are family, my lord. May God withdraw his grace from me should I ever want to avoid any hardships on your account, whether good or bad. [1410] A mutual feeling of loyalty exists when a lord and his companion are of the same mind."

Curvenal then departed, as his courtly sense told him, and he thought a great deal about these two. He went back so secretively that no one knew where he had been. The day was ending as King Mark came riding up. [1420] He was in the best of moods, because he had been successful in everything. He told his people, the young and old alike, to enjoy themselves with various entertainments like reciting and singing, dancing and running, talking and playing music. There were plenty of amusements, and whatever people wanted [1430] they could find, and no one was bored.

"So tell us, Antret, how did it go? Where is the queen?"

---

26. This word *tiergarte* (l. 1398) must refer to some sort of animal enclosure or an area where game is plentiful.

27. These rewards are the gifts of property and goods that a vassal may expect for service provided to a lord. There is no sense that Tristan has "bought" Curvenal's loyalty, or that Curvenal's motives are in any way mercenary.

"Oh dear, my lord," Antret said with evil intentions, "she is feeling very unwell."

"Why?"

"You did not ride to where the thornbush was. She was so angry she almost died."

[1440] "Oh no, Isolde is near death. Who can make her well?"

"The one whose love has wounded her. He will heal her wounds and share her body until she is healed of her sorrow."

"Antret, you're telling me stories that are unseemly and make me very unhappy. Where is her pavilion set up?"

[1450] "On the other side of the stream, by the spring. She doesn't like all the noise here. The trees there are blossoming and there is a nice fragrance in the air."

"If it is the right thing to do, then I would like to go see Isolde and ask her what I did to her." Brangane had meanwhile joined them. "Brangane, tell me what I should do. How is Isolde?"

[1460] "She was practically dead when I left her, she was in a lot of pain. She doesn't want to live like this anymore. Her red cheeks and her sweet red lips are completely without color. I don't think anyone who saw her perfectly healthy when she left would recognize her anymore."

[1470] "She will quickly be revived," said disloyal Antret, "once she is given the medicine that filled her with such happiness.[28] Once her doctor does the same for her in short order we will have her back on her feet."

Brangane said, "Thanks be to God. Sir Antret, you are being sarcastic." The young woman said, [1480] "May God grant that you might someday be just as ill. People say 'Whoever wants to bring shame to a woman will be unpopular with others.' So my only wish for you is that my wish comes true."

"Antret, you are a deceitful character and enjoy spreading evil rumors. [1490] You only hurt yourself this way, and you have my enmity as well," said King Mark. "You bring shame only on yourself, and it won't so quickly be forgotten. If the love of my life Isolde should die, it would be the end of all my happiness. Oh, dearest Isolde, I would gladly take on your suffering so that your burden [1500] might be made lighter."

"That would serve you right," said Melot. "Never has a woman treated a man worse than she has done her whole life."

He gave the dwarf a slap to the head. "Both of you, shut up. Enough. I don't want to hear another word about it."

---

28. Antret's words, of course, have a double meaning, in that Isolde will be cured by her reunion with Tristan. Brangane calls him out for his sarcasm and insincerity.

She then took her leave. [1690] Camele did exactly as Queen Isolde told her. She shoved the little pillow under Kahedin's head, and he was so incapacitated that he slept the entire night. Camele thought it was funny that he was too timid to lay a hand on a beautiful maiden lying right next to him. [1700] Would you like to hear how Isolde and Tristan made love? I think that they enjoyed the best of loves. Their senses were lost in love's spell. No one had ever enjoyed a better night than Tristan and Isolde. They were intent on doing for the other [1710] what each wanted most. Their arms and legs were entwined, the love between them was powerful indeed. Oh, how passionately they kissed each other's mouths and held each other close. They knew how gently to give and to receive, and so the two of them lay together in blissful exertion. [1720] Their love was so evenly matched that each received the same. Whoever knows how to balance love this way has indeed found happiness and joy. They both aimed for the same goal, which opened itself to them. There is nothing like enjoying love if it's done right and if love wins out in lovemaking. I could say a lot more about love, [1730] but I don't want to make this story too long. Love is better than riches. If it's done right, there is nothing that can compare to love. Isolde, the queen, lay with her Tristan. Whatever love has been enjoyed in the past, it could never compare with what these two had then, lying there together. In the end, though, [1740] the pain of parting neared. The night rushed to become day, and this haste brought them nothing but heartache.

Camele, the noble virgin, slept next to Sir Kahedin, who had not laid a hand on her, and day was now upon them. The maiden took the pillow away, [1750] and Kahedin soon woke up. He thought, "What happened to me? If I admit the truth, then I failed to win the prize. A beautiful virgin was in my bed and I didn't even touch her. I will forever have to live with this disgrace. Who could have tamed my heart so? I'm really astonished. [1760] My reputation is shot, and I can see that I've lost my nerve. I won't ever be able to live this day down. If I was born a man, it isn't apparent anymore. Kahedin, you fool, you'll never find happiness again. Fortune denied me its favor, [1770] as a beautiful virgin lay next to me offering her love. The whole world will mock me that I didn't take up her offer. Now I have to come up with a plan to gain her love again. She doesn't need to worry that I'll run from her again."

Camele, the maiden, went up to him and said, "Thank you for the gift of love [1780] that I received from you. I will repay you with my love as long as I live. Never before was a woman so satisfied as I was by you. I could hardly survive so much love." He turned bright red as she spoke. She went on, "Tristan and Isolde are up already."

Kahedin was so embarrassed he couldn't even look at her. [1790] He said, "Lady, something has happened that has forever robbed me of happiness, unless I can arrange it so that I can win back your love through my service."

"You've already served me. Lady Love herself created this wonder. When a mature woman gives herself to a young man and she remains a virgin, [1800] I think that speaks poorly of the man. I'm not blaming you or anything. If you don't like the way I look, I don't like you either. I don't want to be your woman. You're much too sleepy. Love should be on guard where you're concerned, Sir Kahedin."

"Lady, please stop mocking me, even though I've earned it. [1810] I would rather be buried alive than take any more of this. This burden is so heavy that it will weigh on me my whole life and take all my joy."

"Sir Kahedin, may God save you. It will be a long time coming before I ever give in to your request. I was forced to accompany you to your bed, [1820] but you let me leave again, sir, without any trouble. This will be the way things remain between us forever."

"Oh dear, I am but poor Kahedin, that I ever saw you. Love broke faith with me when it led me to you and then destroyed all my happiness. I never touched you [1830] and left you a virgin. That's something that I will regret my whole life."

Tristan and Isolde saw that day was dawning.[30] Isolde said, "Sir Tristan, get up, my beloved man. Tristan, you have to leave. Our parting, which must separate us, [1840] pains me to the core. My dearest lord, now say something, dear man, when will I see you again?"

"Whenever you command it, Lady Isolde. Whatever your page Peliot tells me from you, I will carry out."

"Now kiss me, and may God protect you."

"Isolde, your wish is my command, my lady."

[1850] "Isolde," said Kahedin, "you have not dealt with me fairly."

"Tell me, friend, how can that be."

"I wasn't able to do what I intended."

"How can I help it if you failed when it was time to enjoy love? Wasn't Camele with you? One thing you can be certain of. She would have lost my favor forever if she had not been with you."

[1860] "I can't deny that the maiden shared my bed, but I didn't do to her what men should do with women."

Lady Isolde replied, "That's not my fault."

---

30. This brings to mind the "dawn song," *Tagelied* or *alba* (Provençal) poems that were popular with troubadours and German *Minnesinger* alike. The knight and lady are awakened at dawn, either by birds, the sun, or a sentry, and the knight is forced to leave before the lady's husband discovers them together. Wolfram von Eschenbach, a poet much admired by Ulrich, wrote a dawn song titled "Sîne klâwen" (MF XXIV,II).

which I have lost through no fault of my own. Now go, and I'll wait for you here."

Paranis left and returned to see the queen. He eagerly told her that Tristan was sorry that he had been falsely accused, and he wanted to tell the true account as proof.

"Tell me, where did you find him, where was he?"

[2040] "Truly, lady, I found him there at the pleasant resting spot, near the stream. I can tell you how it happened that he was waiting there. Early this morning Pleherin rode up and attacked his squires. He chased them all the way into town."

"Tristan told you to say that," said Queen Isolde. [2050] "He paid you to help him with his lie. For this he will suffer my anger. He has lost my respect, and he will have to live with that for a good long while."

"Tristan begs you for your mercy, he is completely innocent."

"As clever as your words may be, you'll never convince me. [2060] He still has my disfavor."

"Don't you think that you might be sorry, my lady, if I tell him about your displeasure? You really are being unjust to him. Fine, I will let him know. Pleherin will suffer the consequences, for he has blamed an innocent man and cost him your respect."

Paranis then left [2070] and went on his way with a heavy heart. He was distressed by Isolde's anger and Tristan's suffering. He told Tristan the news, who in turn was greatly saddened by Isolde's anger and her vow never to change the way she felt.

"What is she accusing me of, my lovely, sweet Isolde? [2080] It is a real tragedy that I, poor Tristan, have lost her favor. Well, things can still work out. The one who caused her anger will now have to fear for his life. May God save this blessed woman and protect her honor. I have to return home now, Paranis, don't argue. [2090] Accompany me to Lytan, and there I will give you something that you can use to convince the queen."

"No, my dear lord, I can't go with you. If I should be recognized, it would cost me my life. Lord, don't be angry. I pray that God [2100] protect your honor and your life."

Paranis left. Tristan then had to go by foot to the town of Lytan, where his crew was waiting for him. Tynas welcomed him warmly, and Tristan told him about his troubles. He, too, was troubled but said, "Lord, be of good cheer. [2110] I will admonish Isolde to regret her anger and forever let it go."

"May God reward you, dear host. This trouble has burdened my heart, something that will surely be noticed here. As much as she has hurt me, I don't want to say anything to anyone until I can regain my happiness [2120] and unburden my heart. Curvenal, come here to me. Pay attention to what I am about to tell you. The two of us will stay here. Tell Kahedin and the others to get on board the ship. You should know that I will not leave until I have seen Isolde, even though she has destroyed my happiness and my future. [2130] Even if she doesn't love me, I will stay here for her sake."

"Explain to me, my lord, how can we defend ourselves? Old or young, everyone here is our enemy."

"You're exaggerating. We'll be fine."

"Why don't you keep the ship here until your problems have been resolved? [2140] Maybe Queen Isolde will grant you her favor and lift your burden."

"I appreciate your advice. Let's leave Kahedin, my companion, out of this. By your faith, promise me that you will do as I ask."

"Lord, what makes you say such a thing? Must I also swear now? [2150] I would risk my life for you. Everything you want, I also want, whether it's of consequence or not."

"Curvenal, that is well said and makes me happy. I am living a life of grief. I have two concerns, both for Isolde and for me. You know, Curvenal, I'm going to dress up tomorrow [2160] to look like I'm sick and suffering from some serious illness. If you advise against this, I will be left to the suffering of my heartache."

"Lord, I think this is a good idea. You are so unhappy that anything that can help would bring me joy. I do have one piece of advice, though. [2170] Let's go back to where the ship is anchored and sail to another location during the night, where we are still close to land and can reach it easily."

"Fine. Let's go tell our captain about our new plan."

[2180] They executed their plan just as they had discussed. Tristan said to his host, "Tynas, may God protect you. You should know, I am at your service wherever I am able. I will gladly do your bidding wherever I can serve you and your honor."

"Tristan, lord, where are you going?"

[2190] "Back to where I came from."

"Don't you want to stay here?"

"Those who hate me without reason will not allow me to stay. I don't think that anyone here is on my side, except for you, Tynas."

"Best of all knights, have you thought about when you might return?"

"Tynas, I don't know. [2200] Just recently I experienced something unforgettable."

"Tell me what it was, Sir Tristan."

"Tynas, I can't tell you. Soon enough people will find out about what has saddened me and filled me with anger."

"I can't imagine what that might be. May the son of the Virgin Mary, who is called Christ, guide you. [2210] I commend you to him, Sir Tristan."

Tynas then left. Whatever Curvenal advised, it was to their benefit. Tristan said to the captain, "Captain, my good man, in God's name weigh anchor.

See to it that your ship sails to a place where I can hide [2220] for two or three days, somewhere close to land. I will not leave this land until I have avenged myself and spoken to the queen."

The captain did as he was told and soon brought him to a place that was, as he had wanted, a secluded and good anchorage.

Chapter 6: Second and Third Reunions

[2229] Tristan left the ship [2230] and did as I will explain. He put on old raggedy clothes wholly unsuited to an honest man. Then something amazing happened. He knew a technique whereby he covered his face in a salve that made him look pale and completely different. He took up a clapper, like the lepers have, and set off for Tintagel. [2240] I'll tell you what he did there. He went to look for the queen, and when she saw the ring on his finger, she knew who it was.

He acted as if he were in pain. "*Belle, blonde Isolde, pour dieu.*[32] You should not refuse the one who seeks your mercy."

The queen responded with anger, [2250] "Paranis, give this leper a good beating. He is coming much too close to me."

Three strong squires came up and told him to get lost and then beat him with their staffs. Queen Isolde thought all this was very funny, but Tristan was not amused. He was hurt and saddened [2260] and returned to the ship, where he told Curvenal what happened. Curvenal sympathized and told him not to lose heart, that everything would turn out alright. "Since she insulted you like this, just forget her and travel on to Arundel, back to Isolde of the White Hands. [2270] You have seldom been so dishonored."[33]

"No, I want to give her the benefit of the doubt.[34] Curvenal, Isolde has become such a part of me that all the women in the world could never tear

---

32. "Beautiful, fair Isolde, for God's sake."

33. Ulrich consolidates and streamlines a fairly substantial part of Eilhart's story from this point on. See the Introduction for a more detailed accounting of his changes. Important to note at this juncture is that after Tristan's beating as a leper, in Eilhart's telling Pylose (Peliot) takes a message to Tristrant that communicates Isalde's true remorse, desire for forgiveness, and penance. Eilhart makes much of the fact that Isalde blames herself and realizes that her anger and the way she laughed at Tristrant's beating were inexcusable, something Ulrich leaves out. Tristrant returns the following May to Cornwall dressed as a pilgrim to be reunited with her, a meeting that Ulrich leaves out altogether.

34. The original phrase is *ich wilz ir gelten mit dem Karles lôte* ("I want to return it to her with Charlemagne's weight"). See the footnote on *Karles lôte* in Gottfried's text (l. 277). The sense is that Tristan wants to be honest in his dealings with Isolde the Fair, just as "Charlemagne's weight" was considered the true standard for the weight of precious metals.

her away from me. It is our fate that we cannot be separated. [2280] I will go see Queen Isolde tomorrow, come what may."

"Lord, whatever you decide to do is fine with me, and I will be by your side."

"Tell the tailor to make us two red robes and cloaks. I will approach her as a squire and see if that will help [2290] her let go of her anger toward me."

"I'm afraid they will recognize us."

"Curvenal, what of it? You only die once, and I would gladly die for Isolde."

"Tell me, lord, what do you have in mind? How do you plan to see the queen? If you claim to be with a lord who is in the town at the time, [2300] then you risk your life if they discover that it's you. My dear lord, please change your mind, truly, they'll kill us both."

"Curvenal, I have made up my mind."

"Oh, my dear lord, I would rather live, if possible."

"Dear friend, take heart. I know that no one wants to die before his time, [2310] but I can put your mind at ease. No one will recognize us, so rest easy."

"How is that possible?"

"I'll show you. I will transform us so that we will be completely unrecognizable."

Tristan then quickly changed their appearance and their hair so that even those [2320] who had traveled with them and knew them well could not recognize them. Tristan took out a small jar and with the contents soon made sure that neither one recognized the other. It was really astonishing that not even those in his company knew who he was.

The two "pages" departed and arrived soon after in Tintagel. [2330] Queen Isolde was sitting beneath a beautiful linden tree, from where she was watching knights and young boys as they played games. There was plenty going on. They were throwing stones and hurling spears, and the young ones were wrestling. The two squires came up to them and stood before Isolde, who welcomed them politely.

[2340] "*Grand merci, belle Isolde,*"[35] said the two pages.

"Who are you squires? Where do you come from? Tell me, I want to know. Do you both serve the same man?"

"No, we don't," said Tristan.

"But you're both wearing the same livery."

"We do this out of friendship, since we both come from the same country."

[2350] "Where is that?" asked the queen.

"It is called Arundel."

"Do you know a lady there whose name is Isolde?"

---

35. "Thank you very much, beautiful Isolde."

Tristan was embarrassed by the question and turned pale and then red. Isolde thought to herself, "Certainly this must be Tristan, even though he has disguised himself so that no one recognizes him."

[2360] "Tell me, what is your name?" said Queen Isolde.

"My lady, I am called Plot."[36]

"Truly, that seems odd to me. Tell me, what is your business here?" she asked and started to laugh.[37]

"We are trying to accomplish something that is difficult to achieve. Before I leave this court I must finish [2370] and cannot leave undone what my lord commissioned me to do when he sent me."

Isolde looked at Tristan and said to him amiably, "*Bon bachelier, écoutez.*[38] I very well know your name. You are Tristan, the man I love with all my heart."

"Have mercy, lady, yes, that is my name. [2380] Your anger and your threats have affected me so that I don't even know myself who I am."

"Now I know for certain who you are. Who taught you how to disguise yourself like this? Your face is foreign and looks nothing like your own. *Beau ami*, Tristan, please forgive me for what I've done. [2390] I denied you my favor after Pleherin told me that he had chased you and challenged you to turn around for my sake, my service, and your own honor. You refused, according to what Pleherin said, and that upset me a great deal."

"What can I do? Regardless of what he said, I am completely innocent of his accusations."

[2400] "Tristan, you have to leave now. Go back to your crew before others find out that you've been back to this country. I recognized you right away when you walked up to me and received my welcome. Now go back," said Isolde, "and whatever Peliot tells you, you must do without hesitation."

[2410] "Lady Isolde, send him to the port of Tribalesen. That, my lady, is where I will be. Whenever he arrives, he'll find me there, and whatever he says, I will do."

"*Doux ami*,[39] that is well said, and if you suffer hardships I will compensate you in full. My friend, you should disguise yourself as a fool and avenge yourself on those who have wronged you."

---

36. No adequate explanation has been presented on the meaning of this name. It seems to be simply a nonsense name. If spelled backwards, though, a kind of trick Gottfried would have appreciated, the name would spell "Tolp," and although not in evidence before the fifteenth century, the root of the modern German word *Tölpel* (fool or country bumpkin) is *Tölp*, from MHG *dörper* or *dörfer*. This is purely speculative, however.

37. This is the second time that Isolde laughs at Tristan, a reaction surely meant to embarrass him, but one that also puts her in an unflattering light.

38. "Listen, young man."

39. "Dear friend."

[2420] "I will do that, my lady," replied Tristan, and with that he departed from Isolde. As he was leaving he jumped into the air for joy. Whether young or old, no one could jump like him. When Tristan arrived at the anchorage, he changed his appearance back to what it was. His complexion was as clear as glass.

After Tristan left them, the knights were mystified [2430] as to who he could be. Such strength was out of place for a common page.[40] King Mark was promptly informed of this incident and immediately set out to investigate who this squire was. Antret and Melot offered this information: [2440] "Lord, the squires spoke excitedly with Isolde. By my faith I think they were sent by Tristan. He is somewhere in our land, near or far. Give the order to find him, my lord. I know that he can be found if we try hard enough."

Mark replied angrily, [2450] "You are provoking me again. If I had him here in front of me, what do you think I would do to him? I would let him go unharmed. I know without a doubt that he is my sister's son. Whoever accuses him of something is blind, whether woman or man. Oh, dear Tristan, wherever you may be, may the one [2460] whom Longinus pierced with a spear in his precious side protect you. Anyone who has ever said anything against Tristan will never gain my favor. Tristan and pure Isolde are free from all malice, even though they have been vilified. Get out of here! Leave me alone! You, my nephew Antret, and you, Melot, have often defamed them [2470] and betrayed your king in the bargain."

Chapter 7: Fourth Reunion: The Fool

[2471] Noble Queen Isolde let Tristan know through Peliot that he should remain hidden for another fourteen days, after which his yearning heart would be recompensed with love, and his bitter life would become sweet again. "Tell him that he should come dressed as a fool. [2480] He should carry a club and fool's clothing, a robe and a fool's cap. His hair should be cropped above the ears, his face dirty and his mouth wide open, just like a fool who is constantly getting into trouble. He should put some cheese in his cowl, and he will have to put up with being kicked and beaten [2490] by foreigners and locals

---

40. This unusual strength can be linked to Tristan's jump, but actually Ulrich has left out a part of Eilhart's narrative in another scene in which Tristrant, disguised as a pilgrim, is talked into participating in some athletic events himself, at which, of course, he excels, only to arouse the suspicion of those around him that a pilgrim could achieve such feats of strength (Lichtenstein, 1877, ll. 7794–855; Thomas, 1978, 136–37).

alike.[41] After that he can do what he likes. Peliot, my dear companion, tell him that he will be doing the right thing by coming to me this way."

Peliot said, "I will do that. Whatever you have me do, I will do to the best of my ability." Soon he arrived where Tristan was waiting and gave him the message, [2500] which Tristan was happy to hear. He did something I would never do. If anyone asked me to do something dishonorable, I would end such a friendship, but Tristan did what his dear Isolde, the queen, asked him to do. He dressed up as a fool, with a gray robe as his clothing and bells all over his body. [2510] He put two pieces of old cheese in his cowl and carried a club with him, which was a chore to lug around. Tristan also acted erratically, as if he really were a fool. Then he went before the queen with a great many children in tow. Even some of the bolder men fled, forsaking their courage, [2520] as soon as he started swinging the club around. Everyone just stared at him.

Tristan said to the lady, "Is it you, the queen? I love you with my whole heart. Lady, you don't need to be ashamed. I am a fool because of you, something your heart knows all too well." He took a big bite out of the cheese, threw a chunk at Isolde [2530] and said, "My dear lady, eat. This fool's food is quite good."

Just as a fool would, he lamented his heartache. King Mark then came along and pulled the fool away by his ears. He told everyone there, friends and strangers, to give him a good beating. The fool ambled over [2540] to sit next to Isolde while Mark watched.

Isolde said to Mark, "Tell him to leave me alone."

But among all the women and men there, no one dared touch him or move him away from the queen. Antret finally came up and tried to take his seat away from him, but Tristan punched him so hard [2550] that he knocked him unconscious. When the others saw this they all ran away, and the king with them. The fool just sat there eating. He didn't care if people were friendly or hated him, it was all the same. His heart was bursting with joy because he could see Isolde. [2560] Antret, who looked more dead than alive, was carried away and mocked all the while. His head was bleeding, and he thought the fool was crazy. The fool, meanwhile, had his way with

---

41. It's difficult to say how this may be related to the previous episode when Tristan came disguised as a leper. Isolde may feel remorse for how she had the leper treated (at least this is the case in Eilhart's version), and although she remarks that a fool, too, is abused, the calculus may be that a fool can be tolerated and remain at court, even performing a function, whereas a leper cannot. In Eilhart, a young boy advises Tristrant to go as a fool, because his hair has been cut short as a result of the treatment Tristrant received for wounds suffered in battle (absent in Ulrich). The cheese is also more logically explained in Eilhart's text as having been received by Tristrant on board the ship on his journey to Tintanjol and kept in his cowl for safekeeping, to be presented later to Isalde.

the court, and no matter what he did or did not do, no one would stop him. Melot barely survived his encounter with the fool, [2570] who grabbed Melot by the leg and dragged him around the courtyard.

"Help save him," cried the king loudly. "I've never seen a fool who was so completely out of his mind. Go get the queen, maybe she can save him."

The fool threw rocks and punches at everyone there at court, [2580] whether they deserved it or not.

Now the queen stepped in, and the fool let the dwarf, somewhat worse for wear, go. The king's table was being set and the fool sat down and took whatever he wanted, roast chicken or fish. Isolde thought he had earned it, but as night fell [2590] the fool began to wonder where he could spend the night. He thought the door of the women's chamber a good spot, and he lay down outside. Isolde, the queen of his heart, was sleeping inside. He pretended to be sleeping, and as much as people yelled at him he couldn't have cared less, [2600] until everyone finally left him lying in front of the door. They kept quiet out of fear. The fool lay there awake and thought of a plan. Lying there he wondered if someone would come along who knew his circumstances, and soon enough Brangane came up to him.[42]

[2610] "Brangane, it's me, Tristan. I'm disguised as a fool."

"Oh dear, that the queen's *ami* should ever be lying here like this. If your mouth ever received a sweet kiss from a noble lover, then it was wasted on you. Does my lady know that you're here? She will be here any minute looking to go to sleep. [2620] We shouldn't be talking here. I'll leave before someone else comes by. I'm glad, though, that I found you here."

At that very moment Isolde appeared. She was sorry for Tristan's plight and wanted to help make his bitter anguish sweeter. Tristan lay there and began to sing [2630] a strange dirge with the queen standing over him. "It is with great pleasure that I hear this plaint. Brangane, tell Paranis to give him something for it. I don't think I ever heard a fool sing better."

King Mark came when he heard the fool's song, but as he was standing next to Isolde [2640] the fool did what fools do. He started singing even louder and his voice was even more off key. No one knew what he was singing. He jumped up as if possessed and everyone ran off. The king himself took off, locking the door behind him, hoping to escape to safety. [2650] Melot took a terrible beating from Tristan. He even had to sacrifice an eye as payment. Isolde was happy to see it, but the king complained bitterly.

In the morning as it was dawning the king rode out into the forest, which Tristan didn't mind at all. The king wanted to hunt [2660] for about fourteen

---

42. In Eilhart's version Brangene has already tragically died by this point (Lichtenstein, 1877, ll. 7560–64; Thomas, 1978, 133). This is not mentioned until almost the end of Ulrich's text (l. 3358).

days. Tristan the fool could finally have his Isolde. A fool has certainly never been granted a better life by any woman. Love gave them both unification, not separation. They were both able to love, to win love there where it should be found. [2670] Love made them both happy. Oh, lovely Love, how you force them both to think only of love and hardly ever bring relief. Love, help these two. They are a yes, they are a no, their hearts together are one yes. They are at your command, [2680] and if you don't help them, they will certainly lose. Love, help your own. Make your loyalty apparent in these two lovers. You have made them into thieves. They are forced to steal love and can hardly keep it a secret. Love, they are captives of your power and their own loving bond.

Now the fool went into town. [2690] Wherever he went, here or there, people gathered around him. What do you think the fool should do? He played all kinds of pranks, some of them harmless, others not so much, and some were even decent. He picked up rocks along the street and carried them on his back to Queen Isolde. She thought this was just nonsense. [2700] She held him in her heart, just as he held her in his. Regardless of what he did during the day, at night he found a comfortable bed where his queen cared for him. One morning, as the two of them were enjoying each other, disaster struck as Antret saw them together in bed. [2710] I'm just sorry that earlier he had survived Tristan's blow.

Antret shouted, "Tristan is here! I saw him sleeping with the queen. The fool has changed back into Tristan. Everyone in the land must make sure that he doesn't escape. [2720] He and the queen will burn at the stake!"

Who will be able to help them? Queen Isolde told Tristan to leave as quickly as possible. "I will," said Tristan, "but I will leave in a way that many may come to regret."

He went to the gate [2730] and, hearing no one outside, forced the guard to open it. Tristan then made his way through the town, and whoever was in his way was soon enough forced to back off with the club that he carried. Next he found himself in a large forest, where he thought he would be safe. [2740] He still had plenty to worry about, though, as people were now hot on his trail. He thought to escape unseen but came to exactly the same spot where Mark was staying. He was saved by luck, in that Mark was lying in a blind and couldn't figure out where the fool had suddenly come from. He didn't know yet about the disgrace that had befallen him. [2750]

Tristan thought, "Let's see if he runs away from me." He raised the club and started to bring it down. The king ducked and then fled from the blow. Next Tristan took to the road and came to a large stream, but he was concerned because there was no bridge in sight. [2760] Meanwhile Sir Pleherin had moved ahead of the other pursuers. Tristan discovered a small row boat at the edge of the stream and was soon rowing across with his club, while his pursuers all yelled at him that he would never escape. Once he had made it to the other side, [2770] Pleherin begged him to turn around for the sake of his love of the queen.

Tristan replied, "You're right. Before I run away, I would rather die for my dear Isolde."

He rowed back again as his manly courage demanded. He attacked Pleherin, who had shouted at him, [2780] without hesitation and hit him with his club so hard that he actually killed him. Mark came running up, and seeing him Tristan rowed back across the stream and escaped. Mark commanded his kin and his men that if they valued their lives [2790] they would seize Tristan and Isolde and burn them at the stake. Tristan escaped, however, and reached his ship. He commanded the captain, if he held him dear, to weigh anchor immediately.

"I barely escaped from King Mark. [2800] He's right on our heels. I would never have made it if I didn't know the land so well."

"I will obey," said the captain and sailed off in God's name.

This is what happened to the king next. He went into the stream and swam over to the other side, and all of his men soon followed him. [2810] The king could see that Tristan was already far out to sea and had no reason to fear him. As he rode back Mark was furious that his nephew Tristan had escaped. The dead man was taken back as well, and the king wanted him to be buried alongside Isolde.

[2820] "We have lost in Pleherin a man of great honor. His death has caused me great sorrow."

The court council advised him to overcome his enmity toward Isolde, since it would not be fitting for the crown to put her to death. "Take a look at the evidence. [2830] Antret is against her and may have accused her of something of which she is innocent. How is it that Tristan took on the role of the fool even though he is widely respected? Lord, we ask you to let your anger be."

"I will allow Isolde to live," said King Mark. [2840] "And anyone who reports something about Isolde that displeases me will be severely punished."

Chapter 8: Kahedin and Cassie

[2843] Oh, if only Tristan knew how Isolde fared and if she were still alive. All the while he was at sea, he thought only of her. "She is there, I am here, and yet we are still together." [2850] In his sorrow he found one great consolation: "At least I know that no one will kill her since I escaped harm."

He said, "Friend Kahedin, I want to stop grieving and regain my purpose. If a woman ever made you happy, then you should remember that [2860] and never waver in your loyalty to her."

271

He replied, "Friend Tristan, I've thought only about one woman since I was a young man. I have never given up the idea over all these years that someday she would give me her love. Even when we were children together, since we were very young we both agreed that we wanted to suffer [2870] good and bad things together, as a couple that loves each other should. Her family married her to a man who was famous. His name is Nampotanis, and Gamaroch is his land, which is next to Arundel. He is of noble ancestry, as am I, and an honorable man. [2880] I don't think that any other woman alive is as beautiful as Cassie. This lady's living quarters are surrounded by three high walls. This is the price for her beauty, and Nampotanis keeps the keys. I have been told, though, that she would reward me if she could. Tristan, I can trust only you in this matter. Give me sound advice [2890] that might lead to success."

Tristan answered him, "I will advise you as best I can. Is it possible for you to speak with her?"

"Yes, when I want to, twice a day. He goes hunting, but he always keeps the keys on his own person, even in the forest."

"If you can speak with the noble lady when you want, [2900] then agree on a time with her when the two of you might talk. You have to convince her to steal the keys from her husband and to take some wax, make an impression, and then give it to you. No matter how securely she is watched, I will guarantee you, if she does her part then you will be rewarded."

"I'm sure that I can achieve that. [2910] She won't let me down, since her heart is well disposed toward me. I'm sure that her womanhood will grant me what I seek. All this time I have never served another woman except my lady Cassie,[43] who is free from all falsehood."

"Once we get to land, I'll see what her heart desires," said the lover Tristan. [2920] He asked the captain when they would reach land. "The sea voyage is not agreeing with me, so please hurry. I will give you a reward that will please you."

"Lord, tell me then how I might make my ship sail even faster. We'll reach land sometime tonight, tomorrow morning at the latest. [2930] I guarantee it."

"Captain, that is well said. When I reach land, I will reward your services more than adequately."

As soon as Tristan set foot on land, he gave his mariner twenty marks of gold. "May King Mark be cursed for pursuing you like this. [2940] If you had

---

43. This statement seems, on its face, to contradict the previous episode with Camele (ll. 1596–832). The operative word though may be *endienete* (l. 2914), or "have not served." Although this is technically true, as Cassie is a noblewoman who can be served, whereas Camele is not, there may also be some exaggeration at work in Kahedin's exclamation of love and devotion for Cassie alone.

been killed by him, I would have been left high and dry. In all my life I have never been so well paid by anyone."

"God be with you," said Tristan. "You served me well."

His friend Kahedin was in a foul mood. "Tristan, my good friend, now what? The house is right in front of us. [2950] Up there is the one who occupies my thoughts all the time but never gives relief."

"Send a messenger up ahead. He should carefully scout out if the lord has gone. Tell your scout to inform her that you are coming and that your yearning is as great today as ever. [2960] Request of her on her faith as a woman that she arrange to speak with you, however she can manage it."

This was quickly arranged. The scout was sent out and did what Kahedin had told him to do.

"My lord has gone into the forest to hunt. I will let my lady know that he is here and see what he wants."[44]

[2970] The scout faithfully executed Kahedin's orders. "Lady, please give me my messenger gift. Kahedin is close by. He would like, with your permission, to arrange to see you."

"Should I admit the truth to you, I would rather see him than he me. Dear man, don't delay. Ask him to come see me. [2980] I want to see him very much, and I will grant him every wish, as long as I am able."

The messenger returned to Kahedin, who, when he heard the report, was overjoyed and said to Tristan, "My messenger has returned, and I have received a report that does my heart good. [2990] Cassie, the pure, kind, noble one, has sent a message that I should come see her."

Kahedin immediately rode off and found his dear lady waiting on the parapet.[45] He rushed up toward her to say that her love pursued him relentlessly. She received him graciously and well, [3000] as a lady should receive her servant, that is, someone who has rendered many services to gain her favor. He began to speak courteously, as Tristan had taught him, "Tell me, my dear lady, could it be that you might welcome me inside?"

The beautiful lady replied, "I would gladly do so."

[3010] Kahedin did not forget to say what Tristan had told him, "I have learned of a certain technique, and if you are willing to help me, then our troubles will be over."

"Kahedin, what is this technique? Whatever it may be, I'll help as best I can. Everything that a woman ever risked for a man, I am willing to risk for you. [3020] I will fulfill your every wish."

---

44. This dialogue is a bit confusing, but the "he" here, referring to Kahedin, probably means that the scout is speaking to an attendant and is then allowed to speak with Cassie directly.

45. The original term, *warte* (l. 2995), can refer to a wall or tower, that is, a place from which to watch, a "lookout."

"Dear lady, please let it be so."

"Kahedin, just tell me what."

"You must steal the keys and then secretly press them into warm wax. Take all three keys and make an imprint and then I can make new keys with the wax."

[3030] Cassie began to laugh and said that she would faithfully and gladly do as he asked. "Come back tomorrow and I will throw the wax down to you. You'll see it there in the moat.[46] Just make sure that nothing happens to you."

"Truly, lady, nothing will go wrong. Whatever may happen, I will surely be back tomorrow morning."

[3040] "Dear Kahedin, do that. Now may he who with his right hand blesses us protect you."[47]

Kahedin departed.

"Tell me then, you happy man," said noble Tristan, "does Cassie truly love you with her whole heart?"

"I bow down to her purity and goodness. She will do whatever I ask. [3050] She has given me the confidence to win happiness. I, most fortunate Kahedin, will find the wax tomorrow lying in the moat in front of the gate."

"You have every reason to be overjoyed, my dear companion. You may well hope for success."

In the morning as the day began, [3060] Kahedin did not forego riding out to find the wax. As Cassie had promised he found it and, not leaving it there, picked it up and rode off again. He said, "Now see here, Tristan, tell me who can make these keys. [3070] If we play it smart, we can make a monkey out of Nampotanis."[48]

"I'll tell you where the smithy, who is a loyal man, lives. His house lies right on the road. He's made lots of keys for me."

When Kahedin arrived at the smith's and told him what he wanted, the smith replied, "Lord, I won't decline to do what you want. [3080] They should be ready in two days, and I'll deliver them to wherever you like, as a favor to you."

Kahedin and Tristan then rode back toward Kark, where the lord, his wife, and Isolde were waiting for them. No one there earned a messenger's reward, because they had come completely unexpectedly. [3090] They were warmly welcomed by him, by her, and by her. Whether or not it was fitting, Tristan and Isolde [of the White Hands] pressed their red mouths together

---

46. Most castle moats were dry, i.e., not filled with water, contrary to the common romantic notion.

47. Christ is often depicted in medieval iconography with his right hand raised in a sign of blessing, with three fingers raised as a sign of the Trinity. Blessing with the right hand has its roots in the Hebrew Bible.

48. The verb is *effen* (l. 3071), to make a fool of, or literally to make into a monkey.

and pleasured each other to their hearts' content. This is what they did. Who would have asked what they both felt in their hearts? [3100] They lay together in bliss, and up until Tristan's death, a man never offered a woman more.[49]

The blacksmith brought the keys, which would give them both joy and an end to joy. Cursed be the calamity that befell these two companions! Kahedin showed the keys to his friend Tristan. [3110] "Tristan, take pity on my agony and free me from this worry. Go with me to see Cassie. She is a budding sprig of beauty. I know for certain that Nampotanis has gone hunting today, as a messenger has just informed me. We should travel in courtly fashion and so guarantee her esteem."

"I'll go with you wherever you like. [3120] I would gladly see your heart satisfied. Let's go, I'm ready. We will take only one squire to care for our horses, and may God protect us," said noble Tristan.

If the world lost these two men, it would be a great loss. Whatever people said against them, [3130] there were no two nobler men than Tristan and Kahedin. When they approached close enough to see Sharize,[50] they left both their horses and went on foot to the drawbridge. Kahedin was wearing a small laurel wreath that the wind blew into the moat. Cursed be that laurel wreath and that it was ever made, [3140] because it caused great harm. Kahedin unlocked the gate and was the very picture of joy when he saw his May flower.

"May God welcome you, Kahedin, and your companion Tristan. I have never been so glad to see two men," said the lovely woman. "I've loved you for a long time with my whole heart. [3150] There are no other men in the castle, because when the lord rides out, no men are left behind until he returns. I suffer greatly from this wicked man. Dear Kahedin, let us go find a place to lie down. The pain that I have suffered for so long will soon be requited, [3160] and I don't care what happens as a result."

That sweet woman and that noble man then did that certain "you know what."[51] Tristan stayed with the other women until the two had ended their sport, which Kahedin was never to play again.

Then the time came when the two had to part, something that was painful to both. They never saw each other again. [3170] Their parting still makes me sad, whenever people read or talk about it. The two had just been together, but it was never to be again. Tristan and Kahedin mounted up and rode away, but their demise was near, their lives about to end. On the left hand they saw

---

49. In Eilhart's version the final consummation of Tristrant and Isalde of the White Hand's marriage comes earlier, after Tristrant was driven from court as a leper by Queen Isalde. "His anger later caused him to make the latter's sister truly his wife, thus ending the quarrel with her father" (Thomas, 1978, 127).

50. Nothing is known about the name of this castle.

51. The original sexual euphemism, *wizzet ir waz* (l. 3163) can still be translated literally.

"Dear Lady, make sure that you bring the salve with you that will save Tristan. And be sure to bring Brangane with you, whose heart is pure and faithful."

"Brangane must stay here. I have never mourned another's death as I did Brangane's. [3360] She was so distressed by my troubles that she worried herself to death. No one will accompany me, I will go alone. My heart and my mind will be bereft of all joy until I set eyes on Tristan."

In the meantime, the Isolde in Kark had made an urgent plea to the merchant's wife [3370] that she should let her know as soon as the merchant was about to return. "You can prove your loyalty by telling me when the ship is about to come into port."

"Certainly my lady, I will do so."

Isolde, the beautiful, the fair, made herself ready for the voyage. It didn't take long for them to reach the port. [3380] As people spread the news that a ship had arrived, Isolde of the White Hands asked Tristan for a messenger's reward,[53] since his Isolde had arrived.

"Lady, please tell me, what is the color of the sail?"

"It is black as coal."

Isolde of the White Hands perpetrated a great wrong when she took his life. [3390] She could easily see that the ship's sail was white as snow. The news was so painful that Tristan turned over and died. Isolde committed a great sin when she killed him without cause.

When Isolde the Fair heard of his death, she thought, "I want to die along with Tristan."

[3400] Both of these Isoldes had never before experienced such great pain and sorrow. A bier was prepared for the dead man, and he was carried into the church. A great lament went up from his friends. Isolde sat next to the bier, but everyone hated her for killing Tristan. Fair Isolde then also approached the bier [3410] on which her Tristan lay. It was a great wonder indeed that the pain did not break her heart when she looked upon the bier. Her bright cheeks were wet with tears.

This anguished Isolde asked the other Isolde, "Why are you sitting here next to this dead man whom you yourself, my lady, killed? [3420] By God, leave this bier at once. You have committed a terrible murder. Go and take your place wherever you like, but not here."

Isolde threw herself onto the bier and breathed her last. It was not the one with the white hands, but Isolde the Fair. I think it would be difficult to find among all women even one woman today [3430] who would give up her life

---

53. This is an especially cruel request since she knows that the news will kill him, and because women do not typically act as messengers for payment.

for the sake of her beloved. Isolde and Tristan died for each other. I still feel sorry that their sense of loyalty drove them to their deaths.

In the meantime King Mark had dispatched a great many ships and barks. [3440] While still at sea the news of Isolde's death devastated him and almost took his will to live. He was told that Isolde was dead, as was his nephew Tristan. He asked the messenger how she had died.

"Lord, did you not know why they were forced to love each other? [3450] A cursed potion from Isolde's mother was the cause.[54] They both drank it for their thirst and loved each other forever after."

"No, oh no, forever no," cried Mark pitifully. "Why did no one tell me when this terrible thing happened to them?[55] I hated Tristan through no fault of his own. [3460] I have lost God's grace forever. Oh, Isolde and Tristan, if you were still alive I would grant you whatever you wanted." Mark beat his chest madly, saying, "Dear God, please allow me to find them both still unburied. [3470] I will have to live in misery the rest of my life."

He wrung his hands so hard that they practically cracked.[56] His household cried, there was no laughter. Mark was also very distraught about his sister's child. By then he had arrived in port and quickly made his way into the town. [3480] He heard a chorus of bells ringing and said to himself, "What does all this bell ringing mean?" He finally reached the church and saw the deceased on the biers. "Is this Isolde and Tristan? I curse the day I was born. I curse that I have lost them. I curse myself!"

[3490] He immediately had two coffins made for them. His people placed them inside and carried them down to the ship. I think that foreigners and the local population alike were filled with sadness. Mark soon after was crossing the sea, taking his wife and his nephew back with him to Cornwall. [3500] What happened to Curvenal? Before he left this world, Tristan gave him authority over all his people and his lands. He also ordered his marshal's children to swear fealty to him. Everyone else's suffering was nothing compared to Curvenal's.

When Mark arrived in Tintagel, he gave voice to his suffering. [3510] He had the dead carried ceremoniously to the monastery where his father lay buried. It is hard for me to describe the grief that spread among the people as the dead were laid to rest. They were not in a single grave, if what I heard is

---

54. This revelation clearly puts Ulrich in the (non-Gottfried) camp that attributes Tristan and Isolde's love solely to the love potion prepared by Isolde's mother. See also ll. 3581–82 following.

55. Mark's reaction is similar to Etzel's (Attila) in the *Nibelungenlied* and the *Klage*, where he laments that he could have prevented the final catastrophe if only he had been told that Kriemhild was bent on revenge (Whobrey, 2018, 202).

56. The following scene of lament is reminiscent of King Etzel's lament and the burial of the dead in the *Klage*, following the catastrophic loss of life at the end of the *Nibelungenlied*.

true. I think that there were two separate graves.[57] Noble Mark screamed terribly in his pain, [3520] as the noble dead, Tristan and Isolde, were interred. The two uncorrupted bodies were placed respectfully in two marble sarcophagi. The king suffered greatly for the two lovers. His heart was nearly broken by the anguish [3530] he felt inside.

He called out loudly, "Ahhh!" and cried, "Will I never see you again in this world? Lord God, what pain I suffer for these two lovers. I don't know what you are waiting for, Death, my heart is broken in half. My joy has been turned to grief. [3540] What I loved most I now see lying in the grave. Lord God, receive them according to your mercy, and may the Archangel Michael take them under his wing as you will.[58] Help me, merciful God, and may they now have a better life."

The king had a rose cutting and a grapevine cutting brought, [3550] which he planted himself, one here, the other there, the grapevine over the pure woman, the rose over Tristan's corpse. After that was done, they were covered with earth until both graves had been filled. Oh dear, that someone must die who has wealth, beauty and youth, a courtly education, and a virtuous character. Tristan had all this. [3560] Whatever else people have read about knights, no one performed such chivalrous acts and was crowned with such praise and fame. I award the crown to Tristan. He was polite and good, loyal and generous, and relentless in the pursuit of distinction. He was courteous and wise, and accorded himself well [3570] in work and play. Ah, how many noble deeds Tristan accomplished in tournaments and battles. There was no one during his time who was more highly praised. He was more famous than anyone. In all my days I have never read or heard of any man who was more renowned [3580] than noble Tristan. If only the love potion had not made him so imprudent,[59] which ultimately ruined his honor. Love can give both joy and heartache. Who ever heard of a more pitiful death of two lovers? Their death still pains me, because they both died [3590] of a broken heart. If only God willed that he were still alive, to whom such high praise was given. I hate Death. Why does our Lord take the good and not punish the bad? That seems very strange to me. I, Ulrich

---

57. This directly contradicts Eilhart, who writes that they were interred in a single grave (l. 9509; Thomas, 1978, 155).

58. Archangel Michael, the angel of death, was known throughout the Middle Ages as the weigher of souls. See also ll. 3728–29.

59. The original word is *unsinne* (l. 3582), which covers a wide range of deficiencies, from being inconsiderate to foolish to irrational to insane. I have chosen a meaning somewhere in the middle, but at the extreme the word can mean "crazy." See also l. 49 in Tristan's opening monologue.

von Türheim,[60] would let a thousand evil doers die [3600] before I let one good man perish.

Whoever has life and wealth and uses both to the benefit of the world, then happiness has blessed him. Whoever can use wealth correctly,[61] both in possessing it and in giving it away, truly, he is a blessed man. Isolde and Tristan loved each other [3610] even as they lay in the ground. I will tell you how this is so. The rose and the vine grew together in the earth.

"How is that possible?" many might ask. "It's nonsense to say that the dead love each other and still think of each other."

Yet it is the truth. [3620] It has often been said that this is what happened with these two. If I were to say that I saw it myself, then I would be lying, but the story declares it to be so.[62] Anyone who doesn't believe it will earn only scorn. This book is all about love's fulfillment.[63] True lovers [3630] will love this story. Where has the power of love ever been greater than in their company? Love demonstrated with these two that two lovers are one.

"Is that so?"

Yes, I hope so. Isolde and Tristan suffered a great deal for each other. His death was the lady's death. Now may God have mercy [3640] on these poor lovers and admit them to his kingdom. For this I sincerely pray. They would have been happy in the world if Love had not made them suffer so. Love truly did make them suffer pitifully. I don't know what debt Isolde had to pay when Tristan's deadly wound caused her death. Where has loyalty been more obvious [3650] than with Queen Isolde, when she left the world from a broken heart? I still mourn her passing. Now may God call them to his kingdom, they have both earned it.[64] Wherever loyalty desires loyalty from loyalty, may God have mercy on them.

The ladies who read this book should pray for my soul [3660] and thank me for the part that I have added to it. I did it for a man who is worthy of all honor. His heart desires great renown. From morning till night he thinks only about how he can help others and win the world's esteem. May God direct

---

60. Here the author names himself *von Tureheim Uolrich* (l. 3598) at the very end of the work, as he comments on the injustice of Death and the permanence of Love.

61. The notion that wealth, or *guot*, could interfere with honor or God's grace and salvation was a common theme and is most famously treated in Walther von der Vogelweide's poem, the so-called First *Reichston*, "Ich saz ûf eime steine" (Lachmann 1820, 8,4).

62. The original term is *âventure* (l. 3625), which could mean source or book. It most likely refers to Eilhart von Oberge's version of *Tristrant*, which was clearly Ulrich's main, though not only, source.

63. The original word is *zil* (l. 3628), which can also mean goal or objective.

64. The *Klage* also emphasizes that Kriemhild deserves to go to heaven because of her loyalty (Whobrey, 2018, 198).

that lady, whom he has always served, to reward him. [3670] His life depends on her favor.[65]

Now listen to how Mark proceeded. He swore by all the saints that he would dedicate his life as a knight to the service of God, to atone for Tristan and Isolde's sins and whatever they had done contrary to his commands. He founded a monastery [3680] with great riches, to which he gave all his property.[66] He even made some wealthy lay people beholden to that house of God. He also built a minster so that it surrounded their graves, and he made sure that the builders built it to his specifications. Mark was afraid of death [3690] and when it would come to take his life, so he fasted and prayed often. He did as one does who is focused on the afterlife and wants to gain eternal life for himself and others.

Over the grave people saw the rose and grapevine intertwined in a way that is hard to believe. [3700] Since the creation of the world, no one has seen two people love each other so much after their passing. The builders followed Mark's instructions exactly. Where was there a loyalty greater than noble Tristan's loyalty? He should get credit for this if he is still in hell, [3710] so that God might recognize it and bring him into his kingdom.[67] This is our constant wish, for Queen Isolde as well, whose loyalty caused her all too soon to share in his fate. May God with his right hand lead her out of damnation.

You have now heard all that Tristan and Isolde suffered. [3720] May God let us enter his kingdom when we depart from here, that we might escape hell and never suffer there. May God care for us in all his perfect goodness and give us strength and the will to deserve his blessing. And when the angel weighs all our sins, [3730] may the Holy Trinity have mercy on us. Amen.

---

65. The lady mentioned here is possibly Konrad von Winterstetten's wife, Guta von Neifen.

66. Founding a monastery to atone for sins or to provide a place of rest for the last years of life was a common practice among the medieval nobility. Ute, Kriemhild's mother in the *Nibelungenlied*, founded the monastery of Lorsch and retired there. Toward the end of his life Ulrich's patron, Konrad von Winterstetten, founded the monastery of Baindt in 1240 for Cistercian nuns.

67. The concept of purgatory came into the theological mainstream in the early thirteenth century, although doctrine wasn't established until the Second Council of Lyon in 1274.

Gottfried von Strassburg's Poem in the Codex Manesse

The following two strophes are found in the Codex Manesse (Heidelberg University Library Cpg 848) among the poems of Ulrich von Lichtenstein (247r). Given Rudolf von Ems's testimony (c. 1240) that Gottfried wrote a poem about "luck made of glass" (l. 2,9) as well as various internal stylistic and linguistic features, it is generally agreed that this poem should be attributed to Gottfried von Strassburg. Its relationship to *Tristan and Isolde* is discussed briefly in the Introduction. The lines 2, 3–6 were copied by Reinmar von Zweter in his poem about the Wheel of Fortune (*Mittelhochdeutsche Sangspruchdichtung*, 2011, 144–45). The text itself appears in *Des Minnesangs Frühling* [MF], 1988, 431–32. The best German translation can be found in the Krohn edition of *Tristan* (1980, 3.209–10). The Nolte/Schupp edition (*Mittelhochdeutsche Sangspruchdichtung*, 2011, 142–45) includes only the second strophe. An English translation of both strophes is available in *German and Italian Lyrics of the Middle Ages*, 1973, 142–3. The rhyme scheme for both strophes is: 6A 6A 5B 6C 6C 5B // 3D 7D 5E 3F 7F 5E, the number indicating the number of stressed syllables. The following translation presents the text as accurately as possible, while resisting any attempts to present the original's metrical or poetic features.

MF XXIII/I "People and Lands" (*Liute unde lant*)

1.
[1] People and lands might live in blessed harmony
were it not for two little words: "mine" and "yours."
They cause a great many strange things to happen in the world.
Everywhere they go they build things up and tear them down
[5] and kick the earth around as if it were a ball.
It seems to me their war will never end.
Accursed greed
grows and grows as it has since the time of Eve.
It corrupts all hearts and all realms.
[10] Neither deeds nor words
are intent on anything but betrayal and instability.
Those who say otherwise and those who follow them are outright liars.

2.
[1] Good luck rises and falls in strange ways.
You can find it more easily than keep it.
It seesaws back and forth if you don't take care.
Whomever it wants to torment gets whatever it gives
[5] at the wrong time or loses it again at the wrong time.
It blinds those to whom it lends too much.
To them, joy gives pain.
Rather than live a life in body and mind free from care,
we find instead our luck is made of glass,
[10] and anything but solid.
Whenever it sparkles in our eyes and shines the brightest,
that's when it most easily shatters into tiny pieces.

Thomas's *Tristran* and the End of the Story

One of the unsolved mysteries surrounding the Tristan story and its telling is why Ulrich von Türheim chose to use Eilhart von Oberge's version as the basis for his continuation of Gottfried's monumental work as opposed to Gottfried's own self-proclaimed source, the version of Thomas of Britain. It is apparent that Ulrich knew Gottfried's text; the manuscript tradition bears witness to that as do Ulrich's specific references to Gottfried's text, and so it should be assumed that he was also aware that Gottfried named his source as Thomas *von Britanje* (l. 150). Around the same time that Ulrich was working on his continuation, a cleric named Robert was translating Thomas's work into a prose version in Old Norse, a work now commonly referred to as *The Saga of Tristram and Ísönd*. Given that Robert dates his translation to 1226, and that we are fairly confident that Ulrich was writing his Tristan sometime between 1230 and 1240 (before his patron Konrad von Winterstetten's death in 1243), it seems unlikely that Ulrich could have been unaware of Thomas's text altogether. It might simply have been the case that a copy of the Thomas text was not available to Ulrich. A comparison of the two versions should be helpful in assessing the extent to which Ulrich's choice of the Eilhart version affected his own interpretation of Gottfried's text and its (presumed) ending. It may also be helpful to compare the ending of the story as told by the two competing traditions, the "common" and the "courtly" as represented by Eilhart's and Thomas's versions, and so gain at least some sense as to how Gottfried might have completed his own text. It is worth remembering that Gottfried knew of Eilhart's version, his own text makes that clear,[1] and also that, while following Thomas's lead, Gottfried was prone to amplify the material he had before him.

Ulrich's and Robert's texts have come down to us as complete works, but the fragmentary transmission of Thomas's text makes a comparison challenging, and unfortunately Eilhart's text is in no better shape when it comes to the fragmentary condition of the few early manuscripts.[2] A brief review of the manuscripts containing Thomas's *Tristran* will help make this clear. The last part of the story—that is, that part of Thomas's version that goes past

---

1. Gottfried's borrowings from Eilhart are summarized by Thomas (1978), 34.
2. The three early Eilhart fragments (late twelfth to early thirteenth century) contain only slightly more than 1,100 unique lines, or about 12 percent of the complete work. Three late manuscripts (fifteenth century) provide the rest of the text, which in Lichtenstein's edition (1877) goes to 9,524 lines. The manuscript transmission of Eilhart's *Tristrant* is detailed in Bußmann's edition (1969), xxx–xxxix.

Gottfried's own fragment (ending at l. 19,548)—consists of a total of 3,144 lines and is transmitted in four groups of manuscript fragments (the Cambridge and Carlisle fragments cover earlier parts of the story). Manuscript D (Oxford, Bodleian Library, Douce d. 6, 21983, "Douce"), dated to the last third of the thirteenth century, altogether twelve parchment leaves containing lines 1268–3087, is the largest single block of lines from the fragments. Manuscript Sneyd (Oxford, Bodleian Library, French d. 16, ms. "Sn"), dated to the end of the twelfth century and therefore the oldest set of fragments, contains lines 53–940—that is, the first part of the Thomas ending (the Cambridge fragment is numbered lines 1–52), and lines 2319–3144, which include Thomas's epilogue. Next, the Strassburg manuscript (Bibliothèque du Séminaire protestant, ms. "St"), thirteenth century and destroyed in 1870, transmits a group of lines in the middle of the last part (1197–264, 1489–94, 1615–88, 1785–854), and finally, the Turin manuscript (Accademia delle Scienze, Documenti Cartacei e Trasscizioni, Mazza 813/43, ms. "T"), second half of the thirteenth century, also covers a middle part of the ending (941–1196, 1265–522). While these four groups of fragments all include parts of the end of the story, and while they are assigned consecutive line numbers based on their position in the narrative sequence, they represent in total only some 20 percent of Thomas's work. The gaps that remain must be filled in by Robert's *Saga*. We have to assume that Robert was fairly faithful in his transmission of Thomas's original, an assumption that is reasonable given the fact that throughout Robert's "translation," as far as we can tell by comparison, he tends to shorten and straighten the French text rather than craft his own additions or deviations.

Despite the less than ideal nature of the manuscript transmission of the various versions of the Tristan legend, we are on fairly solid ground in stating that certain elements of the story were universal and a part of every story line. Focusing just on the last part of the story, an outline of the narrative elements that all versions have in common is as follows: Tristan is in Brittany and marries another woman, Isolde of the White Hands; he fails to consummate the marriage, thereby dishonoring her and her family; he makes several trips to King Mark's court (either in Cornwall or England) in disguise to see Isolde of Ireland; Tristan and Kahedin are falsely accused of cowardice; Tristan is poisoned in a battle, a wound that only Isolde can heal; Tristan dies after being led to believe that Isolde is not coming to save him; Isolde arrives after Tristan's death and subsequently dies. This very basic outline contains all the common elements of this part of the story, but there is considerable variation in the number of reunion episodes and the characterization of the primary protagonists' motivation. Finally, and to some extent most importantly, the portrayal of the aftermath of the deaths of Tristan and Isolde, especially with regard to Mark's role in their burial and the "life" after death that the two lovers share, is markedly different among versions and has an important bearing on our interpretation of the author's intent.

There has been much speculation as to how much further Gottfried would have taken his own text. That he would have continued using Thomas as his source should be assumed. That what we have is not the end is also a near certainty. No epilogue or final authorial comments follow, and the end of the story, on which all sources agree, is missing: the deaths of Tristan and Isolde. It is possible, however, that Gottfried did end a major section of his composition at this juncture, given a proposed organization of the entire text into parts as distinguished by manuscript initials and interspersed four-line strophes with unique rhyme schemes.[3] According to this scheme, Gottfried's text ends at exactly one of these main partitions at line 19,548.

Gottfried's text ends with Tristan deep in thought, pondering his dilemma: Does Isolde still love him or not? This interior monologue begins with line 19,424, so we have some 125 lines in which Gottfried details Tristan's internal struggle to reconcile pain and love. He considers that another love, with Isolde of the White Hands for example, might help mitigate the suffering for the one he cannot have. He rationalizes this further with the presumption that Isolde could have found him by now if only she had tried hard enough, a thought that echoes the extraordinary lengths to which his foster-father, Rual, went to find Tristan at Mark's court after his kidnapping as a boy. Finally, Tristan opines that Isolde no longer cares for him and that he himself could not "ask of her what would most give me joy and a happy life on this earth" (l. 19,548). What exactly this is that Tristan cannot ask of Isolde is not entirely clear, but one likely meaning is that, even though Tristan has forsaken all women for Isolde's sake, he would not ask her to do the same, because she is married to Mark and would have to abandon him, and her honor, to be with Tristan.

Ulrich's text begins where Gottfried's narrative leaves off, with the exception of a short prologue wherein Ulrich introduces both his reason for attempting a continuation of the great master's work (Gottfried's death) and his patron, Konrad von Winterstetten, a high Swabian official at the Hohenstaufen court in the first half of the thirteenth century. Ulrich presumes that his audience or readers already know the story of Tristan and Isolde and their illicit affair and so continues with Tristan ending his monologue in short order by resolving to let Mark keep Isolde in Cornwall, while he moves on and takes Isolde White Hands as his wife. He announces his intention to Kahedin to ask for

---

3. This is based on Gravigny (1971). See the Introduction in this book for more detailed information on Gottfried's textual structure. The Table of Contents to this translation follows this scheme.

his sister's hand and stay in Brittany. This follows Eilhart's narrative fairly closely, starting around line 6106 (Lichtenstein, 1877), with the exception that Eilhart has none of Tristan's monologue but moves instead directly from the end of the battle for Karahes (Kark) to Kahenis (Kahedin) asking Tristan to propose to his sister and stay in Brittany.

Thomas's text, opening with the first Sneyd fragment at line 53, begins with Tristran's[4] lengthy monologue (178 lines from ll. 57–234) in which he questions Ysolt the Fair's faithfulness and asks himself why he should not let go of this love and move on. The answer to the question, what good is love that brings no joy, is simply that one should not want what one cannot have, and conversely that one should want what one can have. This is followed by consideration of the power of carnal desire (OF *delitier*) to induce forgetfulness in matters of love. While there is no answer to this question, it seems to Tristran that it might be worthwhile to put this hypothesis to the test. Thomas follows up with his own commentary on Tristran's internal disputation (to line 420). Couched in terms of the conflict between will and desire, Thomas's argument boils down to what we might characterize as the "grass is always greener" argument—that is, we reject what we already have even if it is good, and we want what someone else has even if it is bad. Thomas remarks that this is irrational, and that if Tristran had truly loved (*fin amur*, ll. 381–82) Ysolt of Ireland, he would not have married Ysolt White Hands. We hear echoes of this in Gottfried's Prologue, ll. 9–16, in which it is argued that people ought to praise and be happy with what they should want to have.

Tristran proposes to Ysolt White Hands' parents, they are married, and the wedding night quickly ensues, a scene shared by all versions of the story in which Tristran cannot, or will not, consummate the marriage, much to Ysolt's chagrin. The scene is dominated by a second, long interior monologue during the course of which Tristran becomes convinced that he has made a mistake in marrying Ysolt White Hands and vows to do penance by not enjoying conjugal relations with his new bride. He sees no good choice, no way out of his dilemma: he can either break his oath to Ysolt the Fair and act as Ysolt White Hands' true husband, or he can dishonor his wife by not having sex and staying true to the Ysolt he loves. Either way he loses, and so he makes a decision that he believes will do the least harm. He follows his notion that love and reason will overcome desire and nature and excuses himself with a lie about an old wound that is acting up that prevents him from exerting himself.

---

4. In the following exposition, the spelling convention of Tristan's name uses that most commonly found in the various versions. Tristran = Thomas; Tristram = Robert's *Saga*; Tristrant = Eilhart; Tristan = Ulrich and Gottfried.

So far the two versions, Ulrich's (and Eilhart's) and Thomas's, have not diverged too much, although Ulrich and Eilhart move the plot along more expeditiously. They avoid the two long monologues and move past the wedding night in no more than 350 lines (even fewer for Eilhart), while Thomas takes about 650 lines to narrate the same story line. After the wedding night debacle, however, Thomas follows another path entirely. After a very brief scene in Ysolt's chambers, where she laments Tristran's absence, he introduces a pair of giants from Africa, Orgillus and his unnamed nephew, into the narrative even though their story has no real impact on the main plot, as Thomas himself admits in line 781. King Arthur makes an appearance in the story in the recounting of a past adventure when he killed Orgillus after refusing to sacrifice his beard to the giant's beard collection. Tristran is later wounded in a fight with the giant's nephew while serving in Spain defending the emperor's (presumably the Holy Roman emperor, although the *Saga* says that it was the king of Spain) honor, and beard. Tristran returns to Brittany to convalesce from his wounds, but Ysolt remains under the impression that he is still in Spain.

After a short commentary by Thomas on the nature of envy and gossip, the action turns to Ysolt the Fair in her chambers composing and performing a sad love song (*un lai pitus d'amur*, l. 833) about Sir Guirun, who is killed by a jealous husband and then served as a meal to his lover. Suddenly Cariado, a nobleman and knight at the court, appears in Ysolt's room with the hopes of seducing her now that Tristran is out of the picture. This Cariado is similar in some ways to the Mariodoc of Gottfried's text, although Ulrich has no such character at all. Cariado has no success with his entreaties and is dismissed by Ysolt, but not before, or perhaps because, he brings news of Tristran's marriage to the rival Ysolt. Here the first Sneyd fragment comes to an end (l. 940), and the French version only comes back into play with ms. T as Tristran is enjoying Ysolt's affections in the form of a lifelike statue.

The *Saga* tells us that quite a bit happens between Cariado's appearance and Ysolt's restoration in the form of a statue. Whereas Ulrich and Eilhart move straight from the wedding night to the so-called Bold Water episode, Thomas, based on the *Saga*, inserted a number of episodes in between. In chapters 73–81 of the *Saga*, we are told an elaborate tale of Tristram's defeat of another giant and his construction of a "Hall of Statues," meant to somehow replace the absent Isönd (Isolde), Bringvet (Brangane), and others. It is important to note here that these chapter divisions of the *Saga* are modern editorial conventions and not part of the original work. Chapter 72 opens with Queen Isönd sitting in her room composing a song when Mariadokk interrupts her and gives her the news that Tristram is married. This follows the Thomas text quite closely to this point. Chapter 73 then introduces a giant named Moldagog, who resides at the edge of Brittany's borders. He and the Duke of Brittany have an arrangement that creates a kind of "cease-fire line" following the river's course that divides their territories. Neither will cross the line on pain of severe punishment. The duke explains all this to Tristram and expects him to abide by the agreement. Tristram agrees at first, but tempted by the fine timber available on the giant's land, he eventually breaks his oath. In the meantime, he and his best friend Kardin (Kahedin) are occupied with defeating other enemies apparently still threatening Brittany, and they emerge victorious in all their battles.

Chapter 75 begins with a scene in which Tristram purportedly goes out to hunt but in fact intends to cross the river and challenge the giant for his land and timber rights. After a harrowing crossing, Tristram meets Moldagog and demands the right to take forty-eight of the tallest trees for his own use. In the next chapter, which continues mid-scene, the giant refuses and of course challenges Tristram to defend himself. A fight ensues, but the giant and his cudgel are no match for Tristram and his sword, which slices off one of the giant's legs, leaving him helpless and begging for mercy. Tristram accepts the giant's surrender and his oath of fealty. Next, Moldagog takes Tristram to his lair, shows him his treasure, in which Tristram has no interest, and the two agree that Tristram will have complete control of all the forest and its trees and furthermore that the giant will comply with any and all of Tristram's commands. Tristram then returns home and tells no one what has transpired, but instead makes up some story for Isönd about a boar in the forest that got away and that he intends to find again the next day.

We now come to Chapter 78 of the *Saga*. There was in the densest part of the forest an old cave that had been elaborately carved out in the past by the Giant of Mont St. Michel, of whom we learn that he, too, was killed by King Arthur. Again, the author concedes that none of this really matters except to explain how the cave came into being. Tristram then engages craftsmen to expand and renovate the vaulted room and what emerges is a kind of hall with a fence around it, decorated with gold both inside and outside, intended to be a sort of museum for a group of statues that Tristram has made to his exact specifications. These statues are incredibly lifelike, and their ingenious design even includes a kind of technology that allows sweet smelling herbs to issue from Isönd's mouth. There are seven statues in all: Isönd, with a dwarf underfoot; Bringvet; the giant Moldagog; the dog Peticriu; the steward Mariadokk; and a lion. The lion and the giant, naked from the waist down and holding a raised club, are meant to scare off intruders. The two women are dressed in fine clothing, Isönd is crowned and holding the ring she gave Tristram, while Bringvet holds the vessel with the love potion, which is explained by an inscription: "Queen Isönd, take this drink which was prepared in Ireland for King Markis." The mechanical dog shakes his head so that the bell around its neck rings constantly.

All of this is interesting enough in itself, but we then learn that Tristram intends to use his statues as stand-ins for the real thing. Visiting them daily, he speaks to them and kisses and embraces the statue of Isönd as if she were alive. When he is in a more despondent mood, he berates the two women along with the statue of the evil Mariadokk. It is at this point, in *Saga* Chapter 81, that we can reconnect with Thomas's original text in the form of manuscript fragment T. In mid-sentence (l. 941) we encounter Tristran kissing or berating the statues as the case may be. Thomas explains this strange behavior as symptomatic of Tristran's love–hate relationship with Ysolt the Fair, his jealousy of the steward, and his fear of losing his love. He goes on to compare the love that each of these four characters, namely Marque; Ysolt; Tristran; and his wife, Ysolt *Blanchemains*, feels. The author's conclusion is simply that he lacks the experience to judge which of these four suffers most, or which one experiences the greatest love or the greatest pain (ll. 1084–91, 1120–23). None of this has moved the action forward in any way. If Ulrich or his source Eilhart knew of this version, they were happy to skip it entirely. It seems that the Hall of Statues acts as a kind of allegory of Tristran's internal struggle, a visible memorial to the drama and emotional roller coaster that is Tristran's state of mind (and heart). It is clear that Ulrich prefers a more plot-driven style that lacks the interiority and reflectivity of Thomas's text.

We come now to an episode common to all versions of the Tristan story— that is, the leisurely ride in the country that humorously uncovers Isolde of the White Hands' secret, often called the episode of the "bold water." All versions agree that, while out riding with her family to a tourney, Isolde's horse steps into a puddle of water and creates such a splash that the water reaches under her dress all the way to her thighs and beyond. Her laughter and exclamation that the water is bolder than her husband is overheard by her brother. She tells him that no man's hand has traveled as far as this water, whereupon the Thomas manuscript fragment ends. So, again, we need to resort to the *Saga* to bridge the gap. We do not, however, discover any major deviations between Thomas and Ulrich. In Chapter 82, the *Saga* recounts the same misadventure on horseback, which ends with Isodd's plea that her father not reproach Tristram for his conduct. Nevertheless, the duke and his son Kardin are distressed and concerned for their family honor. The next two chapters are broadly similar in content to what we are told by Ulrich, namely that Kardin confronts Tristram about his neglect of his sister's honor, and Tristram confides that he loves another woman who is more beautiful than any other woman and whose attendant, Bringvet, is so beautiful that she could be a queen, which leaves his own wife barely fit to be the lady of a castle. Ulrich argues a bit differently, claiming that Isolde of the White Hands treats Tristan worse than Isolde of Ireland treats her own dog. What would justify such a claim is left unexplained, and in fact Tristan's failure to make Isolde White Hands his true wife cannot be excused by Isolde the Fair's beauty or Isolde White Hands' mistreatment, which seems fabricated. In both versions, the agreement is that there will need to be material proof of Tristan's assertions. This is where the Hall of Statues comes back into play. Rather than take Kardin to see the real queen, in the *Saga*, Tristram takes his friend to his secret hall and shows him the statues as proof of his claims concerning the two women's beauty. Kardin is convinced, and upon seeing Bringvet's likeness, is thrilled that Tristram promises him Bringvet's love (chapters 85–86). This interlude only delays what in fact must still happen, that is a journey by both men to England to see their women in the flesh.

At this point, as they get underway for their journey on what will be the first reunion of Tristan and Isolde, the first Strassburg fragment helps us rejoin Thomas's original text. With some deviation in detail, the action is similar to Ulrich's telling, except that Ulrich invents a magical deer to act as a messenger for a letter from Isolde. Furthermore, the preparations for the journey and a stop in Lytan are somewhat more elaborately detailed by Ulrich, but in the end, the two comrades make their way to King Mark's, accompanied by two squires. Rather than hiding in a thornbush, Tristran and Kaherdin hide up in an oak tree, from where they can observe the king's and queen's retinues passing by below them as if on parade. Unfortunately, the first Strassburg fragment only goes to line 1264, leaving the two still up in the tree. The *Saga* Chapter 87 tells of the two walking up to the queen's carriage, at which point Isönd immediately recognizes Tristram and returns the ring. As we would expect, the two later rendezvous with the queen and Bringvet and spend the night, although Bringvet rebuffs Kardin's advances through the use of a drugged sleep pillow. This is repeated for two more nights, but on the third Bringvet gives in to Kardin and they become lovers. They are discovered but given enough warning so that Tristram and Kardin can flee, but on foot and without their weapons or horses. Mariadokk discovers the two squires tending the horses, and assuming that they are actually Tristram and Kardin, challenges them to stop, but the pages keep riding and escape.

This case of mistaken identity leads to charges brought by the steward to Isönd and Bringvet that their lovers are in fact cowards. Bringvet at first defends Kardin, but then takes her doubts and anger out on Isönd. Although the *Saga* summarizes the exchange between the two women in a short paragraph, Thomas makes much of Brengvein's anger and the accusations she levels against Ysolt. Ms. D now takes over, from line 1268, and its contents guide us from here almost to the very end of Thomas's text, so that we no longer need to consult the *Saga* to fill in missing content. This, along with the other fragments, gives us a fairly reliable reading of the rest of the Old French poem. Brengvein's and Ysolt's confrontation, and Brengvein's eventual involvement of the king take up almost five hundred lines (ll. 1265–752). This has no counterpart in Ulrich or Eilhart and is much abridged in the *Saga*. Instead, Ulrich describes Kahedin's failed attempt to seduce Camele, an attendant of the queen (instead of Brangane) and then Curvenal's (instead of the page's) escape from Pleherin (instead of Cariado). Ulrich's Isolde doesn't believe a word of Pleherin's accusations (Brangane is nowhere to be found) and sends her messenger Paranis to find Tristan and tell him about his alleged loss of honor.

What comes next in the French text must truly be one of the most remarkable scenes in all of medieval literature. The clash between Ysolt, the queen, and Brengvein, her faithful assistant, handmaiden, and adviser has no parallel in its emotional intensity, wide-ranging argumentation, and reversal of class roles. Brengvein's tirade and her accusations seem at first out of character, seemingly coming out of nowhere. In a sense they do, because we have no earlier material from Thomas with which to compare it, or any previous clues as to Brengvein's true feelings. Gottfried paints a picture of Brangane as a noble, forgiving, and completely loyal handmaiden. Thomas's Brengvein, on the other hand, is unmasked as a vindictive, moralistic, ungrateful servant who is at the end of her rope. She feels betrayed by Ysolt, recalls the murder plot against her, and accuses Ysolt of duping her by foisting Kaherdin on her. All of this rests of course on a false accusation: Tristran and Kaherdin did not run away as Cariado claimed. Brengvein's accusations are built on a foundation of past wrongs that come to a head in her liaison with Kaherdin and Ysolt's persistent amoral affair with Tristran. The upshot of it all is that Brengvein tells the king about Ysolt's latest transgression and is appointed by the king as Ysolt's watcher, or better, jailer.

The story moves on to Tristran's and Ysolt's second reunion, or the leper episode. In all of our versions, Tristran and Kaherdin have by now returned to Brittany. Tristran, determined to find out more about Ysolt's situation after his hasty departure, disguises himself as a leper, complete with a clapper. He returns to the court and places himself at the entrance to the palace in the hopes of gaining some news about Ysolt. On the occasion of a festival the king and queen come out of the palace, allowing Tristran to make his appeal directly. He is abused by the court servants, but as he enters the cathedral behind the royal retinue, Ysolt recognizes him and wants to give him a ring. Brengvein turns out to be the villain in this scene as she, too, recognizes Tristran but then berates her lady for even considering giving a gift to such an outcast. In Ulrich's and Eilhart's versions, it is Isolde who has Tristan beaten and then laughs about it to add insult to injury. Tristan quickly leaves the court and returns to Brittany, in what ends up being a very brief encounter. With Thomas, Tristran goes away convinced that Brengvein is the enemy. What happens next seems atypical for a strong and manly knight such as

Tristran, but the reader can see that the hero is at his wits' end. Tristran hides himself under the steps of an old castle ruin, weeping and bemoaning his fate and longing for death. There he is discovered by a watchman and his wife, taken into their humble abode and comforted. Tristran tells them his story, and so the watchman takes a message to Ysolt, but Brengvein remains heartless and unmoved. Ysolt asks for forgiveness for her past sins and eventually convinces Brengvein to go see Tristran. She then learns from him that Kaherdin's running away was a lie, and the truth leads to a reconciliation of the three, with Tristran spending the night with Ysolt. The next morning he departs and returns home.

Thomas turns his attention to Ysolt, who is left behind to grieve Tristran's and her own pain and suffering. Determined to share in his pain, she takes on the role of contrite penitent, even wearing a hair shirt. She sends a minstrel to Tristran with a message describing her penance and misery, at which point he resolves to see her again, this time dressed as a pilgrim. Back at court he and Kaherdin apparently make contact with Ysolt and take part in a festival in which a disguised Tristran competes in all sorts of physical competitions, besting all other competitors. Almost as an afterthought, the reader is told that he and Kaherdin killed two lords in the course of a joust, one of them being Cariado (!), killed by Kaherdin as revenge for his false allegations. Pursued by a posse of Cornish knights, the two make their escape in the thickets of the forest and sail back to Brittany. This third reunion is missing from Ulrich altogether, even though his source, Eilhart, does include the episode (ll. 7445–864), minus the joust and the steward's death, because it is Curvenal and not Kaherdin who accompanies him. Eilhart furthermore provides us with the information that Brangene has died (l. 7560). Ulrich instead has Tristan regroup after his beating as a leper to return to court soon thereafter with Curvenal, both dressed as squires or pages. This time Tristan is recognized by the queen, even though he gives his name as "Plot," and Isolde gives him instructions to come back disguised as a fool.

Thomas goes another way. In what is sometimes called the episode of the "poisoned spear," we start with a revealing discussion by Thomas of his sources. It seems appropriately timed, given that this is another critical juncture where the two traditions diverge. Thomas begins by telling his readers:

> My lords, this tale is told in many ways, so I shall keep to one version in my rhymes, saying as much as is needed and passing over the remainder. But the matter diverges at this point and I do not wish to keep too much to one account. Those who narrate and tell the tale of Tristran tell it differently—I have heard various people do so. (Hatto, 1960, p. 338)

He goes on to dispute a version about a dwarf's wife loved by Kaherdin, in which the dwarf wounds Tristran with a poisoned spear. Thomas's counterclaim turns on a twist of narrative logic, or rhetorical sleight of hand. He tells us that this other version has Guvernal being sent to England as an emissary to Ysolt on account of Tristran's wound, but this is of course impossible because Guvernal was so well known at court that he could never have acted as a secret emissary. Thomas instead calls on the authority of his source, a certain unknown and probably fictitious "Breri," and promises his readers that he will hold to the truth and that "the tale will bear me out" (Hatto, 1960, p. 338). The frustration for us as modern readers is that we don't have this other version to which Thomas refers. The *Saga* has no such telling, nor do the various prose versions.

So Tristran and Kaherdin, back home in Brittany, go about their chivalric duties, garnering praise and honor throughout the land in deeds of glory. For entertainment, they have the statues back in the giant's forest to keep them company. In what is framed as a typical tale of chivalric questing, they encounter one day while hunting a gallant knight in the distance. When they meet, the knight asks directions to where he might find Tristran *l'Amerus*, or "the Lover." The knight gives his own name as Tristran *le Naim*, or "the Dwarf," even though he is described as "tall" (OF *lungs*, l. 2187) of stature. It is unknown how this relates to the dwarf mentioned previously in other versions that Thomas promises to avoid. The *Saga* merely calls the name a "misnomer," as it obviously does not describe his height. This second Tristran complains of having lost his wife, or his *amie*, to an evil knight named Estult l'Orgillius of Castle Fer, who kidnapped her. After some discussion Tristran agrees to come to the aid of this knight and battle Estult and his brothers, of which there are six (seven in the *Saga* Chapter 95). After laying an ambush in which two brothers are killed, the rest ride out from the castle and attack the two Tristrans. A tough fight ensues in which Estult and all his brothers are eventually killed, but Tristran *le Naim* is also dead, and Tristran is wounded by a poisoned lance. With his remaining strength he makes his way back to Brittany, where his doctors unsuccessfully try to heal him, given their inability to fight the poison. It soon becomes clear to Tristran that he has received a fatal wound unless Ysolt can once again cure him of this poisonous infection.

Ulrich's episode with Tristan the Fool plays no role whatsoever in the Thomas story, nor does his story of Kahedin, Cassie, and her husband Nampotanis, except that at the end Tristan, too, is wounded by a poisoned weapon in his fight with the jealous husband, a fight in which Kahedin likewise finds his demise. We arrive at essentially the same point in both versions: Tristan/Tristran is wounded and needs Isolde/Ysolt to heal him. Kahedin/Kaherdin is not killed in Thomas's story and so is able to take on the role of messenger, whereas Ulrich and Eilhart engage a local merchant. The final sequence of events begins to unfold toward the inescapable tragic ending. Here the two traditions share many of the same points. Thomas tells us that Tristran in his desperation sends Kaherdin once again across the sea to find Ysolt and bring her back to heal him. His plea is heartfelt, and we have the sense that Tristran really is at an end without Ysolt. After a long monologue by Tristran on the nature of ill-fated love (ll. 2395–571), Kaherdin is given his instructions and makes his way to England disguised as a merchant. Unknown to either Tristran or Kaherdin, Ysolt White Hands has been listening to their entire conversation behind a wall. She hears for the first time about the other Ysolt and Tristran's undying love for her. Thomas makes a few comments along the lines of "a woman scorned," then has the "evil" Ysolt of the White Hands feign innocence and complete devotion to Tristran even though she has secretly sworn herself to vengeance. Meanwhile, Kaherdin arrives in London, described as a great and wealthy city (*Lundres est mult riche cité*, l. 2651) that is without equal in all of Christendom. He makes his way to Mark's court, presents the king with gifts to secure his safety, and then finds the queen. Kaherdin explains Tristran's plight and arrangements are quickly made for the voyage. Ysolt and Brengvein make their way to the ship under the cover of darkness and with favorable winds quickly sail past Normandy to Brittany.

All versions now move inexorably to the end. In Thomas, Tristran waits for the ship that brings him life to return, with a white sail if Ysolt is on board, a black sail if she is not. The message is intercepted, however, by Ysolt, his wife, and when the ship finally arrives off the coast after a long storm, she tells her husband that the sail is black, even though she has not yet seen the ship. Tristran turns over and dies of grief in the belief that Ysolt the Fair has abandoned him, with "dearest Ysolt" as his last words. A great cry goes up in the city, and as Ysolt the Fair finally arrives on land she quickly discovers that the lament is for Tristran. She goes to view the body and, believing that she has caused his death with her late arrival, dies in his arms. Thomas ends the story by telling us that "Tristran died of his longing, Ysolt because she could not come in time. Tristran died for his love; fair Ysolt because of tender pity" (Hatto, 1960, p. 353).

We are faced with one last mystery at the tragic end of the story. The Sneyd fragment that we have, which includes Thomas's ending, skips over any mention of a burial and goes from Tristan's and Isolde's deaths directly to the epilogue. Friar Robert, however, first adds a fairly long prayer to his *Saga* ending, in which before her death Isönd beseeches God's mercy for Tristram and forgiveness of her own sins, what is in essence a final confession and prayer for absolution for them both. The *Saga* then goes on to report that Markis had the two lovers buried apart, on opposite sides of the church so that they would remain separated even in death, but that a tree grew out of each grave and their branches became intertwined overhead. This was a demonstration, a sign of the power of their love. The Ulrich/Eilhart version has a variation of the burial scene in which the two are buried close together, and King Mark, less vindictive here, plants a grapevine over one and a rose over the other's grave. These two then grow together and become one. The question as to the "true" Thomas ending remains unanswerable. Did Thomas include a burial scene at the end which is now lost, but that was the basis for Robert's inclusion of just such a scene in the *Saga*? In other words, is the French manuscript transmission somehow defective, or did Thomas intentionally go against convention by remaining silent on the lovers' fate after their death?[5] And what would have been the message in such an omission?

Of course, Tristan and Isolde die tragically in all versions, but the depiction of their "life" after death matters. In his final remarks, Ulrich laments the inequity of Death and the fact that a knight as chivalrous as Tristan should have to die so young. He is sympathetic to Isolde and praises her loyalty above all. Tristan, too, is praised for his loyalty, a quality that should raise him from hell (or purgatory) into God's kingdom. Mark is exonerated by Eilhart and Ulrich when he is told that it was the love potion that made Tristan and Isolde love each other (Lichtenstein, 1877, ll. 9470–73). Ulrich is especially sympathetic in the end to Mark, who looks to his own salvation with penance and the founding of a monastery. On the other hand, Ulrich seems to follow Thomas's ending in its condemnation of Ysolt of the White Hands. Eilhart, on the other hand, is quite benign in the role he assigns his Isolde of Brittany. Her lie about the color of the sail is motivated by foolishness and lacks any kind of disloyalty or falsehood (Lichtenstein, 1877, ll. 9380–81). Should the Sneyd fragment present Thomas's original ending, however (and there are no gaps between its final lines and the epilogue), then the ultimate message would seem to be one of condemnation and hopelessness. The two fated lovers die without ever seeing each other again, there is no reunion in the grave or beyond, and they are doomed by the love that enslaved them. On the other hand, the tradition of a reunion beyond death, symbolized by nature and its power to heal and unite, gives hope and at least a measure of redemption. Even without including the burial scene, Thomas says as much in his epilogue. He concludes that he has written the true story in the hope that lovers "may find some things to take to heart. May they derive great comfort from it, in the face of fickleness and injury, in the face of hardship and grief, in the face of all the wiles of Love" (Hatto, 1960, p. 353).

We still don't know how Gottfried would have finished his magnum opus. If we're honest, we don't even really know how Thomas ended his work.

---

5. In the Haug/Scholz (2011/2012) edition of Gottfried's work, which includes in the second volume a new edition and German translation of the Thomas fragments, the editors opted to insert the *Saga* ending from Chapter 101 concerning the burial before the Epilogue, essentially hedging their bets that Thomas might have originally included such a scene himself. No such gap exists, however, in the Sneyd manuscript fragment. Hatto (1960) makes no mention of these variant endings in his translation of Thomas.

Following Thomas, Gottfried most likely would have included the Hall of Statues. Would he have expounded on the obvious metaphorical similarities to his Cave of Lovers? Would Brangane, widely praised by Gottfried, have attacked Isolde and reported her to the king? How would he have interpreted the leper episode, with Tristan in the depths of despair beneath the ruined steps? How would Gottfried have used Isolde of the White Hands as the instrument of Tristan's death? And finally, how might the burial of the two lovers and his own epilogue have exonerated Tristan and Isolde, or even Mark? It seems likely that Gottfried's purpose would have found its apotheosis and reaffirmation in the epilogue. The project made clear from the very beginning was to justify a forbidden love in a realm beyond convention, beyond society and its narrow constraints, its intrigues, and its suspicions. In this he and Thomas agree, that their story is meant to provide comfort to lovers despite hardship, pain, and grief. Hope is Gottfried's message, hope that love in its highest form can indeed become a bread of life for noble hearts, even in death.

Place Names in Gottfried's *Tristan and Isolde* and Ulrich von Türheim's Continuation

Entries marked with (UvT) are found only in Ulrich von Türheim's Continuation, those with (GvS, UvT) are found in both works. Entries without either annotation are found in Gottfried's work only.

Africa, the homeland of Gurmun, Isolde's father.

Allemania (*Almanje*), Germany, or German-speaking lands of the Holy Roman Empire.

Anferginan, a valley near Wexford in Ireland, home to the dragon killed by Tristan.

Aquitaine, Melot the dwarf's homeland.

Arabia, legendary source of fine gold.

Arundel, duchy belonging to Duke Jovelin, Isolde of the White Hand's father; situated somewhere between Brittany and England, most likely on the southern coast of England. (GvS, UvT)

Avalon, home of the magical dog Petitcreiu; fabled island from Arthurian legend; the home of Morgan le Fay. The name is probably Celtic for "apple" island.

Babylon, an ancient name used by Gottfried to mean Baghdad.

Britain (*Britanje*), used as both a reference to the ancient name of England and as contemporaneous with the terms England and Cornwall as the larger land mass, probably the entire island of Britain.

Brittany (*Britanje*), a land adjoining Tristan's homeland of Parmenie, mostly synonymous with the current region of that name in northwest France.

Caerleon, town and site of Isolde's trial by hot iron; also known through Geoffrey of Monmouth as King Arthur's capital. A town by that name is located today in southern Wales.

Canoel, major castle and town belonging to Rivalin, Tristan's father; located in the fictional realm of Parmenie; possibly named after Canuel in Brittany or Canoel in Cornwall. The name gives Rivalin the epithet "Canelengres."

Champagne, region in northeastern France famous in the Middle Ages for its fairs; mentioned as adjoining Germany.

Cithaeron, Mount, located in central Greece; especially sacred to Dionysus.

Cornwall, King Mark's kingdom by birthright; borders on England, which Mark also rules; according to legend founded by Corinaeus of Troy.

Denmark, land mentioned in itinerary of Rual's search for Tristan.

Doleise, the homeland of Rugier, one of the barons that attacks Arundel; probably somewhere near Brittany.

Dublin (*Develin*), capital of the kingdom of Ireland; home of Isolde and her parents and uncle Morold.

England, land ruled by King Mark; supposedly named by the Saxons, who drove out the previous occupants, the Britons.

France, kingdom in northwestern Europe, named by Tristan along with Normandy, Cornwall, and England.

Gales, most likely synonomous with Wales, but also the original land of the Saxons.

Gamaroch, Nampotanis's realm; adjacent to Arundel. (UvT)

Greece, land of the dawn and legendary home to perfect beauty.

Hante, Nautenis's homeland or town.

Helicon, Mount, in Greek mythology, seat of the muses.

Ireland, also known as Hibernia; island kingdom founded by Isolde's father, Gurmun the Bold, a Germanic noble from Africa. Its capital is Dublin. (GvS, UvT)

Kark (*Karke*), castle in Arundel; site of final battle between Jovelin's forces and those invading from Gamaroch. (GvS, UvT)

Lohnois (*Loinois, Lyonesse, Lothian*), Tristan's homeland in some traditions, including Eilhart's version.

London (*Lunders*), major town in England founded by the Romans; gathering place for Mark's council and Isolde's trial.

Lud (*Lût*), possibly an alternative name for London, although based on the context in Gottfried's usage, it could be a town in Brittany known for its music.

Lytan, town and castle, near Cornwall; home of Sir Tynas, a supporter of Tristan. (UvT)

Mycenae, used by Gottfried as basically synonymous with Greece.

Nante, a town or land; home to Rigolin.

Normandy, land adjoining Parmenie; a duchy in northwestern France established by Duke Rollo in the early tenth century.

Norway, home to merchants who kidnap Tristan.

Parmenie, homeland and duchy of Rivalin, Tristan's father; located somewhere near Brittany and Normandy; possibly a misspelling of Ermonie (*Sir Tristrem*) or Ermenia (*Saga*). Its capital is Canoel.

Rhine, major river between France and Germany.

Rome, capital of the ancient Western world; anachronistically still Gurmun of Ireland's overlord.

Salerno, town in southern Italy known as a center for medical studies.

S(c)harize, Nampotanis's castle in Gamaroch; residence to his wife Cassie. (UvT)

Sens, town in north-central France, mentioned as a center of music.

Sidon, Phoenician city ruled by Queen Dido.

South Wales (*Swâles*), home of Duke Gilan.

Spain (*Spanjenlant, Hispanje*), land in southwestern Europe; fabled for its fine breed of horses.

St. Denis (*Dinis*), royal monastery and chapel near Paris, mentioned as a center of music.

Thames (*Thâmîse*), town or location, possibly taken from the river's name; seat of the Bishop of Thames.

Thrace, homeland of Phyllis, a character from Ovid's *Heroides*.

Tintagel (*Tintajôl*), capital of Cornwall and seat of the Cornish court. (GvS, UvT)

Tribalesen, port town in Ireland. (UvT)

Tyre, Phoenician city ruled by Queen Dido.

Wexford (*Weiseford*), important royal center in Ireland.

Personal Names in Gottfried's *Tristan and Isolde* and Ulrich von Türheim's Continuation

Entries marked with (UvT) are found only in Ulrich von Türheim's Continuation, those with (GvS, UvT) are found in both works. Entries without either annotation are found in Gottfried's work only.

Adam, biblical figure, first man.

Antret, knight at King Mark's court; identified as both Isolde's and Mark's nephew; betrays Isolde along with Melot. (UvT)

Apollo, Greek god of the muses.

Arthur, King, legendary hero and king; leader of the Round Table.

Aurora, Greek goddess of the dawn.

Blancheflor (*Blanscheflûr*), King Mark's sister; Rivalin's wife; Tristan's mother; dies in childbirth.

Bligger von Steinach, German writer of love lyric and possibly epic poetry; from what is today Neckarsteinach near Heidelberg.

Brangane, close relative and lady in waiting to Isolde; counselor to the royal family of Ireland. (GvS, UvT)

Byblis, character in Ovid's *Metamorphoses*; falls in love with her brother, Caunus; commits suicide in some versions.

Camele, lady in waiting to Isolde. (UvT)

Canace, female figure in Ovid's *Heroides*; commits suicide after an incestuous relationship with her brother, Macareus.

Canel or **Canelengres**, an epithet for Rivalin based on his coming from the town of Canoel.

Carsie, Duchess of Arundel; wife to Duke Jovelin; mother of Isolde of the White Hands and Kahedin.

Cassandra, mythological character of Troy; daughter of King Priam; given the gift of prophecy by Apollo.

Cassie, wife of Sir Nampotanis; lover to Kahedin. (UvT)

Corinaeaus, Trojan hero and eponymous founder of Cornwall.

Curvenal, Tristan's tutor and trusted companion. (GvS, UvT)

Dido, Queen of Sidon and Tyre; tragic subject of legend and a medieval lay.

Eve, biblical figure, first woman.

Florete, Rual's wife; Tristan's foster mother.

Gandin, baron from Ireland, aka the Rote Player; attempts to win Isolde from Mark through a wager for his rote playing; outwitted and defeated by Tristan.

Gaviol, merchant; Tristan's landlord in Kark; messenger to Isolde. His (unnamed) wife informs Isolde of the White Hands when Gaviol returns with Isolde of Ireland. (UvT)

Gilan, duke; Tristan's friend and first owner of the dog Petitcreiu; lives in South Wales.

Gottfried, named by Ulrich von Türheim as the (deceased) author of the Middle High German romance about Tristan and Isolde.

Graelent, the Gallant, subject of an anonymous Breton lay; falls in love with a fairy. The plot is closely related to Marie de France's *Lanval*.

Gurmun, the Bold (*Gemuotheit*), king of Ireland; Isolde's father; originally a Germanic warrior-prince from North Africa.

Gurun, subject of a Breton lay; main character in *Le Fresne*, a lay composed by Marie de France.

Hagenau, the Nightingale from (Reinmar der Alte), German lyric poet; praised by Gottfried as the (deceased) leading *Minnesänger* of his day.

Hartmann von Aue, medieval German lyric poet and composer of several Arthurian romances based on French sources along with other stories.

Heinrich von Veldeke, early German lyric poet and composer of the *Eneit*, an epic based on the *Aeneid*.

Hiudan, Tristan's hunting dog; accompanies him into exile at the Lover's Cave.

Isolde, queen of Ireland; wife of King Gurmun; mother of Isolde the Fair; known for her knowledge of the healing arts, especially against poison, as well as magical potions.

Isolde (*Îsolt, Îsot*), the Fair (*la belle, la blonde*), queen of Cornwall and England; wife to King Mark; Tristan's lover. (GvS, UvT)

Isolde, of the White Hands (*aux blanches mains*), wife to Tristan; daughter of the Duke of Arundel; sister to Kahedin. (GvS, UvT)

Jovelin, Duke of Arundel (king in Eilhart's version); Isolde of the White Hands and Kahedin's father. (GvS, UvT)

Kahedin (*Kâedîn*), the Noble (OF *li frans*), Jovelin's son; brother to Isolde of the White Hands; Tristan's friend and confidante; killed in fight with Nampotanis. (GvS, UvT)

Konrad von Winterstetten, d. 1243; patron of Ulrich von Türheim and his continuation; Swabian nobleman in the service of the Hohenstaufen court; Cupbearer (*Reichsschenk*) to the king. (UvT)

Longinus, Roman soldier who pierced Jesus's side with a lance.

Mariodoc (*Marjodô, Marjodoc*), seneschal to King Mark; Tristan's friend; Isolde's secret admirer.

Mark (*Marke*), king of Cornwall and England; husband to Isolde; brother of Blancheflor; Tristan's uncle and lord. (GsV, UvT)

Melot, *le petit* of Aquitaine, Mark's dwarf; plots against Isolde and Tristan. (GsV, UvT)

Morgan, Duke of Brittany; Rivalin's liege lord; killed by Tristan.

Morold (*Môrolt*), duke in Ireland; Queen Isolde's brother; Isolde the Fair's uncle; King Mark's enemy; collected Cornish tribute for King Gurmun; killed by Tristan in judicial combat.

Nampotanis, knight from Gamaroch; husband of Cassie; killed by Tristan. (UvT)

Nautenis of Hante, leader of forces against Arundel and Duke Jovelin; defeated and taken captive by Tristan.

Orpheus, known in Greek myth as the "father of songs."

Paligan, a knight in Kark; travels with Tristan, Curvenal, and Kahedin to Cornwall. (UvT)

Paranis, chamberlain to Isolde; employed as a go-between to Tristan. (UvT)

Pegasus, mythical winged horse; its hooves created the font of the muses on Mount Helicon, the *Hippocrene*.

Peliot, page to Isolde. (UvT)

Petitcreiu (*Petitcriû*), magical dog from Avalon; given to Duke Gilan, who gives the dog to Tristan as a gift, who in turn gives the dog to Isolde the Fair. (GvS, UvT)

Phyllis of Thrace, a character in Ovid's *Heroides*; married to King Demophon of Athens; commits suicide during his absence.

Pleherin, knight at King Mark's court; adversary to Tristan. (UvT)

Plot, Tristan's cover name while disguised as a fool at Mark's court. (UvT)

Rigolin of Nante, count and knight; one of the leaders in the attack against Arundel.

Riol, count; probably the same person as Rigolin of Nante; Ulrich takes the name from Eilhart. (UvT)

Rivalin (*Riwalîn*), nobleman and knight; Morgan's vassal as ruler of Parmenie; husband to Blancheflor; Tristan's father.

Rual, the Faithful (*li Foitenant*), Rivalin's marshal and second-in-command; Tristan's foster father.

Rugier of Doleise, one of the leaders in the attack against Arundel.

Tantris, Tristan's cover name during his first voyage to Ireland.

Thisbe, subject of a lay; character in Ovid's *Metamorphoses*; commits suicide after Pyramus's death.

Thomas of Britain (*von Britanje*), Anglo-Norman writer active in the middle of the twelfth century; named by Gottfried as his source for the true story of Tristan and Isolde.

Tristan, son of Rivalin and Blancheflor; adoptive son of Rual and Florete; nephew of King Mark; lover of Isolde; husband of Isolde of the White Hands; ruler of Parmenie; killed by a poisoned lance in battle with Nampotanis and his brothers.

Tynas, Mark's seneschal; supporter of Tristan; lives in Lytan. (UvT)

Tyntarides, in Greek legend Helen of Troy's stepfather.

Ulrich von Türheim, German poet; composed first ending to Gottfried's story around 1230; also wrote a continuation to Wolfram von Eschenbach's *Willehalm* titled *Rennewart* and a version of Chrétien de Troyes' *Cligès*. (UvT)

Urgan, the Hairy (*le velu*), a giant and overlord of Duke Gilan's lands; killed by Tristan.

Vogelweide, the Nightingale from (Walther von der Vogelweide), prolific medieval German poet and social critic; praised by Gottfried as the worthy successor to Reinmar.

Vulcan, god of fire; master smith and armorer in Greek mythology; maker of Tristan's armor.

Manuscripts Containing Gottfried's *Tristan and Isolde* and Ulrich von Türheim's Continuation

This manuscript inventory is presented in two formats. The first is more conventional and lists the complete and fragmentary manuscripts by date, the earliest first. The second format groups the manuscripts according to Wetzel's stemma (1992) into three groups: X, Y, and XY mixed. Based on convention, the letter abbreviations of the manuscripts are capitalized for the complete manuscripts, and lowercase letters designate the fragmentary manuscripts. For further convenience, the corresponding numbers to the online *Handschriftencensus*, which lists manuscripts alphabetically by current location, are provided in square brackets. Several of these manuscripts can be found online in digitized format, including at the time of publication manuscripts HMBO and fragments enpqrt.

Manuscripts Arranged by Date

Complete manuscripts (11):

M, Munich, Staatsbibliothek, Cgm 51. Second quarter, thirteenth century, around 1240–1250, illuminated; with Ulrich von Türheim. [18]

H, Heidelberg, Universitätsbibliothek, Cpg 360 (combined with Cpg 349). Fourth quarter, thirteenth century; with Ulrich von Türheim. [12]

F, Florence, National Library, Cod. B.R. 226. First half, fourteenth century; with Heinrich von Freiberg. [9]

W, Vienna, Nationalbibliothek, Cod. 2707,3. Early fourteenth century. [23]

B, Köln, Historisches Archiv der Stadt, Best. 7020 (W*) 88. 1323, illuminated; with Ulrich von Türheim. [15]

N, Berlin, Staatsbibliothek, mgq 284. Mid-fourteenth century; with Ulrich von Türheim. [6]

O, Köln, Historisches Archiv der Stadt, Best. 7020 (W*) 87. 1420–1430, paper; with Heinrich von Freiberg. [14]

E, Modena, Biblioteca Estense, Ms. Est. 57. 1450–1465, paper; with Heinrich von Freiberg. [17]

R, Brussels, Royal Library, ms. 14697. 1455–1460, paper, illuminated; with part of Ulrich von Türheim. [7]

P, Berlin, Staatsbibliothek, mgf 640. 1461, paper; with fourteen lines of Ulrich von Türheim; Eilhart von Oberg. [3]

*S, Private ownership, Johann Georg Scherz, Straßburg. 1489, paper; with part of Ulrich von Türheim. Original lost. [30] S, Hamburg, Staats- und Universitätsbibliothek, Cod. germ. 12. Copy from 1722.

Seven manuscripts with Ulrich von Türheim's continuation, three with Heinrich von Freiberg's continuation.

Fragmentary manuscripts (19):

t, Tübingen, Universitätsbibliothek, Cod. Md 671. Second quarter, thirteenth century. [22]

a, Innsbruck, Landesmuseum Ferdinandeum, Cod. FB 1519/III. Second third, thirteenth century. [13]

f_1/f, Augsburg, Staats- und Stadtbibliothek, Fragm. germ. 31. Mid-thirteenth century. [1] Köln, Historisches Archiv der Stadt, Best. 7050 (Hss.-Fragm.) A 44.

m, Berlin, Staatsbibliothek, mgf 923 Nr. 4. Mid-thirteenth century. [4]

ff, Frankfurt a. M., Universitätsbibliothek, Fragm. germ. II 5. End thirteenth century. [10]**

h, Private ownership, Antiquariat Ludwig Rosenthal, München, Nr. 1889/65,491. Thirteenth century. Lost. [29]

z/z_1, Zürich, Staatsarchiv, C VI 1, VI, Nr. 6a. Fourth quarter, thirteenth century, 1270s. [28]

r, Frankfurt a. M., Universitätsbibliothek, Ms. germ. oct. 5. Around 1300. [11]*

l, Berlin, Staatsbibliothek, mgf 923 Nr. 5. Around 1300. [5]

s, Strasbourg, Bibliothèque Nationale Universitaire, ms. 2280 (previously L, germ. 321.8°). Around 1300. [20] [Bechstein, 9785–825; 9907–47]

e/e_1, Tomsk, Research Library of the State University, B-4146 (previously Hamburg, Staats- und Universitätsbiblithek, Cod. germ. 15, Fragm. 3). Early fourteenth century. [21] Hamburg, Staats- und Universitätsbiblithek, Cod. germ. 15, Fragm. 3.a. Early fourteenth century.

ö, Augsburg, Universitätsbibliothek, from Cod. III.1.4° 8. Early fourteenth century. [2]*

v, Würzburg, Universitätsbibliothek, M. p. misc. f. 35. Early fourteenth century. [27]*

w, Vienna, Nationalbibliothek, Cod. 2707,1 (bound with Cod. 2707). Early fourteenth century. [24]

q_1/q, Dillingen, Studienbibliothek, XV Fragm. 25. First quarter, fourteenth century. [8]* Private collection Eis, Heidelberg, Ms. 63.*

p, Wiesbaden, Hauptstaatsarchiv, Abt. 1105 Nr. 42. Second quarter, fourteenth century. [26]** [not listed in Haug/Scholz]

b, Vienna, Nationalbibliothek, Cod. 15340. Mid- fourteenth century. [25]

g, Linz, Landesarchiv, Pa I/3b. Second half, fourteenth century. [16]*

n, Munich, Staatsbibliothek, Cgm 5249/75. Third quarter, fifteenth century. [19]

*Not in Ranke's stemma; ** also not in Wetzel's stemma

Two fragments lacking Gottfried's text, but with Heinrich von Freiberg's continuation:

Wolfenbüttel, Herzog August Bibliothek, Cod. 404.9 (3) Novi.

St. Pölten, Stadtarchiv, no signature, present location unknown.

Manuscripts Arranged According to René Wetzel's Stemma

"X" Manuscripts:

M, Munich, Staatsbibliothek, Cgm 51. Second quarter, thirteenth century, around 1240–1250, illuminated; with Ulrich von Türheim. [18]

a, Innsbruck, Landesmuseum Ferdinandeum, Cod. FB 1519/III. Second third, thirteenth century. [13]

h, Private ownership, Antiquariat Ludwig Rosenthal, München, Nr. 1889/65,491. Thirteenth century. Lost. [29]

H, Heidelberg, Universitätsbibliothek, Cpg 360 (combined with Cpg 349). Fourth quarter, thirteenth century; with Ulrich von Türheim. [12]

q_1/q, Dillingen, Studienbibliothek, XV Fragm. 25. First quarter, fourteenth century. [8]

e/e_1, Tomsk, Research Library of the State University, B-4146 (previously Hamburg, Staats- und Universitätsbiblithek, Cod. germ. 15, Fragm. 3). [21]
Hamburg, Staats- und Universitätsbiblithek, Cod. germ. 15, Fragm. 3.a. Early fourteenth century.

B, Köln, Historisches Archiv der Stadt, Best. 7020 (W*) 88. 1323, illuminated; with Ulrich von Türheim. [15]

b, Vienna, Nationalbibliothek, Cod. 15340. Mid-fourteenth century. [25]

E, Modena, Biblioteca Estense, Ms. Est. 57. 1450–1465, paper; with Heinrich von Freiberg. [17]

"Y" Manuscripts:

s, Strasbourg, Bibliothèque Nationale Universitaire, ms. 2280 (previously L, germ. 321.8°). Around 1300. [20]

z/z_1, Zürich, Staatsarchiv, C VI 1, VI, Nr. 6a. Fourth quarter, thirteenth century, 1270s. [28]

l, Berlin, Staatsbibliothek, mgf 923 Nr. 5. Around 1300. [5]

r, Frankfurt a. M., Universitätsbibliothek, Ms. germ. oct. 5. Around 1300. [11]

ö, Augsburg, Universitätsbibliothek, from Cod. III.1.4° 8. Early fourteenth century. [2]

W, Vienna, Nationalbibliothek, Cod. 2707,3. Early fourteenth century. [23]

w, Vienna, Nationalbibliothek, Cod. 2707,1 (bound with Cod. 2707). Early fourteenth century. [24]

v, Würzburg, Universitätsbibliothek, M. p. misc. f. 35. Early fourteenth century. [27]

F, Florence, National Library, Cod. B.R. 226. First half, fourteenth century; with Heinrich von Freiberg. [9]

N, Berlin, Staatsbibliothek, mgq 284. Mid-fourteenth century; with Ulrich von Türheim. [6]

n, Munich, Staatsbibliothek, Cgm 5249/75. Third quarter, fifteenth century. [19]

O, Köln, Historisches Archiv der Stadt, Best. 7020 (W*) 87. 1420–1430, paper; with Heinrich von Freiberg. [14]

R, Brussels, Royal Library, ms. 14697. 1455–1460, paper, illuminated; with part of Ulrich von Türheim. [7]

P, Berlin, Staatsbibliothek, mgf 640. 1461, paper; with fourteen lines of Ulrich von Türheim; Eilhart von Oberg. [3]

*S, Private ownership, Johann Georg Scherz, Straßburg. 1489, paper; with part of Ulrich von Türheim. Original lost. [30] S, Hamburg, Staats- und Universitätsbibliothek, Cod. germ. 12. Copy from 1722.

"XY" Manuscripts:

m, Berlin, Staatsbibliothek, mgf 923 Nr. 4. Mid-thirteenth century. [4]

f_1/f Augsburg, Staats- und Stadtbibliothek, Fragm. germ. 31. Mid-thirteenth century. [1] Köln, Historisches Archiv der Stadt, Best. 7050 (Hss.-Fragm.) A 44.

t, Tübingen, Universitätsbibliothek, Cod. Md 671. Second quarter, thirteenth century. [22]

g, Linz, Landesarchiv, Pa I/3b. Second half, fourteenth century. [16]

Not in Wetzel's Stemma:

ff, Frankfurt a. M., Universitätsbibliothek, Fragm. germ. II 5. End thirteenth century. [10]

p, Wiesbaden, Hauptstaatsarchiv, Abt. 1105 Nr. 42. Second quarter, fourteenth century. [26] [not listed in Haug/Scholz]

Selected Bibliography

Editions and Translations (listed by date)

Gottfried von Strassburg

"Tristran: Ein Rittergedicht aus dem XIII. Iahrhundert von Gotfrit von Strazburc zum erstenmal aus der Handschrift abgedruckt." In *Samlung deutscher Gedichte aus dem XII. XIII. und XIV. Iahrhundert*. Edited by Christoph Heinrich Myller. Volume 2. Berlin: C.S. Spener, 1785. 1–141.

Tristan von Meister Gotfrit von Straszburg: Mit der Fortsetzung des Meisters Ulrich von Turheim. Edited by Eberhard von Groote. Berlin: Reimer, 1821. [with Ulrich's continuation]

Gottfrieds von Strassburg Werke: Aus den beßten Handschriften mit Einleitung und Wörterbuch. Edited by Friedrich Heinrich von der Hagen. 2 volumes. Breslau: J. Max, 1823. [with Ulrich's continuation]

Tristan und Isolt von Gottfried von Strassburg. Edited by Hans Ferdinand Massmann. Leipzig: Göschen'sche Verlagshandlung, 1843. [with Ulrich's continuation]

Tristan und Isolde: Gedicht von Gottfried von Strassburg. Translated by Hermann Kurtz. Stuttgart: Becher, 1844.

Tristan und Isolde von Gottfried von Strassburg. Translated by Karl Simrock. Leipzig: Brockhaus, 1855.

Gottfried's von Strassburg Tristan. Edited by Reinhold Bechstein. 2 volumes. Deutsche Klassiker des Mittelalters 7/8. Leipzig: Brockhaus, 1869/1870.

Tristan und Isolde von Gottfried von Strassburg. Translated by Wilhelm Hertz. Stuttgart: Kröner, 1877.

'*Tristan und Isolde' und 'Flore und Blanscheflur.*' Edited by Wolfgang Golther. 2 volumes. Berlin and Stuttgart: Spemann, 1888. [with a summary of Ulrich's continuation]

Tristan und Isolde: Höfisches Epos von Gottfried von Strassburg. Translated by Karl Pannier. Leipzig: Reclam, 1903.

Gottfried von Straßburg. *Tristan*. Edited by Karl Marold. Teil 1: Text. Teutonia: Arbeiten zur germanischen Philologie 6. Leipzig: Avenarius, 1906.

Gottfried von Straßburg. *Tristan und Isold*. Edited by Friedrich Ranke. Berlin: Weidmann, 1930 (2nd revised edition 1949).

Tristan und Îsolt: A Poem by Gottfried von Strassburg. Edited by August Closs. Oxford: Blackwell, 1944. [abridged]

Gottfried von Straßburg. *Tristan und Isolde*. Translated by Günter Kramer. Berlin: Verlag der Nation, 1966. [with a full German translation of Ulrich's text]

Gottfried von Straßburg. *Tristan: Nach der Ausgabe von Reinhold Bechstein*. Edited by Peter Ganz. 2 volumes. Deutsche Klassiker des Mittelalters Neue Folge 4,1/2. Wiesbaden: Brockhaus, 1978.

Gottfried von Straßburg. *Tristan.* Translated by Xenja von Ertzdorff, Doris Scholz, and Carola Voelkel. München: Wilhelm Fink, 1979.

Gottfried von Straßburg. *Tristan und Isold: Nach der Übertragung von Hermann Kurtz (1844).* Edited by Wolfgang Mohr. Göppinger Arbeiten zur Germanistik 290. Göppingen: Kümmerle Verlag, 1979. München: C.H. Beck, 2008. [abridged version]

Gottfried von Straßburg. *Tristan und Isolde, mit der Fortsetzung Ulrichs von Türheim: Faksimile-Ausgabe des Cgm 51 der Bayerischen Staatsbibliothek München.* Edited by Ulrich Montag and Paul Gichtel. Stuttgart: Müller und Schindler, 1979.

Gottfried von Straßburg. *Tristan: Nach dem Text von Friedrich Ranke neu herausgegeben, ins Neuhochdeutsche übersetzt, mit einem Stellenkommentar und einem Nachwort.* Edited and translated by Rüdiger Krohn. 3 volumes. Reclams Universal-Bibliothek 4471/4472/4473. Stuttgart: Reclam, 1980. [Ranke's text]

Das Tristan-Epos Gottfrieds von Strassburg: Mit der Fortsetzung des Ulrich von Türheim nach der Heidelberger Handschrift Cod. Pal. germ. 360. Edited by Wolfgang Spiewok. Deutsche Texte des Mittelalters 75. Berlin: Akademie-Verlag, 1989. [with Ulrich's continuation]

Gottfried von Strassburg. *Tristan und Isolde.* Edited by Wolfgang Spiewok. Texte des Mittelalters 2. Greifswald: Reineke Verlag, 1994. [Ranke's text]

Gottfried von Straßburg. *Tristan und Isolde: Roman.* Translated by Dieter Kühn. Frankfurt: Fischer Verlag, 2003. [with a partial translation of Ulrich von Türheim's continuation]

Gottfried von Straßburg. *Tristan.* Volume 1: *Text. Unveränderter fünfter Abdruck nach dem dritten, mit einem auf Grund von Friedrich Rankes Kollationen verbesserten kritischen Apparat besorgt und mit einem erweiterten Nachwort.* Edited by Werner Schröder. Volume 2: *Übersetzung.* Translated by Peter Knecht, with an introduction (in German) by Tomas Tomasek. Berlin: de Gruyter, 2004a. [Marold's text]

Gottfried von Strassburg. *Tristan und Isolde: Diplomatische Textausgabe der Zimelien-Handschrift Codex Vindobonensis 2707 mit Konkordanzen und Wortlisten auf CD.* Edited by Evelyn Scherabon Firchow and Richard Hotchkiss. Stuttgart: Hirzel, 2004b.

Gottfried von Straßburg. *Tristan und Isold: Mit dem Text des Thomas.* Edited by Walter Haug and Manfred Günter Scholz. 2 volumes. Bibliothek des Mittelalters 10/11. Bibliothek deutscher Klassiker 192. Berlin: Deutscher Klassiker Verlag, 2011; Insel Verlag, 2012. [Ranke's text]

Translations into English (listed by date)

The Story of Tristan and Iseult: Rendered into English from the German of Gottfried von Strassburg. Translated by Jessie L. Weston. 2 volumes. London: D. Nutt, 1899. [prose retelling, much abridged]

The 'Tristan and Isolde' of Gottfried von Strassburg. Translated by Edwin Zeydel. Princeton, NJ: Princeton University Press, 1948. [much abridged, with prose summaries]

Gottfried von Strassburg. *Tristan: With the Surviving Fragments of the Tristran of Thomas.* Translated by A. T. Hatto. New York: Penguin Books, 1960.

Gottfried von Strassburg. *Tristan and Isolde*. Translated by A. T. Hatto, edited and revised by Francis Gentry. Foreword by C. Stephen Jaeger. The German Library Volume 3. New York: Continuum, 1988. [republication of Hatto's translation, but without his introduction, appendices, or Thomas's text, and with some important revisions]

Gottfried von Strassburg. *Tristan: A Musical Translation*. Translated by Lee Stavenhagen, 2004. Online at: stavenhagen.net.

Other Adaptations, Continuations, and Translations of the Tristan Legend

Ulrich von Türheim

Kerth, Thomas. *Ulrich von Türheim's 'Tristan': A Critical Edition*. Dissertation, Yale University, 1977.

Ulrich von Türheim. *Tristan*. Edited by Thomas Kerth. Altdeutsche Textbibliothek 89. Tübingen: Niemeyer, 1979.

Ulrich von Türheim. *Tristan und Isolde*. Edited and translated by Wolfgang Spiewok and Danielle Bushinger. Texte des Mittelalters 4. Greifswald: Reineke Verlag, 1992 (2nd edition, 1994).

Heinrich von Freiberg

Heinrich's von Freiberg 'Tristan.' Edited by Reinhold Bechstein. Deutsche Dichtungen des Mittelalters 5. Leipzig: Brockhaus, 1877.

Heinrich von Freiberg: Mit Einleitungen über Stil, Sprache, Metrik, Quellen und die Persönlichkeit des Dichters. Edited by Alois Bernt. Halle: Niemeyer, 1906.

Heinrich von Freiberg. *Tristan und Isolde*. Edited by Danielle Buschinger and Wolfgang Spiewok. Texte des Mittelalters 5. Greifswald: Reineke Verlag, 1993.

Béroul

Le Roman de Tristan. Edited by L. M. Defourques. 4th edition. Paris: Champion, 1966.

Béroul. *The Romance of Tristran*. Edited and translated by Norris Lacy. New York: Garland, 1989.

The Romance of Tristran by Beroul and Beroul II. Edited and translated by Barbara Sargent-Baur. Toronto: University of Toronto Press, 2015.

Eilhart von Oberg

Eilhart von Oberge. Edited by Franz Lichtenstein. Quellen und Forschungen zur Sprach- und Culturgeschichte der germanischen Völker 19. Strassburg: Trübner, 1877.

Eilhart von Oberg. *Tristrant: Synoptischer Druck der ergänzten Fragmente mit der gesamten Parallelüberlieferung*. Edited by Hadumod Bußmann. Altdeutsche Textbibliothek 70. Tübingen: Niemeyer, 1969.

Eilhart von Oberge's 'Tristrant.' Translated by J. W. Thomas. Lincoln: University of Nebraska Press, 1978.

Eilhart von Oberge. *Tristrant und Isalde.* Edited by Danielle Buschinger and Wolfgang Spiewok. Greifswalder Beiträge 27. Greifswald: Reineke, 1993.

Eilhart von Oberge. *Tristrant und Isalde nach der Heidelberger Handschrift Cod. Pal. Germ. 346.* Edited and translated by Danielle Buschinger. Berliner sprachwissenschaftliche Studien 4. Berlin: Weidler, 2004.

Thomas

Le Roman de Tristan par Thomas: Poème du XIIe siècle. Edited by Joseph Bédier. 2 volumes. Paris: Didot, 1902/1905.

Gottfried von Strassburg. *Tristan: With the Surviving Fragments of the Tristran of Thomas.* Translated by A. T. Hatto. New York: Penguin Books, 1960. 301–53.

Les Fragments du Roman de Tristan. Edited by Bartina Wind. Geneva: Droz, 1960.

Thomas of Britain. *Tristran.* Translated by Stewart Gregory. Garland Library of Medieval Literature. New York: Garland Publishers, 1991.

"Thomas's *Tristran.*" Edited and translated by Stewart Gregory. *Early French Tristran Poems.* Volume 2. Edited by Norris Lacy. Cambridge: D.S. Brewer, 1998. 1–172.

Bédier, Joseph. *The Romance of Tristan and Iseult.* Translated by Edward Gallagher. Indianapolis, IN: Hackett Publishing, 2013.

The Saga of Tristram and Ísönd

Die nordische und die englische Version der Tristan-Sage. Edited by Eugen Kölbing. Heilbronn: Henninger, 1878 (reprint Hildesheim: Olms, 1978).

The Saga of Tristram and Ísönd. Translated by Paul Schach. Lincoln: University of Nebraska Press, 1973.

"Tristrams Saga ok Ísöndar." Edited and translated by Peter Jorgensen. In *Norse Romance: The Tristan Legend.* Edited by Marianne E. Kalinke. Volume 1. Arthurian Archives 3. Cambridge: D.S. Brewer, 1999. 25–226. [with Norse text]

French Prose Romance

The Romance of Tristan: The Thirteenth-Century Old French 'Prose Tristan.' Translated by Renée L. Curtis. Oxford: Oxford University Press, 1994.

German Prose Romance

Tristrant und Isalde: Prosaroman. Edited by Alois Brandstetter. Altdeutsche Textbibliothek Ergänzungsreihe 3. Tübingen: Niemeyer, 1966.

Middle English Sir Tristrem

"Sir Tristrem: A Metrical Romance of the 15th Century." In *The Works of Walter Scott.* Volume 6. 2nd edition. Edited by Walter Scott. Edinburgh: Ballantyne & Co., 1806.

Sir Tristrem. Edited by George McNeill. Scottish Text Society 8. Edinburgh: William Blackwood and Son, 1886.

Other Primary Works

Hartmann von Aue. *Arthurian Romances, Tales, and Lyric Poetry: The Complete Works of Hartmann von Aue*. Translated by Frank Tobin, Kim Vivian, and Richard Lawson. University Park: Pennsylvania State University Press, 2001.

Marie de France. *Poetry: New Translations, Backgrounds and Contexts, Criticism*. Edited and translated by Dorothy Gilbert. New York: Norton, 2015.

Des Minnesangs Frühling. Edited by Hugo Moser and Helmut Tervooren. 3 volumes. Stuttgart: Hirzel, 1988. [MF]

Mittelhochdeutsche Sangspruchdichtung des 13. Jahrhunderts. Edited by Theodor Nolte and Volker Schupp. Stuttgart: Reclam, 2011.

The Nibelungenlied: With the Klage. Edited and translated, with an introduction by William Whobrey. Indianapolis, IN: Hackett Publishing, 2018.

Ovid. *The Erotic Poems*. Translated by Peter Green. Harmondsworth: Penguin, 1982.

Ovid. *Heroides*. Translated by Harold Isbell. Harmondsworth: Penguin, 1990.

Ovid. *Metamorphoses*. Translated by David Raeburn. Harmondsworth: Penguin, 2004.

Publilius Syrus. *The Moral Sayings of Publius Syrus, a Roman Slave*. Translated by Darius Lyman. Cleveland, OH: Barnard & Co., 1856.

Wolfram von Eschenbach. *Parzival*. Translated by Hellen Mustard and Charles Passage. New York: Random House, 1961.

Secondary Literature in English (listed alphabetically by author, with a few of the more important references in German or French)

Altpeter-Jones, Katja. "Love Me, Hurt Me, Heal Me: Isolde Healer and Isolde Lover in Gottfried's *Tristan*." *The German Quarterly* 82,1 (2009): 5–23.

Anson, John. "The Hunt of Love: Gottfried von Strassburg's *Tristan* as Tragedy." *Speculum* 45 (1970): 594–607.

Asher, J. A. "Hartmann and Gottfried: Master and Pupil?" *AUMLA* 16 (1961): 134–44.

Battles, Dominique. "The Literary Source of the *Minnegrotte* in Gottfried von Strassburg's *Tristan*." In *Neophilologus* 93 (2009): 465–69.

Batts, Michael. "The Idealized Landscape in Gottfried's *Tristan*." *Neophilologus* 46 (1962): 226–33.

Batts, Michael. *Gottfried von Strassburg*. New York: Twayne, 1971.

Bekker, Hugo. *Gottfried von Straßburg's Tristan: Journey through the Realms of Eros*. Columbia, SC: Camden House, 1988.

Blodgett, Edward. "Music and Subjectivity in Gottfried's *Tristan*." In *Analogon rationis. Festschrift für Gervin Marahrens zum 65. Geburtstag*. Edited by Marianne Henn and Christoph Lorey. Edmonton: University of Alberta Press, 1994. 1–18.

Brockington, Mary. "The Separating Sword in the Tristan Romances: Possible Celtic Analogues Reexamined." *Modern Language Review* 91 (1996): 281–300.

Caples, Cynthia. "Brangaene and Isold in Gottfried von Strassburg's *Tristan*." *Colloquia Germanica* 9 (1975): 167–76.

Chinca, Mark. *History, Fiction, Verisimilitude Studies in the Poetics of Gottfried's Tristan*. London: Modern Humanities Research Association, 1993.

Chinca, Mark. *Gottfried von Strassburg: Tristan.* Cambridge: Cambridge University Press, 1997.

Clark, James, Frank Coulson, and Kathryn McKinley, eds. *Ovid in the Middle Ages.* Cambridge: Cambridge University Press, 2011.

Clason, Christopher. "Deception in the Boudoir: Gottfried's *Tristan* and 'Lying' in Bed." *The Journal of English and Germanic Philology* 103 (2004): 277–96.

Clason, Christopher. "Gottfried's Continuator Ulrich von Türheim: Epistemology and Language." *Tristania* 24 (2006): 17–36.

Clason, Christopher. "A 'Courtly' Reading of Natural Metaphors: Animals and Performance in Gottfried's *Tristan.*" *Mediaevistik* 28 (2015): 141–59.

Classen, Albrecht. "Female Agency and Power in Gottfried von Straßburg's *Tristan*: The Irish Queen Isolde, New Perspectives." *Tristania* 23 (2004): 39–60.

Cole, William. "Purgatory vs. Eden: Béroul's Forest and Gottfried's Cave." *Germanic Review* 70 (1995): 2–8.

Collings, Lucy. "Structural Prefiguration in Gottfried's *Tristan.*" *Journal of English and Germanic Philology* 72 (1973): 378–89.

Dalby, David. *Lexicon of the Mediæval German Hunt: A Lexicon of Middle High German Terms (1050–1500), Associated with the Chase, Hunting with Bows, Falconry, Trapping and Fowling.* Berlin: de Gruyter, 1965.

Dayan, Joan. "The Figure of Isolde in Gottfried's *Tristan*: Toward a Paradigm of Minne." *Tristania* 6/2 (1981): 23–36.

Decker, Frances. "Gottfried's *Tristan* and the *Minnesang*: The Relationship Between the Illicit Couple and Courtly Society." *The German Quarterly* 55 (1982): 64–79.

Deighton, Alan. *Studies in the Reception of the Work of Gottfried von Strassburg in Germany During the Middle Ages.* Dissertation, D. phil., Oxford, 1979.

Deist, Rosemarie. "The Description of Isolde and Iseut and Their Confidantes in Gottfried von Strassburg and Thomas de Bretagne." *Bibliographical Bulletin of the International Arthurian Society* 48 (1996): 271–82.

Dick, Ernst. "The Hunted Stag and the Renewal of Minne: *Bast* in Gottfried's *Tristan.*" *Tristania* 17 (1996): 1–25.

Dickerson, Harold. "Language in *Tristan* as a Key to Gottfried's Conception of God." *Amsterdamer Beiträge zur älteren Germanistik* 3 (1972): 127–45.

Dickhut, Johannes. "Gottfrieds *Tristan* in der Forschungs- und Ideologiegeschichte des 19. Jahrhunderts." In *Rezeptionskulturen: Fünfhundert Jahre literarischer Mittelalterrezeption zwischen Kanon und Populärkultur.* Edited by Mathias Herweg and Stefan Keppler-Tasaki. Berlin: de Gruyter, 2012. 248–70.

Dickson, Morgan. "The Image of the Knightly Harper: Symbolism and Resonance." In *Medieval Romance and Material Culture.* Edited by Nicholas Perkins. Woodbridge: D.S. Brewer, 2015. 199–214.

Dietz, Reiner. *Der* Tristan *Gottfrieds von Straßburg: Probleme der Forschung (1902–1970).* Göppinger Arbeiten zur Germanistik 136. Göppingen, 1974.

Dimler, G. Richard. "*Diu fossiure in dem steine*: An Analysis of the Allegorical Nomina in Gottfried's *Tristan* (16923–17070)." *Amsterdamer Beiträge zur älteren Germanistik* 9 (1975): 13–46.

Eisner, Sigmund. *The Tristan Legend: A Study in Sources.* Evanston, IL: Northwestern University Press, 1969.

Eming, Jutta, Ann Marie Rasmussen, and Kathryn Starkey, eds. *Visuality and Materiality in the Story of Tristan and Isolde.* Notre Dame, IN: University of Notre Dame Press, 2012.

Ferrante, Joan. *The Conflict of Love and Honor: The Medieval Tristan Legend in France, Germany, and Italy.* Berlin: de Gruyter, 1973.

Finlay, Alison. "Intolerable Love: Tristram's Saga and the Carlisle Tristan Fragment." *Medium Aevum* 73,2 (2004): 205–24.

Fourquet, Jean. "Le cryptogramme du *Tristan* et la composition du poème." *Études Germaniques* 18 (1963): 271–76. Translated into German in *Gottfried von Strassburg.* Edited by Alois Wolf. Wege der Forschung 320. Darmstadt: Wissenschaftliche Buchgesellschaft, 1973. 362–70.

German and Italian Lyrics of the Middle Ages: An Anthology and a History. Translated by Frederick Goldin. New York: Anchor Books, 1973. 142–3.

Gottfried von Strassburg. Edited by Alois Wolf. Wege der Forschung 320. Darmstadt, Wissenschaftliche Buchgesellschaft, 1973.

Gottfried von Strassburg and the Medieval Tristan Legend: Papers from an Anglo-North American Symposium. Edited by Adrian Stevens and Roy Wisbey. Cambridge: D.S. Brewer, 1990.

Gravigny, Louis. "La composition de *Tristan* de Gottfried de Strasbourg et les initiales dans les principaux manuscrits et fragments." *Études Germaniques* 26 (1971): 1–17.

Grimbert, Joan Tasker, ed. *Tristan and Isolde: A Casebook.* New York: Garland, 1995.

Hall, Clifton. *A Complete Concordance to Gottfried von Straßburg's Tristan.* Lewiston, NY: Mellen Press, 1992.

Harris, Sylvia. "The Cave of Lovers in the *Tristramsaga* and Related Tristan Romances." *Romania* 98 (1977): 460–500.

Hasty, Will. "Tristan and Isolde, the Consummate Insiders: Relations of Love and Power in Gottfried's *Tristan.*" *Monatshefte* 90,2 (1998): 137–47.

Hasty, Will, ed. *A Companion to Gottfried von Strassburg's Tristan.* Rochester, NY: Camden House, 2003.

Haug, Walther. "Reinterpreting the Tristan Romances of Thomas and Gotfrid: Implications of a Recent Discovery." *Arthuriana* 7,3 (1997): 45–59.

Hexter, Ralph. "Ovid in the Middle Ages: Exile, Mythographer, and Lover." In *Brill's Companion to Ovid.* Edited by Barbara Boyd. Leiden: Brill, 2002. 413–42.

Huber, Christoph. *Gottfried von Straßburg: Tristan.* Klassiker Lektüren 3. 3rd edition. Berlin: Schmidt, 2013.

Huot, Sylvia. "A Tale Much Told: The Status of the Love Philtre in the Old French Tristan Texts." *Zeitschrift für deutsche Philologie* 124 (2005): 82–95.

Jackson, William T. H. "The Literary Views of Gottfried von Strassburg." *PMLA* 85.5 (1970): 992–1001.

Jackson, William T. H. *The Anatomy of Love: The Tristan of Gottfried von Straßburg.* New York: Columbia University Press, 1971.

Jacobsen, Evelyn. "Biblical Typology in Gottfried's *Tristan and Isolde.*" *Neophilologus* 69 (1985): 568–78.

Jaeger, C. Stephen. "The 'Strophic' Prologue to Gottfried's *Tristan*." *Germanic Review* 47 (1972): 5–19.

Jaeger, C. Stephen. "The Crown of Virtues in the Cave of Lovers Allegory of Gottfried's *Tristan*." *Euphorion* 67 (1973): 95–116.

Jaeger, C. Stephen. *Medieval Humanism in Gottfried von Strassburg's* Tristan und Isolde. Heidelberg: Winter, 1977.

Jaeger, C. Stephen. "On Recent Interpretations of Gottfried's *Tristan*, Lines 17031–17057." *Monatshefte* 70 (1978): 375–83.

Jaeger, C. Stephen. "The Barons' Intrigue in Gottfried's *Tristan*: Notes Toward a Sociology of Fear in Courtly Society." *The Journal of English and Germanic Philology* 83 (1984): 46–66.

Jaeger, C. Stephen. "Gottfried von Strassburg." In *The Arthurian Encyclopedia*. Edited by Norris Lacy. New York: Peter Bedrick, 1986. 249–56.

Jaeger, C. Stephen. "Mark and Tristan: The Love of Medieval Kings and Their Courts." In *In hôhem prîse: A Festschrift in Honor of Ernst S. Dick*. Edited by Winder McConnell. Göppingen: Kümmerle, 1989. 183–97.

Jaffe, Samuel. "Gottfried von Strassburg and the Rhetoric of History." In *Medieval Eloquence: Studies in the Theory and Practice of Medieval Rhetoric*. Edited by James Murphy. Berkeley: University of California Press, 1978. 288–318.

Johnson, L. Peter. "Gottfried von Straßburg, *Tristan*." In *New Pelican Guide to English Literature*. Volume 1, part 2. *Medieval Literature: The European Inheritance*. Harmondsworth: Penguin, 1983. 207–21.

Johnson, Sidney. "This Drink Will Be the Death of You: Interpreting the Love Potion in Gottfried's *Tristan*." In *A Companion to Gottfried von Strassburg's* Tristan. Edited by Will Hasty. Rochester, NY: Camden House, 2003. 82–112.

Kern, Peter. "Gottfried von Straßburg und Ovid." In *Swer sînen friunt behaltet, daz ist lobelîch: Festschrift für András Vizkelety zum 70. Geburtstag*. Edited by Márta Nagy and László Jónácsik. Budapest: Péter-Pázmány University Press, 2001. 35–49.

Kerth, Thomas. "With God on Her Side: Isolde's *Gottesurteil*." *Colloquia Germanica* 11 (1978): 1–18.

Kerth, Thomas. "The Dénouement of the Tristan-*Minne*: Türheim's Dilemma." *Neophilologus* 65 (1981): 79–93.

Kerth, Thomas. "Kingship in Gottfried's *Tristan*. *Monatshefte für deutschen Unterricht, deutsche Sprache und Literatur* 80 (1988): 444–58.

Knopp, Sharon. "*Daz honec in dem munde*: The Narrator and His Audience in Gottfried's *Tristan*." *Colloquia Germanica* 16 (1983): 131–47.

Kragl, Florian. *Gottfrieds Ironie: Sieben Kapitel über figurenpsychologischen Realismus im* Tristan. *Mit einem Nachspruch zum* Rosenkavalier. Berlin: Schwabe, 2018.

Krohn, Rüdiger. "Gottfried von Strassburg and the Tristan Myth." In *German Literature of the High Middle Ages*. Edited by Will Hasty. Rochester, NY: Camden House, 2006. 55–73.

Kucaba, Kelley. "Gottfried von Straßburg." In *Medieval Germany: An Encyclopedia*. Edited by John Jeep. New York: Garland, 2001. 303–6.

Kunitzsch, Paul. "Are There Oriental Elements in the Tristan Story?" *Vox Romanica* 39 (1980): 73–85.

Kunzer, Ruth Goldschmidt. *The Tristan of Gottfried von Strassburg: An Ironic Perspective.* Berkeley: University of California Press, 1973.

Lachmann, Karl. *Auswahl aus den hochdeutschen Dichtern des dreizehnten Jahrhunderts.* Berlin: G. Reimer, 1820.

McDonald, William. *Arthur and Tristan: On the Intersection of Legends in German Medieval Literature.* Lewiston, NY: Mellen Press, 1991.

McDonald, William. "The Boar Emblem in Gottfried's *Tristan.*" *Neuphilologische Mitteilungen* 92 (1991): 159–78.

McDonald, William. "*Tristan, der je manheit wielt*: Heinrich von Freiberg's *Tristan* as Emblem of Medieval Masculinity." *Tristania* 19 (1999): 97–113.

Miller, John, and Carole Newlands, eds. *A Handbook to the Reception of Ovid.* Hoboken, NJ: Wiley-Blackwell, 2014.

Müller, Jan-Dirk. "The Light of Courtly Society: Blanscheflur and Riwalin." In *Visuality and Materiality in the Story of Tristan and Isolde.* Edited by Jutta Eming, Ann Marie Rasmussen, and Kathryn Starkey. Notre Dame, IN: University of Notre Dame Press, 2012. 19–40.

Newstead, Helaine. "The Origin and Growth of the Tristan Legend." In *Arthurian Literature in the Middle Ages: A Collaborative History.* Edited by Roger Sherman Loomis. Oxford: Clarendon Press, 1959. 122–33.

Norman, Frederick. "The Enmity of Wolfram and Gottfried." *German Life and Letters* 15 (1969): 53–67.

Ober, Peter. "Alchemy and the *Tristan* of Gottfried von Strassburg." *Monatshefte* 57 (1965): 321–35.

Okken, Lambertus. *Kommentar zum Tristan-Roman Gottfrieds von Straßburg.* 2 volumes. Amsterdamer Publikationen zur Sprache und Literatur 58. 2nd edition. Amsterdam: Rodopi, 1996.

Padel, Oliver. "The Cornish Background of the Tristan Stories." *Cambridge Medieval Celtic Studies* 1 (1981): 53–81.

Palmer, Craig. "A Question of Manhood: Overcoming the Paternal Homoerotic in Gottfried's *Tristan.*" *Monatshefte für deutschsprachige Literatur und Kultur* 88 (1996): 17–30.

Peyton, Henry. "Brangäne: Isolde's Alter Ego." *Arthuriana* 11 (2001): 93–107.

Picozzi, Rosemary. *A History of Tristan Scholarship.* Bern: Lang, 1971.

Poag, James. "Lying Truth in Gottfried's *Tristan.*" *Deutsche Vierteljahresschrift für Literatur und Geistesgeschichte* 61 (1987): 223–37.

Ranke, Friedrich. "Die Überlieferung von Gottfrieds Tristan." *Zeitschrift für deutsches Altertum* 55 (1917): 157–278; 381–438.

Rasmussen, Ann Marie. "*Ez ist ir g'artet von mir:* Queen Isolde and Princess Isolde in Gottfried von Strassburg's *Tristan and Isolde.*" In *Arthurian Women.* Edited by Thelma Fenster. New York: Routledge, 2000. 41–57.

Reid, Thomas. *The Tristan of Beroul: A Textual Commentary.* Oxford: Blackwell, 1972.

Sayers, William. "Breaking the Deer and Breaking the Rules in Gottfried von Strassburg's *Tristan.*" *Oxford German Studies* 32 (2003): 1–52.

Sayers, William. "Celtic Echoes and the Timing of Tristan's First Arrival in Cornwall." *Neuphilologische Mitteilungen* 108.4 (2007): 743–50.

Schlegel, August Wilhelm. "Tristan: Erster Gesang." In *Poetische Werke, Erster Theil.* Heidelberg: Mohr und Zimmer, 1811. 98–134.

Schultz, James. "Why Do Tristan and Isolde Leave for the Woods? Narrative Motivation and Narrative Coherence in Eilhart von Oberg and Gottfried von Straßburg." *Modern Language Notes* 102 (1987): 586–607.

Schultz, James. "Clothing and Disclosing: Clothes, Class, and Gender in Gottfried's *Tristan.*" *Tristania* 17 (1996): 111–23.

Schultz, James. "Bodies that Don't Matter: Heterosexuality Before Heterosexuality in Gottfried's *Tristan.*" In *Constructing Medieval Sexuality.* Edited by Karma Lochrie, Peggy McCracken, and James Schultz. Medieval Cultures 11. Minneapolis: University of Minnesota Press, 1997. 91–110.

Schultz, James. "Why Do Tristan and Isolde Make Love? The Love Potion as a Milestone in the History of Sexuality." In *Visuality and Materiality in the Story of Tristan and Isolde.* Edited by Jutta Eming, Ann Marie Rasmussen, and Kathryn Starkey. Notre Dame, IN: University of Notre Dame Press, 2012. 65–82.

Schulz, Monika. *Gottfried von Straßburg:* Tristan. Stuttgart: Metzler, 2017.

Sneeringer, Kristine. *Honor, Love, and Isolde in Gottfried's* Tristan. Studies on Themes and Motifs in Literature 61. New York: Peter Lang, 2002.

Snow, Ann. "*Wilt, wilde, wildenaere:* A Study in the Interpretation of Gottfried's *Tristan.*" *Euphorion* 62 (1968): 365–77.

Spahr, Blake Lee. "Tristan Versus Morolt: Allegory Against Reality?" In *Festschrift Helene Adolf.* Edited by Sheema Buehne, James Hodge, and Lucille Pinto. New York: Ungar, 1968. 72–85.

Stackmann, Karl. "*Gîte* und *Gelücke:* Über die Spruchstrophen Gotfrids." In *Festgabe für Ulrich Pretzel.* Edited by Werner Simon. Berlin: E. Schmidt, 1963. 191–204. Reprinted in *Mittelalterliche Texte als Aufgabe: Kleine Schriften I.* Edited by Jens Haustein. Göttingen: Vandenhoeck & Ruprecht, 1997. 106–19.

Starkey, Kathryn. "From Enslavement to Discernment: Learning to See in Gottfried's *Tristan.*" In *The Art of Vision: Ekphrasis in Medieval Literature and Culture.* Edited by Andrew Johnston, Ethan Knapp, and Margitta Rouse. Columbus: Ohio State University Press, 2015. 124–46.

Stavenhagen, Lee. "The Raw and the Cooked in Gottfried's *Tristan.*" *Monatshefte* 76 (1984): 131–42.

Steinhoff, Hans-Hugo. *Bibliographie zu Gottfried von Strassburg.* 2 volumes. Berlin: Schmidt, 1971–1986.

Stevens, Adrian. "The Renewal of the Classic: Aspects of Rhetorical and Dialectical Composition in Gottfried's Tristan." *Gottfried von Strassburg and the Medieval Tristan Legend: Papers from an Anglo-North American Symposium.* Edited by Adrian Stevens and Roy Wisbey. Cambridge: D.S. Brewer, 1990. 67–90.

Stevens, Adrian. "Killing Giants and Translating Empires: The History of Britain and the Tristan Romances of Thomas and Gottfried." In *Blütezeit: Festschrift für L. Peter Johnson.* Edited by Mark Chinca, Joachim Heinzle, and Christopher Young. Tübingen: Niemeyer, 2000. 409–26.

Thomas, Neil. "The *Minnegrotte*: Shrine of Love or Fools' Paradise? Thomas, Gottfried and the European Development of the Tristan Legend." *Trivium* (1988): 89–106.

Thomas, Neil. *Tristan in the Underworld: A Study of Gottfried von Strassburg's 'Tristan' Together With the 'Tristran' of Thomas.* Studies in Mediaeval Literature 10. Lewiston, NY: Mellen, 1991.

Tomasek, Tomas. *Gottfried von Straßburg.* Stuttgart: Reclam, 2007.

Tubach, Frederic. "The *locus amoenus* in the *Tristan* of Gottfried von Straszburg." *Neophilologus* 43 (1959): 37–42.

Tubach, Frederic, and Gareth Penn. "The Constellation of Characters in the *Tristan* of Gottfried von Strassburg." *Monatshefte* 64.4 (1972): 325–33.

Van D'elden, Stephanie Cain. *Tristan and Isolde: Medieval Illustrations of the Verse Romances.* Turnhout: Brepols, 2017.

Walworth, Julia. *Parallel Narratives: Function and Form in the Munich Illustrated Manuscripts of* 'Tristan' *and* 'Willehalm von Orlens.' King's College London Medieval Studies 20. London: King's College London Centre for Late Antique and Medieval Studies, 2007.

Werner, Jakob. *Lateinische Sprichwörter und Sinnsprüche des Mittelalters aus Handschriften gesammelt.* 2nd edition. Edited by Peter Flury. Heidelberg: Carl Winter Verlag, 1966.

Wetzel, René. *Die handschriftliche Überlieferung des 'Tristan' Gottfrieds von Strassburg: Untersucht an ihren Fragmenten.* Freiburg, Switzerland: Universitätsverlag, 1992.

Wharton, Janet. "*Daz lebende paradis?* A Consideration of the Love of Tristan and Isot in the Light of the *huote* Discourse." In *Gottfried von Strassburg and the Medieval Tristan Legend: Papers from an Anglo-North American Symposium.* Edited by Adrian Stevens and Roy Wisbey. Cambridge: D.S. Brewer, 1990. 143–54.

Willson, H. B. "The Old and the New Law in Gottfried's *Tristan.*" *Modern Language Review* 60 (1965): 212–24.

Wisbey, Roy. "The *renovatio amoris* in Gottfried's *Tristan.*" *London German Studies* 1 (1980): 1–66.

Wisbey, Roy. "Tristan: On Being the Contemporary of Gottfried von Straßburg." *Modern Language Review* 98 (2003): xxxi–lx.

Wolf, Alois. *Gottfried von Strassburg und die Mythe von Tristan und Isolde.* Darmstadt: Wissenschaftliche Buchgesellschaft, 1989.

Wright, Aaron. "Petitcreiu: A Text-Critical Note to the *Tristan* of Gottfried von Strassburg." *Colloquia Germanica* 25 (1992): 112–21.

Zak, Nancy. "The Portrayal of Isolde in Gottfried von Strassburg's *Tristan.*" In *The Portrayal of the Heroine in Chrétien de Troyes's* Erec et Enide, *Gottfried von Strassburg's* Tristan, *and* Flamenca. Edited by Ulrich Müller, Franz Hundsnurscher, and Cornelius Sommer. Göppingen: Kümmerle, 1983. 56–103.

Ziegler, Vickie. "A Burning Issue: Isolde's Oath in its Historical Context." In *The Germanic Mosaic: Cultural and Linguistic Diversity in Society.* Edited by Carol Blackshire-Belay. Westport, CT: Greenwood Press, 1994. 73–82.

Ziegler, Vickie. "The Ordeals of Tristan and Isolde." In *Trial by Fire and Battle in Medieval German Literature.* Edited by Vickie Ziegler. Columbia, SC: Camden House, 2004. 114–45.